Also by Chelsea Quinn Yarbro

Ariosto
Blood Games (forthcoming)
A Flame in Byzantium
Hotel Transylvania
The Palace
published by Tor Books

Crusader's Torch

Chelsea Quinn Yarbro

TOR
HORROR

A TOM DOHERTY ASSOCIATES BOOK
NEW YORK

This is a work of fiction. All the characters and events portrayed in this book are fictitious, and any resemblance to real people or events is purely coincidental.

CRUSADER'S TORCH

Copyright © 1988 by Chelsea Quinn Yarbro

A TOR BOOK
Published by Tom Doherty Associates, Inc.
49 West 24 Street
New York, NY 10010

Library of Congress Cataloging-in-Publication Data

Yarbro, Chelsea Quinn, 1942–
    Crusader's torch.

    I. Title.
PS3575.A7C78   1988   813'.54   88-4806
ISBN 0–312–93088–7

First edition: October 1988

0 9 8 7 6 5 4 3 2 1

This one is for my good friend in Dallas
Dan Fry

Author's Note

Few military undertakings are as puzzling to modern students as the Crusades. Coming at the end of the Romanesque period, they provide an historical watershed that is more easily noticed than understood in twentieth-century terms.

The First Crusade began in 1096, two years after El Cid took Valencia from the Moors in Spain. Its first exponents were Geoffroi de Bouillon, Duke of Lorraine, and Tancred, nephew of the Norman Robert Guiscard who conquered Palermo, among other things. Pope Urban II proclaimed the First Crusade the year before and offered various inducements to the nobility if they were willing to participate. The First Crusade lasted roughly three years; the Crusaders defeated the Turks at Doryalaeym, Nicaea, and Antioch, and in 1099 captured Jerusalem. Geoffroi was appointed Advocate or Defender of the Holy Sepulcher, and went on to defeat the Egyptians at Ascalon in the same year. A European presence established itself in the Near East as a result. In 1104 Acre was taken by Crusaders as part of the general expansion of their power base at the time, although the First Crusade was officially over. Pope Paschal II, who reigned until 1118, was more involved with European affairs than with Near Eastern, and aside from granting a charter for the founding of the Order of the Knights Hospitalers of Saint John, Jerusalem for the protection, housing, and medical care—such as it was—of pilgrims in the Holy Land, did not concern himself overmuch with Crusading.

The next several Popes (Gelasius II, 1118–9; Calistus

vii

II, 1119–24, during whose reign priests were officially forbidden to marry; Honorius II, 1124–30, who officially recognized the Order of the Poor Knights of the Temple of Jerusalem, or the Knights Templar; Innocent II, 1130–43, and the antipope Anacletus II, 1130–38; Celestine II, 1143–44; and Lucius II, 1144–45) were more active in matters of European politics and Church restructuring; it was not until 1145 that Pope Eugene III proclaimed the Second Crusade. Two years later, as Queen Mathilda left Britain, the Second Crusade failed when a significant portion of the Crusaders died, more of disease and thirst than from fighting, in Asia Minor. But although the Crusade did not succeed, the European presence in the Near East was not significantly reduced.

Pope Eugene III was succeeded in 1153 by Anastasius IV, and a year later the only English Pope, Hadrian IV, ascended the Throne of St. Peter; in the following year he essentially gave Ireland to Henry II of England. On the Continent, Frederick Barbarossa was the major military/diplomatic leader. While Henry II was starting to have problems with his former chancellor and friend Thomas à Becket, Barbarossa was carving out an empire in Europe. The same year that Becket became Archbishop of Canterbury, Barbarossa sacked Milan. Four years later (1165), while Becket remained a self-exile in France, Byzantium and Venice made common cause against Barbarossa, fearing (and not without justification) that they might be next on his list.

Alexander III, one of the great reformer-Popes (reigned 1159–1181), was not terribly concerned about the state of affairs in Jerusalem, although he did express fear for the safety of Christians in Moslem countries as the influence of Saladin increased. While the Orthodox and Catholic Churches were very separate bodies, there was a shared sense of danger from the expanding forces of Islam, and apparently a fair amount of diplomatic negotiation took place between the two Churches at this time. One of the most lasting influences of Pope Alexander III was his establishment of the rules for canonization of saints: one of the first canonizations under the rules was of Thomas à Becket, only two and a half years after his murder in Canterbury Cathedral.

In 1178, Frederick Barbarossa was crowned King of Burgundy for the first time (he repeated the ceremony eight years later); he had already been made Holy Roman Emperor by his own antipope, Paschal III, in 1167. Despite his defeat at the Battle of Legnano, Frederick's star was still regarded as rising. The shift of power in Europe was heightened in 1180 with the death of Louis VII of France; his son, Philippe II Augustus, was only fifteen at the time and was an unknown quantity. Frederick's power reached its zenith in 1184 at the Great Diet of Mainz, and with the possible exception of Moslem Spain, most of Europe had come under his direct or indirect influence.

In 1185, the Shi'ite Moslems took over Egypt, bringing a more zealous regime to the Islamic part of the Mediterranean. Norman French forces from Sicily, then under Norman control, campaigned against the Byzantines, and after a fairly successful invasion were defeated at Demetritsa by a Byzantine army under the command of Alexius Branas. With two major European factions—the Sicilian Franco-Normans and the Holy Roman Empire under Frederick I Barbarossa—as well as Moslem forces on expansionist programs, the situation was volatile in many ways. The new Byzantine Emperor, Isaac II Angelus, though a capable politician, was unable or unwilling to curb the corruption in his government, aware that to undertake reform at such a time was to invite treachery. Through various clandestine channels, he approached the new Pope, Urban III, apparently encouraging another Crusade, which would provide an effective wedge between the beleaguered Byzantine Empire and the armed might of Islam.

Matters worsened steadily. By 1187 Saladin had defeated the Christians at Hittin and had taken Jerusalem. The rivalry between France and England was sharpened when the heir to the English throne, Richard, was required to do homage to Philippe of France for English possessions in France; Henry II of England, fifty-three years of age, was offended enough to turn this episode into a fracas, the result of which was that he was forced to accept all the French demands and to give full recognition to Richard as his heir and as partial vassal to France.

Pope Urban III was succeeded in 1187 by Pope Gregory VIII, and, in the same year, by Pope Clement III, who proclaimed the Third Crusade, charging all Christian chivalry to reclaim Jerusalem and once again restore European rule to that city. Frederick I Barbarossa made certain his reign and succession were in order with a triple coronation at the end of 1186, and began to prepare for war. In France, the first tax ever imposed on the French people, called the Saladin tax, was levied to raise money to pay the enormous cost of the Crusade.

In May of 1189, Barbarossa, with his Holy Roman army, set out from Regensburg for the Holy Land. The French were almost ready to leave for the war when circumstances changed again; on July 6, Henry II of England died at Chinon shortly after surrendering the territories of Gracy and Issoudon to France. He was succeeded promptly by Richard Coer de Leon, who all but broke off diplomatic relations with France, repudiated his lifelong engagement to Alais, the sister of Philippe, and announced his intention of retaining all French territory held by the English. Only the two kings' intention to Crusade kept either from direct hostile action, and by the end of the year, they had pledged mutual good faith for the Crusade.

While both Richard and Philippe spent the winter of 1189–90 preparing for the Crusade, Frederick had already reached Greece, where he drowned in the Calycadnus River on June 10, thus leaving his men, and the entire Third Crusade, temporarily without a leader. Richard, determined to take advantage of this, effectively mortgaged part of his kingdom in order to raise and equip an army of 4,000 men-at-arms and 4,000 footsoldiers for the Crusade. Philippe, not to be outdone or outmaneuvered, established the means to allow him to continue to rule France while he was away from Paris: he relied on a complex system of personal heralds to relay his messages from the Holy Land.

By the following winter, both Richard and Philippe were under way, but because of weather and diplomatic circumstances, spent a good portion of time in Sicily quarreling. When Richard was able to leave, in March of 1191, he conquered Cyprus (which had only recently won its independence from Byzantium) where on May 11 and 12, 1191, he married Barengaria of Navarre, then sold the island to the Knights Templar. Richard and his English army went in June to join Leopold of Austria at the siege of Acre; Leopold was as favorably impressed by Richard's military capabilities as he was offended by Richard's arrogant conduct.

Philippe of France became ill and withdrew from the Crusade, making excellent time in his homeward journey, even though he detoured on the way to Paris to form an anti-Richard alliance with Frederick I Barbarossa's heir, Henry VI, the new Holy Roman Emperor.

In the Holy Land, Richard's campaign continued successful, and before the end of the year, the Crusaders were within a few miles of the gates of Jerusalem. This became the limit of the Third Crusade's achievements; the following year, between treachery, plague, famine, desertion, and unreliable intelligence, the number of fighting men, once approximately 100,000, was reduced to little more than 5,000.

Finally a truce was arranged between Saladin and Richard which would permit the Crusaders, unarmed and on foot, free access to the Holy Sepulcher in Jerusalem. The coastal towns then in European hands were to remain in European hands. Richard, thwarted and chagrined, started for England in October, only to be captured December 20, 1192, in Vienna by Leopold of Austria, who surrendered Richard to Henry VI, the Holy Roman Emperor. A ransom of 150,000 marks was demanded for his return. Although only a portion of the ransom was ever paid, Richard returned to England in March of 1194. Of his approximately ten-year reign, Richard spent less than a year of it in England, and this occasion was typical of that pattern. As soon as he had re-delegated authority, he returned to the English possessions in France.

In 1195, Isaac II Angelus, Emperor of Byzantium, was replaced by his brother Alexius III Angelus, who had organized a palace coup. The new Emperor of Byzantium did not get on well with the Holy Roman Emperor, and Henry VI was prepared to go on crusade against Alexius III Angelus when he fell ill and died, September 28, 1197.

Richard Coer de Leon, determined to regain the English lands in France, completed Chateau Gaillard on the Seine in the same year, in effect throwing down the gauntlet to Philippe II. In 1198, he declared that England —and the King of England—were not vassals of France, but nevertheless lost ground to Philippe, who was having trouble of his own when the new Pope, Innocent III, excommunicated him for repudiating his marriage to Ingeborg of Denmark. During this dispute between the Pope and Philippe of France, Richard disputed with the vicomes (viscount) of Limoges, and the following spring he besieged the castle of Chalus, where he was wounded by a crossbow quarrel and died of gangrene on April 6 after apologizing to his wife Barengaria that God had not made him a lover of women. He was thirty-two years old.

In 1202, Pope Innocent III proclaimed a Fourth Crusade and for the first time the Venetians—who were actively engaged in commerce with Islamic countries— were persuaded to participate beyond providing transport. Manrico Dandolo, Doge of Venice, formidable still at age ninety-four, finally agreed, but on the condition that the Crusaders sack the city of Zara on the Dalmatian coast. The Crusaders accepted the condition, and were excommunicated for the act by the same Pope who had proclaimed the Crusade. The Crusaders, undaunted, proceeded to Constantinople, and restored the blinded Isaac II Angelus to the throne with his son Alexius acting as regent. After six months, both father and son were deposed by the general Mourzouphles who took the title of Alexius V Ducas, and for this usurpation, the Fourth Crusade besieged Constantinople, and as a result a short-lived Latin kingdom was established in Byzantium. Two separate Byzantine Empires were established, one at Trebizond, one at Epirus; the former lasted until 1461, the latter less than ten years.

The Fourth Crusaders fell victim not only to their

excommunication, but to Bubonic Plague, and the forces never reached Jerusalem.

For the purposes of this book, I have used Norman French for names of people and places wherever such information is available and fairly consistent. In the case of Richard Coer de Leon, since he never learned to speak English, I have used his own usual Norman variant of his name. For help with Norman French of the late twelfth century, I wish to thank Jeanet Simeon and R. L. Hansen for their assistance; providing other research material, thanks as always to the indefatigable Dave Nee. Whatever errors may be in the text are not theirs but mine. I would also like to thank Jill Sherman and Paul McNutt for their assistance. And, of course, thanks to the good people at Tor for their support and encouragement of my vampire tales.

PART I

Valence Rainaut

Text of a letter of the Venetian merchant Giozzetto Camar-marr from Cyprus to the Benedictine scholar Ulrico Fionder.

My dear cousin and esteemed teacher, I fear your apprehensions were well-founded. As you warned me, the situation has become worse. It is not only the presence of the Islamites that brings trouble to this island, but since the people reclaimed this place as their own, there has been an alarming increase in piracy, and the venture our united families were so hopeful of I must now recommend we abandon, at least until more order is restored here.

The great Islamite warrior Saladin has demonstrated his capacity for conquest now that Hittin has fallen and Jerusalem is in his hands. I am far from certain that this will be the limit of his expansions; one has only to think of Spain to know that Christian countries are not beyond his plans. I, for one, do not agree with those who say that the Byzantines will be able to hold his forces back. Consider that the Cypriots have already defeated them. The armies of Saladin are more formidable than the people of Cyprus.

Of course one hears rumors. When does not the world buzz with them, like bees and mosquitos? It is said that Isaac II Angelus desires the aid of his Christian brethren in the West. There are those who have denied the chance that there will be another Crusade. Most kingdoms cannot afford the expense, according to what I have heard. The loss of life in the last one has given many leaders pause, and the disharmony between kings has become so great that few kingdoms are able to sponsor such an expedition. However, it may be that with Saladin in Jerusalem, the Pope will decide that Christians must demonstrate their faith by restoring Catholic rule to that most holy of cities. Unlikely though many think it may be, I believe that the Christians must act; since the Byzantines are not inclined to fight the Islamites alone, we must assume that it will fall to good Catholics to defend the Holy Sepulcher.

I wish to make a suggestion to you and to our families: on the chance that there is another Crusade, rather than take the kinds of risks that are currently entailed in trade, we might instead invest in transport ships, for troops bound for the Holy Land will need our assistance, not only to carry them to Acre and Tyre, but to keep them supplied once they are there, for it can hardly be expected for the Catholic communities there will be able to supply an entire army.

It is true that many of the Crusaders are likely to take the overland route through Hungary, but many others will prefer the faster sea routes, and all will rely on transport ships for additional arms and supplies. I realize that there are those who frown on Venetians profiting from such holy undertakings as Crusades, especially since we do not take up the Banner of Christ. To those, I say that the Crusaders would be the worse for lack of our support, and that as long as la Serenissima trades with Islamite kingdoms and cities, then we must be careful to be sure our conduct does not worsen the conflict. By shipping and supplying the Crusaders, we fulfill the obligations we have as Christians as well as maintaining our necessary positions as Venetians.

You are more knowledgeable in these matters than I am, but if I have understood what you have told me, there is nothing in this proposition that is contrary to the laws of our Repubblica or the dictates of the Church. If I have erred, I pray you will tell me of it and aid me to correct my faults.

I solicit your prayers and instruction, and upon my return I will avail myself of your company. I miss the solace of learning and the joys of our families. To be two years away from wife and children is a trying thing for a man; I long to return. May God send me a swift and safe passage to Venezia. I will depart in two weeks. You will have this in good time so *that our families need not delay in coming to a decision in this matter.*

Your cousin and most devoted student,
Giozzetto Camarmarr
On the Feast of the Holy Anchorites, in the 1188th year of Our Lord, by my own hand and under my seal.

· 1 ·

Most of the shutters had been closed over the windows by the time the squall reached Tyre. The few that were not secured banged and rattled until the household slaves tended to them, and then only the eerie wails of the wind and the spattering of rain disturbed the house that stood a little apart from the rest, between custom's station and the Genoese quarter of the city.

"I wish you wouldn't insist that I leave," Niklos Aulirios said to Atta Olivia Clemens as he left the slaves packing his belongings to speak with her in her private apartments.

"You know I can't take the risk of arriving in Roma without preparation. Be sensible, Niklos." She was frowning slightly, her hazel eyes vexed. "We've been over this; I won't change my mind because you repeat yourself."

He was about to protest when he saw the slave from Antioch standing in the door, hand raised to knock. There were two long copes folded together in his hands. "Not like that," Niklos told the slave. "I want them separate, and I want them in my saddle bags, so that I can reach them. If there's going to be more weather like this, I'll need them."

The slave gestured to acknowledge his mistake, and set about following Niklos' orders. "We can't find the leather chest," he said to Niklos, showing respect to the major domo by keeping his eyes lowered.

"I'll help you search for it shortly." Niklos turned to

Olivia once more. "You don't know that there will be more fighting. I don't like to think of you taking unnecessary risks." He looked toward the slave in the doorway. "You have duties to attend to, haven't you?"

"I do," the slave said and withdrew quickly.

"I like the risks no better than you do," said Olivia. "Which is why I am determined to return to Roma. If I am wrong, there will be no harm in the change, and if it turns out that I am right, then the sooner we are gone from here, the better. Was the slave listening?"

Niklos made an irritated gesture. "Even if he were, he did not hear anything that has not been said before. And who would he tell?"

"That worries me," she said wryly. "I wish I knew. And all the more reason for me to leave. It isn't very safe here." She waved her hand toward the window. "Out there everyone is troubled. They expect the worst. I would as soon avoid that if I am able."

"You will need escort for your journey. Have you thought about that?" Niklos did not wait for her answer. "Many of the Templars and Hospitalers are as rapacious as the robbers they are supposed to guard you against. Don't argue with me," he warned her before she could interrupt. "You know that it's true, especially if they're escorting a woman."

"I know it's true for some of them," Olivia conceded with a faint smile. "Why are you so angry with me, Niklos?"

He rounded on her, his burnished skin darkening with emotion. "Because I'm afraid for you, Olivia. After all these years and years, I dread what might become of you."

"I am not entirely defenseless." Her hazel eyes locked with his dark ones unflinchingly and she took two steps toward him. "You may take credit for some of my skills. You taught me well, Niklos. For that I thank you."

"If you think to distract me with compliments, Olivia—I know you too well. It won't work." He folded his arms and did his best to glower at her.

"Oh, Niklos, Niklos; old friend." She turned away from him, her gaze directed at a point some distance beyond the shuttered window. "If that were all there was to fear. If the only worry would be the venality of Christian knights, there would be no reason to leave Tyre. But that is the least of it, and you know it as well as I."

"It is enough," said Niklos, coming and laying his strong, square hands on her shoulders before he turned her toward him. "How are we to manage?"

"As we have in the past, I trust." She said it distantly, her attention divided between him and some unknown factor, a sound or a memory or a nameless impression. "The trouble is," she went on as she studied the bondsman's collar around his neck, "I don't like the necessity of separation any more than you do. With you I am safe, I have no secrets. Among strangers, well,"—she shrugged without dislodging his hands—"there can be difficulties. There have been before."

"You will take slaves with you, at least," he said, his desperation giving his words the force of a command.

"If I am permitted more than a body-slave, yes, at least as far as Greek territories. The Hospitalers and Templars do not permit extensive retinues." Olivia leaned her head against his shoulder. "I would rather travel with you. You know that. But I need you to arrange . . . everything. I rely on you to find me a place to live, one that is secure and where I will have to answer as few questions as possible. With Crusading fervor rising again, there are always greater risks. You've said yourself that if I remain here, eventually suspicion will develop, either among the Christians or the Islamites, and that would not bode well. I need to find a haven where the zeal of my neighbors is not a threat." She smiled faintly. "At least in Roma you will not need to import earth for me."

"Roman that you are," he said, his sternness giving way to affection.

"There was a time it was an honorable thing to be," she said, the words wistful.

"And now?" He held her off. "Never mind. We both know what has become of Roma."

"Yes," she agreed, and moved away from him. "That is why I am depending on you to act for me. I don't want to have to repeat what we endured when we came here from Alexandria. By comparison, leaving Constantinople was a simple . . . swim."

Somewhere on the floor below, a shutter banged once,

twice, and there were muffled shouts as the household slaves rushed to close it once more.

"It's taken care of," Niklos said when the voices beneath them quietened.

"They're frightened. They know that there is danger. I hear them speak of Saladin, and they say he will not be content with Jerusalem." Olivia stared around her apartment, looking at the two crucifixes on the wall. "I hate having to stay here, especially now, to keep to three rooms on the second floor because I am a widow and I must not be seen abroad except to go to church."

"Will Roma be better?" Niklos asked, not quite concealing the cynicism he felt.

"It is where I was born," she replied obliquely. "If I have to remain here, waiting, until either the Crusaders come and butcher us all, or the Islamites come and butcher us all, I will go mad. I feel here I am walled up in a tomb." Her voice grew hushed and she caught her lower lip between her teeth. "I had help then, in Roma. But he is far away and I cannot wait for his rescue now."

As gently as he was able Niklos asked, "Do you think he will return?"

She smiled, her face world-weary. "What you are asking, Niklos, is do I think that he is dead, truly dead?" She shook her head. "No. I would know. There is a bond between us, and if it were broken, I would know."

Niklos kept his thoughts to himself, his eyes directed toward the very old Persian chair rather than Olivia. "How soon do you insist I go? I'll be prepared in two more days."

"As soon as weather and shipping permits. There are three Genoese merchants who are arranging transport; you could travel with them. The Hieronomite monk at the sailors' chapel will handle it if you ask him. My Confessor has spoken to him on our behalf already." She said this quickly, anticipating his reaction.

"You wish me to go by ship?" It was difficult to tell whether he was annoyed or upset at the suggestion.

"It is faster, and more direct. If you travel overland, it will be some time before you reach Roma. Going by ship, you should arrive at Genova in no more than a month." She spoke in her most sensible tone, but her eyes were pleading with him.

"Assuming we encounter no pirates and the winds are fair, that no Byzantine ship seizes us for invented taxes and no Christian ship demands that we be put ashore on some remote isle so that they can commandeer the use of the ship for the transportation of pilgrims or knights," Niklos added as he started to pace the confines of the room.

"Yes," said Olivia with asperity. "Assuming that. Overland there would be robbers and Islamites and slavers to contend with, and more time for them to strike, more places for them to take you, more ways for you to disappear. On the sea, you will be safer. Please, Niklos." She reached out to stop him and shook her head in exasperation as he pulled free of her hand. "You know how much I hate to travel by water," she went on, her patience wearing thin. "But if I had to leave today, I would arrange to go by ship."

"Then come with me when I leave. We'll make provision for you, arrange for you to be an invalid, so that you might keep to your quarters all day." He stopped pacing to address her directly. "Is this why you've been avoiding me, delaying this discussion—because you want me to travel by ship? I tolerate it better than you do, Olivia."

"You could scarcely do worse," she interjected with a little humor.

He was not distracted. "If it must be by water, it will be. Once I am in Roma, give me two months, and everything can be arranged for you, including your passage."

"Yes, everything here can be ready. But you haven't been in Roma in a very long time. What makes you certain that you can settle matters for me so quickly?" That last question lingered in the air like the last echo of a gong.

"I will manage it. Roma can't have changed that much," Niklos said.

"All right," Olivia told him. "You probably will not be able to secure passage for a week at least; I do not want you setting out at the dead of winter. If, in that time, you have managed to make arrangements for Roma and can gain permission for me to sell this house, as well as ship my goods, there should be no difficulties to hamper either of us." She indicated a large, leather-bound and iron-clasped book on the low table beside the Persian chair. "I want to take my library, if I can. It's always difficult, shipping books. No matter what they are, someone inevitably wants to burn them."

"I'll address the Court of Bourgesses." Niklos stood still a short time, then shook his head. "All right; I'll make the arrangements you ask. I'll leave for Genova with the merchants."

"Thank you," Olivia said reluctantly.

"You don't want me to go, do you?" Niklos asked her, long familiarity making her expressions transparent to him.

"Yes, I do. I know it is the sensible thing to do. I know that if we leave without preparation, it might be unpleasant in Roma, and that is something I do not want. Having you go ahead and make all the arrangements necessary will serve both our purposes well. And while all that is true," she said, her voice softening, "still I will miss you while you are gone, and I will worry about you until I have word you are safe."

Niklos laughed once and shook his head slowly. "Well, you've said what I wanted to hear, I suppose. But I still don't like having to leave you."

"I know." She went to the Persian chair, but hesitated before sitting down. "It seems strange to me, to have to think of Roma as a foreign city, to treat it as if I had never been there. It is my home. I was born there."

"It has changed, Olivia," Niklos said with hard kindness.

"Yes."

He watched her, aware of her inwardness. Over the years these brief withdrawals to her memories had increased, and though they were still infrequent, they happened more often. At such times Niklos was at a loss. He started toward her, then stopped. "Olivia?"

She gave a little shake to her head at the sound of her name, and took a moment to answer, "What?"

"Is it Roma?" He knew the answer, but wanted her to tell him.

"Of course," she said ruefully. "What else would it be? Oh, I don't relish moving, and the thought of an ocean voyage makes me ill, but the thorn is Roma." She fingered the tooled leather on the worn arm of the chair. "It was strange to me long ago. I don't know why it has upset me to remember it now."

"Perhaps because it is strange?" he suggested.

She turned toward him. "You know me too well."

"After all this time, I hope so," Niklos said, rallying her.

"You're right," she said. "If I am ever to get out of this house, you must put your plans in order." As she rose, she smoothed the Babylon skins that trimmed her mantel-a-parer.

Niklos caught the gesture. "You love that fur, don't you?"

"It is soft and warm," she said at her most neutral.

"And you love it," Niklos added.

"Yes," Olivia said, nodding once. "But I may have to leave it behind."

*   *   *

Text of an unofficial letter from the secretary of the Metro-politan of Hagia Sophia to the Abbot of the Benedictine monastery on Rhodes.

To my devout fellow-Christian, I pray that you will set aside the differences that divide Christendom long enough to read what I have to impart to you, for our faith, in all its forms, is again in the gravest danger, and at the behest of my most pious master, I approach you in the hope that you will consider what I tell you with all the wisdom that God can give imperfect men.

Surely, since the Knights Hospitaler share part of Rodhos with you, you are aware of the increasing menace of the desert followers of the banner of Islam, and have yearned to come to the rescue of the True Church, which is the Heart of Our Lord. So we in the Greek Church feel as we learn of the fall of Jerusalem into those terrible hands. In spite of the concession made to the Greek Church, and the returning of the Holy Sepulcher to us, the ploy is an obvious one; all Christendom can agree that the presence of Saladin in Jerusalem besmirches every one of us who have accepted salvation in the name of the Christ. Who can be certain how long Saladin will grant us this sop? No Franks have entered Jerusalem since it was taken, and there is no reason to believe that this will change.

While the Knights Hospitaler are not formed for the purpose of war as are the Knights Templar, they still hold in sacred trust the protection of Christians and the holy sites of Our Lord's life. You share similar rule, and certainly you may understand the need for increased vigilance on the part of those knights giving protection and escort to pilgrims. Those who embrace the Rule of Saint Benedict accept absolute dedication, life-long fidelity and chaste humility as the outward manifestation of inward devotion. As you have done, so these good Knights have done also.

They differ from you in their knightly vows, in their mandate to take up the cause of God and the Church as they would take up the cause of King and country. How much greater an honor to defend the most sacred shrines of our faith than to vindicate the claims of a King, anointed only on earth and not in Heaven. It is possible for the Hospitalers to do more than aid the injured and ill, to guard and protect Christians. Now they may protect Christ Himself through helping to restore Jerusalem to Christian hands. It is true enough that the Kings of this world have clamored and battled for possessions and honors, and that their chivalry has been foremost in taking up the fight. How much greater cause would they find in fighting for the preservation of our faith.

You and I must content ourselves with prayers and trust in God's great mercy; those who have been chosen for more strife have an opportunity now to vindicate their souls through their might of arms against an enemy so enormous that Satan must surely be the evil angel guiding all that the pernicious Saladin does.

With your guidance, the Knights Hospitaler can bring about the transformation of Jerusalem from vassalage to triumph again. Those of us in the Greek Church must take care so that our actions will not be misconstrued. Chivalry breeds suspicion, and in crises such as this one, knights will not listen to the timely warning of those they have never known as friends. The heritage of arms and honor teaches men to put the trust in their weapons and their oaths of fealty rather than the unity of faith in God. It is possible that the Knights Hospitaler would regard this message with doubt or anger. You, being given to a more contemplative and prayerful life, have a greater comprehension of the peril we face, and for that reason, I beseech you to address the Knights Hospitaler and urge them to be more militant in their actions, to do more than they have done to bring about the end of the vile bondage that holds Jerusalem in thrall to Saladin.

I will offer prayers for you and your Brothers, and for your success with the Knights Hospitaler. I will thank God for your aid and wisdom that comes not to succor the Greek Church, but to cast off the yoke of shame that touches all Christians.
Alexios from Salinika
At the behest of my master, by my own hand and under seal, on the day after Epiphany, in the Lord's Year 1189.

· 2 ·

A squabble had started between a man leading a donkey-cart and a French Bourgess in his official collar; since the streets were narrow, this stopped traffic in both directions. Under the roof-high awnings that provided some respite from the inexorable sun, faces began to appear in window slits, adding their shouts of derision and encouragement to the exchange.

"Is there another way?" Valence Rainaut asked of the sarjeant at his side.

"We're blocked behind, Bonsier," the sarjeant said, apparently inured to problems of this sort.

Rainaut tugged at the black-and-white cote that identified him as a Knight Hospitaler of Saint John. "How long will we be detained by this?"

The sarjeant shrugged. "If it becomes a fight, it could be some time. But they don't appear to be the sort to fight," he added with a wink, for the man with the donkey-cart was a white-haired ancient with hardly a tooth left in his head and the Bourgess was portly. "Of course," the sarjeant went on when he had considered the rest of the crowd, "there's no telling what the rest might do. Tyre is a volatile place."

"Does that please you?" Rainaut challenged, hearing satisfaction in the sarjeant's comment.

"It pleases me to serve God and His Knights Hospitalers," said the sarjeant, suddenly circumspect. "When you have been here a while, good Knight, you will understand that these coastal cities are all . . . well, they are hazardous. If they were not, there would be no need for Hospitalers here, would there?"

Rainaut was tempted to give a short answer to the sarjeant's insolence, but held his tongue; what he had said was true enough, and there would be other occasions when Rainaut could reprimand the sarjeant if he deserved correction. He rubbed at his neck, glad that he was not wearing armor, for his clothes, more appropriate for France than Tyre, stuck to his body, soggy with sweat. "Is there anyone who could end this?"

"Lord God knows," said the sarjeant, blessing himself in case Rainaut might think he was swearing.

"How far is the chapter house?" Rainaut asked, having to shout now to be heard over the din.

"Not far." The sarjeant pointed down the street. "A little way further, then right at the corner. The chapel is there, and the chapter house is directly behind it. The hospice is nearby."

The ancient with the donkey-cart had picked up a wad of dung. With a screeching outburst, he hurled this at the Bourgess, who bellowed and launched himself at his opponent. The spectators howled and cheered as the battle was joined in earnest.

The sarjeant began to look worried. "I think perhaps that we might—" He tried to move backward, but he and Rainaut were wedged in by the press of the crowd at their backs.

"What is it?" Rainaut inquired, one hand on the hilt of his sword.

"A fight like this, it could turn ugly. Then the Templars would settle it; they restore order by cracking heads." He rapped on the closed shop door beside them, but there was no response. He pointed upwards. "Look. They are leaving the windows."

"Does that mean it is over?" Rainaut had to admit to an instant's disappointment.

"No, it means that it will get worse," said the sarjeant fatalistically. "They are leaving the windows so that they will not be struck by—" He broke off.

At the core of the fight, where the old man and the Bourgess flailed at each other with fists and feet, the donkey pulling the cart began to bray and kick in an effort to escape the battle. It was like a signal to people jammed into the street. Fists were raised, weapons drawn where there was room to do so. A few of the more intrepid dropped to their knees and attempted to crawl between the legs of the others.

"Sweet Virgin," Rainaut breathed as chaos erupted. He had drawn his short-bladed forked dagger from his sleeve scabbard and now held it low and at the ready. "What now?" he yelled at the sarjeant to make himself heard at all.

"Pray," suggested the sarjeant, bringing his hands over his head and his elbows out. A section of brick hit his shoulder and he stifled an oath.

"This is impossible," Rainaut declared, though no one heard him. As the mob surged, trying to break the confines of the street, Rainaut searched for an opening. "How near is the closest alley?" he demanded of the sarjeant.

"It's useless, sir," shouted the sarjeant. "We can't make it."

"Of course we can," said Rainaut, and started to move backward, prodding for the smallest openings between the tightly packed bodies, and sliding through them, dragging the sarjeant after him. For the first time he was grateful that most of his goods were still on the ship that had brought him, along with his two horses, his bard, and battle harness.

A yowl went up from somewhere behind him; Rainaut turned and had to resist the urge to stop and look for the cause of it. He held his two-bladed dagger against his leg and continued his slow withdrawal. "Do not be frightened, sarjeant. We will do."

"If you'll pardon me, Bonsier, I think we're for it now." He was able to make a grimace that was intended for a battle-smile. "There are too many here, and the way is blocked now."

"There are some means to win free," said Rainaut. "How far will this take us out of our way?" he asked the sarjeant.

"Not far, I hope," the sarjeant muttered, repeating his words as loudly as possible when Rainaut demanded it.

"There are stalls set up for craftsmen, I remember seeing them." He had to lean almost into the sarjeant's face to hear the response. The noise and the press was alarming, but he had been warned that the streets in Tyre could be volatile.

"They'll have got out of the way by now, sir," the sarjeant said. His face was beaded and his mouth was white. "There'll be blood shortly, sir."

"That's no concern of ours, sarjeant, if we are not stopped or harmed. We may pray for them later." Rainaut had eased them a few steps farther away from the riot. "Is there a house or a church where we can take shelter if this gets worse?"

The sarjeant shook his head vigorously. "No, sir. They're shut up, the churches, like the houses. Here, that's what they do." This last ended on a sharp hiss as someone stepped on his toes.

"The churches as well?" Rainaut asked, not expecting an answer. There were elbows and knees pummeling him, and as he tried to ease them further back in the crowd, he found more resistance than before. From one of the close-packed men a sudden punch came that left Rainaut with a bloody bruise under his eye. "For the Saints!"

"Are you hurt, sir?" asked the sarjeant automatically; in fact, at the moment he did not care. The battle around him was troublesome and he sensed that it would worsen quickly.

"You say the churches are closed to us?" Rainaut demanded, hoping that there would be some respite to this melee.

"Most especially," said the sarjeant. "I don't like to tell you what happens in churches when the streets go mad this way. The monks and the priests all do what they can to save their treasures and guard those within their gates."

Rainaut had drawn them into the slight protection of a doorway, pressing himself and the sarjeant back against the iron-hasped door. It was the only cover he could find the length of the street. "Stay still; I am looking for a way out."

A square-bodied man in Byzantine clothes, a bruise forming on his chin and his hand pressed to his bleeding nose, stumbled against them, cursed them as he gasped, then was pulled away by a lurching Islamite.

"Damnation to them all," the sarjeant burst out, provoked beyond all resistance. "This is supposed to be a Christian city, not one of those godless Islamite camps where—" He stopped, staring at Rainaut, knowing that such words in the presence of a knight were inexcusable.

"In the heat of battle," said Rainaut with a grim twitch of his lips which was intended to be a smile, "a man forgets."

At the far end of the street a shriek went up, and in an instant the crowd changed. Those who had been trying to push forward were now as anxious as the most timorous to escape. Shouts of outrage became cries of alarm.

"What is it?" Rainaut asked, baffled at the abrupt shift.

"Templars," said the sarjeant comprehensively. "We'd better leave as quickly as we're able." He attempted to get away from the shelter of the door. "Hurry. If they catch us—"

"We're Hospitalers," said Rainaut. "We're fellow-knights."

"Say that when you have seen how they do their work," the sarjeant insisted, plucking at Rainaut's sleeve. "Hurry. They will be upon us soon."

At the far end of the covered street there was, impossibly, the sound of iron-shod hooves, and the unmistakable clang of steel. High wails and prayers rose above the rest of the clamor.

"They'll be upon us shortly," said the sarjeant, blessing himself automatically.

"But . . ." Rainaut tried to see over the crowd in order to learn if what the sarjeant claimed could be true.

"Hurry." This time he tugged Rainaut's arm without apology.

"We ought to await them," said Rainaut, but with less certainty. He stared down at the flagged streets where three men now lay, two of them trying to escape the kicks and blows of those still standing, one of them quite still.

"If we don't leave, they'll have us," said the sarjeant, his plain, hound's face now sagging and pale. "Now, Bonsier."

Reluctantly Rainaut moved into the crowd as if he were entering a swift-running river. He tried to choose his way, to find where there were breaks in the pack of bodies, but even as he moved the crowd shifted, and once again he and the sarjeant were at the mercy of the others, tossed like boats on a flood. Quickly they were separated, the sarjeant all but disappearing in the narrow way: Rainaut, less than two arm's-lengths from him, could neither see nor reach him.

Where the old man with the donkey-cart had been there was now a mounted, armored knight, his sword drawn; his white surcote was blazoned with the red cross of the Knights Templars. As Rainaut watched, the Templar clove a path for himself and his horse with the relentless scything of his sword.

A man in Egyptian garments beside Rainaut began to recite prayers in a monotonous sing-song as he sank to his knees.

Rainaut turned to the fellow but was plucked away from him by the increased flight of the crowd. Now that it was clear that the Templars would maim anyone in their path, everyone trapped in the confines of the street rushed to flee them.

The windows above the street were empty and shuttered.

Rainaut stared in dismay as the relentless knights came nearer. Pride and his schooling told him that no Templar would harm him, but there was blood on the flagstones. He hesitated, then was tugged away by others running from the knights.

The Egyptian had fallen over, and the drone of his prayers were interrupted with a high, brief shriek.

Two broken support rods of a hastily abandoned vendor's stall rolled and clattered under Rainaut's feet. He almost tripped on them, then, more out of habit than inspiration, he bent and picked one up as the relentless mob drove him on. As a skinny man with a scarred face lurched against him, Rainaut fended him off with the short stick. In that moment, he steadied himself against the human tide and turned to face the Templars, the rod held in both hands, angled across his body. This time, as he was jostled, he did not move.

It did not take long for the mounted Templars to reach him; one instant they were five paces away, the next they were within striking distance: four mounted knights, swords reddened, horses blowing.

"Stop," Rainaut ordered, not at all certain he could be heard over the noise.

A muffled, angry burst came from one of the following Templars, and a maul was lifted.

The Templar in the lead motioned for his companion to be still. "A Hospitaler?" he asked, his Norman French flavored with the whispering accents of Burgos. "Stops *us?*"

Stung by the Templar's amused contempt, Rainaut lifted his makeshift weapon a little higher. "Whatever has happened here now is over."

Two of the Templars laughed, and the leader cocked his head the little bit his armor permitted. "Do you tell me that you protect swine like these cowards?" The gesture with his sword indicated all the people who ran from them.

"That is our mandate," said Rainaut, adding quickly, "Put that down!" to the last Templar who was drawing his mace-and-chain from its holster.

"But to waste your courage for filth . . ." The Spanish Templar sighed. "A Hospitaler. From?"

"Saint-Prosperus-lo-Boys, sworn vassal of His Grace Henry of England." He did not let go of the broken staff he held to touch the hilt of his sword, although it was proper he do so.

"Ah." The Spanish Templar signaled to the others and they put up their weapons. "No more sport today, my lads. We're answerable to this . . . fellow." Whatever he had intended to say first, he prudently substituted a less inflammatory word. With obvious disappointment the Templars did as they were ordered, one of them grumbling about milksops in armor. Rainaut pretended to misunderstand. "Tell me," the Spanish Templar went on when he had wiped the blood from his sword and sheathed it. "What would you do with that bludgeon of yours? We have swords and maces and mauls. What would you do with that?"

"I would have smashed your horses' legs with it." He said it bluntly; he knew that for knights in the Holy Land, horses were more rare and valuable than wives, and the damage of one was worse than the loss of armor.

"So." The Spanish Templar regarded Rainaut in the silence of restrained fury. "So. I will not forget you, Hospitaler from Saint-Prosperus-lo-Boys." His accent was stronger and Rainaut had the uneasy sensation that he could see the shine of dark eyes behind the shadow of the heavy cervelliere-with-aventail which effectively concealed his features.

"Nor I you," Rainaut said, but with less certainty. He could not see the Spaniard's face, and aside from the Spanish accent, he had no means to identify the voice.

As if acknowledging this, the Spaniard laughed. "We have done for now." He raised his arm and signaled his men to turn and leave. "God give you good day, Bonsier," he said in mockery, dragging his horse around with a tug on the rein and a jab from one of his long-roweled spurs.

As the Templars clattered down the street, those unfortunate enough to lie in their path were run over with less concern than if they had been dead geese.

Moans, which had been inaudible moments before, now filled the stone street, and those casualties who could cry out for aid entreated every aid they could think of; at least three called for their mothers; one—the Egyptian—continued to beg God. The old man with the donkey cart lay still on the paving stones, blood congealing around him. His donkey, his off-hind leg broken, gave off a series of soft, high squeaks. The Bourgess was huddled against the wall, his garments reduced to rags, his face leaden.

"Sir?" the sarjeant said, and Rainaut jumped at the sound.

"I thought you were—" Rainaut accused, to cover his own sudden lack of bravery. It had happened to him before, this unaccountable nausea and chill that seized him now; as always, he felt shamed by it, and vowed it would not possess him again.

"That was amazing, sir," the sarjeant said with honest humility. "I never saw anyone stand up to Templars that way. Not without full harness on, anyway."

Rainaut tried a ghost of a smile. "It had to be stopped," he said distantly, reaching out as he did to steady himself against the wall. "It went too far."

The sarjeant grinned without mirth. "Well, stop it you did, sir. But you had better be on guard."

"Why?" Rainaut asked, anticipating the answer.

"Because the Templars won't forget. They're the rulers here, for all they tell you otherwise. That devil Saladin is less feared than they are. They're supposed to fight to defend the honor of Christ and the Holy Sepulcher—they fight for the love of battle, not the love of Christ. And they're not all well-born, the way Hospitaler Knights are. There's all manner of graceless sorts who—"

"Yes; I know." Rainaut dropped the broken rod he had been holding, watching it as it hit the flagstones and split down half its length. "Do you know who they were?"

"I can find out. There aren't that many Spaniards in the Holy Land, not with all those Moors in Spain," he scoffed.

"Why are they here, then, if what they want is to fight Islamites? Aren't there enough in Spain for them, that they must come here to find them?" Rainaut slapped the front of his surcote, noticing for the first time that it was blood-spattered. "I will have to have this washed." The stain would never leave it, but treated with urine, it would fade.

The sarjeant led the way cautiously down the street, taking care not to touch any of those who had fallen to the Templars. "As to that, sir, there's no saying what that Spaniard would do in Spain. If he is a priest's son, he would come here now that the Church has made him a bastard. If he is a bastard already, then he would not be welcome among the company of knights in Spain. They send only legitimate sons to chase out their Islamites."

"Foolish of them," said Rainaut absently. He had stopped beside a man in German dress. "His shoulder is out of its socket. We should lend him some aid."

"It's not wise, sir," warned the sarjeant.

"Hospitalers are mandated to care for Christians, to protect them. This man is a German merchant, from the look of his clothes. He is a Christian and . . ." He was troubled that he had not rendered more assistance during this fracas, and now he wanted to make amends, if only through something as minor as this token gesture to this one injured merchant.

"There will be a place for him," sighed the sarjeant, knowing that it was pointless to argue with a knight. "We can sling him between us—we haven't far to go."

A few of the upper windows had been opened once more, the shutters folded back against the stone fronts of the houses. At one of the windows a pair of curious faces appeared.

"You take his legs," Rainaut instructed. "I will try to carry him so that I will not pull on his shoulder any more. It is fortunate for him that he has swooned." He did his task efficiently; only the darkening of his face revealed the effort of his work.

The sarjeant, the merchant's feet caught in the crooks of his elbows, toiled along, puffing with each step. "The turn's coming up, sir. Have a care. The street is a busy one."

"Not as busy as this one has been, I reckon," said Rainaut grimly. "Who tends to the streets when we have gone?"

"It will be done," said the sarjeant vaguely. "There are those who . . ."

The next street was more than twice the width of the covered one they left. Here the sun was merciless where people bustled and jostled.

"This is a griddle," Rainaut protested as he and the sarjeant lugged the German merchant toward the hospice of the Knights Hospitalers.

"Not much further, Bonsier," panted the sarjeant. "Have a care—there's goats ahead of you."

Rainaut had heard the animals in the general din of the street. "Thank you, sarjeant." He continued to back up, and though the German merchant seemed to grow heavier with each step Rainaut took, he did not permit himself to complain of it. "Where now?"

"Five more steps," the sarjeant told him. "Bonsier, my back is aching like I've fallen down stairs."

"You say it's not much farther." It took an effort to speak evenly.

"A little way, yes, Bonsier," the sarjeant said, suddenly resigned to his situation. "Not much more. Have a care, Bonsier." This last warning was for a pushcart filled with hot stuffed breads; the man behind it, a slave, struggled with the unwieldly vehicle while his owner walked at the front, clearing the way and crying his wares into the cacophony of the street.

"Offer the ache to God," Rainaut recommended when the food vendor was safely past them.

"The church will be on your right, Bonsier. Take him there. There are those who will know what to do." The sarjeant's steps were faltering and he grunted with the effort of walking.

"Tell me the way, sarjeant," Rainaut ordered.

A gaggle of ill-dressed children hurtled, screaming and laughing, down the street, careless of where they went. One of them knocked against the German merchant, and the unconscious man seemed to moan.

"A bit more to the right. There are three steps, and the narthex opens immediately to your right." He took a deep, ragged breath. "Hey, you there! Get us some help!"

Rainaut heard steps behind him rush, echoing, away. The shadow of the church fell across him, blocking out the hot weight of the sun. Then, as he struggled up the steps, he heard footsteps approaching, and a voice at his side said, "We will take him, my son." As confused as he was relieved, Rainaut gave over his burden to the priest and two men in the black-and-white cote of the Knights Hospitaler of Saint John, Jerusalem. "Be careful," Rainaut said. "His shoulder's out."

"We'll tend to it," one of those beside him said.

"Deo gratias," Rainaut said, blessing himself with an effort.

A Premonstratensian monk approached Rainaut, his face worn as leather and his head all but bald. "God give you good day, sir knight. You have had a most propitious beginning here."

Rainaut was suddenly too fatigued to respond.

*   *   *

Text of a letter from Niklos Aulirios in Roma to Atta Olivia Clemens in Tyre, written in archaic Latin.

To my esteemed bondholder and friend, Olivia, I send you greetings and what word I can from Roma. Little as I like to admit it, you were surely right when you decided that arrangements were necessary.

I have rarely seen Roma in such disarray as I find here now. It is not only that barbarians have done what they could to destroy it for the last five hundred years, but the Romans themselves appear to have forgot who they are, and are content to house themselves in filth and rubble. Not even the worst and poorest of the underground insulae of your youth were as dreadful as much of what I have seen here.

When I left, I told you I would have all your affairs here in order in two months at the most. You warned me at the time that I was being too optimistic, and that you feared with the change in the world that I would require more time, and possibly more money. Sadly, I must confess that you are right. I will not only need more money in order to do what must be done, but I will have to have more time if you are to occupy a place that is suitable to you in all the ways you require.

What is most shocking to me is the disrepair of the aqueducts, for now there is danger of fever from poor water. It is worse than when the Ostrogoths were attacking, and there is no real battle going on. There are German knights everywhere, because of that travesty, the Holy Roman Empire, which is not aptly described by any of those words. I will strive to find you a villa outside the city walls—although the walls are in such disrepair in parts that they might as well be torn down and the stones used to make worthwhile houses for the poor wretches who haunt the streets. I have heard of a number of such villas, and I will inspect them all, taking care not to stray too far from Roma, and I will determine the quality of wells in all the locations I inspect.

I have found a monk here who will arrange for you to be carried on a Spanish ship and brought to Ostia, which they are now calling Ostia Antiqua. Proper escort will be required, but it has been suggested that you yourself petition the Hospitalers for that. They are prepared to render such service and they have chapter houses in many places. It would relieve me to know you are in the hands of a sworn knight —such a man would be less likely to try to rape you or sell you into slavery, and if it comes down to a fight, he will know what to do—than at the mercy of a ship's captain who might strike bargains with pirates, or worse than that.

No, I do not mean to alarm you. That is not my intention. But you have warned me for years and years that prudence is necessary for those of your kind and my kind, and I am only repeating your own precautions for your benefit. After so long, it would be more dreadful than I would like to think to know you had come to any harm.

Niklos Aulirios

By my own hand on the eve of the Passion, in the 1189th Christian year.

・ 3 ・

This chapel, huddled against the south wall of Tyre, was smaller than most; hardly larger than a box stall. The altar was little more than a polished wooden table, and the crucifix hanging above it had been hewn by unskilled hands. In so close a place, the odor of incense mixed with that of the unwashed monk who tended the chapel, making a living presence in the air.

"You were right to seek aid," said the Cistercian monk who knelt on the stone floor beside Olivia. "A woman of quality, a Roman woman, must not undertake so arduous a journey without proper escort."

"But I have none," Olivia said, wishing for an excuse to rise; it felt to her that she was demonstrating simple letters to a wayward child. "I explained that when I arrived."

"Pray you, tell me again. I do not entirely understand."

Inwardly Olivia reminded herself that she needed the monk's good will and assistance if she were to arrange passage for Roma. She kept her tone quiet and stilled the sharp retort that she longed to utter. "My husband's family has been important in Roma, but I do not think that I, as his widow, could request help from his relatives at this time." She had chosen her most restrained and Norman clothes—for this occasion, none of the wide embroidered sleeves of Antioch and Damascus silks; her bliaud was of saffron-rinsed linen, dyed the color of sand. Her fawn-brown hair was braided and covered with a tied veil of cotton, all of which was held in place with a widow's black wreath.

"There is always an obligation—" the Cistercian monk began.

"Pardon me, but I doubt any of my husband's relatives would be able to make a voyage to escort me," she said, her head lowered. She stared at the seashell embedded in a splendor of gold that hung from a flat gold chain around her neck. "Not many of them are inclined to be pilgrims on my behalf."

"There is estrangement?" the monk asked neutrally.

Olivia nodded. "I have not been in Roma for many, many years. There was never such closeness that their duty could survive so long a separation." She did not add that the separation could be counted in centuries, or that her husband had met his end while the elder Titus Flavius Vespasianus wore the purple.

"These developments are always lamentable," said the monk. "I can petition my Order for—"

Once more Olivia held up her hand to stop him. "Again, your pardon, Fraire Herchambaut. Do forgive me for this second interruption." She saw the monk nod acceptance. "My travels are not as simple as for some pilgrims. I have many household goods which must also be sent to Roma. Because I know how little concern religious men have for such concerns, I would rather not burden them with such responsibilities. Also, if I were to be set upon because of the goods I carry, I would never feel at peace if any harm came to any monk of any Order because of my possessions." She joined her slender hands.

"A very pious thought," said Fraire Herchambaut with approval.

"There is another factor as well," added Olivia thoughtfully. "I do . . . poorly . . . in the sun. I am one of those who cannot endure its rays. And worse"—she managed a faint, self-deprecatory smile—"I am ill when sailing."

"Many well-born women are similarly delicate," Fraire Herchambaut said as if impressed. "All the more to your credit that you undertook the pilgrimage you have made."

"I did not feel that I had much choice in the matter. For many widows, the loss of their husbands entails special burdens beyond their grief. Circumstances being what they were, I realized I must come here." She did not add that she had arrived in Tyre not from Roma but from Alexandria.

"You have lived here for some time, or so I am informed." He was clearly curious about her, but had learned to treat all but the poorest pilgrims with circumspection.

"I have lived here more than twelve years," said Olivia with a gesture indicating that she had little concern with the time involved. "I sought a haven."

"A long time." Fraire Herchambaut lowered his head, more in thought than in prayer. "You say you have a servant in Roma already?"

"My major domo. He is my bondsman, a Greek. He has served me faithfully a long time." This time her smile was more apparent but still secretive.

"Faithful servants are one of the greatest of God's blessings," Fraire Herchambaut declared. He rocked back on his heels. "I pray you, do not be alarmed. At my age my bones grow tired quickly."

"That is unfortunate for you," said Olivia, trying to guess the monk's age. Was he forty, forty-five? The desert aged many people fiercely, and it had been centuries since Olivia had met a physician worthy of the name.

He rubbed his hands on the front of his habit. The rough woolen garment was grimy and stained, the fabric almost stiff in places. Only the narrow scapular was relatively clean. "I was thirty-one when I left Languedoc for the Holy Land. There were seventeen of us, and we walked the distance, through Germany and Hungary. Four died on the way. I do not know what became of the rest of us, for each of us has a chapel like this one, and each in a separate town or fort. Two of my Fraires remained at Caesarea, and two at Castel Montforte. From time to time I hear of the others."

"You must miss them," said Olivia, as always puzzled by the monkish urge to withdraw from all familiar society.

"We are together in God," said Fraire Herchambaut automatically. "When we pray, we are not alone or lonely." He regarded Olivia. "Surely you have learned that peace?"

"Not . . . not to the degree I would like," said Olivia.

"No," agreed the Cistercian, "it is the burden of women, the heritage of Eve." He blessed himself. "Well, tell me what you require and I will do what I may to assist you. Little as I wish to say so, I think that it is wise for you to leave Tyre. If the demonic Islamites attack here as they have in Jerusalem, who can tell what would happen to you?"

"Precisely," said Olivia brusquely, which she modified at once. "What frightens me is what could happen if we fall into the hands of the Islamites." For all her years in Alexandria she had never been abused, but that had been before the Shi'ites came. Now she doubted she could rely on the protection of her household or the assistance of the scholars she had known there.

"All Christians must pray that time will never come," said Fraire Herchambaut. "It is not only a defeat for the honor of Christians, it is a defeat for the Holy Spirit as well."

"To say nothing of the body of the Christian," added Olivia.

"The body is not the concern of Christians, only the soul." He blessed himself. "You are a pilgrim. You know this."

This time Olivia made herself give the answer that the monk wanted to hear. "I care little for my body, but I despair of what would happen to it, and to my soul on its account, should I be taken by the Islamites."

"You are a woman of excellent sense," approved Fraire Herchambaut. "And a prudent one." He rose. "Do not rise on my account," he went on. "I have to prepare the Mass." He bowed to the altar and stepped into an alcove. "I will have to be silent while I prepare."

"Of course," said Olivia, trying to find a good reason to leave before the Mass began.

"Also, because only you are present, and you are a woman, I must ask you to leave. When women pilgrims attend Mass, there must be more than one present or we are not allowed . . . it is part of the new Rule, the same one that forbids priests to marry." He coughed. "I will offer prayers for you, and if you permit, I will visit you this evening. I am allowed to carry out the tasks of my calling after the streets have been closed."

"What of robbers?" Olivia asked, knowing better than most what desperate men roamed Tyre once curfew began.

"Robbers do not trouble themselves with monks," Fraire Herchambaut said with a laugh. "Saints and Angels, why should they? What we carry has little use in this world." He indicated his simple monstrance and a small silver pyx. "Neither is worth more than a few coins, if that is how you measure the value of such objects."

"Men have been killed for far less, Fraire." Olivia blessed herself and got to her feet. "You need take no risks on my account. And you will be welcome in my house whenever you come there." She bowed to the altar and backed the few steps to the chapel door. "God give you wise counsel, and aid you in all your deeds."

"And you, Bondama," replied the Cistercian, his attention more on his religion than on her.

Two of Olivia's slaves waited for her, sheltered against the wall out of the sun. The older, a square-bodied eunuch from Ascalon, indicated Olivia's small palinquin. "Mistress," he said as he drew back the curtains to help her into it.

"I suppose I must," she said. "Alfaze, the monk of this chapel has said he will visit me. I wish him to be announced and admitted at once." She adjusted one of the cushions so that she was more comfortable, then slowly pulled the curtains closed. As she felt the palinquin lifted by her two slaves, she cursed the laws that limited her. It was not so long ago, she thought—hardly more than a century—that she would put on Arab's robes and ride with Niklos through the countryside behind Alexandria. She had not dared to do that more than twice in the last five years, and with the Templars increasing their patrols, the joy had gone out of such escapades. How she missed those few, reckless hours of freedom! Had someone told her in her youth that she would have to live this way, she would not have believed them. But then, she added to herself, if she had been told at the same time the kind of husband she would have, she would not have believed that, either. "It's just as well I'm going back to Roma," she muttered, and then, in answer to her slaves' questions, said, "Nothing, nothing. I pray for our deliverance." In a sense it was true enough.

By the time Fraire Herchambaut arrived at Olivia's house, the streets had been closed for some time, and the Cistercian apologized for the lateness of his visit.

"You are welcome at any hour," Olivia assured him when he had been shown to her reception room. "My household has been told to admit you whenever you call, as I said they would. My footmen—there are three slaves who take that duty—will open the door to you at any hour."

"You have a slave at the door at all times?" Fraire Herchambaut asked, startled at such irregular courtesy.

"A Roman habit. My father always had such a footman at

the door, day and night," Olivia said, refraining from adding how long ago that had been. She recalled, fleetingly, the few slaves who had been left to care for her mother, before Justus sent her away from Roma and Olivia. In those days, it was a footman's duty to be sure every person entering the house stepped over the threshold with the right foot, to avert bad luck for everyone.

"Romans have their own traditions," said Fraire Herchambaut vaguely, unwilling to admit that he was unfamiliar with them. "As do others."

"Yes," Olivia said, clapping her hands to summon one of the household slaves still up. "I'm afraid the fare here is very simple, but you are welcome to share—"

"A little bread and wine will be very welcome, and God will bless you for your charity," said Fraire Herchambaut. "I eat no flesh at night. Bread and wine are food enough for any true Christian."

Olivia did not speak at once, and when she did, there was an odd catch in her voice, as if she had been about to cough, or laugh. She addressed her slave, "Bread and wine for Fraire Herchambaut. And fruit."

The slave bowed. "At once, mistress."

Fraire Herchambaut had been looking around the room, and said now, "I had heard you are a widow of means, but I was not aware how . . ." Words failed him as he indicated the silk hangings on the wall, the Persian carpet underfoot as elaborate as a garden, the small gold crucifix over the door.

"I have been fortunate in some ways," Olivia said. "Pray be seated. I am eager to hear what you can tell me about the requirements for my return to Roma. The sooner I attend to whatever the Bourgesses wish, the sooner I may be gone from Tyre."

"Certainly," said Fraire Herchambaut. He chose one of the three Frankish chairs. "How did you come by these?"

"There was a French Bourgess who offered them to me some time ago." She thought back to the man, and the year of his persistent courtship she had endured. What an impossible creature he had been, she thought, all greedy for her body and her possessions as if they were the same thing.

"And the brass chests?" As soon as he had asked, Fraire Herchambaut waved his own question away. "No, it is not right that I should ask, or that you tell me. I am not your confessor, nor am I retained by your kinsmen. You are in an awkward situation, with so much to attend to on your own." He made a self-deprecatory sound between a chuckle and a snort. "You are almost a chatelaine without a castle, and your duties are more than most women expect. I see why you are careful about your move; it is wise of you."

"This move needs more dispatch than wisdom, and that is proving to be hard come by. Everywhere I turn I am blocked or diverted." She made an effort to control her frustration, and in a calmer voice went on, "I am willing to sell some of these things, of course, and I plan to make donations to the Orders in Tyre, but there is so much—"

"And doubtless your family expects you to preserve these goods as well," said Fraire Herchambaut. "You have that obligation, of course."

Olivia was about to answer incautiously when her slave returned carrying a brass tray. "There is wine, dates, and honey cakes, mistress."

"Present it to my guest," she said, nodding toward Fraire Herchambaut.

The Cistercian tried to defer to Olivia, which was what courtesy required, but was more because he felt intimidated in her presence. He was not used to elegant, self-contained women who managed their own affairs. The Queen of England was said to be such a woman, but Fraire Herchambaut had never seen her. "It is not necessary."

"Of course it is. Zahdi, tend to my guest." Olivia concealed her impatience with what grace she could muster.

The slave obeyed, bringing a little table to the side of the monk's chair. He bowed as he put down the tray, then, at Olivia's signal, withdrew from the reception room, hoping that one of the other slaves would be called when the Fraire left.

Fraire Herchambaut looked at the food. "This is too lavish, good widow. I would be sinning in gluttony if I ate so much after my supper."

"Take what you want," said Olivia, concealing her annoyance at the satisfaction the Cistercian took at his self-denial. "If you want nothing, have nothing."

The monk nodded. "You have a sense of charity, which is

most laudable. It is the virtue of women, isn't it?" He had lifted the wine jar, then said, "I have only one cup. Surely you would—"

Olivia held up her hand. "I do not drink wine."

Fraire Herchambaut hesitated and then poured for himself. "I must tell you that I think your abstention shows your good sense. Women are easily overcome by wine, and then they are prey to their lusts far more than any man." He held up the cup in salute to his hostess. "To your kindness and goodness, in Our Lord's Name."

"Thank you," said Olivia without inflection. How long, she wondered, would it take this tedious monk to tell her what she wanted to know.

"Excellent vintage," Fraire Herchambaut approved when he had finished the wine in three long sips, in tribute to the Trinity. "Now, let us turn our thoughts to the ending of your predicament." He wiped his mouth with the end of his sleeve. "I have considered carefully everything you have told me, and I am reasonably certain that you can leave Tyre in six to eight months." He folded his hands over his belt, obviously pleased with this declaration.

"Six to eight months? *Months?*" Olivia echoed, dismayed.

"There is, as you have said already, much to be arranged, and if you have goods to be disposed of, they must be handled by the authorities in a proper manner." He took one of the honey cakes and broke it into three pieces before popping the largest into his mouth and chewing vigorously. He went on, less clearly, "If you commence at once, you will be able to be finished before the end of summer, and once you have accommodated the requirements of the Bourgesses, you will be able to travel as soon as proper escort is available."

Olivia suppressed the urge to shout at her guest; instead she averted her face so that he could not see how angry she was. "Would it not be possible to issue an authorization for the disposal of such goods as I leave behind after I've gone?"

"I have made inquiries on that point. Unfortunately, you have said yourself that your major domo is in Roma, and not able to attend to such duties. To appoint another would take almost as long as the task itself." He was working on the second piece of honey cake. "I realize you wanted to be gone sooner, but with the Islamites abroad in the land, and danger all around us, the Bourgesses are more careful than ever, and more resolute. They have redoubled their efforts to protect all Roman Christians in the Holy Land, and we are wise to abide by their edicts."

"I see," Olivia said, clenching her fists in the folds of her bliaud. "How Roman, to seek a solution through complexity."

Fraire Herchambaut chuckled. "Roman women have great wit. It is not always appropriate in women, but I doubt you have given offense through yours."

Only, Olivia said to herself, because I am learning to contain my temper. "When I was a child, my father educated me as he educated my brothers. It was the custom in his family." She was able to keep her eyes lowered and her manner calm. "So," she continued more briskly, trusting herself at last to speak to Fraire Herchambaut directly, "tell me what I must do to satisfy the Bourgesses and be gone from here."

Fraire Herchambaut, who was starting on his second cup of wine, cleared his throat. "First, the Bourgesses will require that you present a complete inventory of your goods, indicating which you intend to sell, which to donate, and which to take with you. This is to prevent any pilfering or substitution of goods, you understand."

As the Cistercian drank, Olivia said, "Very well. Is that to include everything in the house, or only the moveables? Such items as the ovens and the troughs in the kitchen are not to be included, are they?"

"Another jest," Fraire Herchambaut said, wagging his head in mirth as he set down his cup. "You must have been the delight of your husband."

"His interests lay . . . in other directions," Olivia said carefully.

"It is often thus with men of affairs," Fraire Herchambaut said, turning abruptly solemn. He selected one of the dates and bit into it experimentally. "Preserved in syrup of . . . ?" He looked to Olivia for the answer.

"Raisins, I believe," said Olivia, irritated at the distraction.

"Superb." He finished the date.

"About the inventory?" Olivia ventured when she thought she had a chance of keeping Fraire Herchambaut's attention.

"Complete, of course, but not to include items that are part of the house as a building. Those items to be sold will be marked by an ancient of the Bourgesses, and then they will be catalogued for sale." He shook his head as he recited this information. "It appears over-complicated, I realize that, but it is to ensure that the goods are protected and that your interests are served."

"If my interests were being served, I would be allowed to leave in a week," Olivia said with asperity before she could stop herself.

"You must pray for patience," said Fraire Herchambaut, one hand lifted to admonish her. "Your husband's family would think themselves and you ill-served if you returned to Roma without the accounts that will indicate—"

"My husband's family, as I've told you already, is not involved in what I do." Olivia paused. "I did not speak to offend you, but in this instance I believe I know my circumstances better than you or the Bourgesses do."

"If you received less than proper treatment, you would discover otherwise," said Fraire Herchambaut as he poured the last of the wine into his cup. "Every family has the family's fortune in mind, from the most august to the most humble. You have an obligation, if not to your family, to the memory of your husband and his heirs to preserve your wealth and to account for how you have spent it." This time his three sips were noisy and rapid.

"Tell me, good Cistercian," Olivia said, feeling desperate, "once the Bourgesses have tended to their accounting, how long will it take to arrange for escort and a ship?"

"Not terribly long, unless another Crusade is called, of course." This afterthought was slightly slurred; the wine was taking hold.

"Oh, Lord," said Olivia, and remembered to bless herself so that she would not be upbraided for profanity. "Isn't another Crusade likely?"

Fraire Herchambaut nodded sagely. "Oh, yes, yes, I would guess that the Pope will preach another soon. We can't have Saladin in Jerusalem. It can't be tolerated."

"And if the Crusade begins, what then? How long will it take me to leave Tyre?" In her desperation Olivia felt an element of the ridiculous and had to bite the insides of her cheeks to keep from laughing.

"That depends if there is fighting here or not. If the Islamites come, then we will be fortunate to emerge alive and with our freedom." He blessed himself. "They make eunuchs of monks, you know? Because we maintain our chastity. They say they do it because we are eunuchs already." He belched. "It blasphemes chastity, castration. The point of chastity," he said with owlish intensity, "is to keep the ability and to offer up the sacrifice of not using it." His expression darkened to a scowl. "Now that priests cannot marry, monks are . . ." He lost the thread of what he was saying.

"Yes?" Olivia prompted. "What of monks, good Fraire?"

"Forgot," he admitted. "It doesn't matter," he went on ponderously. "You make that inventory. That's the first step."

"Yes; all right." She considered sending for fruit juices with peppers but decided against it; the monk would not be sober until morning no matter what she did. "And the escort."

"It will be arranged." He reached out to put his cup down and succeeded in oversetting the entire tray. The last of the honey cakes and five marinated dates sprayed over the floor. "Jesu," said Fraire Herchambaut in a bemused tone.

"My slaves will attend to it," Olivia told him. "About the escort? My escort to Roma?"

"You must have one," said Fraire Herchambaut distantly. "The Devil's in my head."

Olivia persisted. "If I will require an escort, cannot this be arranged in advance, so that once my accounting is approved here, all will be ready for my departure?"

Fraire Herchambaut rubbed his brow in concentration. "It's irregular," he decided at last.

"But is it possible?" Olivia had risen to her feet and was pacing the confines of this room.

"I don't know," Fraire Herchambaut said when he had considered the possibilities. "It might be."

She stopped, her hands locked together, her hazel eyes glittering in the flickering brazier light. "If it is possible, and if it is allowed, will you make such arrangements for me, Fraire Herchambaut?"

"Part of my task," he said to her just before his head lolled to the side and a stentorian snore rumbled out of him.

Olivia stood and glared down at Fraire Herchambaut. She would have to arrange for the monk to be awakened before dawn, and to be escorted back to his chapel by one of her slaves. As she clapped for assistance, she hoped that the Cistercian would be able to remember what he had said this evening. She looked up as one of the footmen came through the door; she indicated Fraire Herchambaut. "Something will have to be done with him," she said. "You see the state he's in."

"I will take care of it, mistress," said the footman.

"And the room must be cleaned, as well." She realized, as she said this, that this was only the first of many extra tasks that would be given to her household in the next days and weeks. The prospect vexed her.

"Do you wish him moved, mistress?" asked the footman, cutting into her thoughts.

"Yes, but you might as well leave him here until morning." She started toward the door. "Is my bath ready?"

"Yes, mistress, as you requested."

"Thank God," she said with feeling. "What ever convinced monks that not bathing was holy?" Without waiting for an answer, she left her footman with Fraire Herchambaut and went off to her private quarters.

*   *   *

Text of a letter from the Chatelaine Fealatie Bueveld to the Abbot of Sante-Estien-in-Gorze.

Most Revered Abbott, my deliverer in this unfortunate time, I will most willingly undertake the pilgrimage you have advocated, for it is acceptable to my husband's kinsmen, to the Comes de Reissac and his kinsmen, and to my family.

I pray you will remember me while I am gone, and will petition Heaven to give me safe passage, for it is agreed that I will travel with an escort of four only, since I am to travel in harness. We will leave from Sante-Ranegonde-in-Toul in a month. It is agreed that we will travel overland and not take ship at Venezia or Genova as some have. I am to offer prayers at every Christian holy place along the way, and am enjoined to bring back to the Comes de Reissac a rose from the walls of Jerusalem.

My cousin Orsin will replace me at Castel Fraizmarch, and will serve in my husband's stead until such time as my husband returns from the service of the Pope in Roma. I accept the decision to remove my authority since I have so greatly abused it.

If God wills, I will send word to you as regularly as I am able, and will entrust my messages to monks and priests alone, not to other pilgrims. Those who travel with me have agreed to send their messages with mine, under seal so that I will not know what they report. Whatever charges are contained in such messages I will answer upon my return to Castel Fraizmarch. It is my greatest hope that the infamy I have brought upon Gui de Fraizmarch and all the House of Bueveld will be forgiven, if not while I live, then at the Mercy Seat. All my faith and my pilgrimage is dedicated to that end.

Fealatie Bueveld
Chatelaine of Gui de Fraizmarch
By my own hand and under the seal of Castel Fraizmarch,
on the last day of May, in the Lord's Year 1189.

· 4 ·

"Most gracious Roman lady," the newcomer said as he dropped to one knee to kiss Olivia's sleeve, "I have greeting to you from a scoundrel in Roma who calls himself your major domo."

Olivia stared at this stranger, arrayed in carnival colors, and speaking with an accent she did not know. "Niklos?"

"In Roma, bribing officials with the best of them," said her visitor. "He approached me because I have a ship, a fast one, and it sails from Valencia to Sicilia and Cyprus and Tyre. Niklos has already purchased space aboard for you on the return voyage, assuming you are permitted to leave at that time." He glanced over his shoulder toward the front of the next house. "I have more to tell you." He spoke a strange version of Latin.

Called out of her thoughts, Olivia opened the door wider. "I ask pardon that my footman did not receive you," she said in a distracted way. "He and four other of my slaves are presenting the inventory to the customs officers at the funda."

"No matter—we Spanish Jews are used to improvising." He stepped inside the door and moved aside so that Olivia could close it.

"Spanish Jew?" Olivia repeated.

"I admit I look something of an Islamite. Most of Spain is part of Islam, and we have learned to take the look. My family is from Cadiz, if you know where that is." He looked around the vestibule and made a gesture of approval.

"Yes; a . . . close associate of my . . . oldest friend is from Gades."

"Cadiz," the stranger corrected. "It was Gades in Roman times."

"Of course," said Olivia, and indicated the entrance to the larger of her reception rooms. "Please, come in and tell me how it is you met Niklos."

"You are most gracious," said her guest, going ahead of her into the luxurious chamber. "First, let me tell you that my name is Ithuriel Dar, and my ship is the *Ondas del' Albor,* and she was built in Lixboa sixteen years ago. She has carried cargo safely ever since. No pirate has ever caught her and no storm has ever drowned her." He smiled, his deep brown eyes lit with true enthusiasm.

"And you say this paragon of a ship is in Valencia now?" Olivia asked, indicating he might be seated.

"Preparing to carry leather and honey to Sicilia," he said. "I came from Caesarea to arrange cargo for a return voyage. I often act as my own agent." He paused to look around the room. "How much of this were you planning to carry back to Roma? Not all of it, I hope?"

"No, not all," said Olivia, beginning to find Ithuriel Dar more amusing than perplexing. "Less than half of my goods will go with me. That is why my slaves are presenting my various inventories at the funda, so that taxes and customs and all the rest of it can be arranged."

"A necessary evil," Dar said, dismissing the process. "Every city on this coast has a funda, and each has its own idea about levying taxes. The Bourgesses' Court is even worse." He stopped and picked up a painted box. "This looks to be quite old."

"It is," said Olivia, and when it was apparent that Dar was waiting for more, she added, "It comes from the time of Heliogabalus."

"That was one of the debauched Caesars, wasn't he?" He put the box down. "Still, the box is very beautiful." As he approached the shuttered window, he said, "I wish I could show you what my ship is like. There are two similar merchantships at the wharves, and—"

"I have seen ships before, Bonsier." She smiled. "Niklos must have told you that."

"He said you had traveled and that you dislike the sea."
Dar gave her a sharp look. "Well? Is that true?"

"Sadly, yes," said Olivia. "If I do travel on your ship, I
will probably spend most of my time in my quarters, trying
not to be sick." Even saying this made her feel slightly
queasy.

"That is because you have not been on such a ship as
mine," Dar informed her with a lavish gesture and a wide
smile. "If you come on the *Ondas del' Albor,* you will change
your mind at once. I promise you, it is not like the rolling
buckets you see every day. This is a ship worthy of the name,
fast as a good horse and with more heart than ten of those
noisy beasts."

Olivia was tempted to tell Dar that her aversion had
nothing to do with ships, but with water. Instead she
remarked, "I have been on the Egyptian ships that ply the
waters from here to Alexandria—"

"Niklos told me you had lived for a time in Alexandria,"
said Dar.

"And in other places as well," said Olivia. "For me, once I
step off dry land, it is always the same."

"You will change your mind." He said it so confidently
that Olivia could not restrain her laughter.

"Very well, let me summon my bearers and you can show
me what makes your ship superior to all the others I have
been on." As she said it, she knew she was behaving badly,
but it did not bother her. She went to the door and called for
Alfaze to ready her palinquin. "They will need a short time
to prepare, but once they are ready, we will depart for the
wharves."

Dar chuckled. "Niklos warned me you might do something of the sort. He takes great pride in how outrageous you
can be."

"I know," said Olivia serenely. She missed Niklos so
much; hearing Ithuriel Dar speak of him was at once
soothing and hurtful. "Was he well?"

"He was the last I saw of him, but Roma is a city of
miasmas in the summer. You know what the fevers can do in
the heat of the year." He shook his head. "Niklos told me
that it was not always so, that in the time of the Caesars
there was less illness, and the wells were pure. They always

tell such tales about the past, don't they? It was always better when no one can remember it. My mother used to say that milk never curdled when Moses was alive."

"Perhaps Roma was a better city then," Olivia suggested as she listened for the signal from Alfaze.

"How could that be?" Dar argued, enjoying himself tremendously. "How could the past have been so much better than what we have now? You can see that some of the buildings once had marble fronts, but that means little."

"If it were simply a question of marble fronts, I would agree," said Olivia, sounding more wistful than she realized.

"Still, if it's your home, it's doubtless preferable to Tyre." He looked up sharply as a bell sounded.

"My palinquin is ready," Olivia explained. "Come with me and my bearers will take me with you." As she started toward the side of her house, she paused to take a small misericordie from its rack on the wall; she tucked the thin dagger in the long folds of her girdle and stepped out of the door.

"We are ready," Alfaze said in his soft voice. "Where are we to carry you, mistress?"

"To wherever this bonsier tells you; somewhere at the wharves." She started to pull her curtains closed, then stopped. "Who is left to watch the doors and guard the house for me?"

"Saniel and Fedyah," Alfaze told her. "And three kitchen slaves."

"That will do for a short time," Olivia said, hoping that whatever Dar offered would be acceptable to the Bourgesses; she was aching to leave. Once she closed the curtains, her bearers lifted her and followed Ithuriel Dar through the crowded streets to the wharves.

At the largest of these, an usciere was unloading its living cargo; knights, equerries, and esquires stood to receive the horses as they were led out, edgy and restless after their long passage in stalls belowdecks. Templars, Hospitalers, and even two men in the yellow cote of the Knights Hospitalers of Saint Lazarus were claiming their precious animals.

"I don't carry horses on my ship—it isn't made for it. Horses belong in uscieres, and that's how it ought to be," said Dar as he watched one of the Templars alternately bully and coax a dark gray destrier down the reinforced rear gangplank. "Ah," said Dar. "Two over—you can see there is a Pisan ship. It has a square and a latin sail, and twelve oars."

Olivia, opening her curtains enough to look out, finally saw the ship Dar had indicated. "Is yours like that?"

"That's a tarida; the *Ondas del' Albor* is a tarida bastarda, with more sail and longer." He braced his hands on his hips. "And my ship is more beautiful."

"I am certain it is," said Olivia, respecting Dar's pride.

"There are two latin sails on the *Ondas del' Albor.*" His expression approached smugness. "Aside from a panfilo or a fusta—and those are armed warships, mind—not even the bergantino is faster. Of course, a saettia is fastest, but there's no room for any cargo on one. I started out with a baleniero, but—"

"Bonsier Dar," Olivia interrupted, "I am sure everything you tell me is true, but I have no great interest in ships. I wish only to get over the water as quickly as is safe, and to have my goods and myself returned to Roma."

Dar sighed and turned away from the excitement on the wharves. "You do not see the beauty in all this, good widow?"

"No, Bonsier, I do not," Olivia said, and then modified her words. "If I did not become ill when traveling by water, doubtless I would come to love it in time."

Dar raised his hand to shade his eyes. "There is another ship, at the edge of the sea; it is bound for this port, I think. It carries blazoned sails."

"How can you tell?" Olivia squinted at the horizon and saw nothing.

"My eyes are farseeing, which for others could be an affliction, but is to my advantage." He favored her with a sidelong glance. "Also, when I was a child, my father taught me to look this way, from the tail of the eye, in order to see things at a great distance."

"How can you be certain that's a ship? What if it is only a cloud?" asked Olivia, curious about his answer.

"A man who has been at sea for as long as I have knows

the difference between a ship and a cloud." He folded his arms over his chest and looked directly at her. "And I know the sails are blazoned because I can see that something is painted on the sails. Surely they are blazoned. Perhaps it is one of the ships of Barbarossa. They say he is bringing an army to recapture Jerusalem."

Olivia kept her voice level, but it cost her an effort. "I have heard something of this as well, Bonsier Dar. The Pope is eager for a new Crusade."

"True enough, true enough," sighed Dar. "Everyone's after poor Jerusalem, but they try to keep us out, whose city it is." He stared out to sea. "Yes, it is blazoned; Norman arms, I think, from Sicilia."

"I won't argue with you, Bonsier Dar." She was relieved that he had changed the subject. "You are, as you have said yourself, the one who has been at sea, and I have already confessed my . . . dislike for traveling over water." She said it lightly, refusing to be drawn into an argument. "I am pleased you are so capable and vigilant."

Dar was not mollified by this. "Save your banter, good widow. I will not be challenged on my skills and my knowledge, least of all by a seasick woman."

"I do not challenge you," she said. "I am curious, in part because I am afraid."

"You have no reason to be. With me, you are as safe as a baby in its cradle." He rocked back on his heels and stared at her, his face a network of creases that revealed his every thought and emotion. "I am not sure you trust me."

"I don't," she admitted without heat. "Or," she amended, "I do not trust you completely. You would not think much of me if I did." This last shrewd touch restored her to Dar's good opinion.

"True enough," he said, showing very white, even teeth. "And who is to blame me for that?"

"Who is to blame *me?*" she countered, waiting to see his response.

"Perhaps," he said speculatively, regarding her with increased interest, "it will not be such a tragedy to have you aboard my ship, after all. You have a good wit. It is a thing I admire in women; wit." He started to stroll along the wharves, paying almost no attention to Olivia's bearers as they struggled to keep up with him in the press of the dockside crowd. "Don't dawdle," he called out to the bearers as they lagged behind.

"For mercy's sake," Olivia replied, "slow down." She cursed the laws of Tyre that required she travel concealed. It was as bad as Constantinople, she thought, which was one of the worst observations she could make of a place. "If my slaves try to go faster, they'll drop me."

"Nonsense," Dar shouted back.

Suddenly one of the horses being unloaded from the usciere broke away from the slaves attempting to lead him. He reared, plunged, whinnied in angry panic, then broke free, rushing headlong down the gangplank into the crowd.

People scattered; screams and shouts cut through the buzz of talk. As the horse grew more terrified, he darted wildly, pawing the air, striking out, trying to find an opening.

"What on earth—?" Olivia demanded as Alfaze lurched, and then the palinquin dropped to the planks of the wharf. As she tried to crawl from the palinquin, Olivia heard one of her bearers shriek, and the hard, implacable sound of hooves pounding on flesh and bone.

"Widow!" Dar shouted from some little distance. "Guard yourself!"

The horse was a big knight's stallion, taller than any of the horses bred in the Holy Land, and heavier of body, a destrier for an armored man to ride in battle. His sorrel coat was sweat-dark and flecked with foam, and the white mane was a long, tangled mat. He was panting with fear.

"Have a care!" bellowed someone in the crowd.

The hooves came down again, but this time Olivia had been able to extricate herself from the curtains and was scrambling to her feet as the horse reared over her. It took all her will to resist the urge to run from the animal. She had a few seconds to act, to save herself from the crushing blows.

She stepped to the horse's side and reached for a handful of mane, holding as the horse pulled; as he reached his full height, Olivia tugged sharply on the mane, dragging the horse sideways and back until, with a scream, the horse fell on his side, legs thrashing. Olivia flung herself on the neck and wrapped her arms over his head, pinning him to the tarred planks of the wharf.

The frenzy around her stopped almost at once. Two of the slaves who had been chasing the horse came running up to Olivia, one of them marked with fresh bruises and cuts. The rest of the crowd gathered around, many expressing amazement that a woman should have brought such a brute under control.

"If you will not get too near," Olivia said in a penetrating voice, "he will remain calm. The animal is terrified, and small wonder."

"He will hurt you, lady," said one of the slaves.

"No, he won't, not if you are sensible," she said, keeping her weight on the neck and head of the horse. The odor of his sweat was everywhere. "He'll be all right shortly, but not if you let him up right now." She spoke to the slaves in much the same tone she would use on the horse, firm and confident but not too loud. "Stand back, and I'll get him up for you. No one is to make sudden moves."

"Widow!" Dar called out from the edge of the crowd.

"Remain where you are, Bonsier," she told him as she crawled up the neck to the horse's head. Only when she was certain she could stand up in front of the animal did she rise, and stepped back as the horse got to his feet, still breathing hard and wet, but no longer insane. Olivia signaled to the nearer of the two slaves. "Hand me a rope," she said, watching the horse closely.

"You cannot manage, lady," said the nearer slave. "Let us bring whips."

"I've done better than the two of you," she reminded him. "Give me a rope and step back."

The horse shook his head, his eyes showing white; he arched his neck, ears forward, legs stiff.

"He's going to attack," warned the nearer slave.

"Not quite yet," said Olivia. "Hand me a rope. Now."

The slave hesitated; a sailor came forward and offered Olivia a length of rough hemp, which she took at once. She stepped nearer the horse, staying to the side so that he could see her, and eased the rope over his neck. "Stand still," she said quietly, calmly.

"He is maddened, lady," the slave pleaded.

"He is frightened," Olivia corrected as she looped the rope under his neck. "If everyone will move away, I will give him back to the slaves who should not have let him go in the first place." This last, pointed remark was heard with mixed feelings.

"Lady . . ." the slave with the bruises began. "He will bolt."

"He will not," she said, holding the makeshift lead in a steady hand. She glanced down and saw that Alfaze had got free of the wreckage of her palinquin, but that her other bearer was tangled in the carrying staves. There was blood on his head. "I am going to lead him away from my slaves," she announced, and moved slowly, coaxing the horse as she went.

"He—" the bruised slave began.

"Stand back and be silent," Olivia said sharply. "Do not speak to me again."

Someone in the crowd whooped; the horse brought his head up and made a sound like a cough as he arched his neck.

"Be silent, I pray you," Olivia said with a calm she did not truly feel. "All of you be silent." She patted his high shoulder. "Come, fellow. Come along." It was a tricky business leading the horse along the wharf. Every noise made him tremble and falter. Olivia held onto the rope and hoped she would not be tested again.

She had nearly reached the usciere when a man in herald's livery of Austria came down from the ship, relief in his face. He watched Olivia with a degree of surprise. "You caught him?"

"Yes," said Olivia, bowing her head in courtesy to the herald's master. "Is he one of yours?"

"Part of a grant to the Templars," said the herald. "I am to deliver them with the compliments of Leopold of Austria." He indicated the arms on his tabard.

Olivia gave her makeshift lead over to a groom with Leopold's badge on his arm. "Very generous of Leopold," she said, aware that she was behaving improperly to speak to the man at all. "I am certain the Templars will be grateful."

"It is prudent," said the herald in a pointed way. "I thank you for your efforts."

Olivia accepted the thanks with a slight smile. "In future you might take greater care in handling those horses. Stallions are worst of all." She started to turn away, then looked back at the herald. "One of my slaves was badly hurt by the horse and my palinquin was ruined. Will you offer recompense, or must I go to the Templars for that?" It was a risk to challenge the herald in this way; Olivia waited for his answer, hoping that she would not be dismissed or upbraided for her request.

"Your slave was hurt?" the herald asked.

"One of my palinquin bearers. He was unconscious when I left him. He may still be unconscious. And I am without my palinquin to return to my house." She stood very straight and her hazel eyes met the herald's uncompromisingly.

The herald hesitated. "You will have escort back to your house, of course," he said heavily. "That is the least that I can offer. As to the slave—"

"The Court of Bourgesses will assess you the cost of his treatment, if you require that I approach them," she told him coolly. Her initial trepidation was fading.

The herald reacted as if a glove had been flung at him. "It will not be necessary," he said with icy propriety. "Who have I the honor of addressing?"

Olivia gave her name. "I am Roman," she said, "and a widow."

"Widow?" the herald inquired, his lifted eyebrow revealing his skepticism. "With a palinquin and slaves. How fortunate."

She ignored the insult. "Who wishes to return to Roma, and finds it more difficult than anticipated."

The herald's stiffness abated a little. "The Pope has called for another Crusade. It is not easy to arrange such matters in such times."

"So I have discovered." She looked toward the groom, who had haltered and tied the stallion. "You had best walk him," she suggested. "Otherwise he is going to break away again, and I will not remain here to assist you." Before the herald could speak, she addressed him. "I . . . inherited a breeding stable, and learned much there." Let the man think her husband had willed her the stable, Olivia thought scathingly. Sanct' Germain would not mind the small mendacity; it was close enough to the truth, for the breeding stable had been a legacy from him.

"I . . . have no doubt, Bondama," said the herald, his voice now respectful.

"My escort?" Olivia demanded, adding, "I am in the company of Bonsier Dar, of Spain. He will accompany me back to my house as soon as you provide me with suitable company." Now that she had achieved so much, she pressed her advantage. "I would appreciate it if you would have my injured slave taken to the Hospitalers and my palinquin replaced."

"Most assuredly," said the herald, clapping to summon aid. "They are esquires, Bondama," he informed Olivia as four youths hurried off the ship. "All are of high family."

"As fits the company of heralds," said Olivia, barely nodding in their direction. "Very well. I wish to leave at once. It isn't seemly for me to stand here where I am exposed to every eye." It was what she was expected to say, not what she believed, for the restrictions placed upon her galled her most of the time and she was enjoying this little sip of freedom.

The herald opened his hands to show his helplessness. "You have only to tell these esquires where you live, and—"

"But we don't know where she lives," one of the young men whispered to the herald in his own language. "How are we to escort her if—?"

Olivia interrupted, her German Latin-accented. "My slave who is not injured will show you the way."

The esquire flushed and the herald craned his neck as if the neck of his camisade had grown tight. Making a point of speaking in Norman French, as he had been from the first, the herald said to Olivia, "On behalf of these esquires, I offer apology for any distress you have suffered on our account."

"I am pleased to forgive you," said Olivia, following the custom.

Ithuriel Dar had made his way to her side; he stood a little behind her, reluctant to bring attention on himself. He said in a low voice, "Your slaves are waiting for you. The eunuch—"

"Alfaze," Olivia said.

"Yes; he said the other slave is badly hurt."

Olivia shook her head, her brows drawing together. "It's all such a waste. If these fools had known more about that horse none of this would have happened."

The herald had come forward with the esquires and waited impatiently to finish his dealings with Olivia. "Bondama," he said as soon as the opportunity presented itself.

"Yes?" Olivia asked, then nodded to the herald. "I will want word of my slave as soon as the Hospitalers can provide it. Bonsier Dar, give me your company."

"As you wish," said Dar, his manner more subdued than it had been, for he distrusted the Austrians.

The herald spoke to the esquires. "See that this bondama reaches her house without further incident. Then go to the Hospitalers and bring me word of her slave." He bowed formally to Olivia. "When I have word, I will send a message to you."

"My thanks," said Olivia, and set out in the midst of the esquires, Ithuriel Dar bringing up the rear. As the little group reached Alfaze and the wreckage of the palinquin, Olivia saw that her injured slave was shivering though his face and arms were slick with sweat; his swarthy face was gray. I must leave this place, she thought. I must leave. I must leave.

*   *   *

Text of a letter from the Venetian Giozzetto Camarmarr to the Benedictine scholar Ulrico Fionder.

My very dear and learned cousin, I have succeeded in leaving Cyprus and have arrived safely at Rhodes. I am making arrangements to take ship home, but now that Barbarossa has his army on the march, it is difficult for a mere merchant to find passage.

Let me offer prayers of thanks for all of the family who gathered the monies to pay my ransom. The pirates who held me would truly have sold me into slavery to some Islamite, which might well have meant they would have made a eunuch of me. To my wife and children, that would be as great a loss as if I had died and been buried. I lament the cost, and I am grieved that my misfortune could impose so great a burden on all who share my name and heritage. In these dire times, who among us can think himself safe? I have learned to my cost and my pain that we may know nothing certain but the Mercy of God.

Now that I am back among Christians again, I realize that what I had feared has come to pass. Everywhere the knights prepare to do battle with the devils of Islam, and everywhere stores are being laid up against the day that these forces meet. I trust that you communicated to our family the sense of purchasing transport ships, for I have seen with my own eyes the tremendous need for them, and the prices that are being paid for their use. If all the Kings under the Pope come here to fight, our fortunes could be made for the next four genera-tions. Such an event might in part compensate for the great expense I have occasioned our family. From the dreadful developments of the last year, I pray we will salvage our name and our riches.

It may be that you do not concern yourself with such

matters, but without doubt there are others of us who do, and they are eager to add to the coffers of Camarmarr and Fionder. Your Abbot would welcome a generous donation, and if one of his monks is part of a family contributing to the success of the Crusade, he will not begrudge us the profits we reap in so worthy a venture. I, for one, would be pleased if we recoup our losses in this way, for it would aid and protect the holiest place in Christendom as well as assist in bringing down the Islamites, who are the direct cause of the losses we have suffered through my capture.

I long for the day that I will see your face again, for the day I will sit with my wife and children in our own house. My captivity, though it was not long, has left me with the most profound devotion to my family, and has given me staunch purpose in my determination to exact full measure from the Islamites for the great torment they visited upon me.

Once I have reached Ragusa, I will send word to you. Look to see me before the summer is over. I fear you will find me much changed, but that cannot be helped. God has imposed His burden on me and I pray for the grace to bear the burden.

Your loving cousin
Giozzetto Camarmarr
By my own hand on the feast of Saint Hippolytus the Martyr of Roma in the 1189th year of Our Lord.

· 5 ·

On the far wall the plaster was broken or missing; the doorframe was warped so that Niklos had to lean on it to close it. All the furniture had been removed years ago.

"The rumor is," said the scribe who accompanied him, "that the building is haunted."

"Haunted?" Niklos repeated in disbelief. "What pagan nonsense is that?"

The scribe looked embarrassed. "Pagan, certainly. What good Christian can believe such gossip?" He glanced over his shoulder toward the window. "The talk has given the estate an evil name. My master has said he wants to be rid of the place. His wife will not come here. His brother will not dare to set foot inside these walls." The scribe suppressed a shudder. "I confess," he went on nervously, "that I would not like to be here after sundown."

"Trust in God," Niklos recommended. "Tell me about this haunting. What is thought to be the cause?" As he listened, he paced the room, assessing the size as he listened.

"It is . . . ridiculous, most ridiculous," the scribe began uneasily. "It seems that the son of the master of the house was going to join with the First Crusaders, with the men Tancred led. But once he reached the Holy Land, he was seized with a passion for an Islamite woman, and for her sake he abandoned Tancred and fled with his siren into the desert." He moved over toward the window so that he could look out into the overgrown garden.

"Such things have happened," Niklos said, amused at the scribe's discomfort.

"Well," the scribe went on after taking a deep breath, "it was said that she was an enchantress who used sorcery to overcome his faith so that he forgot his knightly oath."

Niklos touched the wall where a little of the plaster remained. He rubbed the residue between his fingers and sniffed at it. "Knights have forgot their oaths for less," he observed to tell the scribe that he was still listening.

"But he was sworn to restore the Holy Sepulcher," protested the scribe. "However it was done, the knight fled with the woman, and when she tired of him, she cursed him with flux and with failing bowels. In despair, he became a beggar, shamed and damned. Only at the end of his days did he return here, hoping that he might find succor in the bosom of his family. It is said that he haunts this place still, that his ghost drove out his own family, for they knew him and it brought his shame upon them."

"How does the ghost make itself known?" Niklos asked, wiping his brow with the back of his hand; the afternoon heat was intense as a lover's embrace.

"They say—I have not heard it for myself—that he can be

heard crying for alms and begging forgiveness for his sins."
He licked his lips. "My master has permitted the house to
fall into disrepair, somewhat."

Niklos' smile was ironic, but the scribe was not looking at
him and did not see it. "That's apparent. At least there is no
trace of rot so far."

"There are cellars, if you must look there. I will show you
where they are." The scribe blessed himself automatically.
"This is not a place I want to live."

"But you are not going to have to," Niklos pointed out.
"It is my mistress who may have to live here. If I find the
place suitable."

"What would your mistress think of this place, if it is
haunted?" His voice had risen a little.

"Has a priest been called to exorcise the ghost?" asked
Niklos. "Have prayers been said for the knight's repose?
Have Masses been offered for his salvation?"

The scribe had nodded to each of these questions. "All
that and more. My master offered this house to a company
of knights, but they would not come here for fear that the
spirit of the knight would cause them to turn from their
vows. Nothing has calmed the ghost."

"Show me the rest of the house," said Niklos, doing his
best to sound bored. "I will want to inspect the stables and
barns as well, and to see what condition the vinyards are in.
My mistress will require a full report from me." Although he
did his best to sound indifferent, Niklos was inwardly
pleased. The house was good-sized, with quarters for eight-
een slaves as well as extra rooms for household. He had
already inspected the chapel built a little distance from the
house, which the scribe had told him was dedicated to Santo
Telesphorus. All of the place needed repair, but did not
appear to be beyond restoration.

"There are ovens in the kitchen, and possibly they are
sound, but it would be a foolish chance to use them unless
they are remortared," said the scribe.

"Most of the house will need that, I think," said Niklos, in
hope that would be the extent of the work needed.

"Some of the timbers in the cellars are . . . not sturdy,"
the scribe went on, determined to be forthright.

"Not surprising," said Niklos. "Tell me, is there a church near?"

"There are two not far. Roma itself is—"

"Quite near," Niklos agreed, knowing that the crumbling walls were visible to the south on the western side of the house. "My mistress is determined to find a house where she will not be far from priests."

The scribe opened another door with difficulty. "Some of the doors will need replacement," he explained unnecessarily.

"She will tend to it," said Niklos, "if she decides that this is the house she wants."

"My master has slaves skilled at such work," the scribe said, as he had been told to do.

"That can be determined later if my mistress purchases this house. My mistress has tastes of her own, and she will decide how they can be best served." Niklos nodded as he looked around, imagining the walls freshly plastered and painted, furniture in place.

"It is a pleasant room," the scribe ventured uneasily.

This room was larger and opened on the far side to a private garden. The plants had gone wild and given way to weeds, but Niklos could see there was an empty stone fountain at the center. Five other doors gave onto the garden, and above the garden there ran a gallery to the upper floor.

"How are the stairs?" Niklos asked.

"Most are safe," the scribe admitted.

"I will want to check them shortly." He forced the garden door and stepped into the tangle of creepers and dry thistles. He looked up at the gallery from this vantage point, and called over his shoulder. "How many rooms on the floor above?"

"Six, I believe. Six or seven," the scribe answered. "One is large. The others are of moderate size." He was growing uncomfortable again. "How much longer do you wish to remain here?"

"Until I have seen all I need to see to make my recommendations," said Niklos bluntly. "Will the other doors open, or ought I to come through that room?"

The scribe folded his hands as if in prayer. "Good bondsman, sadly I am not as sanguine as you are, and I am more distressed—" He stopped as something banged in the depths of the house. "Salva me," he muttered as he blessed himself.

"It is probably that shutter we had to pry open. I warned you that it might happen; the wood around the bolts was rotten." Niklos walked through the garden and tugged on the larger of the two doors. At first it would not budge, but finally, with a groan of protest, it opened, and would not be closed.

"It will need—" began the scribe unhappily as he followed after Niklos.

"It will need replacement. All the wood will need replacement," Niklos said affably.

"A costly business," the scribe observed. "For a house with such a reputation as this one, perhaps too much cost."

Niklos laughed. "Your master charged you with the task of showing me this house, not with damning it," he said. "Where is the door to the cellar? I want to find out how much damage there is."

The scribe sighed heavily. "It is near the kitchen. There is a pantry and the cellar door is beyond it."

"Is there a holocaust?" He did not expect to find one. Most of the larger rooms had fireplaces, which indicated that the old Roman system of heated floors had been lost before the house was built.

"A what?" asked the scribe, confirming Niklos' suspicions.

The kitchens were in disarray, and there was a lingering odor of burnt meat that made the scribe cough. The pantry was nothing more than a small room of empty shelves. The door to the cellar hung on a single hinge.

"Not very promising," Niklos said in faint amusement as he started toward the opening.

"Be careful," the scribe warned sharply. "It may not be safe to go there."

"It may not be," Niklos agreed, and stepped through into the darkness.

"Must I accompany you?" the scribe called out, ill-concealed dismay in his question.

"I will manage for myself," Niklos answered cheerfully. "I should not be long." He moved cautiously as his eyes adjusted to the dimness. He heard a muffled slithering, and the chitter of rats, but neither sound concerned him. He made his inspection quickly and thoroughly, noting the timbers that would have to be replaced, the sagging floor and the cracked supports. As he looked around, he was more and more convinced that this would be the place for Olivia. It was not so new that she would feel ancient inside it, and it was neglected, so that she could make it her own without attracting criticism or condemnation. Best of all, it was close enough to Roma that the earth would nurture her. He brushed off his hands before he emerged from the cellar, not wishing to add to the scribe's unease.

The scribe was nowhere to be seen. The pantry and kitchen were empty. Apprehensive, Niklos went looking for the scribe, searching the house before looking in the gardens. Eventually he discovered the man kneeling in the chapel, his head pressed against the dusty altar.

As Niklos approached, he looked up in shock, then tried to remedy this with a lopsided smile. "I thought you would be some time. I didn't mean to leave you . . ." He indicated the house with a frightened lift of his hand. "Have you seen enough?"

"I wish to inspect the stables, the barns and the slaves' quarters. And I want to see how stout the compound walls are." Niklos was at his most matter-of-fact, speaking sensibly and without any suggestion of apprehension.

The scribe fretted. "You could come another time. It is afternoon, and the sun will be setting—"

"The summer sun is long," Niklos said evenly. "I have been charged with a task by my mistress and I am bound to carry it out." He looked around the chapel. "Is the roof intact?"

"The stones are in place. No one has been up on it to see." He coughed. "My master could arrange it, if you insist."

"It is not what I insist," said Niklos. "I am a bondsman and my mistress has given me a task. It is she who insists, and I who will answer." He studied the floor, realizing that under the dust and litter, it was of rosy marble. "One of the churches will be willing to supply a priest?" he asked.

"If a living is provided. Otherwise it isn't certain." The scribe had mastered himself and was standing very straight, as if his lapse had been the act of someone else. "My master can tell you what to do, if your mistress decides to come to this place." His tone indicated that he considered this highly unlikely.

"Let us go to the stables," said Niklos. "One can buy slaves in Roma, I know, but are there craftsmen there who could be put to work making repairs?" The more he learned of this place, the more convinced he was it would be what Olivia wanted. As he and the scribe came out of the chapel, Niklos asked, "How much land is included in the sale?"

The scribe sighed. "From that hill"—he indicated a long ridge to the east—"south to where the road comes, then follow the road to the tower there; that's the western boundary, there, from the tower to the foot of the broken aqueduct, then along the edge of that field to the crest of the hill."

"It includes the vinyard?" Niklos said, to be sure.

"Yes, and there is a spring on the eastern slope that gives water year round. In the days of the pagans, it was thought to have magical properties, but Romans would believe anything."

"So they would," said Niklos with a quick smile. "Show me the stables."

It was almost sunset by the time Niklos had finished. The scribe was markedly uncomfortable and his attention strayed constantly to the house, as if he expected the dishonored beggar-knight to appear in one of the windows. Niklos ignored the scribe's distress for a while, then said, "If you would rather wait for me outside the gate, do so."

"I have been instructed to stay with you," the scribe informed him miserably.

"You went to the chapel earlier, and left me in the cellar. I will not mention that if you will not." He wanted to put the scribe at ease, but failed.

"My master is most adamant," said the scribe stubbornly. He looked toward the house, his eyes glazing with fear, and then he looked directly at Niklos. "I will escort you."

"As you like," Niklos conceded. "I want to see the gates of the compound. We will be through then."

"There are five gates," said the scribe. "Follow me."

The compound enclosed house, gardens, the slaves' quarters, the barns, the stables, and the chapel. All but one of the gates were in need of replacement.

"Your master has been lax here," said Niklos when he and the scribe went to their tethered horses. "If it was his obligation to see that this land is kept in good heart and the house maintained, he has not done well."

"It has been a difficult time in Roma," said the scribe stiffly. His mount was an old mare, slow and cantankerous, but even then, the scribe handled her badly.

Niklos watched the scribe drag himself into the saddle, and checked his impulse to offer some suggestions. Instead he waited while the scribe dragged the mare around, then set out toward the estate of the scribe's master. "Is this the last of the holdings you are to show me?"

"There is one other, but it is a day's ride from here. You said you must have a location within sight of the walls of Roma, and if that is truly your requirement, then the other estate will not do for you or your mistress." He squinted in the fading light, trying to make out the turns in the road.

"I see well at night," said Niklos as soon as he realized the scribe's predicament. "I will be happy to guide you."

"It is appreciated," said the scribe shortly.

They rode in silence for a short time, and then Niklos asked, "How long do you think it would take a crew of skilled artisans to restore that house and the other buildings to usable condition?"

"You're not seriously interested in the place, are you? Your mistress would not want to have a house with a ghost in it, you can be certain of that." The scribe laughed tentatively. "Or do you ask for some other reason?"

"That house, ghost or none, most closely fills my mistress' requirements. It is a most suitable place, the ghost aside, and she is not easily troubled." Niklos smiled as he spoke, but it was too dark for the scribe to read his expression. "That smithy in the stables, that needs more change than the rest of the buildings, but that is not so urgent as the rest."

"You're serious, aren't you?" the scribe demanded. "You intend to advise your mistress to purchase that holding." The scribe waited for an answer, and when none came, he was outraged. "You say you are her sworn bondsman and you are her true servant, and yet you would bring her to a house known to have a malign ghost within its walls. You are willing to recommend a house that is dangerous to her body and soul."

"Your pardon, scribe," said Niklos sternly, "but my mistress follows the teaching of the Church Fathers and puts her faith in God, not in spectres, which the Church teaches us are immaterial." He took a deep breath. "We're near your master's house."

"I will tell him what you have said." The scribe was rigid now, his words like stones.

"So will I," Niklos said easily, as if he were unaware of the disapproval of the scribe. "Eugenius," he said as they turned in at the gate, knowing that his breach of good conduct would give him the scribe's strict attention. "I am not unaware of your good intentions, but I have a mandate from my mistress, and I am bound to fulfill her orders, no matter what you or I may think of them."

The scribe started at hearing his name spoken by this foreigner. He was so shocked that no rejoinder occurred to him and he said only, "You mistake me."

"If I do, then you must excuse my failing," said Niklos as he pulled his horse in at the entrance to the stableyard. He swung off the gray and offered the reins to the stable slave who approached, lantern in hand. "What I might select as a house is not the issue; what my mistress has said she desires in a house is all that concerns me."

Eugenius made as bad a job of getting off the old mare as he had getting on. "Then your mistress is a fool."

"Oh, I don't think so," Niklos said, speaking so lightly that the scribe grew wary, hearing the warning Niklos intended.

"As you say," Eugenius said as he walked away from the horses, "you must carry out her orders, I suppose. But you must warn her of the ghost. Otherwise you will advise her irresponsibly and her fate will be on your head."

Niklos fell into step beside Eugenius as he led the way to the entrance to his master's house. "True enough," he said at his blandest. "But permit me to know more of my mistress, who I have served for most of the years of my life, better than you, for you have never met Bondama Clemens."

A slave opened the door and the major domo came at once to guide Niklos to the smaller reception room where his master would meet him shortly.

"Well," said the scribe, "I have done all that I might to dissuade you."

"I know. And I know you have done so for the best reasons, but I must obey my instructions." He nodded to the scribe, and hoped that this little courtesy would make up for the gaffe of addressing the scribe by his name.

"May God guide you, then, for there is danger all around you if you occupy that house." He turned on his heel and walked away toward the servants' wing of the house.

This was a much grander establishment than the house Niklos had just inspected. It was three stories tall and had more than fifty rooms within its stout walls. Frederick Barbarossa himself had stayed here once, and had pronounced the place satisfactory. Doca Arrigo Benammo di Cruceclare was the fifth of his family to own it; he had doubled the family holdings in the last ten years as much through his astute political manipulation as through riches, and his title was secured not only through the endorsement of the Pope, but through the mandate of Frederick Barbarossa.

Doca Arrigo was in his study when his scribe and Niklos returned. His major domo escorted Niklos there as soon as the scribe had given his report. Unlike many of his contemporaries, Doca Arrigo was literate and read extensively, which was why his failing eyesight troubled him so much. "Ah, Aulirios," he said, when Niklos was more than a blur. "My scribe tells me that you were impressed with the villa he showed you today." He indicated a wooden chair for Niklos as he waved his major domo away.

"I was. Your scribe told me the place has a sad reputation, and that is unfortunate," Niklos said smoothly, aware that for Olivia's purposes the state of the villa was to her advantage. "However, it is by far the most in accord with the demands of my mistress, and for that reason, I wish to discuss purchase with you."

"Just like that?" Doca Arrigo raised his tufted eyebrows.

"No questions, no assessments, you simply wish to discuss price?"

"In a word, yes," Niklos said as he tugged at his slitted short cote as he sat down. "If that is agreeable to you. That way, I can commence implementing my mistress' instructions in regard to putting the place in order to her liking, so that when she arrives, she will be able to live as she . . . ought."

"Commendable, I suppose," said Doca Arrigo. "She is in Tyre, still, your mistress?"

"Her last letter said she had not completed all her arrangements for departure." This careful answer was deliberately vague, and both men knew it.

"My son Egidio is with the Emperor. He took the Cross when the Emperor called for men. They left for the Holy Land not long ago." He sighed. "Egidio is twenty, and passionate in his love of God. I pray for him."

Niklos hesitated. "I will send word of this to my mistress, if it pleases you. It may be that the Crusaders will reach Tyre before my mistress leaves it." He hoped that this would not be the case, but dared not say so aloud.

"I have another son, of course. But Andrea is so young— only ten—and his sight is as afflicted already, as mine has become." He leaned back in his chair. "Enough of that. You say you intend to offer for the villa. It is called Sanza Pare, incidentally."

"I will inform my mistress." Niklos thought the name would amuse her, for Olivia herself was "without equal."

"How much of the holding is she planning to buy?" Doca Arrigo asked as he drew out a sheet of vellum.

"The entire holding, I should think," Niklos replied in his most pragmatic manner. "And of course, I will need to make arrangements for proper repairs and rebuilding."

"Naturally," said Doca Arrigo as his brows rose again, like two inquisitive caterpillars. "The purchase of so much land, and those buildings as well, will require . . . a goodly sum." He had taken a wax tablet from the drawer in his writing table, and with an iron stylus, he started to figure.

"You have in your care the funds Bondama Clemens authorized me to bring for such a purchase. I doubt the cost could exceed what I have with me." His manner was nonchalant, but his brown eyes with the faint ruddy tinge, were not.

"Oh, certainly, certainly," agreed Doca Arrigo. "More than enough. The jewels alone are sufficient to buy Sanza Pare twice over, but—" He stopped abruptly, cleared his throat, and put the wax tablet aside. "Look here, Aulirios, if the fortune you brought with you is the sum total of her wealth, then she would be better served if you purchased half the land, so that your mistress could establish an income before risking everything. These are uncertain times, and it may be that crops will fail, or there will be more . . . more disruption."

"The Emperor will come back from the Holy Land and make new demands on Roma? Is that what you fear?" Niklos asked, coming directly to the point.

"In part, yes," Doca Arrigo said uncomfortably. As an Emperor's man, he was not inclined to speak to Barbarossa's discredit.

"Is there concern that the death of Henry of England changes things?" Niklos inquired.

"The death of Kings always changes things," answered the Doca. "His heir is already causing difficulties." He shook his head.

"But that is for the future," Niklos said, his voice softer. "What is sure is the present." He blessed himself and watched while Doca Arrigo did the same. "And what is the price for Sanza Pare today?"

"The casket of jewels will pay for the estate and all the work you wish done on it." He set the stylus aside. "I will call an advocate to record this in the morning, and copies of the deed of sale will be carried to Roma."

"My mistress will be most grateful," said Niklos with a quick smile.

"It is to be hoped that she will be, for in these times, finding another suitable estate in the vicinity of Roma might not be possible for some time." His face grew drawn as he spoke and his forty-one years lay heavily on him.

Niklos rose in order to bow with full courtesy. "That will not be necessary," he said. "She will be pleased."

"I trust she will," Doca Arrigo said. "It is a great expense."

"My mistress has a personal fortune, one that has yet to be touched." He kissed the thumb of the Doca's hand. "It pleases her to know that you were concerned on her behalf."

Doca Arrigo shook his head. "It is a bad time to travel."

Niklos bowed again. "All the more reason for her to come home."

*   *   *

Text of a note from a Byzantine ship's captain to Ithuriel Dar.

To the master of the Ondas del' Albor, *the master of the* Illion *sends his greetings and thanks, and informs him that if at any time he might be of service, he need only ask.*

Your warning arrived in time, and because of the information you provided, we were able to arrive in Cyprus without another battle with those pirates who have become the bane of all voyagers. I have been told that they have collected more than forty ransoms in the last year alone, and I offer thanks to God and you for our deliverance.

While it is true that we are supposed to obtain permission for dealings with Jews, let alone Jews from Islamite kingdoms, still, the debt I owe you is greater than the laws of the state. If you had not warned us, I know that my cargo would be lost, my crew would be in slavery, and I would be held for ransom or dead. I am beholden for so much more than my own life and fortune that the requirements of my faith make it necessary that I pay no attention to the laws of my King. The laws of God are the first that any man must obey.

My ship is the support of my family and the families of nine other men. Had it been lost, all would have suffered greatly, and if ransom had been paid, then it would have reduced us all to penury. Your name will be remembered in the prayers of everyone you have spared through your timely warning.

It has been suggested that you learned of this because you occasionally resort to smuggling. I am certain that every cargo you carry is lawful. I will say so to any Court officer in any port of the sea. A man who is so honorable, who saves the lives and livelihoods of so many, must be within the law. That some of those laws are reserved to Christians is clearly a question of misinterpretation, and one that I will gladly aid in setting straight, should the occasion ever arise.

Never doubt that my aid and the aid of my family is yours from now until the grave.

Ezekias of the Illion
By the hand of the pope of Hagia Irene at the end of August in the 1189th year of Our Lord.

· 6 ·

When the eunuch showed him to the larger reception room, Valence Rainaut was shocked by the luxury he saw around him. He had heard rumors about the wealth of the East, but he had never thought that a Roman widow could live in such splendor. He took a deep, slow breath; the room was perfumed, and for once, he felt uncomfortable in his Hospitaler's mantel. His own arms were embroidered on his surcote: or, an arm bent erased at the shoulder gules.

"Hospitaler?" spoke a voice from the inner door.

He turned, feeling like a child discovered in mischief. "Yes?"

Olivia, in a muted gold samite bliaud, her hair covered with a tissue veil of golden gauze, stepped into the room. "God give you good day, Bonsier," she said, her eyes fixed on his.

Rainaut could not bring himself to speak; he hardly moved. Then he recalled where he was and his errand, and he dropped to his knee and kissed her sleeve. "Tell me what I may do to serve you."

"First, you may get up," she said playfully. "There are chairs—choose whichever suits you." She sank onto her favorite Persian chair and waited while he tore his eyes away from her long enough to decide where to sit.

"Fraire Herchambaut came to—" he began, lost the line of his thought and had to start again. "Fraire Herchambaut said that you wish to leave Tyre, that you have prepared the documents for the Court of Bourgesses and the funda, and that you lack escort."

"Yes; I trust he explained the circumstances to you?" When he said nothing, she went on. "The Court of Bourgesses have approved my departure only when I can demonstrate suitable escort for myself and my household. Without that, I will not be given permission unless I leave everything behind and bribe a captain to carry me away from here."

Impulsively Rainaut leaned forward. "You would not do that? Bondama, give me your word that you would do nothing so reckless."

"Probably not," said Olivia after a little consideration. "But it grows increasingly tempting. I feel I am in prison here. Everything conspires to hold me within these walls, like a dungeon. While I agree that it is a pleasant prison as prisons go, it does not alter the fact that I am confined. With another Crusade upon us, I wish to be gone from here."

"It is understandable," said Rainaut, his voice as soft as music; he was startled.

"Fraire Herchambaut has told me that one of the Hospitalers might be spared for this task." She looked directly at him.

"Actually, Bondama, two of us are required for proper escort." He flushed without knowing why. "It may present a problem, since at present I cannot be spared, not any one of us can, let alone two of us. It is the Emperor, you see."

Olivia did not understand why that should interfere, so she said, "Barbarossa. What about him?"

"His army is at the edges of Byzantine territory, and because of this, there has been a great increase in pilgrims, as the mission to free the Holy Sepulcher is renewed. Monks and pious leymen come overland and by ship, merchants strive to make arrangements in preparation for the Crusade, and so all the roads are crowded, and there are more ships of every kind on the seas. We haven't enough men here to accommodate all the demands being made. There are more Hospitalers coming, and once they arrive it might be—"

"Coming when?" Olivia interrupted.

"With my King, Richard of England."

"The one they call Coer de Leon," Olivia said, frowning. All she had ever heard of the man made him appear to be hotheaded and impetuous. "He has not been King long."

"Yes, that is true, but he is my liege, and he has sworn to join the Emperor on Crusade," said Rainaut, putting his hand over his blazon in homage. "He and Phillippe of France have declared themselves Crusaders."

"It is September," said Olivia. She brought her hands together as fists. "When do you think these Hospitalers will arrive? How much longer must I wait? When will I be able to leave?"

"Surely by the end of the year," said Rainaut, gazing at her, taking in the lines of her face and the promise of her body in her silken garments. She captivated him as no woman he had met before had, and her nearness was dizzying. He knew he would have to visit Joivita that night, or he would not sleep for desire.

"The end of the year," Olivia echoed. "It will then be more than a year since I made my plans. My major domo is already in Roma, finding a house for me and attending to my affairs there. You tell me I must wait."

"I will explain the urgency of your—" Rainaut said with feeling. He wanted to perform a service for her, to show his devotion and his honor. "I will speak on your behalf."

"That has been done before," Olivia told him. "Fraire Herchambaut addressed the Bourgesses already." She saw the expression on his face, the despair in his eyes, and she relented. "But my case had not been pleaded by a Hospitaler. Forgive me. I did not mean to speak against you."

"You have reason for curtness." He again leaned forward, as if drawn on invisible wires.

"But not at your expense." She loosened her hands and made herself calmer. "You come to offer me aid and I make complaint to you, when you are not concerned with what has gone before."

"I wish I had been," he said, inwardly damning himself for speaking so rashly. "I wish I had known from my first day in Tyre that you needed my help, for then, I . . . I—"

Olivia smiled, her face changing subtly. She tilted her head, thinking he would go on, and when he did not, she said, "I wish I had spoken to you before now, as well. You are kind, Bonsier, and I have grown unused to that."

His throat ached with words he could not speak. He took her hand, then released it. "I am a sworn Hospitaler, and to conduct myself otherwise dishonors us both."

"Does touching my hand mean so much?" Olivia wondered aloud. "It does not seem so to me, but Romans, you know, have their own standards for such things." She looked at him differently now, noticing his dark blue eyes and his tawny hair. His voice was pleasant, and he was not so very young that he seemed little more than a child to her, as so many did now. "Tell me, how old are you?"

He stared at her, bemused. "I am twenty-seven," he said after a moment. "I am from Saint-Prosperus-lo-Boys."

"Isn't twenty-seven a trifle old for the Hospitalers?" Olivia asked, intrigued.

"For some, perhaps. I have fought for my King, and it . . . it . . ." He looked away from her, shamed by what he was going to say to her. "It sickened me."

"Small wonder," said Olivia.

"I became a Hospitaler in the hope that God would forgive me if I rendered honorable service in His cause." He was whispering now, as if he sat in confession. "It has not happened yet; look. I have not courage enough to face you."

"Am I so terrible?" Olivia asked, taking care to keep all trace of humor from her voice, so that he would not think she mocked him.

"Most terrible," he said, staring down at his hands. "Your look is . . . mortal."

Olivia was taken aback. "Mortal?" Her laugh was short and hurt-filled. "Surely not."

At last he was able to turn toward her again. "What do you mean?"

She shook her head, then tentatively reached for his hand. "There. If anyone is dishonored, I am." She looked down at his straight, long, blunt fingers, his wide, heavily lined palms. "You are something rare, something I did not expect to find inside a knight's cote."

"A coward," he said, making a halfhearted attempt to pull away from her.

"Oh, no. Not a coward." Whatever else she might have said was put aside as Alfaze came into the reception room. She released Rainaut's hands and rose. "You have brought the documents?"

"Yes, mistress," said Alfaze. Nothing in his manner showed he had noticed what had passed between her and Rainaut. "There are true copies of all the inventories and of all bequests, as well as your indication that you have access to a ship for your journey, and the owner has reserved space for you, your goods, and retinue for the voyage." He bowed to the Hospitaler. "God save and keep you, Bonsier."

"And you," Rainaut said automatically, hardly able to think for the turmoil within him.

Olivia took the vellum sheets and looked them over. "Yes, they are all here. Thank you, Alfaze, for bringing them." She paused. "Have refreshments been prepared for my guest?"

"You have only to send for them, mistress," said Alfaze.

"Will you give the order for me, when you leave?" She knew that Alfaze wanted to guard her, and with another man she would have welcomed his intrusion. The Hospitaler had surprised her and she wanted more time with him. "In fact, I wish you to bring the refreshments yourself." She looked toward Rainaut. "Would that suit you?"

"You . . . whatever suits you," Rainaut said in confusion.

"That will give us a little more time to review the documents I have prepared. If you can read—" She did not know how best to frame the question, and left it open for him.

"I have some skill at letters," he said. "But I am no scholar." It had never troubled him until now; faced with so captivating a woman, he longed to match her learning.

"Then review these"—she handed him the vellum sheets —"and tell me what more is needed to satisfy the Court of Bourgesses."

Rainaut was glad for the diversion of puzzling out the lists in the inventories. It gave him a respite from her tantalizing nearness. Mercy of Christ, he asked himself, what is happening? What sorcery does this Roman woman possess that she disturbs me in this way? His eyes moved down the page, though he made sense of little of it. One line—the number of holy ornaments she was donating to various churches and chapels—he read four times without understanding it, though he knew the words and what they meant. I am like a child, he thought. I am like a blind man newly given sight. In a strange voice he said, "They appear sufficient to me."

"And what am I to do?" Olivia asked, some of her earlier exasperation returning.

"Let me speak for you. It is strange that the Court of Bourgesses should withhold permission." He attempted to speak properly, with correct respect and deference, but he could not manage it. "I will do everything I can, Bondama."

"Thank you, Bonsier," said Olivia, waving Alfaze away. "Return with refreshments," she said over her shoulder as the eunuch left her alone with Rainaut once more.

"I *will* do everything I can," he repeated more forcefully.

Olivia watched him, feeling the intensity of his eyes as if she stood near a fire. "Free me?" She had said the words before she realized she spoke. With a quick, dismissing motion of her hand, she continued. "No; that isn't your burden to take up. If you will assist me, I will be thankful and—"

"I would take any burden you give me and count myself privileged beyond dreams," Rainaut said impulsively. "It is no burden to fight your cause, Bondama."

For an instant, Olivia missed Niklos so intensely that the effect was a pain. "You . . . you surprise me, Sier Valence," she said quietly, and it was no less than the truth. "I pray you will never have cause to regret those feelings."

"It would not be possible," said Rainaut with increased emotion. As every knight his age knew, Rainaut had been told that in the presence of the beloved it was proper to become faint. Until that day, he had considered such things to be troubadors' nonsense. He looked toward the shuttered window where the narrow bands of rose-colored light came in as the lowering sun at last gained access to the room. Where the brightness cut the scented gloom, the atmosphere seemed about to burst into flame. "I must leave soon," he said, his voice remote as he tried to secure some distance from Olivia's presence.

"There are refreshments being brought for you," Olivia said politely, knowing better than to press him while he was still so visibly confused. "You will offend my cook if you refuse them."

Rainaut looked toward her again, making himself appear at ease, hoping her attraction would lessen; it did not. "I want never to give you the least offense." It was said without emotion, as if he were speaking the words he had been ordered to speak, not the conviction of his heart. "But I must not stay much longer. We Hospitalers have duties and devotions." It was an excuse, and an insignificant one, if he allowed himself to think about it. "I will come again, in a few days, if you will permit."

"Since you are taking up my cause," said Olivia, "I rely on you to keep me apprised of what has happened." She brushed the gauze back from her face as if it was a tendril of hair. "You have a better knowledge of how I might proceed than I do; I'm aware of that. So. What can I do to help you? You say you will aid me; what am I to do to assist you?"

"You have done so much already." He said the words angrily, but there was no anger in his face or the lines of his body. He looked away from her again, once more fascinated by the glowing fingers of light.

"Unsuccessfully," she appended. "Sier Valence," she said a short while later, "I meant what I told you, that I feel I am a prisoner here. No one yearns more for release than I do. No one is more willing to—"

Rainaut still did not look at her. "I will arrange escort, I will see that you are given permission to leave, I will accompany you, by land or water, and I will stay with you until you are safely arrived in Roma. On my life's blood." He reached out blindly, his hand brushing her samite bliaud before catching her wrist. "Listen to me." He turned toward her as inexorably as a lodestone turns north. "You have a right to this: I give you my pledge. On my honor, on my sword, on my life, that I am your true knight; only God is a greater sovereign than you are to me." What had come over him? he wondered as he offered this vow. What had happened, that he made such a vow? What had possessed him? The idea of possession hovered in his mind, malignant as a vulture. Did this Roman widow have command of magical powers that perverted his knightly purpose to her own ends? The question banished his doubts. Olivia had asked nothing of him—he had offered service, had wanted to give her service. He admitted to himself that if she had refused his service, it would have been the cruelest wound he would ever take, worse than his knowledge of his own cowardice.

"You do not need to do this, Sier Valence," Olivia said as his grip tightened on her wrist. "I do not ask this of you."

He stared into her eyes. "You know of my shame, of the weakness in me. You have not dismissed me, or castigated me, although if you had done either, you would be blameless for it. I make no excuse for . . . If I am to expiate this failing, then I . . . I cannot abjure my oath. This is not your doing. I give you my fealty willingly. If you refuse, then—" He released his hold on her.

"I fear that without your help, I will be here forever." She shuddered as she said the last, trying to imagine what all the years she had lived would be to her had she passed them within the walls of this house.

"No; I will arrange your passage as soon as possible." He brought her hand to his lips, thinking that Joivita would be a poor substitute now for his appetites. Even so oblique a recognition of his passion shamed him. He let go of her hand and moved away from her. "It is said that all knights, to be true knights, must serve ideal as well as worldly goals. From my youth I was told that without a lady for . . ." He did not finish; instead he continued in a different tone, "I thought that it would be better to serve Heaven and the King's Grace. But I did not know the wisdom of my teachers. It is better to have a lady. My King's mother said so, years ago, and she has always been accounted wiser than most women."

Olivia knew something of Eleanor of Aquitaine, and would have held her tongue, but she saw that Rainaut was looking at her once more, waiting for what she would say. "I have heard that she is devoted to her son Richard." It was a cautious comment, one that seemed safe.

"And Henry liked John, or so they say," Rainaut remarked. "She put her hopes in Richard when her husband failed her."

It was difficult for Olivia not to ask "Which husband," but she restrained herself. "If Richard is coming on Crusade, what of his mother? Will she follow him, do you think?"

"She has said she will," Rainaut said, glad for the respite such impersonal subjects gave. "But she is not young, and France longs to claim the Plantagenet lands for their own, leaving only the English Islands to Richard and his heirs."

"Richard has yet to—" Olivia stopped.

"I have heard he is to marry. His mother has urged it, since Richard will not have Alais; he will not take his father's leavings, he says. So there must be another, and Queen Eleanor is determined that the line will be preserved. Richard must have a Queen: that is the greatest protection for England. Eleanor will preserve her son's heritage. If Richard is married and his throne assured, his mother may remain to guard the kingdom."

"And you, Sier Valence? You come from . . . where is Saint-Prosperus-lo-Boys?"

"In Aunis, a day's ride from Niort." He smiled faintly. "Our family has a fortified holding there, not quite a castle. It is very old."

"And your family?" Olivia asked with interest. "What of them? Are they as old as your not-quite-castle?"

"They say we came with the men of Charlemagne, and that we gave good service, and were rewarded. We have lived at Saint-Prosperus-lo-Boys for eleven generations, or so the records of the monastery show. God is good to us. In my generation, only one of us died in youth. Another two have died in battle, but still, there are seven of us, my father's children, alive and well." He blessed himself. "My father was a younger son, and my mother was his second wife."

"Then your lands have already been divided. It is difficult

to cut up an estate into many pieces; younger sons fare badly. You have others to consider. No wonder you have come to the Hospitalers," said Olivia.

"It isn't quite so bleak. I have lands from my wife," said Rainaut, feeling his face grow hot.

"Then you are married?" Olivia said without surprise.

"I was. It was some time ago. My wife died less than a year after we . . . There was a fever, and she took it. Three of my cousins died of it as well." It seemed to Rainaut that his hands were shaking; he looked at them and was astonished to discover they were steady.

"That was unfortunate," said Olivia sincerely. How long ago it was that Sanct' Germain had warned her about the terrible brevity of the lives around her! And how keenly she sensed it now.

"It was nine years ago, and my wife was over thirty." He continued to stare at his hands, as if some reason might appear between his palms. "The physicians at the monastery said that at her age she . . ." He raised his head as Alfaze came into the room with a tray.

Olivia got to her feet and moved away from him. "I am sorry about your wife. It is . . . painful to lose those you love."

"It was not a question of love, Bondama," said Rainaut, the words soft, indistinct. "It was a good marriage."

"A good marriage." She waited, her hand raised so that Alfaze would not yet present the food.

"For both our families. And she was not displeasing to me. I have known others who fared less well than I did." He knotted his hands together. "We knew our duty."

"I see," said Olivia, thinking of her own long-ago marriage that was supposed to serve family expediency. She no longer shut the memories away, as she had done once, but she did not want to remember Justus while in Rainaut's company. "While you eat," she told him in a different voice, a trifle breathlessly, "I will find the records you will need for my departure."

"And Roma?" asked Rainaut, his attention divided between her and the lavish supper Alfaze had brought. Six different dishes were laid out on brass plates, and two different sorts of breads were wrapped in thick cloths. The meals served to Hospitalers were austerely simple; this assortment of exotic viands intrigued him. Little as he wanted to admit it, he was hungry.

"I will inform you as soon as I learn something. My major domo is authorized to purchase a house and lands for me." She hesitated, realizing she did not want to leave him. "Sier Valence?"

His blue eyes grew more intense as they met her hazel ones. "Yes, Bondama?"

"I thank you for . . . for coming to my aid." He was so tempting. It had been a long time since she had felt her special need become longing, and that alone confused her. If only she was intrigued, or only he, it would be so simple. She knew he would welcome her in what he would recall as a dream, for there was no mistaking his ardor. With a start she realized that for once that would not be sufficient for her; she would need more than his satisfied dream to fulfill her.

"What is it?" he asked, seeing some reflection of her thoughts in her eyes. He took a step toward her, then held off. "Bondama?"

Her smile faltered. "Nothing, Sier Valence. Nothing . . . important." She shook herself inwardly and went on in a brisker tone. "Enjoy your meal. I will return when you have done."

He indicated the meal with a sweep of his hand. "This is most gracious, Bondama. It is hardly necessary."

"It is hardly necessary that you appoint yourself my champion, but you have," she rallied. "The least I can do in return is . . . feed you." Before he could speak again, while she was able to ignore the implications in her own words, she turned away and left him alone with his meal and the turmoil of his thoughts, sensing that his were as distracted as her own.

*   *   *

Text of a letter from Arrigo Benammo di Cruceclare to the bishop at San Jacoppo degli Agnelli.

To the reverend Bishop Niccolo Sassi at San Jacoppo degli Agnelli, the Doca Arrigo Benammo di Cruceclare sends his greetings and requests that the bishop will be kind enough to record and keep this notification, and for that service and the honor of his family, the Doca sends six golden angels for the benefit of the work of the Duomo.

You are familiar with the extent and nature of the various holdings and estates of mine, and you have documents of title at your chapter house where such records are maintained. The accuracy and veracity of these documents are beyond question and are deemed correct in every particular. Therefore this letter will serve to be placed among them as legally binding on me and mine, as well as on the purchaser.

I have accepted payment from one Niklos Aulirios, a Greek bondsman who is major domo to the Roman widow Atta Olivia Clemens, for the purchase of the house, attendant buildings and lands of the estate known as Sanza Pare. You will find it among those lands obtained by me within my period of tenure as Doca. The full nature and extent of the sale accompanies this letter, as well as the current condition and state of Sanza Pare, the buildings and the lands. The price of sale is based upon the current agreed value of the estate with additional money for the requirements of the purchaser. Further, I have provided artisans and slaves for the renovation of said house, buildings and lands, against the arrival of the Bondama Clemens from Tyre, where she is currently living. This transaction is complete with the payment received, and no further claim from me or mine can be recognized as binding.

My assurance has been given to Niklos Aulirios that the

funds given are sufficient for the work that has been ordered, and I relinquish all further claim to money for work being done providing that the terms laid out in the enclosed statements are not exceeded or altered. The instructions of Bondama Clemens have been copied and are appended here.

In case of dispute, I pray that you, good Bishop, will be willing to adjudicate the matter; I state now that I am willing to abide by any ruling you make at that time, and I further bind my heirs and their heirs to honor this condition. Should you not be available for such a decision, your successor is hereby deemed worthy to be your deputy in these dealings.

True copies of this letter, as well as all attendant documents, maps and renovation plans, notarized and under seal, are being sent to Roma, as were copies of the original terms of the negotiations that have led to this letter culminating the sale of the estate.

In the event that I or my heirs perish before the completion of the ordered renovation, those who inherit my position and title are strictly enjoined to uphold the conditions of the agreement and to honor the commitment made by me, both in regard to the sale of the estate and its renovation as outlined elsewhere. Any failure to do so forfeits at once the sum of three thousand golden marks to Niklos Aulirios and Bondama Clemens, should she be in residence at the time, as well as bearing a penalty of a thousand golden marks to be paid to the Church for the cost of the dispute.

May God show favor to you, reverend Bishop, and to all those who serve God at San Jacoppo degli Agnelli, and bring you to His rewards in Heaven. May He preserve the Pope and all the Princes of the Church who serve Him on earth. Praises to our Emperor Frederick and to the Empire God has been pleased to give to him. May long life and victory attend him, and may the triumph of the Emperor be the triumph of our faith as well.

Arrigo Benammo di Cruceclare, Doca

By the hand of my scribe Eugenius, endorsed by my sigil, verified and notarized by Fra Marius, and under my seal, on the Feast of Advent, in the 1189th year of Our Lord.

At the door to the room of the Bourgesses' Court in the funda there stood three armed men, two of them with swords, one with a maul. All wore light chain mail; their surcotes had the blue anchor badge of the city of Tyre. Inside this guarded door there were three separate chambers, one of them large, the other two smaller but as impressive.

It was in one of these two smaller rooms that Jaufre Chartier waited for Olivia to arrive. He had passed most of the previous day reading over all the inventories and similar documents which had been presented to the funda by the French Hospitaler, Sier Valence Rainaut. Now the vellum sheets were laid out in three neat stacks, and Chartier tapped his fingers over them. Although it was not quite the hour for the widow's visit, he was impatient to have the entire interview over so that he could return to his business, which he treated as a sacred calling. Born at Sidon forty-five years before, he considered himself wholly and utterly French, as did the rest of his family.

His personal servant came into the chamber carrying a small writing table with vellum and ink laid out for recording all that was said during the interview. He bowed to Chartier and proceeded to trim quills. He knew better to address Chartier directly unless the Bourgess required it.

"This is an unnecessary procedure," Chartier remarked to the walls. "It is an intrusion." He drummed his fingers more loudly. "Why did that Hospitaler insist?"

The servant said nothing, knowing that he was expected to remain silent. He kept busy at his task.

"What prompted her to involve the Hospitalers?" Chartier said, then slapped the high table where he sat.

From another part of the funda came the sound of a bell,

two crisp notes that were selected more for their carrying quality than their beauty. There were clamors of opening and closing doors, and a loud cry from the direction of the customs rooms at the other end of the building.

"She's late, as well," grumbled Chartier.

There was a sharp rap on the door, and the guard with the maul stepped through the door. He bowed, his mail creaking and jingling. "May I admit the Widow Clemens?" he asked without a trace of inflection.

"Certainly, certainly," said Chartier in a weary voice. "We might as well settle things."

The guard stood aside. "You are admitted to the presence of the Bourgess Chartier."

The first person to enter the room was not Olivia, but Fraire Herchambaut, who bowed to the Bourgess and stood aside for his companion. "May God give you good day and wise counsel," he said as he motioned Olivia to join him. "Bonsier Bourgess Chartier, I have the honor to make the Widow Atta Olivia Clemens known to you." His strict and courtly formality was at odds with his unwashed habit and unkempt appearance; he treated Bourgess Chartier with respect usually accorded to a noble.

"Yes; get on with it, get on with it," said Chartier impatiently.

Olivia had dressed more circumspectly than usual; her bliaud was of simple linen dyed to the color of slate. Her hair was covered by a veil that was secured by a widow's black wreath. Her only jewelry was a bracelet of silver set with rubies, which was a keepsake from her oldest and most treasured friend. She showed courtesy to Bourgess Chartier before she approached his writing bench. "May God grant you favor," she said when she was sure she had Chartier's attention.

"And you, and you," Chartier said, casting a single, wrathful glance at Fraire Herchambaut. "I suppose you believe that we have been lax here at the funda in dealing with your petition."

"Not precisely," Olivia said, thinking that they had been a great deal worse than lax, but in such a manner that Chartier could misunderstand if he wished.

"Well, there are extenuating circumstances. These are not

ordinary times, are they?" His expression dared her to contradict him.

"That is why I wish to leave Tyre," Olivia responded, refusing to be goaded into sharp speech. She looked toward the small table where the servant was busy scribbling. "What is that fellow doing?" she asked innocently.

"He is making a record of our conversation," was Chartier's curt answer. "He is required to do this."

"Is he in the employ of the funda, or is he your servant?" Olivia asked with deceptive naivete.

"My servant, of course," snapped Chartier, caught off-guard by her inquiry. "All Bourgesses of the Court must employ such a servant."

"Why does the funda not provide such scribes?" asked Olivia, not willing to let the circumstances go unremarked. "Why employ a man who must show favor to his master, when the funda could provide scribes who were much harder to influence?"

Chartier glowered, looking in the space between Olivia and Fraire Herchambaut. "That is a matter for the Court to discuss, if ever it is thought necessary. Each Bourgess of the Court is expected to provide his scribe a living, and for that reason—" He stopped. "This is not to the point."

"It would be if what we say is ever disputed by either you or me," Olivia contradicted him in as mild a tone as she could manage.

Fraire Herchambaut was growing distressed by this exchange and was about to stop it, when the scribe timorously made a suggestion.

"I could provide you with your own copy of what I have written, and you could sign each. I am certain the monk will be willing to determine the accuracy of the copies—"

"I read and write," said Olivia, not adding that she had more than twelve languages at her command. "That arrangement suits me very well." She looked back at Chartier, waiting for him to approve or disapprove of the recommendation.

"Very well, yes." He sighed. "Yes, I agree." He motioned toward his scribe. "I will want to read the two copies as well." He turned back toward Olivia. "Is that your only complaint about this proceeding?"

It was not, but Olivia saw the obstinate set of Chartier's mouth and decided to make the best of things. "The arrangements are acceptable," she said, not quite answering his question. "I wish to review my inventories with you, and determine when I am to be permitted to leave this place."

"It will be attended to," said Chartier with the appearance of boredom.

Olivia was no longer willing to go along with the delay and obfuscation. "When?" she challenged.

Chartier looked at her, mildly annoyed. "What concern is that of yours?"

"Good widow Clemens," Fraire Herchambaut said, in an attempt to divert her. "I pray you—"

"It is my concern," said Olivia, cutting off the monk and addressing the Bourgess with no trace of her earlier submissive attitude, "because it is my life. When I first requested permission to tender these forms, I was put off. When I asked for reasons, there were none. When I made a second petition through this good Cistercian, there were more delays, unconscionable delays. And now you cannot tell me when you will have the response from you Bourgesses. I find this inexcusable. I have been patient, I have complied in every particular with the requests made by the Court of Bourgesses, I have given documents to support every statement and claim. What more do you need of me? Do you require I die of old age?" She laughed harshly, as if in sudden grief.

"We will attend to it in good time," said Chartier with irate dignity. "You speak as if we have nothing better to do than to review the endless number of lists you have sent us."

"Lists you asked for," Olivia reminded him pointedly.

Chartier ignored this. "You come in here, bringing this monk and imposing on his good nature, and now you shout at me because you think it is inconvenient for you to wait a few days while we conclude the business we are chartered to do."

"If it were a few days, I would not be bothered," said Olivia emphatically. "It is almost a year, good Bourgess, since I first requested permission to leave Tyre. I explained then that I wished to be away from here in no more than three months, which was denied when seven months had gone by. I have arranged escort, as I have been told I must. I have submitted lists of those items I wish to sell, those I wish to donate, and those I intend—with your gracious permission, of course—to take with me. I have paid a shipowner for transportation. All that is left is for you to assess the taxes I must pay, and for the funda to accept those items I am selling. I am willing to leave the goods here and arrange for the payments to be sent later." She knew even as she spoke that if she did this, she would gain less than a third of what the goods had sold for, but that no longer mattered. "What possible reason can you have for denying me permission to leave?"

Chartier regarded her as if she had metamorphosed into an insect. "You are beyond your knowledge and authority," he said.

"If by that you mean I no longer comprehend the actions of the Court of Bourgesses, you're right, Bonsier Chartier," said Olivia with sarcastic politeness.

Fraire Herchambaut had come to Olivia's side and had taken her arm. "You are overwrought. You need time for prayer and reflection, and then you will wish to ask the pardon of this good Bourgess for the insult you have—"

Olivia rounded on him. "I am the one who is being insulted, not this insufferable sham of an official!" Her eyes were bright and her mouth almost square with rage. "If anyone has been insulted, I have been. Take your hands off my arm, good monk, or I will do you an injury." This last was spoken softly, but without gentleness. "Now."

Confused, Fraire Herchambaut stepped back, blessing himself as he did. "You are in error, Bondama, and will understand that presently."

"And this fellow?" Olivia demanded contemptuously as she pointed to Chartier. "What of him? What is his error that he cannot prepare three simple documents for one widow to leave this city? Or is it that this particular widow is wealthy, and there are those who want to wring every bit of gold and silver they can out of me? Is that it?"

"You're raving," said Chartier coldly, and reached for the bell that stood at the end of his writing table. "When you are cooler, Bondama, I will speak to your representative. Fraire Herchambaut or the Hospitaler will do. I will not permit you to enter my presence again." He rose as he said this last, ringing the bell as he did.

From his little table, the scribe looked up, white-faced, grateful to be regarded as invisible. He looked at the pages in front of him, at the point he had stopped copying what was said for fear of repercussions later. He moved closer to the wall.

The door opened and the guard with the maul entered the room with suspicious promptness. "Yes, Bourgess Chartier."

"This woman is leaving now. The monk is to accompany her, because she is not responsible for herself." He held up both hands as Olivia started to speak. "No more. You have disrupted my work enough already."

Olivia took a deep breath and said quite steadily, "How strange, since you have accomplished so little." She turned abruptly and looked at the scribe. "I wish to watch you destroy whatever you have written. Immediately." Her stance was uncompromising and she folded her arms, her gaze fixed on the scrawled sheets before him. "There is a brazier near you. You may burn the sheets there."

"This is not proper," protested Chartier.

Fraire Herchambaut blessed himself again and said to Bourgess Chartier, "In this instance, given the heat in which you both have spoken, it is wisest."

"The monk's probably right," said the guard, giving Olivia his unexpected support. "It's what comes of trying to do business with women. Better to leave it to men, who understand it."

Olivia was tempted to rail at the guard, but her good sense told her that it would be useless. She lowered her head, telling herself that the interview would not be recorded to be used against her, and that given her difficulties, this was a reasonable compromise. Her face darkened, but she made herself say, "No doubt you are right. It was my impetuosity that drove me to this interview. But I am eager to be granted permission to leave."

"Yes," said the guard with sympathy. "For a widow, the talk of Crusades must be terrifying." He gave her an avuncular smile. "I tell you what, Bondama. I will have a word or two with the Court of Bourgesses when your representatives come again, and perhaps we can find a way to have you on your way in a month or two."

"A month or two?" Olivia repeated, trying not to let her outrage be too apparent. "Is that all?"

"It is possible," the guard said blithely, unconcerned with the disguised anger Olivia offered. "The Bourgesses are always much too busy, and they do not have enough help to work quickly, but still, I think two months may be—"

"Possible," Olivia finished for him. "I understand." She was relieved to leave the room. "I don't know what to say to you, Bonsier, for your help."

"It hardly warrants thanks," the guard replied, nodding in the direction of Fraire Herchambaut. "Give the monk a donation for me, and I will be well pleased." He indicated the galleried corridors of the funda. "This is the heart of the city, no matter what else you may hear, and everything passes through the funda, one way or another. That is why the Bourgesses are too busy and why you have not been granted permission to leave yet."

Olivia closed her eyes. "I wish I could . . ." Her tone changed as she began once more. "I wish I could persuade the Bourgesses that I have no wish to put them at a disadvantage, that I desire only to be allowed to leave without abandoning my house and goods here, in accordance with the laws that they have made. I don't want to . . . to cheat them."

"I'm sure that the Bourgesses know that," said Fraire Herchambaut before the guard could say anything.

"Perhaps," Olivia allowed sarcastically. "Come, good monk. I must ask you to help me to prepare yet another petition to present to the Bourgesses. I will see that you have a copy as well as Bonsier Dar and Sier Valence of the Hospitalers." She glanced at the guard to see if her intentions impressed him.

"An excellent plan," enthused Fraire Herchambaut. "Most excellent. I am convinced that this is the better way, for the Bourgesses will prefer to hear from your deputies rather than you yourself. It isn't seemly for you to press your own case."

"It isn't seemly," Olivia repeated. "There was a time, Fraire Herchambaut—it was a long time ago, but still—

when no one would have thought it strange that I pursued my own interests for myself. There was a time when none of this endless circumlocution would have been warranted just because I am a widow."

Fraire Herchambaut chuckled indulgently. "What time was this, Bondama?"

"When the Caesars ruled in Roma, when—" She was about to say *when I was young* but stopped herself.

"Those are nothing more than legends. The Caesars were evil and Godless men who persecuted Christians." He folded his arms and tucked his hands into his sleeves. "If you have heard otherwise, it is nothing more than wild tales. After all, it has been said that the houses of the Romans were kept warm by hot floors. Warm floors!" he scoffed. "A foretaste of Hell, rather."

Olivia wanted to tell the Cistercian exactly how the Roman heating method worked, but knew there was no point. She needed this monk's help, not his censure. She loosened a corner of her veil and let the soft folds cover her face. "Fraire Herchambaut, I pray you come with me to my house. I need your guidance and assistance."

"Surely," said Fraire Herchambaut. "Your palinquin is over there, in the far corner of the courtyard." He pointed down to the ground level. "If we take that staircase . . ."

"Yes," said Olivia. She longed for the chance to move about the streets on her own. "My slaves are waiting."

"You do well by them," Fraire Herchambaut said as they made their way down the narrow, twisting staircase.

"Who?" asked Olivia, as she gathered more of the voluminous folds of the skirt of her bliaud into her hands so that she would not trip.

"Your slaves. You treat them very well, more as servants than slaves, in fact." He looked back over his shoulder at her. "Do you never think that your attitude is over-indulgent? Slaves that are permitted too much liberty become lax and corrupted."

"Really?" Olivia marveled. "And yet my father taught me that slaves were to be treated with respect, given all the rights to which they were entitled, and—" She saw that Fraire Herchambaut disapproved. "I honor what my father taught me," she said defiantly.

"As well you ought. It is fitting for you to honor your father, no matter how odd his instruction. But permit me to say that what you have told me indicates that your father lacked wisdom in the matter of slaves." They had reached the ground level; the noise was too intense to carry on conversation, so Fraire Herchambaut nodded toward Olivia's palinquin.

"Thank you, good Fraire," said Olivia, raising her voice to make herself heard.

Alfaze was the lead bearer, and he bowed to his mistress, the words he spoke lost in the babble around them. He lifted the curtain so that Olivia could take her seat in the palinquin, holding out his other hand to her for balance.

The streets were as noisy as the funda and only marginally less crowded. A caravan from Damascus had arrived at mid-morning, and the merchants were just completing their dealings with the customs officers of the funda; vendors of food and drink gathered near the funda, shouting out the prices and virtues of their goods. In addition to these, a group of thirty pilgrims—from Bohemia, by the look of them—were trying to reach the Court of Bourgesses before seeking the Hospitalers and a place to rest.

As she was carried away from the din, Olivia held her hands to her ears to shut out the sounds. Had the fora of Roma been this noisy? She could no longer remember. At least the Romans had bathed more often and had swept the streets frequently. Here in Tyre the smell of the place was as intrusive as its noise. No matter how long she lived here, or in what circumstances, it remained foreign to her, more foreign than Alexandria had been, or Fraxinetum, or Ortranto, or Tunis, or Phasis, or Constantinople, or any of the other far-flung places she had made her temporary home. Tyre had been a haven once, long ago, but that city had vanished as surely as if it had been covered over with desert sands. Now her house, Tyre itself, was a cage.

"Bondama," said Fraire Herchambaut as he hurried along beside her palinquin. "Who among the Hospitalers has offered to escort you to Roma?"

"A French knight, vassal of England: Sier Valence Rainaut. He has already spoken to the Bourgesses." Her own mention of Rainaut's name brought a strange longing to her, still unexpected in its intensity. At another time she might have sighed; now she discovered she was repeating his name over and over in her thoughts, like a prayer.

"I will find him," said Fraire Herchambaut. "The Court of Bourgesses are not entitled to delay your permission to leave unreasonably unless they have reason to suspect you are a criminal or owe monies in Tyre."

"I owe no money," said Olivia stiffly. "That has been made plain more times than I care to discuss."

Fraire Herchambaut did not find it easy to match the pace of the bearers and talk at the same time. "Bondama . . . I think it would . . . be best if you do not . . . press the matter."

"Why?" Olivia asked with deliberate bluntness.

"Because it is not becoming . . . for women to act so. You . . . are not the Queen of England . . . you are not . . . free to pretend to rule the world." He was panting heavily now, and Olivia took mercy on him.

"Alfaze, slow down a trifle," she shouted, and felt her bearers drop back to a walk. "As I recall," she went on to Fraire Herchambaut, "she was confined by her husband for some time. That is hardly ruling the world."

"Only because she had consistently tried to usurp his authority," said Fraire Herchambaut, less breathlessly than before. "Had she kept to her proper role in life, Henry would not have confined her. She gave favor to one of her sons and made no effort to aid her husband in his work. It was Richard who had her loyalty then, not Henry. Now that her son is King, she is showing again that she is unwilling to accept the place in life assigned her by God."

"Reis Richard," said Olivia, giving the King his preferred French title, "has made it apparent that he depends on his mother. That is what the rumors say."

"It is fitting that a son honor his mother," said Fraire Herchambaut, his voice carrying better now that they had turned off the main thoroughfare. "It is good that a King show favor to those who bore him. But . . . Richard is . . ." His voice trailed off.

"Yes," said Olivia dryly, "I have heard such rumors, too."

Fraire Herchambaut did his best to recover his composure. "It is only rumor, and therefore suspect. Foolish and malicious people will say anything about a King."

"Including that he has an aversion to women and a hankering for men?" Olivia asked with feigned innocence. "A strange rumor to spread, I would have thought, when there are others that might be more—"

"King Richard is about to be married," said Fraire Herchambaut baldly. "The arrangements are being made. Rumors of this sort and at so critical a time are worse than most others might be." He moved toward the rear of the palinquin as they neared Olivia's house. "I do not want to hear such scandalous allegations repeated," he said in a loud voice which carried to several others in the street and caused a brief fuss.

"If even part of it is true, I should think that his prospective bride would want to know of it," said Olivia, much more to herself than to Fraire Herchambaut. "If these rumors are heard in Tyre, what are they saying in England and France, I wonder?"

"What?" shouted Fraire Herchambaut as the door to Olivia's house was opened for them.

"Nothing," Olivia yelled back. "Nothing at all."

Then the door closed behind them and the palinquin was set down now that Olivia was once again safely inside.

"Gracious mistress," said Alfaze as he opened the curtains for her. He held out his hand in case she wanted to steady herself.

Olivia stared at the walls surrounding her and shuddered.

*   *   *

Text of a letter from Niklos Aulirios to Atta Olivia Clemens.

To his much-missed bond-holder, Niklos sends greetings from her house Sanza Pare in Roma.

First, you will receive a shipment of six barrels of Roman earth with this letter; you indicated that your supply was getting low. You have risks enough already without that hazard, and with Barbarossa so determined to reclaim Jerusalem, who knows what will happen in Tyre? Since there was no difficulty in getting the earth—especially with all the repairs at Sanza Pare—I have sent more than you requested, and I hope they serve your purpose. If you think I have done more than you required, consider my reasons, Olivia.

Every day there are rumors, and each of them is more ferocious than the last. Judging from what you hear in the market, the entire world of Islam is about to be eradicated by the pure vengeance of Christian knights for the intolerable insult done to the Holy Sepulcher. The people of Roma are in the mood for blood again, and they are no longer content to see it spilled in the arena. For that reason alone, I am horrified to learn of the continued and senseless delays which plague you. What do the Bourgesses want—a writ from one of the Kings? Or an endorsement from the Pope? Perhaps a command from the Emperor demanding your presence in his Italian territories? The New Year has already come, and you are yet in Tyre. Who would have thought it would take so long? I have asked Doca Arrigo Benammo di Cruceclare to send a copy of the deed of sale of Sanza Pare to the Court of Bourgesses, in case they are unconvinced that you have the land in question.

On a different note: the repairs to the main house of Sanza Pare are more than half completed. The place has a much different aspect now, not so abandoned and bare. I have requested that all the rooms be painted and that there be frescos in the major rooms, with the exception of the kitchen, of course. I have discovered four gifted artisans who have done such work before. I asked more than ten of them to give me sketches; the four are the best of the lot. They have agreed to begin work in the spring, and all of them will stay at Sanza Pare until their frescos are complete. The monies required are on deposit and all the artisans have seen the pouches sealed. As you instructed, each of them has been told to examine the mosaics left in the two ancient villas nearby. Whether or not they are able to capture the flavor of those scenes will be discovered when their works are complete.

And speaking of that, I have found two apprentice stonemasons who are willing to do the mosaic inlays for the floors in the rooms you have requested. I have also ordered the marble you wanted from the quarries in the north. I have seen samples of a rose marble, and one of pale green, and both are appropriate to your house, I am sure. I have already specified the rose-veined marble for your private baths. Incidentally, I have not mentioned the installation of the baths to any of the monks and priests hereabouts—they do not approve of bathing, and I do not want them curious about you.

I have used your authorization to sell off part of the stock at your stud farm near Canossa, and have an accounting waiting for you. The sum realized will more than cover the remaining work to be done here, and will also satisfy the requirements of di Cruceclare, who has been worried about increasing costs and the wages being paid. He informed me he had not expected you to use so little slave labor. Since the money is held by him in your name, he is more cooperative. I still have the authorizations for the canvas-makers in Ostia and the goldsmith in Verona, in case there should be reason to convert more of your holdings to ready gold. Also, there are the shares in the boat-building partnership on Sardinia, but I doubt this is a good time to sell those shares, either politically or financially. Once this latest Crusade is at its height, there will be a chance for profit and you may want to be out of the whirlpool.

If you wish, I can make arrangements with Ithuriel Dar to bring you here, and we can try to straighten out the rest of the confusion with Tyre at another time. Dar is willing to do this—in fact, I think he would enjoy it—but I realize how little you want to leave behind everything you own. Knowing you as well as I do, I suspect that part of the trouble by now is that you are in no mood to give up anything to the Court of Bourgesses. However, if you decide that you are too much at hazard there, you have only to tell me and I will make arrangements with Dar at once. I urge you, Olivia, to consider Dar's offer, for with the new Crusade, Tyre could become a slaughterhouse and even you are not immune to cold steel.

The winter so far has been a stormy one, and I have seen more heavy rain here than any time during our last prolonged stay in the Roman environs. Word has it that many of the smaller ships are not leaving port for fear of the storms, but most of the larger ships are setting out in greater numbers now that the chivalry of Europe is venturing to the Holy Land.

While we are on that subject, let me recommend to you that you accept that Venetian merchant's offer and buy into the dyes-and-spice business. I know you are wary of Venezia. The city cannot help it, Olivia, if it had the ill-grace to be founded after the end of the Western Empire. Not all cities in Europe have links to old Roma. Venezian or not, this merchant clearly needs more funding if he is to be able to expand his enterprise, and you will earn a good return on your silver. From what I have seen, the only worthwhile legacy of the first two Crusades has been a hunger for spices and for bright clothes and fine fabrics. Those two tastes will not be easily sated now, no matter who rules in Jerusalem.

Have a care, Olivia. You say you are not in danger, and that may be so, but you know as well as I do that Tyre is no longer a safe place for you or anyone. I hope you will be here by the Spring Passion; I will do all that I can to ensure it. In the meantime, know that my thoughts and good wishes are with you and that I miss you as I would miss my arm if it were struck off.

Niklos Aulirios

By my own hand the day before Epiphany in the 1190th Christian Year.

· 8 ·

Her voice was still low and breathless, but the softness of a moment before was gone. "What did you call me?" Joivita demanded as she started to shove her lover off her.

Rainaut blinked, puzzled by her sudden change. "I . . . I

said nothing," he told her, worried that perhaps she was right and he had let slip the name of the woman he saw in his mind as he possessed himself of Joivita's body.

"You said a name. It wasn't mine." She glared at him, her delicate vixen's face no longer tempting.

"I . . . I might have said . . . my wife's name." He knew it was not so, that her memory was as far from his mind as Joivita was, but any other admission would lead to more ire than she was showing now.

"Your wife?" Joivita asked sarcastically. "This is news."

"She's dead," Rainaut said quietly without mentioning how long ago she had died. He could feel his flesh change, his need growing as his organ shrunk.

"How unfortunate," Joivita sulked, showing no trace of sympathy.

"It was God's Will," said Rainaut, guilt making the words difficult to speak. He had no right to the sweet images that had haunted him only moments ago. He dishonored himself to use his wife's memory as a mask for his lust; he would have to confess it. If only he felt remorse instead of guilt!

"And you, a good Hospitaler, never question God's Will," said Joivita as she pulled her saffron-scented sheet up under her chin. She shook out the tousle of her hair in provocative defiance. "And when you're with your mistress, you think of your dead wife. What virtue! How devoted you are."

"I don't always think of my dead wife when I am with you," said Rainaut, not quite coaxing her. "Most of the time you fill my thoughts."

"But tonight I reminded you of your dead wife," she pursued relentlessly. "Grand mercie, Sier Valence." She made a movement like a courtsy, pulling the sheet aside to reveal most of her thighs. "What is it proper for a dead wife to offer her husband? Or do those in Heaven—you assume she is in Heaven, don't you?—offer bodies as a sign of respect and honor? Perhaps they only do such in Hell."

"Is that what you will give me now?" Rainaut asked, doing his best not to sound impatient or to goad her to more outrage. Out of his own guilty misery, he wanted to throttle Joivita for what she forced him to see. And how dared she calumniate his wife's memory: what a dreadful time for the

little whore to take on airs! It would not do for Joivita to
know how much she had upset him. He leaned back against
the mass of pillows. "Since you are clearly insulted, though
such insult was not my intent, will you accept my apology
and forgive me?" It was a speech that might have been found
in a troubador's tale, yet he said it as sincerely as he could.

"I am not a dead woman and I am not a priest," she said
primly. "Though it appears you confuse me with both."

"Joivita—" He started to reach out for the curves her
body made in the sheets.

She slapped his hand. "No. You treat me as if I am a
common street woman, and I am not. If all you want is a way
to remember your wife, find another." As she folded her
arms, her breasts rose under the thin cotton. "You are no
gentleman, Sier Valence, if you treat me thus."

He stared up at the timbered ceiling of her room. He felt
tired now, and the game she demanded of him vexed him as
it intruded on his more distressing thoughts. "I did not
intend to say her name."

"You were so moved that you thought it could only be that
dead woman," mocked Joivita, starting to enjoy the discomfort she was giving to her lover; nothing pleased her as much
as the power she exerted with men, either through her body
or in spite of it.

Rainaut held back the sharp retorts that slipped through
his mind as quickly and unwelcome as Olivia's image had
been. "I am in a faraway land. You made me feel I was home
once more," he said with the same ease he would have
spoken to his aunt who lived with the nuns. "I never
intended to give you displeasure of any kind."

"Certainly not," said Joivita. "You intended to plough
me."

This was so baldly true that Rainaut could not keep from
chuckling once. "And instead, this."

Joivita peered at him suspiciously over the gathered sheet.
"And what would you call this?"

"A misunderstanding," said Rainaut with a touch of
humor. He was resigned to completing the game, for he
knew with utter certainty that he would have need of Joivita
again. "You and I both have misunderstood."

"So I see," she responded with a direct look at where the sheet covered his loins. "A misunderstanding. Something is not standing, is it?" She smiled at her own joke.

"No," Rainaut said brusquely.

"And?" Joivita sensed the conflict in Rainaut. "Sier Valence?" she offered.

"If I say I want you, you will tell me that I make you my whore, and you will turn me from your bed. If I say that I do not want you, you will call me a priest or a eunuch and turn me from your bed. If I say I want you but cannot take you, you will laugh me out of your house." He recited these possibilities in a flat, unemotional voice. "So, I beg you, tell me what I might say to you that would return me to your esteem." It was another troubador's phrase, but this time Joivita heard it favorably.

"Very clever," she said, as much to herself as to him. "You are not quite a dolt, then." Her smile was predatory. "And yet you falter when you could—"

"I am not a barbarian, Joivita," Rainaut said, growing angry with her again. "If you want me to force you to do the thing we both desire, I will do so." As he said it, the idea became appealing. There were times, he knew, when the love-making of poets and courtiers had no place between sheets, unless those sheets belonged to a book.

"I will fight you," she announced as her face flushed, turning dark in the light from the braziers. "Oh, Sier Valence, I will fight you." She held her hands up, the fingers curved like claws. "I will leave marks on you."

"You may try," said Rainaut, feeling his body respond to her challenge. He reached out and pulled the sheet away from her. "You may try," he repeated as he moved over her, his weight pinning her to the bed.

Her hands rose, ready to scratch his face, but he caught them and stretched them over her head, keeping them out of range.

"You are hurting me," she protested eagerly. "How you are hurting me." Her attempts to free her hands were only token effort; she moved beneath him to give him more access to her body.

"Be silent," Rainaut said, knowing that it was what she wanted to her, and hoping that if both of them said nothing, he could not forget himself again. Roughly he tugged her knees upward, feeling her sigh at this use. He braced himself and then pressed into her.

At his penetration, Joivita gave a little shriek and pulled her hands from his, reaching down to score his back with her nails. She felt the strength of his desire and it filled her with more delight than his flesh did. To be able to drive a lover to madness, to violence, was a sign to Joivita of how great her power was. Only an implacable enemy could evoke more passion than she could, and no enemy could control another as she controlled her lovers. She rocked with him, her nails drawing blood now. Her eyes were closed, and she imagined that Sier Valence Rainaut was Richard Coer de Leon; she wanted Richard lo Reis more than she wanted any other man in the world, for she had heard that he could not abide the bodies of women and took his pleasure with his men. At Richard's dreamed surrender, Joivita's body spasmed and twisted beneath Rainaut's, and her cry was hard and high, like a shout in battle.

Moments later, Rainaut was finished. As soon as his semen was out of him, Rainaut was off Joivita and staring up at the ceiling once more. He was panting and he stank of sweat. His flesh was sated now; his senses were famished.

"Impressive," said Joivita softly, but whether she spoke to him or to her own hopes she did not know.

Rainaut said nothing. Inwardly he cursed himself for permitting Joivita to spur his lust as she had, and for his own lack of will that let him succumb so easily. He laced his fingers together behind his head and tried to follow the meanderings of the patterns on the beams.

"What now—contempt?" teased Joivita as she rolled to Rainaut's side, her breast against his arm to tantalize him.

"It is not good for the soul to use women," said Rainaut, recalling everything that Fraire Huon had said to him in the five years he had been his tutor.

"Tell that to your body, Sier Valence," Joivita said as she ran her finger up his arm to his chest and along the collar bone, pausing to circle the knot of an improperly healed break. "How old were you when this happened, Sier Valence?"

He moved her hand away. "I don't remember—fourteen, fifteen."

"So long ago," she said, the mockery back in her eyes. "So very long ago."

He refused to look at her. "And who remembers so long ago?"

Her finger continued up his neck, pausing where a thin flake of skin came loose as she touched it. "Your armor is chafing?"

"It's the heat," he said, turning away from her.

"Is it hard, Sier Valence, to wear such armor and to fight in the sun? Does the acton grow heavy with blood and sweat?" She ran her tongue over her lips. "Does it? And does the mail cut through the acton and score your skin? As I've scored your skin?" This last was her own triumph, and as she said the words her eyes glowed.

"I have not had to fight," Rainaut said stiffly.

"Oh, yes. I forgot. You Hospitalers can fight only when attacked; you are not permitted to make the first assault, are you? Is that what happened to you tonight?" She laughed and moved closer to him. "You're not like the Templars. No wonder you have so many graces."

"Joivita, don't." He faced her at last. "If all you want is to jeer, then let me find a dwarf for you."

"Oh, a dwarf would not serve me at all," she said, so blatantly obvious in her intentions that Rainaut opened his hand to strike her. "I need much more than a dwarf."

"To jeer?" he challenged.

"Possibly," she answered, her finger on his lip. "When there is nothing else to do." She reached out and drew her sheet back around her. "There's blood on your side." Her eyes brightened. "Sit up, Sier Valence."

Rainaut had started to move, but her eager command stopped him. "Why?"

"I want to see your back. I want to see my handiwork." She pulled at him, nothing gentle or seductive in her actions now. "Hurry. I want to see."

Reluctantly, Rainaut swung his legs out of bed and sat up, facing the door, away from Joivita. "Well?"

Her face was luminous, and her breath quickened as she saw the long gouges she had made in his back. "Very good," she said to herself. "Oh, very, very good." Deliberately she put her hand on the most severe of the scratches and drew it across the torn skin. Though he made no sound, Joivita could feel Rainaut wince as she did this, and she was pleased. "You will not forget me, either, Sier Valence. Like your dead wife, you will remember me."

Slowly Rainaut started to get up. "I must leave."

"Now that you have taken what you wanted, you are going away," she corrected him, suddenly petulant.

"If that is how you will have it, Bondama, then that is what I am doing." He got up slowly, not certain how Joivita would respond.

"Will you return?" she asked as she adjusted her sheet around her.

He hated himself for answering "Yes," but he could not bring himself to lie.

Joivita grinned. "When?" She could see his resistance and gloried in the knowledge that she would be able to wear him down, that his need for her was too strong for his will to contain it.

"I . . . I don't know," he said as he looked for his clothes. His Hospitaler's mantel was draped over the clothes chest by the door, but where had he put the rest of them? Staring at his mantel, he could not help but feel he had dishonored the cross on it.

"Soon," she said, making it an order. "If you wait too long, I will have to find another." She pouted, hoping he would look at her and see her displeasure, but he did not. "I will not send you a message; you will have to send one to me."

"Of course." He was weary, body and soul. He saw the wadded heap in the corner of the room and went to sort out his clothing. Now all that was missing was his belt.

As he dressed, Joivita sat watching him, appraising him as he prepared to leave her. He was well-born, and that was an improvement on the Templars she brought to her bed. He admitted he had no fortune, but wealth was measured more ways than in gold. He was not as young as some of her lovers, but he was no graybeard, and he was tolerably good-looking, being taller than most men, and of regular but angular features. All in all, she decided, she would have to regard him as her most promising lover yet. When at last he looked at her, she moved back, stretching out on the bed, the sheet draped artfully to reveal more than mere nudity would have done. "I am desolate," she said.

"You will find consolation," said Rainaut with unhappy certainty, since he had no illusions about Joivita.

"Nothing so sweet as you, Sier Valence." She lowered her voice, making it more musical. "If I know others, it is for my bread; you I know for delight."

Rainaut bowed. "You are gracious, Bondama." He knew she was not entitled to be called bondama, but he sensed she was flattered by it, and he hoped that flattery would permit him to escape without another disagreement.

"So are you, Sier Valence." She raised one arm and let it drop languidly above her head, deliberately reminding him of how he had held her down. "You are many things."

He did not want to have to listen to her catalogue nor to think of his own, so he gathered up his mantel. "I will send you word again, when it is possible for me to visit you," he told her, loathing the desire that drove him to her.

"I will count the hours in my prayers," she said, reaching out to touch his hand.

He pulled away from her. "It will not be before Sunday. I have duties, and I am to go with the Franconian pilgrims for one day on the road to Sidon." He did not add that he had requested the task.

"Only a day of escort? Only two days away from Tyre?" she asked, amused at his discomfort.

"It is what was requested. There are two knights with them who are making the pilgrimage on foot, at the order of their bishop, so they are not without protection. The robber bands will be sorry if they attack them. Those who take slaves will not find what they like among the Franconians, for all save the disgraced knights are crippled or disfigured in some way." He fastened his mantel with a square brooch that was decorated with his arms.

"Poor unfortunates," said Joivita without sympathy. "Has the pilgrimage given them back their arms and legs, I wonder, or restored their—"

"Stop," said Rainaut very quietly. "You are not to speak so again in my presence. It is blasphemy and heresy to say such things, even in jest, and I am sworn to defend the honor of Our Lord and God."

"I—" Joivita did her best not to appear as much taken aback as she was. "I never meant—"

Rainaut nodded. "Certainly."

"I have never intended any—" She saw his face and fell silent.

He came to the side of the bed and looked down at her. "Understand me, Joivita. I am a slave to your body, but when you seek to touch my soul, then I am your executioner, though it bring me to my own death. I will risk my allotted time in Hell for you, but not my salvation."

She nodded, afraid to speak. It was delicious to feel this fear, to know beyond question that she would make him pay dearly for it. Carefully she rolled to her side and looked up at him from under her lashes.

"Your tricks are damning, Joivita. Use them at your peril." He turned away from her, his hewn countenance looking as if it had been carved out of the heart of stone.

Joivita watched him go, sighing as she heard the front door of her little house slam closed. She leaned back, propping herself on her elbows, and clicked her tongue several times in quiet irritation. More than ever she was determined to bring Sier Valence Rainaut under her heel, and through him to reach Reis Richard Coer de Leon. What better means, she told herself, than through the King's vassal knight who was completely in her thrall.

A discreet knock at her door interrupted her thoughts.

"A moment," she called out, neither surprised nor confused. When she sat up, she had abandoned her sensual airs and had much more the look of an expert thief, which her father was. She pulled a barbaresque robe around her shoulders and said, "Enter, Meniques."

The man who came through the door was her cousin, and like Joivita, had been born at Narbonne. He was fifteen years her senior and had not spent those years well: his nose had been struck off and he was missing three fingers on his right hand. "Was it a good night, little cousin?"

She shrugged. "It was not bad."

"He excites you, this one, doesn't he?" Meniques asked with a knowing look.

"What he is excites me," said Joivita shortly. "He is no mere Templar, he's with the Hospitalers, and he's a vassal of Richard's."

"Poor fellow, if he gets too close to his king," said Meniques with a very unpleasant chuckle. "Someone as handsome as that would not be able to escape the king's . . . favor." The last word was so salacious that Joivita flushed.

"That has nothing to do with us," she snapped, unwilling to hear anyone speak so crudely of Richard Coer de Leon. "I have learned a little from Sier Valence, as we agreed."

"And the pilgrims? What of them?" Meniques' manner changed abruptly, now all business. "How many and how guarded?"

"I don't know the number. They're Franconians, all cripples or disfigured, and two are knights on foot, for protection as for penance. The Hospitalers will accompany them for one day and then return." She looked speculatively at Meniques. "Worth the picking?"

"It's hard to say," Meniques answered. "Possibly. Franconians. All disfigured or crippled. That's not promising. Nothing much for a slave market and . . . what about ransom?" This last was the only idea that Meniques could salvage from the unpromising news.

"So far as I know none of them are worth much," said Joivita, secretly glad that this was the case, for it did not suit her plans to have Rainaut hurt or killed in a skirmish before she had achieved her purpose.

"But it's possible?" Meniques pursued.

"I suppose so. But if that was the case, there would be a greater escort. What well-born pilgrim would want to be in the company of the disfigured or knights on foot?" It was a sensible question, and Meniques considered it carefully.

"Well, we will have to delay, then. Probably just as well. With the new Crusade, there's no telling how much ransom we can collect on knights. I'll need more men with me if we're going to try that, but—" He reached out and patted Joivita's arm in a proprietary way. "You're doing very well, little cousin."

Joivita could feel the familiar tightness in her gut at Meniques' touch and told herself that she had long since passed the place where she had to be afraid of him any longer. When she was ten and had no means to fight him, she was entitled to fear, but no longer. Now she knew his weaknesses and would use them against him. "I am doing better than you could dream," she corrected him haughtily.

"Are you?" He did not move his hand.

"And my body is not for the likes of you any longer," she insisted with hauteur. "You may go back to your slaves and camp followers."

"Why should I do that, when you're here?" he asked, starting to push her shoulder.

"Because," she said very distinctly, "if you touch me when I do not demand it of you, I will never again tell you what I have learned from my lovers. I will lie to you and betray you and I will laugh when they cut off your hand and your ears. I will say that you are a blasphemer and they will peel the skin off your feet and pour salt on the meat for goats to lick." She laughed as Meniques turned pale. "And you dare not punish me. I am not a whore, I am a courtesan and my lovers would not let my death go unavenged."

"Are you so certain?" Meniques had turned ugly but beneath his belligerence there was fear. "What if I took you with me now, what then?"

"My slaves would kill you," she said with a certainty she did not feel. "And they would take you to the Court of Bourgesses for murder. You would be flayed alive then." She crossed her arms and waited for her cousin to step back.

Slowly, angrily, he did. "I curse the day I had your maidenhead," he said.

She responded with great sweetness. "Dear cousin, so do I."

*   *   *

Text of a letter from Sanct' Germain Franciscus in Karakhorum to Olivia in Alexandria, sent eight years ago; written in archaic Latin.

Greetings to my dearest Olivia, from one of the most forsaken places on the earth. It reflects my present humor. Karakhorum is said to be a city, but it is more of a Mongol camp with walls. Why is it that the more desolate and unaccomplished a place is, the grander the titles are that are heaped on it?

Luckily I will be leaving here in two days, bound at last for Lo-Yang, where your letters will find me eventually if you will entrust them to cloth merchants bound along the Old Silk Road. Rogerian has found a reliable caravan going to the old capital and they have agreed—at an enormous fee—to permit the two of us to ride with them.

I know your opinions of my actions. You made them very clear in your last letter. But surely even you can see that the world is changing, and that the continued clash of Christianity and Islam has only served to make each side more zealous and unyielding. There is precious little room for reason or moderation now, and you will not convince me that the skirmishes will not continue until once again there is war, presented in the more flattering guise of Crusading.

That madness is contagious, Olivia. Remember what happened to those of our blood who died in a flaming barn. Neither you nor I would escape their fate if we were revealed for what we are. I am sick of the waste and the treachery. When I thought, in our trek over the desert, that at last I would die the true death, I was not troubled; in fact, I was relieved that only the relentless sun would claim me, and not the axe or the sword or the fire.

As you see, I survived. And yet, aside from the loss of you, there was little binding me here. I could not have withstood it all, but for you. Not even the few scattered remnants of our blood could hold to life as you did. Perhaps I will have the respite I seek in Lo-Yang. You need not remind me that I will be a stranger there—I am always a stranger everywhere.

This is much longer than I intended, and I will not compound my fault. If this reaches you, answer me when it is safe for you to write. In this hopeless world, my treasured friend, you give me hope.

Sanct' Germain
his seal, the eclipse

By my own hand on the 14th or 15th day of April in the Christian year 1182.

· 9 ·

As he gazed at the roughly carved crucifix, it seemed to Fraire Herchambaut that the Body of Christ moved, and that for an instant the wood was not wood at all, but bleeding flesh. He made the Sign of the Cross and whispered a prayer that was not part of his devotions. Now he could not recall the numbers of the Hosts of God, or their designations and ranks. He squinted, his eyes stinging from sweat, and tried to resume his orisons, his voice croaking out the words by rote, all sense or true understanding faded from his mind.

It was mid-afternoon before someone came to the chapel and found Fraire Herchambaut lying on the floor, nearly unconscious, fever giving his grimy features the ruddiness of false health. The page, coming from the Templars, blessed himself and hurried away, shouting that the monk had fainted from plague.

By sunset, two monks from the Hospital of Saint Lazarus had come and pronounced Fraire Herchambaut clean, having no taint of leprosy about him; they could not care for him, for their work was only with those most unfortunate souls afflicted with the disease that visited corruption on the body before death claimed it.

The Knights Hospitaler had no room for Fraire Herchambaut, for their hospital was already filled with pilgrims suffering from almost every malady known in the Holy Land.

"We cannot return him to his chapel," said the senior infirmarist to his assistants. "Left to his own devices, he will die for lack of care. There is no one who—"

"He is a monk," one of the assistants pointed out. "He has placed his life in God's Hands, and—"

"That is enough," said the senior infirmarist as he glared at the young man in the stained white habit with the black cross on the sleeves. "You have your task, which is the care of those Christians suffering in the body. This monk prays for those who are suffering in the soul. It would be a great failure if we were to neglect him." He continued to scowl.

"He has no other Cistercians to tend his chapel," said their page, a twelve-year-old boy from Ravenna. "He maintained it by himself, and provided comfort to those few who sought him out."

The senior infirmarist shook his head. "A bad business." He turned back to the pallet where Fraire Herchambaut lay, not quite asleep, fretting and muttering. "There is no room here."

"There are Islamites who—" one of the others suggested, but was cut off at once.

"What are we that we would send our monks to the followers of Islam, whose soldiers are massing now to fight our Christian chivalry?" the senior infirmarist demanded, not at all pleased with the question that was almost asked.

"What of the others? What of those who came to him?" This was one of the older infirmarists, a carter's son from Paris.

"He's a monk, not a priest," one of the others scoffed. "Who came to him, except poor travelers?"

"There were a few who . . ." the page began, then hesitated. "The Roman widow knows him. She might be willing to pay for his care."

"The Roman widow?" repeated the senior infirmarist. "What woman is this?"

"The one who lives near the rug-merchants' market, the one with the palinquin with sea-colored hangings," said the page. "She is over thirty, they say, and was married to a Roman noble older than she."

"I know nothing of her," said the senior infirmarist. "I ought to speak to one of our superiors." Like all infirmarists, he was a lay brother, not bound by the more stringent vows of the knights of the Order. "To release a sick man to the care of a widow—" He shook his head.

"Who may not have him in any case," said the page. "Still, she knows who he is. That may mean . . ." The movements of his hands ended his thoughts.

By morning, Fraire Herchambaut was delirious, his words rambling and his fervid eyes glazed. He tossed on the narrow pallet in the infirmary hall where he had lain all the night, unaware of where he was or how ill he had become.

"Has the widow been approached?" asked the aloof Premonstratensian who supervised the chapel. "We cannot permit Fraire Herchambaut to remain here."

"Word was sent shortly after dawn," said the senior infirmarist. "There is no answer yet."

The Premonstratensian stared at the suffering monk. "At least he is not a leper."

"There is no room in the Hospital of Saint Lazarus," said the senior infirmarist. "I was warned last week when those three pilgrims were discovered to be lepers." He blessed himself. "I would embrace any affliction, even the bite of a mad dog, rather than leprosy." He saw the expression in the Premonstratensian's eyes. "Truly, I would. I know it is wrong of me, for Our Lord washed a leper clean, but—"

The Premonstratensian sighed. "Whatever the cause, death comes to all of us, and for those who have lived in God, they will live again, as the others will be lost to Hell for eternity." He looked down once more at Fraire Herchambaut. "Has he been able to take water?"

"He hasn't been given any. You see the state he is in." The senior infirmarist cleared his throat. "Whoever cares for him, he will not need help long, not with his condition. Two, perhaps three days, and he will stand at the Mercy Seat." The Premonstratensian nodded. "We are always in the Hands of God." He hid his hands in his sleeves and moved around the pitiful figure of Fraire Herchambaut on his way to the main infirmary.

By mid-morning, Alfaze presented himself at the Hospitalers' infirmary along with a scribe from the Court of Bourgesses. On the orders of his mistress, he went in search of Sier Valence Rainaut, carrying a formal statement from Olivia declaring that she would take Fraire Herchambaut into her house as an act of charity through ministering to those diseased.

"I knew nothing of this," said Rainaut when he had taken the time to look over the statement. "She is trying to leave Tyre. We are arranging it." He stared at Alfaze as if the slave would provide him an answer.

"She said the monk has aided her," Alfaze said in his high voice. "So long as she remains in Tyre, she intends to offer the protection of her house to the Cistercian Brother for as long as he requires it." He spoke precisely as Olivia had instructed him, but he was not prepared for the heat of Rainaut's response.

"What is the matter with her?" he shouted, making the narthex of the Hospitalers' church ring and the worshippers within look around in vexation. Uncaring and undismayed he went on, "What is her purpose? And do not tell me that it is charity, for she could practice that any way she pleased. She already has donated a third of her goods to the use of religious Orders and Houses; there is no doubt of her piety or sincerity. Why this?"

"She did not tell me, Bonsier," Alfaze said, making his voice as soft as possible as if it would quiet Rainaut's.

"Why tell a slave?" Rainaut asked of the air. "But she will tell me, by all the Saints in the calendar." He started past Alfaze, but turned back. "Where is she?"

"She awaits at her house. She is preparing to receive the monk." He looked down at his feet. "I must do what my mistress orders me to do," Alfaze apologized to Rainaut indirectly.

CRUSADER'S TORCH · 107

"Certainly," Rainaut said. "But I will speak with her at once." He stormed out of the church and along the crowded street toward the funda. His anger was so intense that he barely noticed the heat of the sun.

Two Egyptian slaves opened the door to Rainaut when he pounded on the door, and they stood silently aside as the Hospitaler thundered into the vestibule.

"Bondama Clemens!" he bellowed.

Olivia appeared at the end of the central hall. "Sier Valence," she said as she came toward him, her shadow-colored linen bliaud soft and ungirdled so that it swirled around her like smoke. "I had not thought to see you."

"No, I suppose not," he said, face thrust forward.

She came up to him. "Is there more trouble?"

"How can you ask that, after what you have done?" he shouted. "What possessed you?"

The two Egyptian slaves had not left their places by the door; they watched their mistress with her unexpected visitor, ready to act at her signal.

"What are you saying?" Olivia asked between amusement and annoyance. "Why are you here, yelling at me?"

He slapped his thighs hard with his hands. "Never mind this pretense, woman. Tell me why you have"—his manner changed abruptly as he met her hazel eyes with his blue ones—"why have you said you would take the Cistercian into your house? The man is dying, Bondama. He is sick. He has a fever and he sweats like a pig." In his concern he touched her arm.

"I am not afraid," said Olivia softly. "But I am . . . I am grateful that you are, for my sake." She wished she knew him better, understood him better so that she could say more to him.

"If you took his sickness, I . . ." He shook his head slowly.

"I will not take his sickness, on my blood I will not." Her faint smile was so distant and sad that Rainaut wrapped his arms around her before he thought of the consequences of his act.

"Listen to me," he whispered fiercely to the soft cascade of her hair. "Listen to me, Olivia. Fraire Herchambaut has the flux. He is mad with fever. Nothing can save him now but God." His arms tightened. "You must not go near him. Don't endanger yourself for one who is already a dead man."

She slipped her arms around his waist, above the studded belt that held his sword-and-scabbard. "I am not afraid," she said simply.

"I *know* that," he muttered. "The Virgin's Tits! No one doubts your courage. I pray I had one half your courage." He drew her more tightly against him. "If anything should happen to you, Bondama, it would be the end of what little honor I have left."

Olivia leaned her head against his shoulder, her face to his neck. "Valence, listen to me," she said in a still, quiet voice, "I will take no harm from Fraire Herchambaut. I have seen his fever before." In the centuries since her death, she had witnessed more epidemics than she could remember, or wanted to. "I will not take it from Fraire Herchambaut, as those who have had the Little Pox do not take the Great Pox."

"But—" His right hand was caught in her hair, the strands falling, glistening, through his fingers like skeins of silk.

"The poor man is in his greatest need and there is no one to help him. It is a little thing for me to do, where others would have to risk much more." It was pleasant to be held this way, to lean close to him, feeling his strength and affection in his embrace. "I worry more for you than you have cause to worry for me."

The Egyptian slaves exchanged glances as they remained rigidly and correctly silent.

"If you are lying to me," Rainaut said at last, his tone growing rough with emotion, "I swear by Christ's Nails that I will strangle you."

Olivia chuckled once. "If I take fever, I won't notice."

"It is no laughing matter," Rainaut protested, drawing back from her just far enough to be able to look into her eyes. "Don't mock, Olivia, I beg you."

Her response was strangely melancholy. "I do not mock, Valence." She touched his face with the tips of her fingers. "I want only to convince you there is nothing to fear. I will not become ill from caring for Fraire Herchambaut."

"You have a sign from God, then?" he challenged her, his voice still low, his eyes volcanic.

"Something of the sort," she replied, giving herself the luxury of leaning against him once more. It had been so long since she had been more than a passionate dream to a man: she reminded herself that it was proper for a widow to be filled with ambivalence, but—

"Bondama?" Rainaut said, sensing her turmoil.

"I am . . . moved, Sier Valence," Olivia said, in proper form once more. Unwillingly she stepped back from him, knowing that to stay in his arms would bring him shame. "And I wish with all my heart you would permit me to . . . to express—"

Rainaut's face darkened. "It is not mete." He moved away from her. "Nothing I have done is mete. You are not some careless woman who—" When he looked at her, his eyes were supplicants in his hardened face.

"You are not a careless man," she said simply. "That you came here out of . . . of compassion, tells me you are not a careless man." She read self-accusation in his expression now, and she wanted to shout at him as he had at her. What absurdity of honor had he traduced now? she wondered. As a Hospitaler, he would have to confess his sins like a monk or a priest, and he would blame himself for the very thing that Olivia treasured most in him. She was tempted to box his ears or pour a jar of wine over his head. How dare he! she railed in her thoughts. How dare he awaken all her longings, all the denied joys she had been able to set aside for years and years! How dare he show her a rapture he would not let her have!

Rainaut was staring at her. "What is it?" he asked.

She caught her lower lip in her teeth before she answered. "I am . . . I am thinking about my household," she lied. "You have reminded me that they are not safe from Fraire Herchambaut's fever." If only Niklos were here, she thought. Between the two of them they could care for Fraire Herchambaut and neither of them would be in danger. As it was, she would have to expose one of her slaves to the disease.

His expression lightened. "Have you changed your mind?"

"No." She considered. "But I will seek out one of the penitent pilgrims. Surely among them there is one who would be willing to help me." His disappointment was so plain that she smiled at last, though it brought her a deep, hidden pain. "Or is that not permissible?"

"It is permissible," he said slowly. "But many of those pilgrims are . . ." His words trailed off and he wandered toward the larger of her two reception rooms. "I will arrange it, if that is your wish," he heard himself say in a tone he did not recognize.

"Thank you," she said, coming after him once she dismissed her Egyptian slaves. "There will be a place made for the penitent."

"Most of them do not bathe," he said after a moment.

"How fastidious," she remarked. "I wouldn't have thought anyone noticed."

"Lice are holy for pilgrims," Rainaut said distantly. He hoped she did not know how disastrously she stirred him. He had been unwise to hold her, to put his hands on her, for now his desire had scope and substance. "Some of my Order bathe rarely."

"But you are not one of them," said Olivia, watching him closely although she appeared to be paying little attention. "Why is that?"

He laughed. "There was an old Roman camp on my family's lands. The baths could still be made to work. My father's apothecary had a theory that bathing . . ." His memories were suddenly very present. "He said that those who bathe had fewer boils and eruptions of the skin. He said that bathing prevented canker and . . . and leprosy." His attempt at derisive laughter did not succeed. "He was a mad old man."

"But you bathed," said Olivia.

"Yes, and pray for my sins now." He turned to look at her, hoping he had enough control not to stare or hunger for her. "I did not mean you any disrespect."

"You showed me none," she said. Had he been nearer she would have reached out for his hand, but he kept a good distance between them so that only their eyes met.

He said nothing for a short while, then told her, "Your eunuch, Alfaze, will be bringing Fraire Herchambaut here. I will find you a penitent, one that has some skill with caring for the sick."

"Why don't you sit down, Sier Valence?" she offered.

"No." He rubbed his fist into his palm. "No, I must not stay. I have . . . I have duties and . . ." Whatever else he was going to say faded from his mind as he looked at her. "If I were . . . other than I am, I would—"

"I don't object to what you are, Sier Valence," Olivia put in quickly. "If that is your question."

"I—no." He paced restlessly, moving away from her and approaching her as he spoke. "You are Roman. You do not understand my position."

"No, I don't, though what Roman has to do with it, I can't fathom." She waited while he wandered a little closer to her. "I don't think you could explain it to me, in any case."

"Possibly not," he said, not paying much attention. "You don't have to . . ." He stared at how her hair shone, at the tendrils that curved beside her ear. When he had touched it, the texture had been finer than anything he could remember.

Olivia returned his look. "One day, perhaps, you will explain it to me, when it doesn't matter to you as much."

"Honor must always matter," he said automatically.

"I suppose so," she said in a thoughtful voice. "But who is to decide what—Yes?" This last was to one of her Egyptian slaves who had appeared in the doorway.

"Alfaze has returned. They are bringing the monk," he said; if he saw Rainaut, he gave no sign of it.

"I must go," Rainaut said at once, starting out of the room.

"Not just at once," Olivia told him. "Let me have a little of your time, please." It was not so sharp a request that it sounded like an order, and for that reason alone, he stopped.

"What may I do for you, Bondama?" He retreated behind polite address, hoping that he would not suffer another lapse while he was in her company; his chagrin was great enough as it was.

"I have prepared one of the slave's rooms—I have six empty now—for Fraire Herchambaut. I want to be certain that it will suit, and to know which of the other rooms ought to be prepared for the penitent." She might have been discussing menus for all the emotion she revealed.

"Certainly, if you consider anything I say of value." He could have cursed himself as soon as he spoke the words. "It is my honor to assist and advise you."

Olivia had risen and now led the way to the slaves' quarters. "I have reduced my household, you know, in preparation for my departure. I still cling to the hope that I will be permitted to leave."

He nodded, watching how she moved. "Permission will be granted."

"If I knew who to bribe, I would do it, and gladly," she continued as they passed through the kitchen and down a side corridor away from the stables. "I have sold off all but two of my horses, and I have kept only nine slaves. I have filed writs of manumission for them upon my departure. With a small grant to aid them in getting on in the world."

"You are very generous," said Rainaut, puzzled.

"I am very Roman," she corrected as she entered the slaves' quarters. "There was a time when not making such provision would have been considered quite odd—as doing it is considered to be now."

The room she had set aside for Fraire Herchambaut was at the end of the corridor, with two high windows to give it light and ventilation. A basin was built into the wall and a plugged iron pipe dripped water from above it.

"It is the coolest of the rooms, and the most remote," Olivia said. "The bed-frame is supported with hemp lines, so Fraire Herchambaut will not have to lie on straw. I have a brazier and two oil lamps to keep the room lit in the night." She touched the cotton blankets set out on the bed. "He will be warm enough to keep from chills, but not so warm that his fever must increase."

"Yes," said Rainaut. "To a Cistercian, you offer luxury." He turned away. "It is wonderful care you offer, Bondama."

She looked at him. "Will you suggest which room would be best for the penitent?"

"Any that is close. But don't trouble yourself with beds and similar excesses; a straw pallet is all that a penitent is entitled to have. If you provide more, the penance will be lessened and salvation will remain far-off." He started to leave the room, then stopped, hardly more than two steps from her. "I wish you would reconsider."

"I know. But think of poor Fraire Herchambaut. If you were afflicted as he is, I would hope that there would be someone willing to care for you as I will care for him." Again she met his eyes without apology.

"For charity?" he asked harshly.

"At the least," was her level answer.

"What greater reason?" he countered, his sarcasm colored by something he did not realize was jealousy. He regarded her, his emotions so confusing that he did not know what to say.

A commotion at the head of the hallway startled them both. Olivia glanced around the room. "Is that—?"

"Your slaves with Fraire Herchambaut," said Rainaut heavily. "They're bringing him in." He took a single, hasty step toward her. "You won't change your mind?"

"No," she said softly. "But thank you."

"Don't thank me, not for letting you throw your life away for this Cistercian who is beyond all remedy but God's." He raised his hand abruptly, as if he might strike her, but instead the caress he gave her face was so light and tender that both sensed more than felt his touch.

"Mistress!" Alfaze called out, his voice echoing in the narrow confines of the hallway.

"Here," Olivia replied. "I must tend to my patient now, Sier Valence," she said, breaking the tension between them. "If you will find me that penitent to aid me?"

He bowed to her. "As you wish, Bondama," he said as he left the room, taking care not to get too near Alfaze, the two Egyptian slaves, and the muttering bundle they carried.

*   *   *

Text of an unofficial letter from the secretary of the Metropolitan of Hagia Sophia to the Abbot of the Benedictine monastery on Rhodes.

To my devout fellow-Christian and defender of Rodhos from the devilish forces of Islam which everywhere seek to bring down the Cross of Our Lord and raise the Crescent in its place, I write to you once more on the instruction of my most pious and saintly master to seek your continued aid in this time of great travail.

It is with joy that we have seen the forces of the Emperor Barbarossa enter the boundaries of the ancient Attic lands, known of old for its heros, and advance with his army toward the strongholds of the foe. We offer prayers for him and for the men that follow him, and for those mighty Kings who are gathering their men-at-arms about them to join in the battle. We are uplifted in our hearts and our souls to know that in spite of the differences which have caused so much sorrow to our Church and your Church, the bonds of Christian to Christian are sustained unbroken. It is as if once again Agamemnon has come to claim his bride—but how much more worthy and chaste a prize is Jerusalem than the woman Helen!

My master has told me often of his hopes for the successes of your great warriors, for well we know that without your succor and strength, we would be defenseless against this ruthless and implacable enemy. We know Islam well, my Christian brother, for we are much nearer to its terrors than you are. Indeed, perhaps only the Christians of Spain can share the feelings that haunt us through day and night that Islam will triumph over our Church and we will all suffer the pains of Hell for it.

How great a loss we would all sustain should such be the

fate we endure! Not only would we all lose our souls to Satan and the pains of Hell, all those souls that we would have brought to God would also be lost because of our failure in this test of our conviction and devotion. If we fall, all of Christianity falls with us, and for all ages to come, we will bear that shame in Hell. The treason of Judas we would have to share for our desertion of the Lord in this time of greatest need. I have heard my master speak eloquently, empowered by Angels, on the glory of sacrifice in the name of God and His Son, and the joy of martyrs before the Throne of God; I have known as I listened that it was the joy of the men of this great Crusade that he expressed. I cannot say how I wept then, for there are no words that could convey the depth of my vision of this gift of Grace that is descending on the Crusaders for the nobility of their fight. Those who battle in His great cause will have reason to lift up their hearts all their lives long, knowing that they are thrice welcome in Heaven, as they will be honored by those of us who worship beside them on earth.

There have been those who have suggested that we of the Eastern Church do not share the devotion of the Western Church and that we are lax in our faith and cynical in our ambitions. Some have gone so far as to suggest that we of the Eastern Church have actively sought these Crusades for our own purposes in order to strengthen our position against Islam without having to fight so that we would not have to give up our profitable trade with either the countries of the Western Church or with the various leaders of Islam. This is patently ridiculous and were it not that a few credulous souls repeat these vilifications, I would not sully this letter with mention of such insinuations. Most certainly we of the Eastern Church are keenly aware of the danger of Islam—it is before us every day of our lives. We are filled with gratitude and thanksgiving for the courage and purpose of your Kings and their armies that are willing to take up this battle.

Just as there are lies spoken about us, so we hear from time to time that in the Western Church the Crusades are approved in order to keep the Kings from fighting one another, and the peoples in the clutches of the Church because of fear of the men of Islam. It is said also that so long as the Western

Church can show to its peoples the encroaching danger of Islam, they can also enforce their hold over the people, for now heresy is seen as the equal of Islam in danger to the Church. No true cleric can believe such lies; by the same token, I pray that what you may have heard of the Eastern Church has not been tainted with doubt as to our motives.

Were our Emperor more secure upon his throne, he would most certainly join with the great Barbarossa even now, and together they would advance to victory at Jerusalem. That such is not possible fills me with suffering, for there is no greater joy for a true Christian than dying as a martyr in the cause of Our Lord. Given the opportunity, I would trade with the most humble man-at-arms for the privilege of fighting with your gallant men against the might of Islam. My master has forbidden me to do this, and so I can only give you my prayers day and night for your success and for the success of your splendid Kings who have come to defend the heart of our faith in its time of direst need.

For the soldier and knights, for the Brothers and Fathers who accompany them, for the greatest to the humblest of men under the Cross, I give thanks with every breath, and I beseech God to give His protection to all who fight beneath His Son's banner, for the glory of all Christians everywhere, from this time until we stand together at the Judgment Day.

In the Name of the Christ we all
adore, I am your servant
Alexios from Salinika

At the behest of my master, by my own hand and under seal, on the 2nd day of May, the Feast of Saint Athanasius of Alexandria, in the Lord's Year 1190.

· 10 ·

Joivita was nervous, though she denied it when Rainaut asked what was bothering her. "You're always thinking
that I am upset when I am teasing you," she chided him
unconvincingly.

"I will beg your pardon," Rainaut said, with enough of a
bow to satisfy her without disturbing the remnants of their
evening meal. "It was not my intention to offend you." He
had been with her for some time, but she had not shown him
the encouragements that she usually offered as soon as he
stepped through the door. He supposed she wanted to
punish him for the days he had not come to see her, days
when Olivia had filled his thoughts so that he dared not
approach another woman.

"Oh, I am not offended," she said quickly. "I am . . . well,
perhaps I am a little nervous. Now that the Emperor has
landed and his army is on the march, I suppose it's not odd
that I could be . . . nervous." She gave a quick, covert glance
toward the shuttered windows as if she suspected all of
Barbarossa's army to be camped outside her house.

"He will not be here for a while yet," Rainaut said, faintly
amused. He was aware of how slowly vast armies moved and
knew that Barbarossa's men were no exception: five to eight
miles a day would be the best they could achieve.

"But all the Islamites have left the city, haven't they? The
Bourgesses gave them permission to leave, no questions, no
delays," she demanded. "They are not so sanguine as you,
Sier Valence."

"The Islamites were not ordered to depart," Rainaut
pointed out, frowning as he thought of it. While it was true
that there had been no official expulsion, there had been no

118 · *Chelsea Quinn Yarbro*

attempt whatever to stop the departures, nor had there been any statements issued to calm the general public. In some instances, the necessary statements for customs had not been required, and from his experiences on Olivia's behalf he knew how remarkable that was; it bothered him that so many people were leaving Tyre.

"But they left," Joivita insisted, hesitating before she spoke. "They know that the Emperor is coming, and they fear for what he and his men will do. We all fear that, even those of us who are good Christians and pray for his soldiers each day." Her voice had grown shrill; she tried to laugh without success.

Rainaut moved two of the brass platters aside, so that there was only a tray of fruit and bowl of saffron rice with nuts, pepper, and ginger between them. "Is there a second jug of wine?"

"Of course," she snapped. "If you are not afraid of drinking too much. A man filled with wine is not always a good lover."

"Spiteful little shrew," Rainaut said mildly, uncertain how much of Joivita's temperament was show and how much was genuine.

"Is that what you think me? That I am spiteful and foolish? That I am a loose woman who has nothing to do but indulge myself with pleasures and have no thought in my head but how to satisfy my whims? Is that how I seem to you?"—she gave him no chance to answer any of the accusations flung at him—"Then why do you stay here?" She started to get up, then sat down. "I'm sorry," she said after a moment. "You know what capricious creatures women are."

Rainaut nodded. "It is one of the many things that men love most about you—how mysterious you can be." He found the second jar of wine and busied himself prying the seal off with his dagger. The evening was not going as he had thought it would, and he could not decide what was best to do now.

This time her laughter was more convincing. "Such gentle answers, Sier Valence. Reis Richard would be proud of you for his mother's sake."

"Why is that?" Rainaut asked, not paying much attention. He almost had the seal now, and he concentrated on it.

"Why, for not disputing with me, for permitting me to say whatever thing is in my thoughts, and for—oh, for keeping silent when you want to rage at me." She leaned back, a little of her usual coquettishness returning. "Am I being cruel to you, Sier Valence?"

"If you ask to cause me pain, then yes." He looked up as he tossed the seal aside. "If you are doing this to repay a pain I have given you without knowledge, then no." Another troubador's answer, he thought as he said it, but allowed that it had some justice to it.

"Very good," she approved. "How well you have learned that."

"Yes," he agreed with a faint smile. "Those lessons that are of merit are the ones we learn most completely." This time it was a priest's answer, but again Joivita did not seem to notice.

"How is it that you had so little time to see me? Or do you know when my blossoms come?" This last was intended to upset him, and succeeded.

"I . . . I am a Hospitaler. There were those needing short escort, and it was my honor, with my fellow-knights, to provide it." He lifted the wine and poured some into her cup before filling his own. "We who have taken Hospitaler's vows ought to remain chaste."

"The way priests are supposed to be chaste now?" she suggested. "Because it is convenient for you not to have a wife or children? Or is it because you would rather spend your time with your fellow-knights, as they say Reis Richard does?"

Rainaut's face darkened. "They speak slander who say such things of my King. And they speak slander who say it of me." This last was very pointed, and he watched her narrowly as he said it. "Those of us who vow to give our lives to the service of Christ and His Victory do not cavil at chastity when we are prepared to give our lives." He meant what he said, but even to himself he sounded pompous and self-aggrandizing.

"Your lives, yes. What knight will not give his life for his liege?" She looked at him with seductive, taunting eyes. "But a death is a single thing, isn't it? Once it happens, it will not happen again," she went on, her smile blighted with malice. "But chastity, that goes on day after day after day, and night after night after night after night, not at all like death—more like prison, I think. Which are harder—the days or the nights?"

"Chastity, when it is for God, is a light burden," said Rainaut, thinking that until he met Olivia, it was true enough. Now, little as he wanted to admit it, sating his body was no longer satisfaction enough, and if he intended to imperil his soul, he wanted more than release: he wanted rapture.

"And do you confess the times you spend with me?" Joivita challenged him, moving so that the side of her cote fell open, revealing her flesh from the outer curve of her breast to the rise of her hip. "Do you?"

"They do not call that fashion the gates-of-hell for nothing, Bondama," said Rainaut, wondering where this angry banter was leading them. He took his cup and drank, noticing that the savor was not as good with this jar as it had been with the first.

"Then do you risk your soul to enter them?" she asked, moving toward him so that he could better glimpse her body. "It has been almost three weeks, Sier Valence. Have you forgot how it is with us? Do you still think of your dead wife when your flesh hardens in the night, or do you blame demons and lust?" She touched his hand, holding him firmly by the wrist. "Do you want to have me? Or have your vows become so important to you?"

"My vows have always been important. That you could bring me to forget them is . . ." He stopped short of accusing himself of laxness, which he knew would infuriate her. Instead he lifted her hand and kissed it. "I have not come because I can offer you nothing, and that shames me more than you."

"You are a knight," she pointed out.

"I am a Hospitaler. As long as I wear the black-and-white, I am bound to my oaths. My . . . my confessor has shown me the error of my conduct and how greatly my sins traduce the honor of the Order." This last was a lie, but an acceptable one, he hoped. Other Hospitalers had been admonished in this way. He was not the only knight who struggled with the demands of the Hospitalers or Templars, and the needs of his body.

"Your men-at-arms are married, and so are your

infirmarists," said Joivita, pouting. "Why are knights different from the rest?"

"Because we are knights," said Rainaut as he drained his cup of wine. "Because we fight for Our Lord above our King, and for that we must become part of His Church so that we cannot betray our fealty." He filled his cup again. "You know this, Bondama. Everyone knows it. Why do you ask me now, when you have known it from the first?"

She laughed, and this time there was nothing false and nothing kind in the sound. "I like hearing you blame yourself. I like hearing your doubts and your despair, Sier Valence. It pleases me, since you will not set your vows aside, to scourge you with them."

"Then you must have great satisfaction now," he said, feeling distaste as he looked at her. "Why do you want me to have to choose?"

"Because," she said, moving toward him once more, her garments showing tantalizing promises of her body, "it makes your fall sweeter. All men lust, Sier Valence, but most of them are content to rut and be done. But you, and those like you—you are not quite the same. Oh, you lust like men, but you do not rut. You drug yourselves, like those who eat syrup of poppies. Some men become the worse for it, taking women in hatred and blood." She cocked her head. "You have seen it, haven't you? The women after the battles, raped and ruined. The others are like you, Sier Valence. They seek to hide their lusts in other guises." She took his hands in hers and pulled them under her cote. "This is what you want, but you will not let yourself have it until your need is so great that you would cross the desert barefoot for me."

Rainaut felt his flesh rise; he was shamed by the ease of Joivita's skill, at the quick and simple way she brought him to this state. "I didn't come here for . . ."

"Yes, you did," she countered playfully, setting his nerveless fingers against the rise of her breasts. "You always come to me for this, but you always lie to yourself, so that you need not blame anyone but me for what happens. Since you are a pleasant lover, it suits my purposes to have you think this. But remember, Sier Valence, that I am not deceived." She kissed him, her mouth open on his closed lips.

At first he tried to push her away, but slowly the resistance went out of him as he felt his passion grow. Hating himself for his weakness and hungering like one famished, he began to pull her cote off her shoulders. He resigned himself to his failing once again, knowing that he was betraying more than his Hospitaler's oath now; he was also betraying his love of Olivia.

When Joivita stood naked, she began to undress Rainaut, her experienced hands divesting him of weaponry before anything else. "You are thinner," she remarked, tossing his cotehardie aside. As she pressed against him, she licked up his neck to his jaw. "Admit it, you have wanted me every day you stayed away."

"Yes," he muttered.

"And you have dreamed of me, haven't you?" She kissed him before she let him answer.

"I have dreamed," he said obliquely, wanting to be through with her. "All men dream."

Her laughter was low in her throat, almost a growl. "Poor Hospitaler, so noble and pious." She was about to kiss him again when she stopped. "Have you been sunburned, Sier Valence?"

"I don't know," he said, perplexed by her strange question and change of manner. "It's possible."

"There's a place like a burn on your cheek. Haven't you noticed?" She tilted his head with her hands, inspecting the patch of skin.

"Hospitalers do not use mirrors; how would I notice?" To his surprise, her apparent indifference was stimulating to him. Before he had not been eager for her, only needful. Now he began to enjoy the game again, to want to take the time needed to make the most of their meeting.

"Your page or squire shaves you," she reminded him.

"Celadon or Huon shaves me," said Rainaut. "They haven't mentioned a burn."

"Perhaps it is from your armor." She touched the place. "Your beard is very light there. It is probably the armor, rubbing, that has caused it." Her smile changed again. "So. You want me after all."

"Yes," he said, reaching for her with more enthusiasm than before. In a small part of his mind, he was curious about Joivita's skill, about her ability to play on his body as some musicians played on harps and rebecs, or beat out rhythms on the tabor that would make a lame man dance. That he would not—could not—resist her was so apparent that he did not make any effort to excuse his actions. Between his thumb and fingers her nipple hardened, and he felt a brief savage pride that he was not the only one captured by the bonds of flesh.

"Not here," Joivita said breathlessly a short while later.

"Where, then?"

"My chamber. The bed is ready. It was filled with roseleaves this afternoon." She took his hand and started toward the door. "The slaves know enough to leave us alone."

"Then why not here?" He wanted no delays now, for his body ached with desire.

"In my chamber," she insisted, almost dragging him from the room.

The scent of roses was cloying, so strong that its sweetness was almost bitter. Two braziers gave the room its light without making it much hotter than the sun in the day had done.

"My clothes—" Rainaut protested, aware that he was two rooms away from his weapons and garments.

"My slaves will bring them when I call for them," Joivita assured him as she sank back on the wilted petals. "Come. I yearn for you."

Rainaut sighed as he sank down beside her. "There had better be no thorns in these roses," he murmured as he pulled her beneath him. He felt her open to him from the soles of his feet to the top of his head. What gave her this power over him, this continued tie when his heart and soul denied her? He pressed into her, shoving her knees back with his shoulders so that he could penetrate further.

"Do not falter, Sier Valence," Joivita urged him, her words coming in single quick breaths. "Hurry."

For an answer he began to move, steadily, deeply, wishing with every thrust that the woman who shuddered under him was not Joivita but the Roman widow, whose love he could not seek, either in honor or in propriety.

Joivita drew her nails along her lover's back, feeling the skin tear and smiling as he tensed and bucked. It was almost over, and she was sure he would not refuse her for so long again. She remembered to sigh and roll her eyes upward as he finished, and to kiss him as he got off her. "You are a marvel, Sier Valence," she said, trying to recall if she had told him that recently. Men became suspicious if they heard the same phrase too often.

"You flatter me," he told her, aware once again of the overwhelming odor of roses, sharper now that the petals were crushed.

"Hardly flattery," she said, moving nearer to him. "You have brought me such pleasure." Her languor was only partly feigned; over the last few days she had not got much sleep.

He did not speak at first. The turmoil, which he had been able to forget for those brief moments they were linked, returned redoubled. "Oh, God," he whispered, bringing his hand to cover his eyes.

"You need not confess quite yet," Joivita chided him lightly. "I wish you would stay, Sier Valence. Who knows, you might have more to confess in an hour or so."

"Then be grateful that I will not stay," he said rather bluntly. "I have obligations tonight." He had been assigned to keep vigil in the chapel from midnight matins to matins-and-lauds; it was a duty every Hospitaler had, and it served both to guard the chapel from possible enemies as well as to provide constant entry to those in need.

"And you will offer up your sins?" she giggled. "What would you do if you ever had a real sin upon your soul—not lust and fleshly weakness, for that is every man's fate—but a true sin, a dark sin: murder or treason or heresy."

"With God's aid, I never will." He blessed himself as he stood, scattering roseleaves in all directions. "My clothes?"

"My slaves will bring them," she said quietly. "I wish you would stay." The plaintive note in her voice almost persuaded him to accept her offer; only the realization that he might be late to his post if he remained with her gave him the impetus to leave.

"I must go," he said, bending down to kiss her.

"Ask your infirmarist for a salve for your face," she recommended as he drew away from her. "The mark is as bad as a scar. And have your squire take more care with your armor."

"Yes, my tribuness," he said as she reached for a bell to summon her slaves.

Once she had given her orders, she lay back, letting the

petals run through her fingers as she played with them. "When will you return, Sier Valence? Will you tell me?" "I . . . I will send you word. There are more pilgrims now, because of the Crusades. More Christians are coming in the hope of seeing Jerusalem and praying at the Holy Sepulcher. We Hospitalers are sworn to protect them and so I am not able to . . . to set my time as I used to." He looked up as one of the slaves came through the door, Rainaut's clothes over his arm, his solers in his hand. Rainaut took them as the slave bowed to him. "I have heard that one of the debauched Roman Caesars once suffocated his enemies in a shower of rosepetals," he remarked as he began to dress.

"If one must die, better that way than many another," said Joivita flippantly. "Rosepetals. How many does it take to smother a person, I wonder?"

"Do you mean that?" Rainaut paused in the act of shaking out his cotehardie. His own arms were embroidered on the pectoral; his Hospitaler's badge adorned the sleeves. "About dying?"

"Certainly. If we must die passing between Heaven and Hell, then to die crushed in rosepetals . . . well, why not?" She let a handful of the petals fall over her face. "It isn't so unpleasant. Better than a sword-thrust, or the rack, or hanging in chains, certainly."

"Hanging in chains! What thoughts for a beautiful woman," Rainaut said as he reached for his belt.

She shrugged. "When I am left to myself I think of death. The troubadors call death the one faithful lover, and we all embrace him in time. If that is a sin, so be it." She rolled onto her side and braced herself on her elbow. "Do you leave me now?"

"I must, Bondama." He gave her the undeserved title out of habit, though now it grated more than it had a month ago. 'Bondama' for a woman like Joivita cheapened the word, so that Rainaut did not want to use it for Olivia once he had given it to Joivita.

"Go, then." She turned away from him and would not respond to him again, though he touched her shoulder and bade her good fortune. When he was gone, she rid her sheets of rosepetals in two angry sweeps of her arms.

Rainaut knew that Joivita was angry; he could not dispute

the justice of her anger, nor could he find a way to lessen it. He stood outside the gate to her house until he heard the slave fix the bolt into place, then he made his way toward the chapel of the Hospitalers, walking quickly in spite of the engulfing heat of the night.

"Sier Valence Rainaut, of Saint-Prosperus-lo-Boys," called a voice from the darkness as Rainaut turned a corner at the edge of the Islamic quarter of the town, near the Jerusalem Gate.

Rainaut stopped, his hand dropping automatically to the hilt of his sword, first and third fingers hooked around the quillons. "Who calls me?"

There was a chuckle in the shadows, and then a man in the cote of the Templars strode into the moonlight. "I do. I have been at pains to learn about you since we met, Hospitaler."

"Why?" demanded Rainaut, staring at the Templar, trying to discover what about the man was familiar.

"Because you bested me once, and I do not permit such things to go unmarked." He came nearer, and Rainaut realized that this must be the Spanish Templar he had encountered his first day in Tyre. "I have a score to settle with you, Hospitaler."

"Not in honor," Rainaut said bluntly. "Alone, here? What true knight would do that?"

"Not all Templars are true knights, are they?" He strolled around Rainaut, his spurs ringing on the flagged street.

"If you care to speak of it." Rainaut gave a hitch to his shoulders that would have been a shrug if he had been relaxed.

The Spanish Templar barked a laugh. "Still, you are in the right: not here and not now, certainly. Your honor would not permit it. You wear no mail, there are no officers to observe, and we are both of knightly Orders, and so we are enjoined to fight only the enemies of God." He came a little nearer. "I am watching you, Hospitaler. I know what you do. I know you. I am watching everything you do, and when I have the means to bring you down, you may be sure I will."

"And who is my Nemesis? Or do you intend to act entirely in secret, with no name to disgrace?" In spite of the Templar's assurances that they would not fight, Rainaut kept his hand at the ready on his sword.

"Think of me as the Avenging Angel. I am Ruiz Ferran Iñigo Foxa. My father has lands near Burgos." He came within an arm's-length of Rainaut and stopped. "You will fall, and I will bring you down."

"Because of a street fight?" Rainaut asked with disbelief. "Because of a dispute between merchants?"

"Because we did not settle it," Foxa hissed.

"But there is nothing to settle," Rainaut protested, amazed at the fury he saw in Foxa's eyes. "At the most it is a misunderstanding, and for that I ask pardon in Christian brotherhood." As he faced the Templar, he grew cold in anticipation of battle, and hated himself for his weakness.

"Pardon? When you have offended me? You may be content, Sier Valence, but I am not," Foxa corrected Rainaut harshly. "But that will not last." He spat at Rainaut's feet, then turned abruptly and strode away into the night.

*   *   *

Text of a formal commendation from the Court of Bourgesses at Tyre addressed to the Knights Hospitaler, the Knights Templar, and Atta Olivia Clemens.

Let it be known by all those in the city of Tyre that we of the Court of Bourgesses agree, all and singly, that the charitable acts of Bondama Clemens in caring for Fraire Herchambaut in his illness and in paying for his burial upon his death have been noted and are held to be of singular importance to this city, for which reason we have caused these notifications to be made, and her name to be added to those of the civic Mass each morning.

Due to the continued petition of Bondama Clemens for permission to leave Tyre for Roma, the Court of Bourgesses has convened to decide what might be done to expedite this unfortunate tangle. The appropriate tariffs have been paid, the donations recorded and the customs records amended, which leaves only the arrangements for departure. The Court of Bourgesses, aware that most ships are being contracted for use of the armies of the Crusaders, may not be able to supply the requested transport that would carry Bondama Clemens to her chosen destination. We have statements from her bondsman and from a shipowner affirming that it is possible to carry her back to Italy. However, since the ship in question has been requisitioned by Crusaders, it is not possible for the ship to be used by Bondama Clemens at this time.

In lieu of such transport, we are issuing a safe passage to Bondama Clemens and her escort to go to Sidon and from there to Cyprus or Rhodes, whichever is the most appropriate once she has reached Sidon. The payments of tariffs will be appended to the safe passage; if further payments are demanded, they are to be assessed against the amounts already paid, and any adjustments will be adjudicated by this Court of Bourgesses once Bondama Clemens presents her complaint, or her duly authorized representative does so in her stead.

It is a sad day for this city when so worthy a widow as Bondama Clemens leaves it, but we cannot place our need over her desire to return to the estates of her husband. The selfless service that was rendered to the Cistercian Fraire Herchambaut commends her to us as well as to Heaven, and we are less than good Christians if we do not honor her petition and grant her requests with all reasonable dispatch. Although it is unusual, we waive the second appearance before this Court required of those Christian citizens who have been residents here and are now leaving Tyre. We also waive the presentation of the travel itinerary, for given the current circumstances, it is not possible for Bondama Clemens to offer such information, and it is not fitting that she should endure a protracted delay. For her generous act, we of the Court of Bourgesses allow her to travel without further hindrance. Our prayers go with her, and we ask Heaven to send her a safe journey.

For the Court of Bourgesses
Jaufre Ivo Chartier
Bourgess of Tyre

By the hand of the scribe Norbert, on the 11th day of June, in the Year of Our Lord 1190, affixed with Chartier's seal.

"If only Barbarossa hadn't drowned," Olivia said to Rainaut as they strolled in her garden. She was dressed in the lightest silk bliaud with huge, square barbaresque sleeves that reached the ground. "I might have had a chance to get away from here before winter. As it is—"

"As it is," Rainaut said for her, "you are well-advised to let us escort you to Sidon, and there, since you will have status as a traveler—"

"Assuming that the Court of Bourgesses honors the safe passage, and that there will be housing, because of all the pilgrims," she interjected quietly.

He chose to ignore her objections. "—it will not be as difficult to arrange passage for Roma. Away from here." The last was hard to say, and he stared down at his hands as he spoke.

"You will escort me there? To Roma?" She had stopped by a bank of Nile lilies. "Have you asked for permission? Sier Valence?"

"I . . . I am permitted to escort you as far as Rhodes or Cyprus. Beyond that, there must be other . . . arrangements." He would not look at her; his eyes moved from his hands to the flowers. "Bondama, it is an honor to escort you, though it be only as far as the Jerusalem Gate." He was relieved when two little finches flew over them, making high piping notes as they went.

Olivia sighed. "All right, I will not press you."

"You . . . you do not press me," he said, not wholly accurately. "I am not able to be pressed. I am bound by the rules of my Order, and they are strict." There was a kind of consolation in his admission, though it left him feeling like a recalcitrant child.

"Still," she said distantly, then made a quick gesture as if to shut her thoughts away. "It was not my intention to press you."

He bowed. "I would know I would fail to resist you if you pressed—you pressed the Court of Bourgesses until they capitulated, no easy accomplishment."

"It took the death of that poor monk to get the Court of Bourgesses to help me," she said. "I am sorry that his suffering was needed in order for me to leave." It was late in the day but the heat rose from the walls, shimmering, and the splash of the fountain gave little relief.

"It is not your fault he became ill. That he died in comfort and with care is to your credit." Rainaut tried to keep from looking at her; with the strength of a magnet turning north he found her eyes. "Olivia."

She smiled fleetingly. "Valence."

"I must not . . ." He ought to bow to her and leave, he ought to go to his confessor at once, he ought to insist that she find another Hospitaler to escort her.

"What is it?" she asked gently, reading trouble in his face. "Tell me?"

He shook his head. "You do not understand."

"About what?" she asked when he fell silent. "What is it, Sier Valence?"

That little formality was enough. "You know." He held her gaze. "It will be difficult to travel with you, Bondama."

"Only because you will have it so," she reminded him. "You wish our travel to be difficult, then it will be." The tension between them had been increasing steadily since they first met. Now it was a force that gave weight to every word they spoke, made each glance significant. "Do you seek—"

He held up his hand. "No. Nothing more."

"Why?" she inquired, catching his hand in hers. "Why, Valence? I am a widow, you are a widower, neither of us is promised—"

"I am a Hospitaler. I have given my word to God that—" He tried to pull his hand away without success.

"But you spend nights with a courtesan, and confess the sin," she said reasonably. "I would not turn you away, if you came to me." The wistful note in her voice was more surprising to her than to him.

"No." This time he pulled free of her. "It is one thing to succumb to lust, for men are lustful creatures. We are made in sin, and sin is with us always. God knows that sin and how men are; devotion is never in question when it is lust we sate." He pressed the hand she had held to his chest as he spoke, feeling the beat of his heart beneath it.

"What is the difference?" she asked, knowing full well what it was.

"I do not lust for you—or rather, I do, but for love." His face reddened, but for the burn-like patch on the side of his jaw, which remained pale.

"Lust is permissible and love is not?" she wondered aloud, not quite teasing him. "Valence, how does that make sense?"

More than a dozen angry answers buzzed in his thoughts, but he spoke none of them, realizing that none of them were more than excuses. "You have the opportunity to leave," he said, his determination giving his voice a hardness it had lacked before. "Even though Barbarossa is dead—"

"And half of his men are no doubt robbing the other half and any traveler they find," Olivia interjected, starting to walk once more.

"They are sworn knights—" Rainaut protested.

"All the more reason to worry; they're skilled fighters, and they came here for plunder." She saw the shock in his face. "Don't pretend otherwise, Valence. For every true Christian seeking salvation, there are a dozen soldiers hungering for battle and glory."

"Some Crusaders are not . . . devout," he allowed as he came after her.

"Some Crusaders are worse than the Islamites," she said roundly. "But you're probably right. Travel will be more difficult with Barbarossa dead. Once the word reaches Europe, every King and Prince will scramble for the chance to assume the leadership of the Crusade." She bent over the five-petaled roses and plucked one for him.

He took this, more careful of not touching her than avoiding the thorns. "You're severe. You do not comprehend the great purpose that carries us on."

"I understand greed and anger and covetousness," she said. "And I understand fear. What else need I comprehend, with war coming?"

He regarded her narrowly. "You have heard tales, and they have frightened you."

"No. It isn't my fear I meant. I've seen so much in the last—" She had almost said she was a thousand years old. "I'm old enough to have seen war before," she amended.

"You mean the Islamites in Alexandria," said Rainaut, stopping while he spoke, then strolling up to her. "That was nothing, Bondama. You are right to fear the Islamites, but in regard to Christian knights, it is not important."

"Not important?" she repeated as her thoughts ranged back through the centuries, her breath quickening at the memories his casual dismissal stirred.

"It is one thing when men battle for loot or favor, but that is not why we are prepared for war. The Crusaders fight for our faith, for our God, against the enemies of our God, for the salvation of our souls and the preservation of our faith." He took a deep breath, his blue eyes growing hot as his emotions became stronger. Purpose showed in the line of his stance and the tone of his words. "There is the strength of Angels in our arms."

"Really?" Olivia turned to him, a bitterness she thought she had forgot filling her. "Because you are doing the Pope's bidding, you think arrows will not penetrate your mail? You think that your wounds will not bleed? Or mortify? Prayers will not keep you whole, Sier Valence. An Islamite sword cuts as deeply as a Christian one."

Taken aback at her outburst, Rainaut stared at her. "What do you mean?" he demanded of her at last.

"I mean that war is a waste: of men, of countries, of peoples, of everything worthwhile and pleasant. To fight against attack is one thing, but to court disaster, to invite the depredations of war"—she raised her fists—"is more futile than feeding a starving man tainted meat."

Rainaut glowered at her. "You say that taking the cause of Christ is futile?"

"If it leads to slaughter, yes, I do," she said, her chin up, her face set. "Any cause that leads to destruction is futile. And if that makes me despicable in your eyes, Sier Valence, then you must despise me; I will not change my mind to suit you—especially to suit you."

Everything Rainaut had been taught said that he should leave her now, that he should know himself blessed to be free of her. He could turn away and feel no shame, no regret. He could then confess and be purged of his love for her. He put his hands on her shoulders. "I cannot despise you, Bondama, though I lose my soul for it."

She swallowed hard, wishing, as she had so many times before, that she could weep. Slowly she reached up and kissed him once, lightly. "I don't ask your soul of you, Sier Valence."

"You have it already," he said, deliberately moving away from her, feeling his resistance weakening. As he reached for one of her trailing sleeves to kiss, he said, "I am your devoted servant for all my life; I swear that on my sword." He had wrapped his other hand around the hilt of his sword, and now he started to draw it.

"I will take your word for it, Sier Valence," said Olivia. He was the most infuriating man, she decided, offering her his soul and his love, but not his passion or his body, because his love and reverence for her were too great to sully her. She indicated one of two low benches near a bed of sweet herbs. "So you will escort me for as far as your Order will permit you to go."

"Yes," he said. He came to the second bench and lifted one foot onto the bench, resting his elbow on his knee. "And I will pray for God to forgive me each day I am in your company, for each day I am with you, I am more your servant than His."

"But you spend your nights with a courtesan," said Olivia.

"Because she is a courtesan and you are not," Rainaut told her. "You may not hold your honor in high esteem, but I do."

Olivia shook her head. "Never mind. You will not convince me, and I will not convince you." She had resisted the urge to appear to him as a dream and rouse him that way; such encounters had sustained her for years. But with Rainaut she continued to hesitate, for fear of his repugnance, or something worse than repugnance. Her manner was deceptively calm; she had learned long ago to mask her feelings, and now she wanted to conceal her longing and her doubt from Rainaut. "Ithuriel Dar's ship has been taken over by the Teutonic Hospitalers."

Rainaut bristled at the mention of the rival Hospitaler Order. "We will find passage at Sidon."

"And if the Crusaders get there first, what then?" She reached over and fingered a drooping massey stalk, watching the pale pink blossoms tremble at her touch.

"We will go to another port," he said, but with less confidence than before. "You have my word that you will not be abandoned and without care for as long as there is breath in my body."

"Of course." She looked up at him, her decision made, though she had never truly doubted she would leave Tyre. "Sier Valence, since you are determined, find out when we will be able to secure room in a ship returning to Italy. I will send my belongings by sea—that is permissible, since crates of possessions do not eat or require slaves to care for them—as soon as possible, if you will . . ." She let her words trail off as her deception became more difficult.

He reached out and let the backs of his fingers brush against her hair. "I will arrange our travel," he said.

"Thank you." She sat very still.

"Olivia," he said in a low voice, "if you knew how much you tempted me."

"Not enough, apparently," she said quietly.

"If I were free, Olivia, and had the permission of my liege, I would find your relatives and I would haunt them day and night, I would do all in my power to gain their approval, and if they refused, I would persevere until they were convinced." He had taken one fine tendril of hair between thumb and forefinger and now he rubbed it absently. "No matter what relatives you have, I would persuade them."

"I have only . . . only one blood relative currently living," she said, a faint, sad frown drawing a line between her brows. "And he is far away."

"That would mean nothing," Rainaut promised her. "I would seek him out and I would gain his permission. He would not refuse me if he is a man of reason."

"But you aren't free, are you?" Her face showed more

pain than she realized, and she was surprised at the response she evoked.

"Olivia," whispered Rainaut, pulling her to her feet and into his arms.

"What is the point?" she murmured as his lips grazed her cheek. "Why do you do this, when you will not do more? Valence?" What would he do, she wondered, if he knew her for what she was? He could not accept her as a widow; what would he do if he ever learned the rest? "It is no kindness to do this, to wake my desires and my hopes, and then to refuse me anything more than these hints. And it torments you as much as it does me."

"It *is* torment," he said, still keeping hold of her. "For both of us."

They stood together in silence, then Olivia sighed. "Valence, you were the one who said that it will not be an easy thing to travel with me. You have told me that being in my company is hard. Yet you do this, which makes it more difficult still." She looked at him, into his bright blue eyes, saying, "You tell me that you must honor your oaths, and I accept that. You tell me that you esteem me, and I almost accept that. But then you spout the nonsense of troubadors. Those tales are not for men and women who breathe, they are for the wraiths conjured up by poets. I am no wraith, and my needs quicken as yours do."

"You are lonely. It is your loneliness that speaks," he said, his words coming unsteadily.

"Yes," she exclaimed. "Yes, I am lonely, and never more so than when I am with you, when I can sense your feelings and know my own, and still *do nothing.*" With an effort she moved away from him. "Perhaps you are right," she said in a changed, subdued tone. "Perhaps it is too difficult for us to travel together and I ought to request other escort, to spare us both."

"It isn't possible," he said sharply, having no idea if it was or not. "You have been assigned my escort, and I and my companion knight will accompany you as far as Rhodes, at least."

Olivia shook her head. "Assuming we get there."

"It will be arranged," Rainaut said firmly. "I will find a way to see your goods are shipped and—"

"Not quite all my goods," she interrupted. "There are a few things that are . . . essential to me, and I will take those with me." They would include two chests filled with her native earth, but she would not mention that.

"Naturally. Women of breeding are not expected to travel like serfs or penitents," he said, doing his best to maintain the distance between them. "You are not to think that you will have to be a pilgrim unless that is what you wish."

"I've seen enough pilgrims to last me . . . a lifetime." A faint amusement lit her hazel eyes. "Escort and one slave should be sufficient; I will supply my own horses."

"And wagon?" asked Rainaut.

"If I must," Olivia capitulated. "I would rather ride. You know that I can."

"Yes," Rainaut said slowly. "But it is not fitting for a woman of your rank to go about on horseback."

"Why the devil not?" Olivia demanded of the air. "The Queen of England does."

"The Queen of England is a law unto herself," said Rainaut awkwardly. "Admirable and irresponsible at once, and unlike any woman in the world."

"A great tribute, Bonsier, coming from you," Olivia said with an ironic lift to her brows. "Or is it that she is mother of your Reis Richard, and that puts her beyond criticism?"

"You are playing with me," Rainaut accused. "You are mocking—"

"Playing I own," Olivia said, stopping him. "But much as I might wish to, I will not mock you, Sier Valence. I might say things to you in anger that are cutting, but not mocking. I hope you will believe that, for it is true."

He looked at her in hungry silence. "I believe you," he told her at last, and the silence between them returned.

Finally Olivia started toward the arched doorway leading back into her house. "There is much to do, Sier Valence, if I am actually to leave this place. I must set my slaves to work and prepare my things for shipping."

Rainaut followed her. "You puzzle me, Bondama."

The shadow of the building fell across them, providing a little relief from the enormous heat; Olivia paused in this twilight and looked back at Rainaut. "Why is that?"

"There are many reasons," he said, striving for a lightness

that might dispel the intensity of their nearness. "What puzzles me now is how you accommodate the shifts in your fortunes. You speak of sending your goods as easily as you might order meat from the butcher."

"In this world, Sier Valence, we must learn to accommodate or we die," she said, going into her house as she spoke.

"But for most, the accommodation is a great burden; for you it seems it is not." He noticed the scent of cinnamon and cloves on the air and thought of the bland fare waiting for him at the chapter house.

"I have had practice," Olivia said, and before he could question her further, she went on, "As soon as you have secured room for my goods, I will want to know of it. I have already provided inventories of what is to go. If you can get me the information about the ship's capacity, I will see that the goods are packed to suit the hold."

Rainaut bowed slightly. "You have only to wish it, Bondama, and it is done." He reached the end of the hall and entered the vestibule. "I will call upon you when I have news or information."

"You needn't wait that long, if you would rather not," Olivia said impulsively, then shrugged. As much as she wanted to see him, she dreaded their being together for the irresolution between them. "Do as you think best, Sier Valence. I do have tasks to keep me busy, and there are affairs to be settled still before we depart. If there are problems or I have questions, I will send one of my slaves to you. If not, then—" She managed a world-weary smile for him.

His expression altered a little, becoming more worried. "About your traveling, your plans: you have not told me yet how you intend to get from Rhodes or Cyprus to Roma, if I cannot escort you." He steeled himself against the hurt he felt at thinking of their parting.

"As you have told me yourself, something will be arranged. There are other escorts, I assume, and ships to be hired. I have learned to improvise, Bonsier." She turned toward him. "It would be more pleasant if we could share each other's company after Rhodes or Cyprus." Perhaps then, she added to herself, something would be settled with them.

He opened the door himself, not waiting for Olivia or one of her slaves to do it for him. "I will return soon."

"As you wish," said Olivia, the wistfulness coming back into her face.

His eyes were like blue sparks. "If things were otherwise, Bondama—"

"Ah, yes, if things were otherwise," she said, crossing the vestibule to close the door.

*　　*　　*

Text of a letter from Fealatie Bueveld to the Abbot of Sante-Estien-in-Gorze.

To the Most Reverend Abbot, my strength and intercessor, I write to you from Antioch, where I and my men-at-arms are currently staying, waiting upon the decision of several of the authorities to continue the pilgrimage you have mandated for me.

For the last month there have been Masses every morning for the repose of the soul of the Emperor Frederick, who drowned on June 10th. So great a leader was he that his men are now in great disorder and it is said everywhere that no one will be able to take his place before the troops disperse and the Holy Sepulcher is lost forever to the Islamites.

Those who came with the Emperor have confessed they are at a loss without their great leader; they will not ally themselves with the Templars or the Hospitalers, for they do not wish to bind themselves for life or to bring possible conflicts of loyalties to their souls. So they wait, those that are not too afraid, for the decision of who is to lead them now. Some have already left the Holy Land, some have formed themselves into bands and have offered themselves under contract to various Christian Courts in this place.

We have had to remain where we are, my men-at-arms and I, because it is not possible to obtain permission to travel from the Court of Bourgesses here, which we must have if we expect to have protection and Christian hospitality on our journey. Of late there have been robbers and other brigands who have posed as Christian knights who have used their hosts badly, so without the proper permission, we would be counting ourselves among those numbers, so far as the Christians here are concerned. This land is too harsh for anyone to travel without the possibility of finding hospitality in the course of a journey.

The Holy Land is forbidding in its beauty. Nothing in Franconia can compare with it, and nothing in France. Here there is desert that stretches for farther than the German forests, and is nothing but sand and rock, and so hot that the rocks sing with it. The winds that come out of that furnace sting like a lash, and they scour the life from the land. Where there are wells—and there are very few wells—they are guarded and treasured more than gold and jewels. If this is the desert Our Lord fasted in, no wonder Satan came to Him, out of the inferno of the sands. What is wonderful is that in this trackless desolation, the words of Satan could make no impact on the Christ. That alone is proof of the deity of Jesus, for any mortal, offered the joys and bounty of the world in this place, would hardly be able to resist so desirable a reward.

You said when I departed that you would remember me in your prayers. For this I am especially grateful now, for our trials are greater than before. With each new hindrance or setback, I offer up my sins, praying that God will aid me. I pray, also, that my husband will forgive me; I never intended to dishonor him or his House; had I been told of his obligation to the Comes, I would have proceeded differently. All that is in the past, and if my pilgrimage is expiation enough, in time my husband may be willing to speak with me again, and give me the shelter of his House once more. If he cannot, I will seek your advice for what to do next, for I will be without recourse then.

It was not my intention to dwell on the past. I am not inclined to such useless thoughts, but there are occasions when I find my memories pile in on me, and then I feel I am in a world haunted by ghosts of what is past. Then I beseech the Virgin to come to my assistance, to cleanse my thoughts from such useless folly, and to direct me to the hope of

Heaven. In this strange and harsh land, I know that I am at the mercy of God more than those who have remained safe in the fields and forests of home.

For your prayers, your intercessions and your great justice, I thank you once more, and thank God for sending you to me when my need was so great. This pilgrimage in penance for my sins is less of a burden than life in an oublette would have been. With the charity of Heaven, my husband will no longer wish to confine me in such a cell when I have come back from Jerusalem.

Fealatie Bueveld
Chatelaine of Gui de Fraizmarch

By my own hand and under the seal of the Castel Fraizmarch, on the last day of August, in the Lord's Year 1190; carried by a messenger of the Knights Templar.

· 12 ·

Over Rainaut's strenuous objections, Olivia donned the enveloping mantel worn by Bourgesses and rode most of the way between Tyre and Sidon, helping to lead the seven mules, two harnessed to an enclosed wagon, that carried her possessions which had not been shipped to Roma, as well as her single body-slave who clung miserably to an old-fashioned saddle.

"It isn't seemly," Rainaut repeated as they drew within sight of the walls of Sidon. "You are a well-born lady, and for you to risk—It is bad enough that you have traveled the road this way, even with our escort, but to enter the city in such outrageous garments—"

Olivia looked from him to his companion, Aueric de Jountuil. "Sier Aueric, am I as shameless as Sier Valence says?"

"You are certainly unorthodox," de Jountuil said with his

usual good-natured cynicism. "Rainaut is right. If you were discovered, it would be awkward. The laws are strict here and we are bound to obey them. Sidon is more Islamite than Christian."

"They would not tolerate this display," Rainaut insisted. "It is forbidden for their women to behave this way. It *ought* to be forbidden for Christian women as well. You might be imprisoned or . . . or worse." The black Maltese cross on his mantel was so dusty that it appeared to be gray. His face was grimy, bits of sand clinging to his beard stubble. "Bondama Clemens, *please,* for your sake if not ours, let your slave help you put on proper women's garments so that you will not be subjected to—"

"To being looked at," Olivia supplied for him. "Gracious, yes, who knows what dangers there might be in a single look." She met his gaze with irritation. "If that is what you wish, then I suppose I must do it, or lose your escort."

"It's not that drastic," de Jountuil said when Rainaut had not been able to answer her.

"Isn't it?" Olivia did not expect an answer. "Very well. It's maddening, all these restrictions. You're probably being more sensible than I am, so I will do as you wish." She indicated the empty track. "I suppose this is as good a place as any we will find. I will have Iyaffa help me change in it while you harness two fresh mules." She swung expertly out of the saddle, and handed the reins up to Rainaut. "Be good to him, he's the strongest of my horses," she reminded Rainaut.

"Another one of those bastard crosses, I suppose; part knight's horse and part desert pony, by the look of him," de Jountuil said, inspecting the bay more openly than he had before. "Rainaut told me you used to breed horses."

"I have, in the past," Olivia said, patting her bay gelding. "He's a little like some of the old Roman cavalry horses."

"Cavalry horses!" scoffed de Jountuil. "I wouldn't think he'd be much use for that. Not strong enough to carry an armed knight."

"True," she agreed. "But he was not intended to carry an armed knight; only me," Olivia went on sweetly as the two knights dismounted. She was already loosening her mantel, feeling the scrape of sand against her skin. "Tell me when

you are ready." She moved a little away from the Hospitalers as they set to work on their task while Iyaffa watched
from her place on the second mule; she strode out on a low
promontory and squinted against the afternoon sun toward
the west and the sea. The walls of Sidon rose up at the
water's edge, with a cliff to guard them.

"Have you been to Sidon before?" Rainaut called to her as
he helped de Jountuil wrestle with the disassembled wagon.

"No, not recently," she replied. Four hundred years had
gone by since she had stayed in that city. It was somewhat
larger now, and the harbor was improved, but it was still
much smaller than Tyre, and it wore more battle scars.
Olivia stared down at the harbor, at the rusting chain that
was raised at the mouth of the harbor every night to keep out
spies and pirates, at the three quays where the bustle was
greatest.

"We're almost ready. There is no one near us on the
road," Rainaut informed her, coming to her side. "I know
you prefer riding, but truly, Bondama, you must not enter
Sidon that way."

"I suppose you're right," she said, retracing her steps to
where the young body-slave stood beside the curtained
wagon, folded garments the same color as a freshly-sliced
peach piled in her arms. "I will need my combs, too, Iyaffa."

The slave bowed stiffly, her careful movements revealing
how sore her muscles were from the hours riding. "I have
perfumes as well, mistress."

"Fine," said Olivia resignedly as she got into the wagon
and drew the curtains closed behind her and Iyaffa.

"I will take your mantel, mistress," said Iyaffa as Olivia
struggled to get out of the garment; the wagon was small and
offered little room for changing.

"In a moment," said Olivia as she unfastened the brooch
that held the garment to the shoulder of her short cote.
"There. Put that aside and take hold of the top of the
sleeves."

Iyaffa did as she was told. As Olivia wriggled out of the
cote, Iyaffa properly averted her eyes. "I do not mean to
offend, mistress."

"You don't offend me," Olivia assured her. "The precautions I have to take infuriate me, but that's another matter,

and they have nothing to do with you. There is no reason for you to worry." She continued her dressing in silence, putting on her woman's clothes as if they were cerements.

"There are armed men approaching from Sidon," called out Rainaut. "Eight of them."

"Islamites or Christians?" Olivia asked, not particularly concerned either way.

"Pegasus badges," de Jountuil said in disgust. "Templars."

"Well, they're not here to fight," Olivia said. "That's a consolation with Templars." The fear she had held in check flared in her; Templars were known to be brutal with women when they found them unprotected: two Hospitalers would not prevail against a company of Templars. She continued to change her clothes, her features impassive, though she felt for the dagger strapped to her leg.

A short time later the party of Templars clattered up to Rainaut and de Jountuil, drawing in and saluting out of courtesy. "Good Hospitalers," said the Templar leader in a voice made rough with years of shouting.

"Worthy Templars," Rainaut answered. "God give you all a good day, and send you victory over your enemies." He did not touch his sword or make any other move to suggest that he viewed them as intruders; his behavior was courtly and impeccable, since the Templars did not wear their famous red-and-white battle cotes over their mail, but were distinguished only with their Pegasus badges.

"On escort, I see," the Templar leader said, his sneer unconcealed.

"A Roman noblewoman, bound for Sidon and thence to Roma," said de Jountuil.

"From?" the Templar leader inquired a trifle too casually.

"Tyre," was Rainaut's terse answer.

"And the woman?" the Templar pursued.

"A distinguished widow, Bondama Olivia Clemens." Rainaut said this with deliberate emphasis on her status and title, which was intended to mislead the Templars. "Her household goods are already on a ship bound for Roma, and she is eager to return to her home."

The Templar leader laughed raucously. "Poor fellows, to have to coddle a widow; better to fight Islamites."

De Jountuil bowed in the saddle. "For Templars, most certainly. But as you have your sworn tasks, so we have ours."

"And you're paying for it now," the Templar leader said, and his troops joined him in rough laughter. "Who are you, that I may enter your names in my records of this journey?"

Rainaut and de Jountuil made full, formal introductions, with titles and fealties, and de Jountuil asked, "Where are you bound now, good Templars, and what is your task?"

"We are to survey Belvoir, to find out how much of the east wall has been rebuilt. Since the damned Islamites seized the place—from you Hospitalers, as I recall—they have made changes in the gates and walls." He glared at Rainaut and de Jountuil as if the two Hospitalers were personally responsible for the surrender of Castrum Belvoir two years before.

"It was a sad day for our Order," Rainaut said, deceptively mild in his tone. "I pray that it will be in our hands again soon, with God's grace."

"It will take Templars to carry out God's grace for you gutless monks," one of the Templars jeered. "Since you say that God forbids you to attack, only to defend. You can't reclaim Belvoir that way."

This time all the Templars laughed without prompting; the tone was edgy and unpleasant.

Olivia, listening to this exchange, frowned. The last thing she wanted now was a melee between Templars and Hospitalers. She made her voice high and quarrelsome. "Sier Valence, Sier Aueric, why this delay? Is it not enough that I am forced to sit here by the side of the road?"

"Bondama Clemens," said Rainaut at once, his manner apparently resigned and irritated. "Have but a little more patience. We will be under way almost at once."

"And see to it that my horse is tended properly. I want no more split hooves." She knew she sounded like a bad-tempered crone, and she smiled broadly.

"Is that her horse?" the Templar leader asked, indicating the bay Olivia had been riding. "Why does she want it? It's a runt."

Rainaut shrugged expressively. "She has a notion about

breeding," he said, shaking his head, then added, "She hankers for the old days of the Caesars, and thinks they rode small horses."

When the Templar laughed again, the nastiness had gone. "I might have been wrong about you; maybe you have a battle on your hands after all."

Rainaut, feeling he was betraying his vows, rolled his eyes upward. "The worst kind; not only can we not attack, but we must not strike women."

Now all the Templars were chuckling, the hostility of a few moments ago forgot in the shared contempt for civilians. The leader said, "If you will have such ludicrous rules of conduct, you must endure your harridan, I suppose. A Templar wouldn't stand for such treatment. Women are easily dealt with. A blow or two, and she would be more cooperative." He looked around for the agreeing nods of his troops.

"There are times it is tempting to use your methods," said de Jountuil. "But she has connections in Roma, and it would be unwise for us to forget that. Not that she would let us."

Inside her curtained wagon, Olivia gave a sly half-smile. In her most forbidding accents, she said, "You continue to chat with riff-raff, Sier Aueric. I will mention this, you may be certain of it."

"What connection can she have to make you endure that?" the chief Templar asked, his voice deliberately loud.

De Jountuil almost whispered. "Very near Saint Piere's Seat, if everything we have been told is correct. Her family is old, very old, and they are powerful in Roma."

"God save me from powerful old widows," avowed the Templar, and was given supporting nods from the men accompanying him. "Very well. Let us get out of your way. We have our journey and you have yours." He dragged on the rein and spurred his horse into motion. "Peace and Grace," he shouted back as an afterthought.

"And with you," Rainaut called, as the Templars went by in rising dust.

Olivia listened to the Templars clatter away, then drew the curtains back on the side of the carriage away from the Templars. "You did very well."

"I did not think we would see them in such numbers," Rainaut said, frowning. "They are moving troops faster than before."

"They're anxious to be fighting again," said de Jountuil, not without a trace of envy. "France and England will be here soon."

"And you wish to fight with Reis Richard," Olivia said for him.

"I am a Christian knight," de Jountuil said curtly, looking Olivia directly in the face. "I honor my King and my Faith with fighting for their protection." He had become flushed with anger as he spoke.

"Then why be a Hospitaler?" Olivia asked, looking from de Jountuil to Rainaut. "Why didn't you become Templars if you so long to fight?"

"We are legitimate nobles," de Jountuil reminded her. "We have obligations to our Houses not to disgrace our name with allying it basely."

"Oh, of course," said Olivia lightly, thinking that the whole question was more foolish than she had supposed possible. "And so you are Hospitalers." She looked back at her slave and said, "You may ride with me, if you wish."

There was no room to bow or to show respect. Iyaffa put her hands over her face and nodded low. "You need not—"

"You didn't like riding the mule," Olivia interrupted the string of protestations she knew would follow. "And when we enter Sidon, we may have to continue our deceptions. It will be easier to make them think that I am an old woman if you ride with me." As she spoke, Olivia thought of the thousand years since her birth: old woman, indeed.

"If you require it, mistress," said Iyaffa. "I will do as you ask." She bent as low as she could in the confines of the wagon, hands once more spread over her face. "You have only to ask a thing of me and I will do it."

"Thank you, Iyaffa," Olivia said, strangely humbled by her slave's devotion. When she reached Sidon, Olivia was determined to give Iyaffa her writ of manumission and a proper pension for the service she had rendered. She shook her head at this quaintly old-Roman decision. It had been eight hundred years since owners treated their slaves thus, but Olivia had never been comfortable with the harsher laws that had replaced the ones she had known in her youth, and she continued to treat her slaves as if the old laws were in effect.

"We're almost ready," Rainaut said. "We'll lead your horse."

"As you wish," Olivia responded, and leaned back on the thin pillows that covered the plank seats.

They reached Sidon by the middle of the afternoon, when much of the city was drowsy with heat. The guards at the gate, often abrupt and demanding, passed the Hospitalers and their train through with little more than the necessary questions and the instruction to report at once to the funda for any taxations that might need to be paid.

"We are faring well," said Rainaut, from his vantage point behind the wagon. "The streets are fairly empty."

"Let us hope that there will be someone at the funda who will tend to us. I do not want to wait forever for this or that official to compute our taxes. We are only visiting here." Olivia did not want to admit she was as tired and uncomfortable as she was.

"We'll attend to that," said Rainaut, his words becoming loud as they entered one of the covered streets. He looked about with marked unease, remembering his first experience with such streets in Tyre.

Olivia looked up at the gathered cloth that was the roof of her wagon. "Find out what ships are leaving, and when. If we do not find out quickly, we may have another long wait to endure."

"Of course," Rainaut assured her. His horse was weary and starting to favor his off-rear foot. Along with all the things Olivia required, he would have to find a smithy and a farrier to tend to the animal. His eyes ached. Perhaps the smithy would have a wheelwright as well, so that the wagon axles could be greased and made true again.

"Ehi! Rainaut!" De Jountuil was in the lead; he turned in his saddle to shout back at his fellow Hospitaler. "The funda is just ahead on the right. Better dismount."

"Right!" Rainaut yelled back, and pulled his horse to a stop. As he climbed out of his saddle, he felt his legs ache as if he were a green rider who had never sat a horse before and who had no experience of long journeys. He held onto the stirrup until he was certain he could stand upright without swaying.

"The funda? Where is it?" Olivia called from behind the curtains. Being within the city walls, she knew it was reckless to draw the curtains back, for Sidon was not a Christian port but an Islamic one.

"Just ahead. We're almost there." Rainaut had brought the reins over his horse's head and was now leading him, walking immediately behind Olivia's wagon. "I can see part of the wall now."

"Excellent," Olivia said. "I feel as if I'd been cooped up for days, not hours."

It was on the tip of Rainaut's tongue to remind Olivia that the precaution was for her own protection, but he stopped the words as three Islamic soldiers approached, their curved swords sheathed across their backs. "Be quiet, Olivia," he ordered her in an undervoice.

"Why?" she asked sharply.

"There are soldiers," he told her in a level tone. "Officers of the funda, I hope."

"And I," Olivia said softly.

The three Islamic soldiers bowed to the strangers. "Hospitalers," said the oldest of the three. "You are welcome in Sidon."

De Jountuil sighed inwardly with relief though his manner did not change. "We are escorting the widow Bondama Olivia Clemens to Cyprus as part of her homeward journey to Roma," he explained when he had finished introducing himself and Rainaut to the soldiers. "We have a safe conduct to this place, and we seek housing here until such time as we may take ship for Cyprus or Roma."

The oldest Islamic soldier pursed his lips. "We will address the officers of the funda, of course, but we are a small city and our inns and hospitals are full." He bowed to express his apology for this problem. "The widow you escort will need more than a tent, won't she?"

"She would," said de Jountuil before Rainaut could speak, for there was an impulsive look about him that troubled his companion. "And we would, as well."

The three soldiers conferred. "You must follow us," said the oldest at the conclusion of their discussion. "We will take you to the officers of the funda." He turned at once and started to lead them forward.

"The streets are damned empty," Rainaut said sotto voce to Olivia.

"It is still their time of rest. In another hour, the city will be completely alive again." She reached out and pulled the curtain back a little so that she could see where she was being taken.

"Close the curtains," Rainaut hissed. "For God's sake, Olivia, these are Islamites. They would cut off your nose if they caught you peeking at them."

She closed the curtains angrily. "Where are we going?" she asked Rainaut. "Since I cannot watch, you have to tell me."

"We're about to enter the funda. The soldiers are leading us to the inner courtyard." He kept his voice low, but no longer feared to be overheard.

"Who are they taking us to?" she asked in a rush.

"I don't know," Rainaut confessed. "But since we are foreigners . . ."

Ahead the three soldiers stopped before a carved and painted door as detailed and luxurious as the most treasured Persian carpet. One of them tapped a brass gong, then stepped back to allow the doors to be opened.

Opulent in his official red robe, the master of the funda strode out to greet them. He was of medium height with large shoulders and chest and a massive neck. His big square fingers were crusted with rings and his short beard was glossy. He made the gesture of greeting and said, "It is an honor to have you in my city. I am Hamal Khouri. What will it be my privilege to do for you?"

*   *   *

Text of a letter from Joivita to Meniques, dictated to the scribe Cortise.

To my dear cousin Meniques, I send word of my most recent attempts at securing a proper alliance, as well as the failure of same brought about by the untimely intervention of none other than my cousin himself.

The knights I have been able to bring to my bed until now have all been here under vows, which has meant that there was little I could do to induce them to take me to wife or make me a proper leman. I would have liked to continue with Sier Valence, but he has left Tyre, and so there are others I have sought out, or who have sought me out and are to my liking. One in particular is a knight who has come from England in advance of the Reis Richard, and who is placed well with his King. He is of good heritage and holds the title of Esquire. Not so great as a knight, you may say, but an excellent beginning. He is not quite nineteen and he burns for me.

We have met now eight times. Each time Taggart has shown more passion than before. He has declared himself my devoted servant and begged me to accept his protection. Which I would do, and gladly, but that you, my foolish cousin, decided that you would beat and rob him for his arms and the few jewels he wears. Now he lies with a broken skull and the infirmarians say that he will not last the week.

Why would you not be content? Why would you not leave my lover alone? You had to have that one extra bit of loot. How much did you get for the armor and the rings? Compared to what I would have brought you through my alliance with him, you have made a very bad trade, and for that, if nothing else, I despise you. There was a chance that this man would have kept me and you handsomely for quite a long time, and you can think of nothing better to do than to hit him over the head and steal his purse.

When Taggart recovers—although as I have told you already little hope is held for that—I will visit him to find out if he has any desire left for me, and if he does, I will do all that I can to be deserving of it. You are another matter, and if ever you speak to me again, or attempt to force me to aid you, I will denounce you in the Court of Bourgesses, though they brand me for it. You have taken everything I loved from me, cousin, and I will not let you have anything more.

Joivita

By the hand of the scribe Cortise in the funda of Tyre on the 10th day of October in the Lord's Year 1190.

· 13 ·

All of the south side of Hamal Khouri's estate was given over to formal gardens, linked by inlaid walkways and narrow, pebbled paths, with fountains cooling the air. Those flowers that bloomed at night glistened at the touch of the moon and the call of birds made music of the darkness.

"You were most gracious to accept my invitation," said Khouri to Olivia as he walked beside her down the widest of the garden's paths. "In spite of your escort's misgivings."

"His misgivings do not concern me," Olivia said, politely but with enough coolness to stop casual inquiry; she was hoping not to be lured into a conversation about Rainaut.

Khouri fingered his beard. "Strange. I observed you both closely and I was under the impression that there was a . . . a closeness between you."

Reluctantly Olivia gave a sad laugh. "There is; of a sort." She fell silent as a nightingale began its plaintive song.

For a little time Khouri listened and smiled. "What I told

you was the truth, you know. You could find no other lodging in the city. There truly is no room for travelers in Sidon just now. It was not a convenient fiction to bring you to this house."

"Would you have offered this hospitality if only the knights had come?" Olivia countered, starting to enjoy the game.

"Of course not," he said. "It would not be correct to do it, for our religions are at war. But then, if there had been two knights only, there is lodging of a sort for them, and they would have to be content with it. Knights may command a pallet in any church in Sidon, or take over a monk's cell. You are another matter." He stared at her, eager anticipation in his large brown eyes.

"Suppose they had escorted a churchman—" Olivia ventured, watching Khouri's face from the corner of her eye.

"It would not have been proper to have him in my house, for either of us." He favored her with an appreciative smile. "And if there had been another woman, it would have depended on my interest. Interest is everything, is it not? Sadly, I do not find most women interesting beyond certain very basic limits."

"But you think me interesting," Olivia said. "Why is that?"

"Ah, if I were to tell you that, you would know too much and would have power over me." He hooked his thumb in his wide belt as he went on. "Most women are creatures of the flesh, which is both superb and unfortunate. Allah endowed them to be creatures of the flesh. While I am fascinated by your body, you are something more."

"Oh?" She was more cautious than flirtatious as she asked this, and she no longer listened to the song of the nightingale.

"You are a woman of some education. I have known few women who were given to study, and most of them chose it because there were no men or children to occupy their thoughts, or because like certain foolish Christian virgins, they had run away from their destinies. This is puzzling in you. There are other Christian women who have the inclination to learn, once the joys of love and children are over. You are a beautiful woman. True, you are not young, but there are compensations that come with age, such as skill and expertise." He moved a step nearer to her. "And you long for that blue-eyed Hospitaler, and he for you, and you remain apart, which is by far the most puzzling part of all."

"It has puzzled me, as well, from time to time," Olivia said, her tone light but not encouraging. She knew that Khouri was using her own longings to draw her to him, yet she could not bring herself to abandon the game. She let her thoughts drift.

"A baffling thing," Khouri went on, "when there is no reason that you cannot take one another as you wish."

"Apparently we cannot do so," Olivia said, becoming withdrawn. "What does it matter?"

"I am a student of the world, good Roman widow, and I have seen how men use the world to their ends. I do not see how this refusal is of use." He smiled swiftly and there was a glint of white in his face.

"I do not either," Olivia admitted. How much she wished it were Rainaut with her in the garden, speaking to her in that gentle, caressing tone. "It distresses me." That was blunt enough, she thought, to make it apparent that she would prefer to discuss something else.

Khouri touched her arm, running two fingers lightly from her shoulder to her wrist. "How do you want Sier Valence to treat you, Roman woman?"

Olivia started to draw back. "That is nothing to you."

"But it is something to you," Khouri said with unexpected kindness. "You burn and there is no help for it; since you have no recourse to what you want, take what I offer you. I will not compromise you to your knight." He stroked her neck, letting his hand drift down the front of her bliaud, over the curve of her breast, along her waist and hip.

Why not? Olivia asked herself. For too long she had taken her pleasure with unknowing men, visiting them in dreams that were as deliriously sweet as they were forbidden. It had been the sensible thing to do, she knew, and had been sufficient for her particular needs. But her desires were unmet and her deeper hunger remained. "I do not care for you, Hamal Khouri."

"You care for Sier Valence Rainaut," he agreed. "You have made him the brightest star in the sky. Tell me the things you want from him, and I will do them. You and I will both benefit." His voice was gentle and persuasive. "If he is fool enough to turn away from you, I am not, and I will show my gratitude." He brushed his lips over her cheek. "Tell me you agree, Roman widow."

Olivia stepped back from him. "You do not know what I want. You tell me you will do as I request, but you do not know what I want." It was all the warning she was prepared to give.

"I will find out," said Khouri in an unperturbed way. "Roman widow, you are not like my wives, you are not like my three concubines, for you are not my servant or my slave." He reached out and took her hand in his. "You are a stranger to me, and I to you. There are times it is best this way."

"And this is one of those times?" Olivia suggested, her manner suddenly blunt. "And why is that?"

"You mistake me," said Khouri, not releasing her hand. "I mean only that we do not have access to each other, and that in a short time, no matter what we may or may not do, we will part, and that will be the end of it." He raised her hand to his lips and kissed the opened palm. "Consider this as a kindness of strangers."

"The kindness of strangers?" she echoed. "Because you desire me?" She had not refused such offers in the past; with Rainaut so near, her feelings were confused, for she knew who it was she yearned for and could not have.

"Of course because I desire you," said Khouri. "I desire you for pleasure and variety and many other things; I do not desire you forever, which is another matter entirely. I have what satisfies and contents me. You are . . . you would not bring me contentment, would you?"

"I don't know," she answered carefully.

Khouri smiled. "How appropriate an answer. You are skilled, Roman widow. I wager you gave your Roman husband much cause for grief."

Olivia's features hardened. "I hope I did," she said, the glint in her eyes like steel.

"Ah?" Khouri had been about to touch her, but his hand withdrew and he looked at her more closely. "How is this?"

"My husband," she said with deliberate bluntness, "had perverted tastes."

"And he let you know it?" Khouri sounded legitimately shocked. "A man may require variety from time to time. A boy or a different woman, or however Allah has formed him; this is not to be displayed for wives, however." He touched her hand and found it clenched and cold.

"Apparently my husband did not know that. His perversion was to see me violated." She broke away from him and moved away down the arabesque patterns of the path. It startled her to feel the intensity of her reaction: Cornelius Justus Sillius had died over a thousand years ago, yet the memories of his use of her still had the power to distress her. She came to one of the fountains and stopped, staring down at where the moonlight turned the splashing water to the brightness of diamonds, letting the music and the beauty of it calm her.

A short while later, Hamal Khouri strolled up to her. "I did not mean to offend you, Roman widow, or to cause you unhappiness." He remained three or four steps away from her. "It was not my intention to—"

"I know," said Olivia quickly. "And there is no excuse for my behavior." She inclined her head, not looking at him directly but watching him closely.

He remained silent. "I trust you will pardon my lapse, but I hope that you found aid then."

In spite of herself, Olivia smiled. "Oh, yes. I found aid." Unbidden, Sanct' Germain's well-loved features formed in her mind. Where was he now? she wondered. It had been more than thirty years since she last saw him, but the sense of him was as strong now as then, as it had been since that first time she spoke to him, when Nero was Caesar. "His eyes are like no others; very, very dark, almost black, like slates at night."

Khouri moved one step nearer. "Like slates?"

Olivia turned toward him. "Yes. You know—of a blue so dark it is black." She took his hand. "Not like yours, Khouri, which are darker than all wood but ebony. Your eyes are brown at its darkest; his are blue at its darkest."

"And this slate-eyed man was your aid?" Khouri reached out and pulled the wisp of a veil from her hair.

"He saved me," Olivia said. "He taught me to"—she laughed—"to . . . appreciate life." She regarded Khouri, thinking of Sanct' Germain, and all he had showed her down the centuries. *To appreciate life* was one of Sanct' Germain's phrases, elegant and equivocal. She had no doubt what he would advise her to do now, if she could ask him.

Khouri was enthralled by her. "How mercurial you are," he exclaimed. "Al zoqh, which influences all other elements, which you call the celestial mercury." He let his hand rest on her shoulder. "Did your rescuer recognize that in you?"

"Better than anyone before or since," she replied seriously, letting her long-denied hunger stir.

"And yet you wish for Sier Valence Rainaut," mused Khouri, fingering the neck of her bliaud. "It is written that the heat of the desert burns less than the passion of women."

She met his eyes. "You may lie with me three times; no more, if we suit one another the first time."

Khouri's face grew deeply intent. "Three times."

"No more," Olivia insisted. "I am not a foolish woman who squanders herself." There was another, more compelling reason, that she would never tell him.

"You changed your mind quickly," he said as he stroked her body through her clothes. "Perhaps you will change again."

"If you suit me and I you, now and two more times I will lie with you. My word on it." She caught both his hands in hers. "My word on it." She waited until he nodded, then she leaned forward and kissed him.

"Surely only Allah is great," whispered Khouri when they moved apart. "You are the fairest moon, the brightest jewel, the most potent perfume. Show me your body, that I may make it my idol for the night."

Olivia loosened the lacings of her bliaud then slithered it down off her shoulders and over her hips. She did not make the error of moving too quickly; each tantalizing motion worked on Khouri more compellingly than the smoke from the waterpipe he used every evening. "Do we remain in the garden, Hamal Khouri?"

He stared at her, devouring her with his eyes. When he spoke, he was breathless. "There is a door. That way."

She bent and scooped up her discarded clothes, only to have him take them from her. "I will need them later."

"My slaves will tend to them," he said. "Come." He had her by the wrist. "The door."

"I have done as you asked; now you will do as I ask," Olivia countered, as curious as she was desiring of him. "I am not chattle."

He stopped at once. "No, you are not," he said, releasing her. "Tell me, then, what you wish of me."

Olivia was mildly surprised at how tractable Khouri had proven to be. She stood staring at him. "It has been a long time since a man has taken pleasure to rouse me."

"Allah has made men fools, O Flower Filled with Nectar." He spoke this endearment in a deeper tone than he had used before. As he said it, he pulled her to him.

Olivia kissed him again, then half-turned and started toward the door Khouri had indicated. Leading him was no difficulty; he moved after her as if bound to her with thongs. As she stepped over the threshold into the incense-sweetened chamber, Olivia at last bent and took the solers off her feet.

"Ah." Khouri stood in the doorway, waiting until she had straightened up. "You are delight to all the senses, Roman widow. How is that, when so many others are not?"

"I am a Roman," Olivia reminded him. "I bathe."

Khouri shook his head. "That is not the whole of it. But, yes, I will allow that it is some of it, certainly." Now that they were in the chamber—which was hardly more than an alcove off the garden—Khouri was less pressing. He approached Olivia slowly but with complete confidence. "It is not your love I am seeking; I want your rapture."

"Then commence your search," she suggested, sinking back into the enormous mound of pillows and cushions that were the principal furnishings of the room. Sliding into a comfortable sprawl, she looked up at Khouri as he tugged free of the last of his clothes. How good it was to enjoy this man! For too long she had confined her encounters to those midnight embraces that were remembered by the men who gave them as dreams—or demons. She recognized some of her hesitation with Rainaut stemmed from her own doubts as well as his. It was so reassuring to be able to have this time with Khouri, to play.

Khouri knelt over her, straddling her without touching her. He kissed her quickly, gently, over her face and neck, then to her breasts. As he tongued one nipple, he tweaked the other between his thumb and fingers. He was deft in all he did; he never rushed or prodded, but continued a slow crescendo in their bodies. "My most precious rose," he murmured as his hand slipped down the inside of her thigh. "You will bloom for me; you will open all your petals."

Olivia reveled in the subtle sensations Khouri awakened in her flesh, at the complexity of responses that filled her. From the brush of his beard on her breast to the warmth and weight of his hand resting between her legs, she was entirely aware of him, and she all but moaned with pleasure. Since she had wakened in her tomb, she had known no malady, but under Khouri's touch she trembled as if with palsy, and her skin burned as if kindled by fever. She held a silken pillow to her face to keep from crying out when at last he slid into her.

"My ruby lily," he whispered. "My heart of all treasure, my most cherished slipper, my honeyed rose." He spoke in cadence with his movements. "My glorious scabbard."

Olivia held him, listening to his poetic compliments without attempting the same thing herself. She gave herself over to his expert ministrations, allowing herself to be carried into aspects of her senses she had neglected or ignored for far too long. Gradually she began to caress him, to slide her hand down his back, along his flank, over his legs, feeling his reaction with all her body. As she felt him tense, and his thrusts suddenly became deep and abrupt, she kissed him, at first on the mouth, and then on the neck.

"Well?" he asked her some while later. "You said if I pleased you and you pleased me, there could be . . . how many was it?" He had pulled a soft blanket of Kashmiri wool over them just before he spoke.

"It was this and two times more," Olivia said, staring up into the darkness.

"Only two?" asked Khouri, teasing and pleading at once.

"Only two," she said. "It is best that way."

"You are a remarkable partner, Roman widow. I have experienced many women, but no one like you." He kissed her softly, affectionately. "Who knows, in time I could come to have a passion for you."

"And what have you now?" She rolled onto her side so that she could look at him.

"A passion for your body, of course," he said, his face momentarily serious. "You are a treasure among women. A pity that you are not a courtesan, for you would own half the world."

There had been a time, three centuries before, when Olivia had been just that, and for twenty desperate years had risked discovery and denouncement while she entertained her lovers. Ultimately she had come to loathe what those years had made of her; since then, she had not considered being a courtesan again. "I have no taste for that," she said.

"And doubtless I am an idiot to say such a thing, after what you told me of your husband." He lowered his head and sighed. "I intended no offense."

Olivia shrugged. "So, there are two more opportunities, if you want them, but only two." She put her fingers to his lips. "No, not yet. Think about your answer."

"Wonderful Roman widow, whether I answer you now or after Allah—certainly His name will be praised forever and ever—has called me to Paradise, it will be no different. Whatever you offer me, be it two or twenty or two hundred million, I will count myself the most fortunate of men." He slipped his arm around her and pulled her to him. "What man disdains such a gift?" Before she could answer, he went on, "That Hospitaler is worse than the fool I thought him. If the fire of your flesh can do so much, what is your passion like?"

Olivia did not answer at once. She touched the place on his neck where her mouth had been. "Passion changes things," she said remotely.

Khouri chuckled. "How careful you are."

She frowned. "You don't understand," she said, turning to look out into the garden shadows and moonlight. "The senses can be . . . fed."

"As hunger is sated and thirst is slaked," agreed Khouri.

"But passion is more than a feast or a display or . . . or anything but itself." She made a sudden, impatient gesture. "There is no way of knowing what passion will do."

"And your foolish knight does not seek for it?" Khouri shook his head in disapproval.

"He seeks it, but not in me." Olivia closed her eyes, feeling defeated.

"Then he is not likely to find it," Khouri decided. "He is not willing to lie with you and he will not embrace Islam. He is hopeless."

Olivia stared at the dark garden and sighed.

* * *

Text of a letter from Ithuriel Dar to Niklos Aulirios.

To Niklos Aulirios at the estate Sanza Pare near Roma, the shipowner Ithuriel Dar sends greetings and some news.

I have made inquiry at Tyre and found from the Hospitalers here that your mistress the widow Bondama Atta Olivia Clemens has left this city for Sidon, with authorization to take ship there for Roma. All inquiry thus far indicates that she is still with her Hospitaler escort in Sidon, since no captain I have spoken with has any knowledge of such a woman taking ship from Sidon. Now that both Phillippe of France and Richard of England are underway, most of the captains agree that space aboard ship will be hard come by for some time, since supplies and materiel are being much increased against the day that the Christians and Islamites meet in battle.

So that we will not lose track of your mistress again, I have left word (and paid several handsome bribes; I include the accounting) at most ports from Ascalon to Attalia, requesting any and all information that might be found about this woman. I am about to leave Caesarea for Sidon, to try to locate her, as soon as the current storm dies enough to take ship, that is.

It may be difficult to get this to you speedily, or to find your mistress with dispatch, for the winter has started out badly, and the storms have not diminished in either frequency or severity. This is fortunate in one sense, in that it means that the French and English Kings cannot travel and thereby commandeer all the boats on the sea, but it also restricts all other sailors as well.

I have the opportunity to meet with the Master of the Hospitalers here in Caesarea, and perhaps he will be able to tell me how best to proceed. Be of good cheer, my Greek friend who is Roman. We will find your mistress and see her returned to your before any harm can come to her. Let me add, too, that your mistress is not without resources, as I have cause to know. As great as our determination is to reach her, so is hers to reach you, and from what I have seen of Bondama Clemens, she is a force to be reckoned with.

Ithuriel Dar

By my own hand, carried by the ship Leocadia, written on the day the Court of Bourgesses in Caesarea declares to be the 22nd day of November, in the Christian year 1190.

· **14** ·

It was the third squall in as many days, and in the lavish house of Hamal Khouri, everyone was growing restless. Word had been brought from the harbor that yet another ship had been unable to leave port: in the last month only the small ships of the fishing fleet had ventured onto the sea, and five of them had been lost.

"It is shameful that we must wait this way, and in the house of an Islamite," de Jountuil said to Rainaut as they prepared to spend the morning practicing at swordplay. "It's bad enough that we are not allowed to defend Our Lord more vigorously, but"—he hefted his long, double-handed broadsword and took two experimental swings with it—"to accept hospitality from an Islamite is beyond bearing."

"There is no room for us in Sidon, unless you want to sleep in the stable with the grooms," said Rainaut tightly.

"It would be a change," said de Jountuil. "Are you ready?"

Rainault swung his sword. "I believe so," he answered, taking the crouched posture used to imitate fighting on horseback. He brought his sword up, balancing the flat of the blade against his shoulder. "At your word."

De Jountuil hopped backward, at the same time bringing his sword down and across in a vicious arc. *"There!"* As he shouted, his weapon clanged off of Rainaut's, which he had brought under and up to intercept de Jountuil's blow.

Both men stepped back, realigned themselves, and took up their stances again. "I am ready," said Rainaut. He flexed his fingers on the hilt and braced his thumb against the quillons.

"And I." This time the two circled each other for a short while before de Jountuil straightened up, his sword raised high and starting to swing directly down.

Rainaut again brought his sword up, and sparks flew where the two blades scraped. He could feel the force of the impact down his arms, across his shoulders and down his back. As he disengaged his sword, he asked, "Again?"

"Of course," said de Jountuil, panting a little. He blotted his forehead against his leather-covered arm. "Take your place." As he brought his sword up to the ready, de Jountuil asked, "Your Roman widow seems to be making the most of our stay here, doesn't she?"

Rainaut hesitated, thrown off balance by the question. "How do you mean that?"

"How do you think?" countered de Jountuil. "She amuses herself and our host. It probably would not pain her if we were forced to remain here all winter." He had found a position that put more sun into Rainaut's eyes than his own; he set his feet and crouched.

"That's a pernicious lie," Rainaut said, trying to make his tone light and bantering, but without success.

"Is it? She has been with him at night three times." He had to slide backward as Rainaut lunged. "I have watched, Rainaut. I know what I have seen."

"And what is that?" His eyes were narrow and his voice taut with anger; he felt the icy fist gather under his belt. "What have you seen?"

"I've seen . . . For God's Fish, Rainaut!" He ducked as Rainaut's blade clove the air a hand's-breadth above his head.

"Tell me." The blade was moving again, and this time de Jountuil moved back several paces.

"I saw Bondama Clemens in the company of our Islamite host. You know what they are with women. All the world knows that they are perverted and hedonistic. They keep their own women prisoners so that they may treat them as they wish." He lowered the point of his sword and let the weapon fall. "Khouri says he admires Bondama Clemens' mind. And he has wives and concubines enough to keep any man satisfied. But they have been alone together at night upon three occasions. Wait and watch with me, and you'll see I am right in my suspicions."

Rainaut flung his sword away from him, so that it crashed into the far wall and clanged to the floor. "May every demon in Hell consume her entrails if you tell me the truth," he vowed.

"Fine, fine," de Jountuil said at once. "Wish all of them happy." He cocked his head to the side. "We don't owe her escort if she is nothing more than a harlot."

"She's not a harlot!" Rainaut's face darkened.

"All right," de Jountuil agreed at once. "Perhaps a harlot, perhaps a courtesan, perhaps only one of those widows who from time to time gets an itch. Whatever the state, unless she is virtuous, she cannot demand our escort."

Rainaut glared at de Jountuil. "You are my fellow-Hospitaler and we are of similar rank; I will not make you accountable to me for what you have said. It is not worthy of either of us that we should come to blows over your jest." He leaned forward. "But so there will be no mistake, I will watch with you, and we will learn together how great your misunderstanding has been."

"If you are so enthralled by her, make her your whore and have done with it," said de Jountuil, making certain that he was out of range of Rainaut's fists.

"No man turns an honest widow to a whore." Rainaut reached for the dagger at his belt and started to draw it from the sheath. "And well you know that."

De Jountuil shook his head. "She's yours for the asking. If you do not believe me, then wait until you catch her in the Islamite's arms." This time as Rainaut came toward him, de Jountuil held up his hands. "Peace, Rainaut. I have no quarrel with you. I only wish to let you see the nature of the widow we are protecting. If I am in error, then I will ask her Christian forgiveness." His smile was slight and cynical. "Is that enough for you, or must I prepare to open a vein?"

"Suicide is a sin against the Holy Spirit," said Rainaut quietly.

"So it is. I am very sure of myself, Rainaut. I know what I have seen." He bent to pick up his sword again. "Shall we continue practice?" It was a deliberate jibe, expertly delivered and timed. "Sier Valence?"

"Yes," Rainaut said through his teeth, going to fetch his sword. "And then we must tend to our horses."

"Twice a day, every day," de Jountuil said automatically. "By Rule of Order. For the sake of a Maltese Cross, we become stablehands and grooms."

"For the sake of pilgrims and the honor of God," Rainaut corrected him. He slipped into his fighting stance. "Are you ready?"

"Strike," said de Jountuil, his sword already moving.

They fought their mock-battle until both were sodden with sweat, then they called a halt by mutual agreement.

"Our host has offered us the use of his bath," said de Jountuil as they cleaned their swords and oiled the blades. "What do you think?"

"I stink like a camel at a hog-wallow," said Rainaut. "I do not think we'd be accused of vanity for bathing now." He plucked at the quilted cotton acton under his chain mail. "This must be washed, too."

De Jountuil snickered. "Not very good company, are we?"

He got to his feet, slipping his sword into its sheath. "I'll tell Khouri's slaves that we will be bathed."

"And we will work out how we are to watch," said Rainaut in a low, determined voice.

"If you insist on giving yourself pain, by all means," said de Jountuil with a half-bow.

In the end, they agreed to keep watch together, at opposite ends of the long corridor that passed both Khouri's and Olivia's bedchamber doors. They kept to the shadows, each just able to see the other, and remained there until the middle of the night. After four nights, when they had watched Khouri's wives and concubines visit him, de Jountuil grew impatient.

"They do not meet because they know you suspect," he told Rainaut while they raked the straw in their horses' stalls.

"They do not meet because they do not meet." Rainaut was no longer angry with de Jountuil, but his patience was worn so thin that he did not trust himself to argue any more.

"I tell you, I saw them," de Jountuil said as they went through the darkened house to their quarters. "I saw them together, in a room off the garden."

"You happened to be there, you happened to see them. And although it was dark, you knew precisely what you saw." He folded his arms as he reached his bedchamber door. "I believe you are sincere and that you do not want me to compromise my name, but I do not and cannot believe that Bondama Clemens would permit such things to happen to her."

"She talked about her husband. She said he was debauched." De Jountuil opened the door to his bedchamber. "You don't believe that either, do you?"

"If what you say is true, all the more reason for her to be virtuous." Rainaut sighed. "We will watch again tomorrow night, but that will be the end of it, de Jountuil."

"Unless she is at that time of moon, when she cannot be touched. Two or three more days, to be certain." De Jountuil glanced back over his shoulder. "The honor of the Hospitalers is imperiled as well as your own. To use our Order to defend those who sin and blaspheme—"

"All right, three more nights," said Rainaut. "But you will

apologize for your suspicions and you will confess the wrong you have done Bondama Clemens, both to her and to your confessor. I am not the only one who might impugn the honor of the Hospitalers."

On the second night of the three, while Rainaut and de Jountuil watched from the shadows, Hamal Khouri paused at Olivia's bedchamber door. He hesitated before he knocked, and waited indecisively until the door was opened enough to let in a gnat. "Have you changed your mind, my flower who blooms unseen?"

"No," Olivia answered. "Please; do not ask me again."

"There could be paradise," he persisted.

"No." She started to close the door against him.

"We could have passion, Roman widow," Khouri said in desperation.

"Three times: you have my answer," Olivia said sadly, then closed the door.

Hamal Khouri stood outside her door for some little time, not moving. Finally he leaned his forehead against the door as if to pierce it with his thoughts. Then, giving a resigned sigh, he moved down the hallway toward the chamber where two of his concubines slept.

When the hall had been empty a short while, Rainaut stepped out of the shadows. He walked directly toward de Jountuil, feeling a triumph he had never found in fighting. "Well then," he said in an undervoice as he approached de Jountuil. "Shall we watch for one more night, or was this sufficient?"

"It does not prove that they did not meet before," de Jountuil insisted.

"Doesn't it?" Rainaut took de Jountuil by the arm and started to pull him from his hiding place. "I say that Bondama Clemens is vindicated and that you must do as you have sworn to do. She will receive your apology; you will be forgiven." He shoved de Jountuil against the wall. "And if ever I hear you breathe one word of shame against her, I will make you pay for that indiscretion in blood."

De Jountuil broke away from Rainaut. "You cannot treat me this way. No Hospitaler can demand satisfaction of another."

"A Hospitaler does not defame the innocent." Rainaut

pursued him down the hall, trying to keep from raising his voice as he went.

"The *innocent?*" de Jountuil repeated. "The *innocent?* What claim does the Widow Clemens have to innocence? You say because we have not caught her in Khouri's arms that she was never there. I tell you she was." He stopped as he saw the way Rainaut was staring at him. "But you are right," he said in a chastened way. "I have nothing to prove what I know to be the truth; I have only my suppositions. They have not been substantiated." He shrugged to acknowledge his defeat. "Very well, I will obtain her pardon and I will confess. It will not change what she has done, but that is nothing to me, is it?"

"When we have taken Jerusalem once more, you and I will pray for her together at the Holy Sepulcher," said Rainaut. "Until then, I will pray for her and for you every morning and evening."

"Through what Saint, I wonder?" de Jountuil asked, making no excuse for his sarcasm. "Never mind. When am I to beg the pardon of your Roman widow?"

"Tomorrow after lauds will be soon enough," Rainaut said curtly. He indicated the door to his room. "I will pray now. You will do well to follow my example."

"What was the story?" de Jountuil asked of the wall, speaking a little more loudly than before. "There was a monk, a very holy man, who saw a courtesan, and conceived a burning desire to save her soul and bring her to a love of the Christ. It was a hard-fought battle, but at last he succeeded and she became a nun, given to fasting and praying and tending to the lowliest needs of lepers and beggars. And only then did the monk realize that he lusted for her—and could no longer take her. Once she had been his for a piece of gold, had he paid it; and now, because of what he had done, she was beyond his reach forever and he was damned." He cocked his head to the side. "There is a lesson in that tale, Rainaut, if you care to find it."

"Is there? I'll consider it," Rainaut said coldly. "And let me offer this parable to you: the story of Susannah and the Elders." He stepped back. "Tomorrow morning, after lauds."

De Jountuil nodded as Rainaut turned away from him.

It took Rainaut longer than he expected to explain the problem to Olivia, who answered his summons in some consternation.

"What is the trouble, Bonsiers?" she asked when she saw the two Hospitalers in the central reception room of Hamal Khouri's house.

"My comrade-at-arms has an apology to offer you," Rainaut prodded, watching de Jountuil narrowly. "I pray you will have the grace to forgive him."

Olivia smiled, her hazel eyes untouched by it. "What is the matter?"

"I . . ." de Jountuil took a deep breath and dropped to one knee, taking the hem of Olivia's saffron-colored bliaud in his hands. "I erred, and I erred to your discredit, Bondama, for which I petition you now to pardon, both for my thoughts and my actions." He brought the hem of her bliaud to his lips and kissed it. "You have only to tell me I am forgiven, and I will remember you in my prayers with gratitude."

"You erred to my discredit," Olivia mused, looking at Rainaut. "Will you tell me the nature of your error?"

The two men exchanged uneasy glances. "It would not be a good thing for you to hear," said de Jountuil at last.

"All the more reason I should," Olivia rejoined. "When men speak well of me, there is no reason for me to listen," she went on, her eyes still on Rainaut. "It serves only to strengthen vanity, which is a sin. But when men speak ill of me, it is to correct my fault or to warn me, and it is wise for me to know of it." She read the expressions of the two men as she spoke and realized she had guessed correctly: de Jountuil was not alerted and Rainaut was convinced.

De Jountuil, confused for the first time, lowered his head. "I . . . I supposed that you and . . . our host . . . had come to a . . . a contract of sorts."

"You mean," Olivia corrected him serenely, "that you suspected I was guaranteeing your safety by giving Khouri my body as bond." It was close enough to de Jountuil's suspicions that he would accept it. "There is truth in that."

Both men stared at her, and she took advantage of their astonishment.

"Yes, I consented. But I would not be made his woman,

and I would not involve either of you. Our bargain was for three nights, and for three nights I lay with him, for I do not abjure my promise. I do not ask your pardon for this, for we are in an Islamite city in the house of an Islamite who could turn us into the streets any time he chose." She disliked the implied lie in what she said, but she could not be more candid without disaster.

"You mean that you submitted to him for us?" demanded Rainaut.

"No, for me. That it protected you as well was secondary," she said. "Do not misunderstand me. I am a widow, and my married life was far from happy. I know what I can and cannot endure." She looked at de Jountuil who still clung to her hem with nerveless fingers. "So you see, you need no forgiveness. And I have incurred no blame." It was difficult not to scream at the two Hospitalers, to demand that they explain themselves to her. But the laws and the customs which had protected her had faded away more than seven hundred years ago, and what little was left was a travesty of the rights she had known when she was young. "Do you leave me now?" she asked of Rainaut. "Do you denounce me?" she asked of de Jountuil.

"I do not leave you," Rainaut answered at once, though his face had darkened with conflicting emotions. "You might give yourself to all the warriors of Saladin and I would not leave you."

She smiled fleetingly. "I suppose I must thank you for that," she said, musing.

"You need do nothing," said Rainaut with more feeling than he had shown previously.

De Jountuil got slowly to his feet. "Was it a sacrifice?"

For once in her life, Olivia answered indirectly, as her cherished first lover might have answered such a question. "What do you think?"

De Jountuil looked down at her. "Roman widow, you are the most acute woman I have ever met. You have wit and you have something more . . ." He stared at her. "I wonder how old you are?"

"Older than you think," was her unperturbed answer.

"Stop this jibing," Rainaut insisted. He came and looked down at Olivia. "You let that Islamite possess you?"

"No; I let him touch my body," she answered, watching him, seeking the blue depths of his eyes.

Rainaut made a fist of his right hand and slammed it into his left. "You ought not . . . I would have defended you."

"And all of us would have been in the street in an Islamite city," Olivia reminded him. "Or would that have pleased you?"

"No—how can you think it?—but to trade . . ." He broke away from her. "Bondama, how could you accept an Islamite in your bed?"

"I have been forced to take worse," she said without any softening of her words. "Perhaps in another time, at another place, it would be possible not to make such . . . concessions. But here and now, being who and what we are, what is left to us?" She looked from Rainaut to de Jountuil. "You wish to condemn me for letting our host have what he wished for. What did I risk? But if I had refused, the lives of both of you as well as my own were at stake. What was to stop him from ruining both of you and making me his concubine in any case?" It was not an unreasonable question; much worse had happened in the last hundred years.

De Jountuil was the first to speak. "I do not condone your actions, Bondama, but I applaud your motives. I will say nothing to your discredit, now or ever. And if I hear any speak against you, I will call them to accounting for it." He bowed and kissed the edge of her sleeve. "If I was in danger, you have saved me."

Olivia shook her head. "There is no obligation, Bonsier."

"There is," he countered, and moved away from her, going toward the hallway that led to the stable.

"How could you do this?" Rainaut demanded when they were alone. "How could you let another man touch you?"

Olivia met his gaze fearlessly. "What was I supposed to do? Long for you, desire you, seek for you, and let you die when it was a simple matter to save you? This man did not touch my soul. He did not desire it. He asked only for my flesh, and the scriptures you uphold and adore say that flesh is dross." There was a challenge in the last, and she waited while he framed his answer.

"You do not understand," he said heavily. "You do not

know what can be accomplished when there is more than lust—"

"And you will not teach me?" she interrupted. "Sier Valence, you refuse me, but you accuse me when I accept another. I would prefer you, but you deny me. Hamal Khouri does not want my soul. Do you begrudge him my body?"

"Yes!" Rainaut whispered through clenched teeth. "Yes. I begrudge the look of your eye, the scent of your perfume, the silk of your hair to anyone." His voice was so low that it was hard to hear him, but his passion was so great that it made him tremble.

"Then it is yours, Sier Valence. Why do you refuse it?" She touched his face, on the place where the beard no longer grew. Here the skin was pale, like a scar from a burn. She leaned forward and kissed him where his ear joined his neck. "Or do you refuse me?"

"I am a Hospitaler," he said, trying to bring himself to move away from her. "I have taken an oath."

"You break it with your harlot. Why will you not break it with me?" Olivia studied his face intently, then moved back from him. "When you know the answer to these questions, tell me, for I do not understand."

"Bondama Clemens—"

"Olivia," she corrected.

He stared into her eyes as if he could drown in them. "Olivia," he repeated as if in a dream. With an effort he made himself look away from her. "Olivia," he repeated, and did not see that she smiled at the sound of her name.

*　　*　　*

Text of an anonymous note sent to the Regent of England, John, written in English.

To my lord John, Prince and liege, the greetings of a friend come to you from Sicilia with the hope that the news is welcome to him, and that what he learns from my poor efforts may be useful in the days to come.

Although Reis Richard and Reis Phillippe pretend to be cordial, their dealings are ever more frayed. With both of them and their armies stranded here while the winter storms rage, the chafing has become so marked that everyone has remarked upon it, even to the most humble village priest. While they have not quarreled in public nor countenanced the battles of their men, the two rulers are not in accord no matter how they strive to maintain the fiction that they are Brothers in the Cross. They are rivals, and all the world knows it.

Reis Richard is more eager than Reis Phillippe to be away from here and into the Holy Land. He is a man itching for blood, who lusts for the clash of arms. Phillippe is of a less excitable temperament, and because he is easily made ill, he is not as anxious as Reis Richard to be under way. He has spent part of the winter in the care of certain monks famous for the cordial they prepare for travelers suffering illness. He claims that his condition has improved. For so young a man, he is most careful of his health; I cannot say the same of Reis Richard, who appears to be inured to physical complaint of any kind.

The cost of wintering in Sicilia is staggering, and it may be that Reis Richard will require more funds before he pushes on to engage the forces of Saladin in battle. As you are doubtless aware, Reis Richard did not anticipate having to pass the winter on this island, but hoped to enter Jerusalem on the eve of Christ's Birth. That has not been possible, and so now he is speaking of the Feast of the Resurrection or some other suitable day. Those who have had experience against Saladin's men have said that it will take more than the mere presence of Reis Richard on the shores of the Holy Land to change Jerusalem. Saladin is a formidable leader and a worthy foeman. He respects those he battles, but he does not concede one length of ground to anyone on reputation alone.

Leopold of Austria has done much to rally the forces of Barbarossa, and the loss of fighting men has not been as great as was feared at first. According to what has been said in recent reports, by the time Reis Richard can bring his men to the Holy Land, there will be sufficient Christian warriors under arms that it will be possible to push back the Islamic enemy. The Islamic forces are more prepared for the terrain than our Christian forces, but our cause and our numbers must eventually prevail. At what cost I do not know.

The commandeering of ships has begun. The English and the French armies are preparing to sail in early spring, so that all requests for monies and supplies must be made quickly or not be made at all until they reach the Holy Land. Burdened as you are, Prince, with the demands of raising the funds to pay for Reis Richard's expedition, I fear you have not heard the last of his demands. If you are able to meet the requirements of the French and Genoese, be aware that there will be more funds needed before the summer is out. I tell you this in the hope that you will not have to impose more tithes on the people of England and English possessions.

Remember me to the Abbot of Saint Giles in Hastings, if that is possible, for it was on his behest that I took the Cross for the sake of God and the sake of England.

A true friend
By my own hand, under seal, in the shadow of Mount Etna, on the 13th day of January in the Year of Our Lord 1191.

· 15 ·

Not long after nightfall Rainaut returned from the wharves, his jaw bruised under the two-day stubble that grew there.

"We were worried about you," said Hamal Khouri after he had ordered his slaves to prepare a bath and a meal for his guest. "You said you would not be gone for more than a day."

"I was prepared to send word to the Chapter House, to

alert those of our Order that you had been taken prisoner," de Jountuil said, a speculative lift to his brow. "We had no word from you."

"I found a captain from Hydros who will carry us—de Jountuil and Bondama Clemens with me—as far as Cyprus. I have given him half the gold he demands, and he has said he will sail on the first stormless day." His eyes were dark with fatigue and his skin was streaked; his cote was rent in two places, the blazon of his personal arms almost torn from the heavy linen.

"You were in a fight," said Olivia, moving closer to him.

"Three," he corrected her. "There are some rough men who sail these waters, and they enjoy a good scuffle." He tried to laugh but coughed instead. "The captain gave me his word that he would send one of his crew to me each day to tell me when or if he would sail."

"You gave the man money?" de Jountuil repeated incredulously. "What is the matter with you, Rainaut? Do you not know that it is money lost that is spent so recklessly?"

"He will do it. I bested him in a fight with knives and he swore on that." Rainaut sat down heavily. "There are rumors that Reis Richard will soon leave Sicilia with his army. I would rather be gone from here when he arrives."

"And who is to say he is arriving here?" de Jountuil asked. "Why not up the Orontes at Antioch, or at Beirut? Why not at Caesarea or even Tyre, where the Christians are still in control? Why Sidon, for all the Saints in Heaven?"

"I meant here, on this shore, not in this city." He rubbed at his forehead. "Have you a barber, Bonsier Khouri?"

"Of course," said his host urbanely. "I will send him to you while you bathe. Allow me to suggest that your hair as well as your beard wants trimming." He fingered his own elegant beard as he spoke.

"That's vanity," said Rainaut, waving the suggestion away. His exhaustion was taking hold of him now, and he moved and spoke more slowly. "There's no need."

Olivia laid her hand on Rainaut's shoulder. "I am sorry you took so great a chance for my sake."

"Are you?" He looked up at her, over his shoulder. "That is some consolation, I suppose."

"The bath," said Khouri decisively, and clapped loudly to

summon his slaves, rapping out orders when they answered his summons. "Ready the bath for the Hospitaler. He is very tired. See that he is attended." When the slaves departed, he regarded Rainaut closely once more. "You may also want a physician."

"There's no need," Rainaut said brusquely. "I manage well."

"You were hurt?" Olivia demanded.

Rainaut almost pushed her away. "It is nothing. A few bruises and a cut or two. I have had worse in sword practice." He took a deep, uneven breath. "It is not necessary to fuss over me."

De Jountuil laughed cynically. "But she will do it, won't she?" He strolled toward the door. "When you're ready, you'll tell us the whole of the plan. In the meantime, I gather we are supposed to pack. I will see to that." He added as an afterthought, "It's a shame we brought no servants. I dislike doing such menial work."

"Why do it at all?" Khouri asked. "I will provide slaves for the task."

Olivia shook her head. "It's part of their Order," she said, lapsing from the Norman French they had been speaking to the language of the Islamites of Tyre. She knew he would understand her better. "Only those who are part of their households are supposed to serve them. They are something like monks and something like soldiers."

"Christian nonsense," Khouri said with amusement.

"Perhaps, but there are men who will die for it, and not all of them will be Christians." She looked down at Rainaut, who was regarding her narrowly. "I am trying to explain to him," she said in French, "why you will not accept his hospitality and permit his slaves to pack your belongings."

Rainaut shook his head. "We have obligations, who wear the Maltese Cross."

"Of course," said Khouri smoothly and uncomprehendingly.

Olivia reached down and touched his face. "You risked a great deal, didn't you?"

"Not as much as you might think," he responded after a moment. He had taken her hand in his and was staring at how their fingers interlaced. "I am very tired."

"Quite an admission for you," said Olivia, teasing him gently. "Come. The slaves will be ready for you shortly." She looked at Khouri. "It isn't proper, but let me lead him back to the bathchamber."

Khouri made an elegant gesture of resignation and bewilderment. "Surely Allah is great," he said.

The bathchamber was cavernous and dark, but the bath, though shallower than what Olivia was used to, was deep enough and wide enough to allow Rainaut to stretch out in the heated water. Soaps and perfumed oils were set out in vials along the inlaid sides of the bath, and two slaves, both young eunuchs, waited to tend to Rainaut.

"One is the barber, the other will massage you when you are through. Khouri understands you do not want bath attendants to wash you." Olivia watched him. "What would you like to wear when you are through? Khouri has provided a robe for you, but if you would prefer something else . . . ?"

Rainaut hesitated, knowing he should refuse the robe and send the slaves away, but instead he muttered, "The robe is welcome."

Olivia's eyes crinkled as she tried not to laugh. "Very good. If you had refused this, you would have insulted him. He has made an effort to accept your ways. It is wise that you have done something to accept his."

"He has shown us great hospitality," Rainaut said, a bit indirectly.

"So he has," Olivia agreed at once. "We are strangers, we are in a country that is at war, and he was willing to take us into his household. Next time you think ill of him, remember these things, also." She started toward the door. "If you don't mind, I'll wait for you in the little alcove of the library. Seek me there before you go to bed."

He sighed. "Very well, if you wish."

She left him to his bath and the ministrations of the two eunuch slaves.

When he finally came to the library, he was almost a different man. His hair, still wet and newly cut, altered the look of his fresh-shaven face, the burn-like patch on his jaw and neck where little beard grew less obvious now that his skin was smooth. His eyes were still set in dark rings, but he no longer looked a fugitive. The long robe of fine, light wool complimented him, and he moved more easily.

"So, at last we will be bound toward Roma," Olivia said quietly. "I am grateful to you, Sier Valence."

"It is my task to take you there, Bondama." He kept his distance from her, not trusting himself near her.

"And it has been more arduous than any of us anticipated," she said, a certain steely anger under her words.

"Amen to that, Bondama."

She let the silence hang between them, then asked, "How soon do you think we will leave?"

He shrugged. "Word is that Reis Richard is on the sea from Sicilia, bound for Cyprus. He wishes to establish the island as a base for the Crusaders, as Rhodes is for my Order. If this is the case, we can reach either Cyprus or Rhodes and be assured that you will find passage to Roma." His eyes, averted before, now met hers. "You will be bound for home."

"And you?"

"I have my oath to serve. If you are in worthy Christian hands, you will have no more need of my escort." He rubbed at his arm through the wool. "Such indulgence is a hazard to the soul."

She took a step toward him. "What are you talking about, Sier Valence?"

"The bath. I realize now why there are such strictures against bathing and indulging the flesh." He seemed distracted, distant; Olivia attributed it to his fatigue. "The Church Fathers knew what the flesh can do, how it corrupts the soul."

"Is the soul so weak that a little soap and water can harm it?" Olivia asked. "You underestimate it, I think."

"It is flesh that is weak. It succumbs to all manner of temptations." He rubbed his arm again, and this time drew back the loose sleeve to look at it. At once an expression of dismay crossed his features.

"What is it?" Olivia came to his side, holding out her hand to him.

"The eunuch must have . . . done something." He was staring at his arm where much of the hair had fallen out and the skin had the same look of burn scar as was on his face. "God and the Saints; I am unclean."

"No," said Olivia at once. "You may have a disease, but you are no leper." She took his wrist and stretched out his arm. "I will give you a salve and bandage your arm."

Rainaut lowered his eyes. "Perhaps you ought not to touch me." He blessed himself automatically, his manner dazed. "It cannot be. God would not curse me so."

"It isn't," Olivia said staunchly. "I have seen leprosy before, many times, and this is not what afflicts you, Sier Valence. Use the salve I give you and you will improve." This last was as much bluff as truth, for the few times she had seen others afflicted as she suspected Rainaut was, there had been nothing that stopped the spreading of the burn-like patches on the skin.

"Very well," he said, as grateful as he was dubious. "I'll use the salve." He moved back from her. "You are kind to me, Bondama. You have my thanks."

"Oh, Valence, you are the most exasperating man!" Olivia burst out. "Your fine manner is a mask, and you know it better than I. What is the matter with you? Do you think that every knight who comes to the Holy Land does so for high purpose and for the Glory of God? Do you honestly suppose that every Hospitaler is dedicated to aiding pilgrims, and never once thinks of lining his pockets or filling his coffers? Do you suppose that the Templars never plunder and loot? Do you think that the Kings are coming for the Holy Sepulcher alone? Are you that willfully blind?"

He took a deep breath before he answered her. "I pray that we may all be made worthy of our calling, and the faith we profess be given us. I pray that every knight and man-at-arms who forgets his mission for God will remember it before he damns himself eternally."

For a few moments it was quiet in the library alcove, then Olivia shook her head. "How do you manage to be so obstinate?" she asked sweetly, and started past him out of the room.

He caught her by the elbow. "If I would not imperil both our souls, I would deny you nothing, Olivia."

"This is not very consoling, Valence." She stared into his very blue eyes. "And well you know it."

"Perhaps I should not go with you on the ship." He spoke softly, dreamily.

"Oh, excellent." She rounded on him, her hazel eyes bright with anger. "When the Captain is taken by pirates and I am sold into slavery, I will recall how careful you were. No, Bonsier, you are not excused from your duty. You have said yourself that escort is required. I believe you. And therefore I must rely on you, whether either of us likes it or not. If it were safe for me to travel alone, I would. But in these times, can you tell me I would not be at risk?" Her words, so cutting, were soft as a caress. "How would you answer that?"

He had gone white around the mouth. "I will not abandon you. You must not travel alone. I only wished to . . . to avoid . . . to avoid . . ." He could not finish.

"You want to avoid being with me," Olivia said directly. "Because you desire me."

"It is more than desire, Bondama," he said with difficulty.

"Perhaps," she responded, breaking the hold of their eyes and moving away from him. "Come to me in the morning when you waken, and I will give you the salve. My goods will be packed by the evening. After that, you have only to tell me when we are to leave."

He nodded, not trusting himself to speak to her, though he listened to the sound of her footsteps and the closing of the door as she left him alone to ponder his responsibilities—to his Order, to his oath, to God, to Olivia.

Tired as he was, Rainaut did not sleep quickly nor easily that night. His thoughts were full of anxiety and conflict, as if he were about to go into battle. He remembered his dead wife, and for a time recited prayers for her repose. He asked God's blessing on Reis Richard. Once he attempted to pray for Olivia, but his petition became so complex and entangled that he gave it up, trying instead to calm himself with the recitation of the Hospitalers' devotional prayers and vows. In the middle of the last, he finally drifted off into uneasy slumber, which ended abruptly when de Jountuil woke him not long after dawn.

"The news is that Reis Richard is truly, now, en route to Cyprus. I had it from a sailor newly arrived from Venezia. His ship stopped at Crete coming here." He was genuinely excited, for once lacking the cynicism that marked his manner.

"A sailor from Venezia?" Rainaut repeated, not fully awake.

"Just arrived. The ship entered the harbor as soon as the chain was lifted. The Leone di San Marco is on the sails, and the crew all speak Venezian." He reached out his arms. "We may have battle yet, my friend. Once the Islamites attack, we can fight as valiantly as any Templar."

"After Bondama Clemens has been safely escorted to—"

"I know, I know," de Jountuil interrupted. "First your precious Roman widow must be put into safe hands. We are honor-bound to see that she is escorted out of Islamite lands. Very well. But then we will see battle." He swung an imaginary sword, whooping at what in his vision was impact.

As he untangled himself from the bedclothes, Rainaut said, "I must go to the harbor. I have to speak to—"

"The Captain. Yes, indeed. Hurry along." De Jountuil whistled a scrap of tune. "If the Venezian ship has got through, there must be others. We'll be out of this place at last."

"We might be gone from here by tomorrow," Rainaut said, his words awed. "We could be on the sea, away from here."

"Then by all means, hurry, hurry," de Jountuil urged lightly. "Get up. Tend to your horse, see that all is in readiness. There is much to do." He picked up one of the huge, soft pillows that were strewn over Rainaut's bed and punched it as hard as he could. "It will be good to fight. I can feel the blood in my veins again."

"It's exciting," Rainaut said uncertainly. He had got to his feet and was staring blankly at the two chests on the far side of the room. "We must visit our chapel as well, for blessing, before we leave."

"To take the contamination of this place off us, yes," said de Jountuil with urgent agreement. "And when that is done, we will be ready for our foe at last."

Rainaut shook his head slowly. "You can engage the Islamites if you wish. While we are in Sidon, I will be at pains to provoke no incident. We are in an Islamite city, and there are but two of us, with a woman depending on us for her safety. Our duty to her and our Order is clear."

"Don't you long to spill a little Saracen blood?" de Jountuil asked enthusiastically. "Despicable as they are, the Templars have a real advantage over us. They are allowed to attack." He stopped and gave Rainaut a quizzical look. "Are you quite well, Sier Valence?"

"Um?" Rainaut made a quirky smile. "I am still tired, I fear. Let me have a little time to wake up, and we may talk again." He scratched automatically at his arm, then forced himself to stop. "Later we must talk, you and I."

"Naturally," said de Jountuil, bowing to Rainaut. "When you are ready, come break your fast with me. Our host has laid out dates and hard cheese for us."

"Very generous," said Rainaut, perplexed at the generosity Khouri was showing them.

"An apt politician, our host. He wants to be certain that the Christians speak well of him, in case the Crusade is successful and he is isolated here. Never say that these Islamites are not canny folk. If we were not enemies and had they not defiled the Holy Sepulcher, I might admire them."

Rainaut was unable to come up with a response. He ran his hands through his hair, then stretched. "I will join you directly." He turned away, but added as if the answer were of no more than passing interest, "Has Bondama Clemens been told of this news?"

"No, not that I know of," said de Jountuil, smirking.

"Then I must speak with her. She will have to speed her arrangements." He was already pulling the Islamite robe over his head, tugging at the seams in his eagerness to be dressed. "She will be glad to be gone. Who would have thought when we came here that it would be almost April before we were able to depart once more."

"You are caught in your own fancy," said de Jountuil. "But I will let her know you have news for her, how's that?"

"I thank you for it," said Rainaut as he rummaged in his larger chest for clean clothing. "Tell her I will be with her once I have set my own things in order."

"Oh, most certainly," said de Jountuil with elaborate and false courtesy. "There is little for me to tend to, in any case. How fortunate I am to have this task wished upon me."

"You don't have to behave so badly," Rainaut warned. "As Hospitalers, we are to welcome humble tasks to aid pilgrims and other Christians. You haven't forgot that, have you?"

"Naturally not," said de Jountuil at his most blithe. "Bring on the chests and cases, and I'm the man for it. Put my other actions out of your mind."

"I didn't mean to rebuke you," Rainaut said, shocked at his comrade-at-arms. "I . . . never mind. I'm not quite awake. I will speak with Bondama Clemens myself. I know you have tasks enough to attend to."

"Generous of you," said de Jountuil, heading for the door, whistling once again.

When he was gone, Rainaut sat for a short while, his elbows propped on his knees, his chin in his hands, his mind amazingly blank. At last he shook himself mentally and he returned to choosing his garments for the day, and to arranging his things for packing. He had just donned his own cote, his arms blazoned on the breast, when Olivia came through his door without knocking.

"Why didn't you tell me?" she asked, not precisely angry, but far from pleased.

"I . . . I learned only a short while ago myself," he said, making himself continue his chores. "I was going to wait on you in a short while, to inform you—"

"Khouri and de Jountuil have both saved you the effort," she said without apology. "So. Does that mean we are to leave for Cyprus, in the hope of meeting your King and his army there?"

"If it can be arranged, yes." He hefted two short swords, debating if he should wear them or pack them away.

"And do you think it can? You are the one who has been making arrangements." She gave him time to answer, and when he did not, she went on, "I have to send notice to my . . . my major domo in Roma."

"We will arrange it," he said distantly.

"When you do," she said, deliberately offensive, "I hope someone will have the goodness to tell me about it." She turned toward the door, then stopped. "I ought to warn you that I am usually seasick when I travel by water."

He looked up at that. "You?"

"Yes," she said, chagrined. "Those of my blood are often so afflicted."

"Seasick." He chuckled. "I pray not, but if you are ill, your slave can tend to you."

"How gallant you are," she told him sweetly, her hand on the door latch. "I will have my goods packed by the middle of the afternoon. That will give us the chance to leave on the evening tide, if it is required."

"It probably won't be until tomorrow," he said. "No matter what, the captain cannot leave until he has his cargo loaded, and that cannot be completed in a day."

Olivia looked at him closely. "You are glad to be leaving here, aren't you?"

"You know my reasons," he replied.

"Some of them," she said before she let herself out of the room.

Rainaut remained staring at the place she had been; the two swords he held he ignored. He had strayed farther from his oaths and his Order than he had realized and only now was the enormity of his transgression becoming apparent to him. He blessed himself and started to pray, addressing his words to Maria for her intercession. But when he reached the formal salutation—o clemens, o pia, o dulcis Virgo Maria—he could not see any face but Olivia's and his heart was touched by despair.

*   *   *

Text of a letter from Niklos Aulirios to Doca Arrigo Benammo di Cruceclare.

From Sanza Pare, I take the liberty of addressing you directly on behalf of my mistress, Bondama Atta Olivia Clemens, to extend her sympathy and our own on the death of your son and heir Egidio. To learn of so unfortunate a development on the eve of this great Crusade must be doubly sorrowful for you, and surely my mistress joins with me in expressing condolence for this most sad of all news.

The church at Ognissanti offered prayers for him at first Mass this morning, which is how I came to know of his death; I have taken the liberty of arranging for five Masses to be said on his behalf, which is as my mistress would have done, had she been here. To lose so splendid a young man to nothing more than a mortified wound in the ankle is a great loss for any family. Yet such is the perfidy of bodily ills that none among us escape them but the dead.

To answer your inquiry of the other day, as far as I am aware, my mistress remains in Sidon, but now that Reis Richard and Reis Phillippe have sailed for the Holy Land at last, I trust it will not be long before she is able to see her new home and to be welcomed here by her staff, her neighbors, and the clergy. It is most lamentable that she will not have the felicity of meeting your son Egidio, as you suggested.

So great has my anxiety been for her welfare that I have sent messengers to those who own ships plying the waters between here and the Holy Land, to discover how quickly it might be arranged to carry Bondama Clemens home. With the Crusade underway at last, such travel is greatly restricted, and most of it is controlled by the Knights Hospitaler, which makes things especially difficult, for recently they have given preferential escort to clergy and other religious. Honorable widows like my mistress are relegated to one or two knights for escort, and such space in shipping that has not already been commandeered by order of the Hospitalers for more worthy pilgrims and more pious errands. My mistress, though doubtless well-served by her escort, is not in a position to request more assistance than what she is already receiving.

Should I or any part of the staff of Sanza Pare be able to assist or aid you in this time of grief, do us the compliment of sending word, and you may be sure your request will be filled at once. If you believe that a little time spent here might lessen your sorrow, you have only to inform me and the estate will be at your disposal. Do not fear that my mistress would countermand such orders; it is her way to keep to the ancient traditions of her gens, whose roots stretch back to the times of the Caesars. She has kept and upheld the old ways all her life. Had I not extended this offer to you, with all humility and *sincere intent, she would reprimand me herself at the first learning of it.*

Know that my prayers and sentiments are with you, and that your loss moves me and all of those of us who staff Sanza Pare. We respect your grief and share your mourning.

Niklos Aulirios

By my own hand on the 9th day of April in the Lord's Year 1191.

· 16 ·

Four days had passed since Ithuriel Dar had landed on Sicilia, but the disorder left in the wake of the departure of the Kings of England and France continued everywhere and as a result Dar had made little or no progress in that time.

"It's bad enough," he said to the innkeeper in Siracusa as they shared a plate of broiled fish that evening, "that the armies were as rapacious as they were, but now everyone is in complete confusion and there appears to be no end to it. First Reis Richard hectors all his men into ships the first break in the weather, and then Reis Phillippe, outraged that Richard had taken the lead, attempts the same thing. You would think that Etna and Stromboli had gone off at once."

"Two Kings are something like two volcanos," the innkeeper agreed as he pulled a bit more of the sweet white fish off the bone and popped it into his mouth. "The same temperament, the same grandeur."

"And the same ruin, by the look of things," said Dar, and immediately laughed to turn his remark to a joke. "But which is Etna and which Stromboli?"

"Reis Richard is Etna, here in the middle of things," said the innkeeper after giving the matter some thought, assisted by two generous swigs of the strong white wine made half a day's ride from the inn. "I think that Phillippe must be

Stromboli, sitting by himself in the sea, with little near him. Perhaps he is really Vesuvio."

"Vesuvio is over the water," said Dar, gesturing in a generally eastward direction.

"So are England and France," said the innkeeper, "or so the soldiers kept saying. Maybe it is the other way around, and Phillippe is Etna, with all of Sicilia around him, and Richard is Stromboli, out in the sea, like England. But Reis Richard has lands in France as well, which Phillippe covets. Of course." He had more fish and gestured philosophically with greasy fingers. "You might as well try to evacuate this city as move those damned armies of theirs."

Dar nodded, permitting himself another cautious sip of wine before he had more fish. "When will the ships be returning from the Holy Land? Is there any news? Have you heard?"

"They have to get there first. And once they are there, they have to unload and deploy. That will take some time, for there are so many of them. They say that Reis Richard is fighting on Cyprus. Why he should bother to do that when he wants to reclaim the Holy Sepulcher, I don't know."

"They say he wants a base," Dar said, repeating what he had heard through his travels. "Cyprus is the best for his purposes. It is ideally located and has thrown off the Byzantine yoke they wore. The Hospitalers already have part of Rhodes."

"Well, that's another thing Reis Phillippe can covet, isn't it?" He chuckled and nudged Dar with his elbow. "They aren't like you and me, are they? Kings don't covet their neighbors' goods and wives, or envy their good fortune, they covet whole countries and envy their armies and kingdoms." He drank down the rest of his wine and refilled his cup, offering the same to Dar, who reluctantly allowed the innkeeper to top his off. "But, I suppose, if what they say about Reis Richard is true, he might as well covet countries, since wives don't tempt him."

"But he's about to be married." Dar knew the rumors as well as anyone, but he wanted the innkeeper to continue to talk, in the hope of gleaning some information from the chaff of words.

"To that poor girl from Spain, yes. Doubtless there are

treaties and agreements and the rest of it to go along with her. It might be contingent upon heirs, in which case Reis Richard will have to put his pageboys aside or deputize one of his cousins. Still, who knows what the Spaniards are like, come to that. She might have some understanding already." He finished off the fish and wiped his hands on the rough, filthy cloth tied to his girdle. "Ehi! Arrigo! More food here. Don't be stingy this time." He reached for his cup and lifted it mockingly. "A happy bedding to Reis Richard and his Spanish Princess."

"Her name is Barengaria of Navarre," said Ithuriel Dar, doing his best not to sound offended.

"Whatever her name, seems to me she's got a poor bargain. Her family weren't thinking of her when they contracted with Richard, that's sure, no matter what contract they concluded." He looked up as his younger cook came up with a platter laden with more fish, small breads, onions and mushrooms, all covered in a pungent saffron-and-pepper sauce. "That's more like it."

Arrigo bowed once he had put the platter down. "Is there anything else, master?"

"Another jar of wine," said the innkeeper.

"If it is for me—" began Dar, only to be cut off by a dismissing gesture by the innkeeper.

"It is for the both of us, for the good of our souls, for it is in Scripture that wine is to be taken for the good of the body. It's in the Old Scripture, so it applies to Jews as well." He winked at Dar. "You're allowed wine with your fish, aren't you? Well, then." He grinned expansively, revealing several blackened or missing teeth. "Have all that you want."

Dar concealed a sigh and hoped he would keep a clear head through the evening. "You are most gracious," he said ironically, knowing it was true. There were some innkeepers who would not permit Jews to stay at their inns, let alone eat in them.

"Well, good fellowship is good fellowship, and after those damned men-at-arms with their camp followers and wives and God-knows-what-all carousing in here all the day and half the night, a sensible Jew is a treat." He indicated the improvised brace on one of the beams across the taproom. "They did that. And the dinner room is a shambles. I won't be able to use it until summer is over. Not only did they take half the carpenters on Sicilia with them, they made off with everything else. They took much of the timber, you know, and nails and hammers and any other tools they could find. They wanted to take the forge from the smithy, but it was too big to move. One of them made off with my best cleaver." He blessed himself, leaving grease spots on his shoulders. "But it's for the Holy Sepulcher, isn't it?"

Dar, who had a mouthful of fish, nodded vigorously.

"If you ask me, there's more going on than saving the Holy Sepulcher." The innkeeper wagged his finger at Dar. "You have eyes, Jew, and you show some sense."

"And some caution," Dar said pointedly, hoping the innkeeper might acquire some himself.

"But you can tell what is happening, can't you?" the innkeeper persisted. "Of course you can. You're capable of recognizing a lie when you're told one. Oh, that's not to say that some of those who've taken the Cross aren't inspired to aid Our Lord—though the priests say that He is in Heaven where *He* is supposed to aid *us,* not the other way around—but there are many who are eager for the adventure and plunder and glory." He belched. "And some are running away—from work, from families, from prison, it doesn't matter. I've had them all in this taproom, and I know what I know." He gave Dar a sudden challenging look, his stubbled chin jutting out and his hooked nose thrust forward.

"There is certainly some truth in what you say," Dar agreed carefully.

"God knows it better than I do," declared the innkeeper, his voice now quite loud.

A Hieronomite monk who had been sitting alone near the hearth making his required evening meal of two dried fish and a small loaf of bread, now looked up, his eyes narrowing as he watched the innkeeper.

"Then pray to God," said Dar, who was dismayed at the attention the monk was paying to their conversation. He had seen people stoned or burned for saying less critical things. "It is for God to guide us from error."

"Strange sentiments from a Jew," said the monk.

"What business is it of yours?" demanded the innkeeper,

his face darkening with choler. "This good Jew and I were discussing things privately. I was not talking to you."

"You were speaking of religious matters, and that concerns me," said the monk, rising from his solitary place and coming toward them.

"We were speaking about Crusaders," said the innkeeper without any change in demeanor. "That's not a religious matter so far as I'm concerned. They were little more than rowdy hooligans in this inn; their conduct was no different than I'd expect of pirates from Tripoli. When they reclaim Jerusalem, then I will believe they are religious." He put his hands on his hips and stared at the monk. "I've said the same to my confessor; he has been here through the winter, too, and he knows I speak truth."

The monk blessed himself. "If you have suffered any abuse at the hands of the Crusaders, then God will reward you for your pains." He lowered his eyes. "I am Fraire Eleus, and I am bound for the Holy Land. It is my intention to join the Hieronomite community near Ascalon."

"There's bound to be fighting at Ascalon," said the innkeeper.

"All the more reason to be there, to pray for those wounded and fallen in battle," said Fraire Eleus. "I had hoped to reach Sicilia before the two armies embarked, but the same storms that held them here all winter kept me at Fraxinetum."

"There are Islamites in Fraxinetum," said the innkeeper. "More shame to France."

Fraire Eleus blessed himself. "Yes, there are Islamites in Fraxinetum. There are Islamites in most of Spain. There are Islamites in Narbonne. If we are not careful, there will be Islamites in Roma and Paris before Jesus Christ comes again."

"And so we take half the unhanged criminals in France and England, put crosses on their arms, and tell them to have at any green banner they see?" the innkeeper asked. He pulled more fish off the bone and bit into it. "Well?"

"Something must be done," said Fraire Eleus.

"Possibly. It appears to me that this is more Byzantium's fight than ours, but we're all Christians, aren't we? Why should the Byzantines have to turn back Islam all by themselves?" The innkeeper laughed aloud at his own humor.

Fraire Eleus shook his head. "You have permitted the experiences of this last winter to blind you to the real enemy. It is understandable, I agree, that you would harbor unkind thoughts for those who have behaved poorly while at your establishment, and certainly if they have caused damage and not supplied the repair, they have acted improperly, but . . . God is not to be mocked, Bonsier Innkeeper."

"Who's mocking God, I'd like to know?" the innkeeper asked of the ceiling. "I'm not. This Jew isn't. You're not. The Islamites pray to God five times a day, every day. Reis Richard says his army is for the honor of God. Reis Phillippe says his men are champions of God. No, it is not God Who is mocked."

Ithuriel Dar wished he could find a reason to leave the inn at once, but none suggested itself. He had more of the wine, and then realized that he would need his wits about him. "Innkeeper, a little bread?" He reached for one of the breads on the platter with the fish.

"Help yourself, help yourself. Have the onions, too. They're one thing the Crusaders didn't raid out of the garden, though they took enough of the rest." He grabbed one of the breads himself, tore it in half and started to sop up the sauce with it. "It's good."

"It is," Dar agreed, following his host's example. "The matter is," he said, turning the conversation—he hoped—from the Crusades to the information he sought, "that I have been asked to meet and accompany a widow returning from the Holy Land."

"Another Jew?" asked the innkeeper with a conspiratorial wink.

"No; she is the widow of a Roman noble." He remembered watching her on the wharf at Tyre and a slight smile played over his features. "She has been trying to find passage from Sidon to Rhodes or Cyprus, and from there back to Roma."

"Not easily done, I'd say," remarked the innkeeper. "Not in these times. Pilgrims and clergy and knights from all over

Europe bustling to and from the Holy Land. One widow, pah! Who cares for one widow?" He glanced at Fraire Eleus. "Not that the rest aren't important."

"You are a very worldly man," Fraire Eleus said, his manner becoming more reserved.

"Well, yes, I should hope so," said the innkeeper. "Someone has to look after the world, Fraire. You're looking after the soul, the Church is looking after salvation in the next world, so it's left to simple fellows like me to tend to the world and all that's in it. Have some more fish, won't you?" This last was addressed to Ithuriel Dar.

"Much appreciated," Dar mumbled as he listened to the innkeeper.

"You mayn't believe it, Fraire, but you need us worldly fellows. We have our uses, you know. You might be more concerned with your prayers, but it's nice to have a warm hearth to say them in front of, isn't it?" He winked outrageously. "Those soldiers, too, most of them were out to make their mark in this world, not the next. Give them a chestful of gold from some Islamite's house and they will let the rest take care of itself."

"You demean them," said Fraire Eleus, shaking his head slowly, ponderously.

"Not I," corrected the innkeeper. "I have no reason to be in sympathy with them. I tell you what I have seen and heard; if it displeases you, that's unfortunate, but it doesn't make what I say less true."

Fraire Eleus sketched a blessing in the innkeeper's direction. "I will pray for you, and hope that God brings you to the light."

"If He does, well and good. If He doesn't, then I will muddle along as I've done before." He picked up one of the sections of bread and squeezed it between his thumb and fingers, watching it ooze sauce. "Excellent," he approved before he ate it. As he chewed, he blessed himself.

Dar wanted to move away from his place with the innkeeper, but was now convinced that if he attempted the move without some explanation, it would draw more, not less attention to his errand. He helped himself to two more onions and tried to be inconspicuous. He still did not know what he hoped to learn about Olivia, and he hesitated to write to Niklos Aulirios until he had something useful to report. "Superb sauce," he said to the innkeeper, to account for his silence.

"I was lucky in the cook. I bought him from a bishop on Sardinia. He had an estate there, where he went when he wanted to get away from Pisa. It was as luxurious as a Persian brothel and as secluded as a hermit's cell."

Fraire Eleus looked offended. "This is worse than blasphemy."

"Hardly that," said the innkeeper. "God witness all I say, it was the way the bishop lived when he was not with his flock. He kept dozens of slaves to care for his guests and to tend to all their wants." He smirked. "A most lascivious man, under his bishop's raiment."

"And how did you happen to be there?" asked Fraire Eleus, clearly skeptical.

"I was sent for, because of the wine I serve here. I have an agreement with the vintner, as did my father and his father before him. The bishop wanted to purchase some of the older barrels. I traded them for the cook, and I believe I had the better bargain." He laughed aloud. "Not to say that the bishop didn't get good wine—he did, but surely he drank it all before the year was out, and I still own the cook."

Dar almost choked on the onions, but managed to say, "How long have you had the cook?"

"Eight years," said the innkeeper. "I'm lucky he's a slave and not a bondsman, or one of those Kings would have commandeered him away from me. As it was, I set the price too high and neither would pay it."

"Do you mean that Reis Richard and Reis Phillippe ate here?" Fraire Eleus asked. "Here, in a common inn?"

"Of course not," said the innkeeper with a disgusted snort. "But their men did, and their officers did, and the knights carried tales. Each King sent their factotums to make an offer for him, but—" He shrugged.

Fraire Eleus gave a ghost of a chuckle. "You almost persuaded me, but I know it must be false, your story. Reis Richard or Reis Phillippe sending their factotums to you indeed! I wonder how many have listened to your tale and thought it true?" He gave the innkeeper a long scrutiny. "I will not forget you, nor will I forget what you have said. The time may come when it will serve me well."

"You want to frighten me?" the innkeeper asked incredulously. "You think that you have heard heresy in my inn? I have said what all the others in Siracusa have said, what all those on Sicilia have said since those two quarrelsome armies arrived."

"They are doing God's work, quarrelsome or not," said Fraire Eleus.

"Then they have a strange way of showing it," was the innkeeper's belligerent response.

Dar reached over and plucked at the landlord's sleeve. "It might be wisest to—"

"I will not be mealy-mouthed for a cowl," said the innkeeper implacably. "If he thinks that his God was served by the soldiers here, let him repair the damage they did." He flung the contents of his cup at the ruined beam. "Damnation on all scoundrels hiding behind crosses, that's what I say. And God would second me, if He were asked about it."

Fraire Eleus retreated a few paces more, then folded his arms into the sleeves of his habit and lowered his head. "I will pray for you," he said before falling silent.

"And that will fix the beam, won't it?" bellowed the innkeeper. He swung around, facing Ithuriel Dar. "What do you make of this, Jew?"

"I hope it will not bring you trouble. Or me." He waited while the innkeeper considered what he had said. "I want only to find Bondama Clemens and see her returned to her home. I want no part of the Crusade. I am a shipowner, and I cannot command my own ships because they are being used to carry the families of the men-at-arms to the Holy Land; there is no payment for this usage, and whatever happens to my ship is my expense."

"It appears you have as much complaint against the Crusades as I do," said the innkeeper. "To say nothing of the widow you are supposed to find. She'll be fortunate to get out of the Holy Land with all her skin, if you take my meaning." He filled his cup once more. "All for the reward in Heaven, is it?"

Dar decided to make one last attempt. "Leaving Sidon, how long should it take a ship to reach here?"

"It depends on the weather, and any stops along the way. And pirates, of course. The pirates are about the only ones to turn a profit these days. Chances are that a ship out of Sidon will stop at Cyprus or Crete, one of the two. If the fighting's still going on on Cyprus, they may make for Crete. There's more pirates there, but it's closer." He peered at the far wall, as if he expected to find an answer written there. "But, if the fighting's over, Cyprus is safer. We'll say Cyprus. From Sidon to Cyprus to here. That would be . . . oh"—he beetled his brow—"twenty-four days, more or less. As much as thirty, as few as twenty-two. It depends on the situation in Cyprus, doesn't it?"

Dar, whose ship had taken nineteen days to go from Tyre to Ostia, nodded. "Yes; it all depends on Cyprus."

*   *   *

Text of a letter from Aueric de Jountuil to his confessor on Rhodes.

To the most worthy and reverend priest, my spiritual father, Meyeul, my greetings and hope of forgiveness for my long silence. It was not my intention to neglect you while I have been carrying out my duties as a Hospitaler, but there has been so little to report that I have been reluctant to disturb you with letters that have no content. As it is, I am making use of the scribe accompanying us on our journey to Cyprus, and from there it is my intention to return to Rhodes for a time, not only to receive any new assignment that might be granted me, but to restore my inner tranquility that has been lacking in my days of late.

It is not that I chafe at the obligation of providing escort, for that is the purpose of the Order, but I am of the opinion that there is no reason for us to spend our time with the Roman widow known as Bondama Olivia Clemens. She is fully capable of fending for herself, and to have to protect her when there are many others more worthy of our aid who languish because we have this widow to tend to is galling to me.

I am not in agreement with my comrade-at-arms, Sier Valence Rainaut, who seems to have fallen under the spell of the woman—and there is no denying that she is a woman of considerable impact—and who is forever finding reasons why we cannot leave her. I know he has remained true to his oath, but I fear for him, because he is so much in the thrall of this widow. If ever a woman exercised a fatal fascination for a man, it is this widow who has captivated Sier Valence.

My other concern for Sier Valence is more worrisome, if that is possible. He has of late complained of an ailment that has changed the nature of his skin. He now has three patches of skin—one on his face, one on his shoulder and one on his arm—that have the white look of burn scars, but where he has never been burned. The hair grows poorly there if at all, and feels scaly to the touch. He has become sensitive to light; bright light hurts his eyes and causes him to have terrible pains in his head. While he has not been examined by a physician, I know he is worried that he might have been tainted with leprosy. It is imperative that we learn as soon as possible what afflicts him so that proper steps may be taken. Should he have become a leper, those of us who have been with him must pray that we have escaped the contagion. I beseech you to pray for me and to beg God to spare me from this scourge. I have upheld my oath and I am faithful to God and my calling; there is no reason for God to punish me as He may be punishing Sier Valence.

It is a terrible thing to be a leper. Only those whose lives have been debauched can count themselves fortunate if this disease comes to them. I have placed no adoration before God, I have sought no prize but the service of God. I am not like Sier Valence, who does not know if God or this Roman widow is more dear to him. Let me be spared. Let God spare Sier Valence if He is able. I ask you to pray for me. I beg you to request an examination of Sier Valence as soon as we reach Rhodes.

In all things I am your obedient son in God's eyes,

Sier Aueric de Jountuil
Knights Hospitaler of St. John,
Jerusalem
By the hand of the scribe Arrin, on the Feast of the Martyr
Sabas the Goth, in the Lord's Year 1191.

· 17 ·

Until the second pirate ship appeared, they had a chance, though a slim one, to get away: as the second saettia nosed in from the west, the first picked up the speed of the oarsmen, so that the long, narrow ship seemed to leap through the water toward them. The tarida, built for trade and heavily laden, had neither the speed nor the maneuverability of the two pirate ships, and the captain, a hatchet-nosed Greek from Hydros, began to swing his boat around to take the attack.

"You must not do this!" Rainaut cried out as the tarida changed direction. "You haven't a chance."

"I haven't a chance running, either," he growled. "At least this way the worst that will happen to us is slavery, and—" He stopped, seeing the rage in Rainaut's face.

"Not for us. Not for Hospitalers, nor the woman we escort. You must fight." He reached for the tiller arm to restrain the captain.

"*Stop!*" roared the captain, bringing the flat of his short sword down on Rainaut's shoulder. "You touch anything else on this ship, and I promise you, you'll be over the rail for the sharks."

"We have our duty," said Rainaut through clenched teeth as he tried to flex his arm.

"And I have mine," said the captain abruptly. "Leave me."

The two saettias were closing quickly; Rainaut knew he

had very little time to warn Olivia and de Jountuil. He turned on his heel and strode toward the rear of the ship, aware of all the sailors around him hurrying onto the deck. He broke into a run.

"Who are they?" Olivia asked as he approached. She was wrapped in a long mantel over her bliaud, and she carried a dagger in her right hand. She was pale and still a little shaky from her continuing seasickness.

"Pirates. We're not far from Cyprus. You can see it, over there to the left." He took her by the shoulders. "They're going to board. They want captives for slaves and for ransom."

She shook her head. "No."

"I am sworn, as is de Jountuil, to defend you until death. I will do so, if it will save you." He cleared his throat. "If you require something else of me . . . ?"

She looked at him. "You mean the quick and merciful sword instead of slavery and worse? No, thank you. I'd rather take my chances with the water, and you know how much I love the water." She was not able to laugh, but her expression was heartening to him. "Water, at least, is clean."

"Whatever you decide, you must hurry. They'll be on us in less than—" There was fear in him, cold and shameful, like something small and hard under his sword belt. He could hear an echo of his fear in the voices of the sailors.

Olivia had been staring at the approaching ships. "They have beaks," she said quietly, hardly audible in the noise and clamor around them.

"What?" Rainaut shouted, unable to hear her over the din.

"The ships coming," she said more loudly. "They have beaks. The corvus, like the old Roman ships. They're going to break this ship apart, and then pick the bones." She shuddered in spite of herself. "There's no choice then. They're going to ram us. We go into the water, like it or not."

Her last words were drowned in a howl of anger and dismay as the oarsmen caught sight of the enormous metal beaks of the two saettias, and the captain swore comprehensively as he realized what was going to happen to his ship. The confusion, which had been under minimal control, erupted into chaos.

"We must go over the side. Now. Before they reach us," yelled Olivia, trying to make herself heard as the ships hurtled together.

"Can you swim?" Rainaut shouted, knowing how seasick she had been, and afraid of her answer.

"No," Olivia replied. "Not very well." There was no time to explain the reason for this. "But I'll try."

Rainaut took a quick look over his shoulder. "Come. Now." He looked about the milling sailors. Nowhere could he see another black Maltese Cross. "Where's de Jountuil?"

"I don't know," Olivia answered. "I haven't seen him."

Three of the deckhands ran past them, one of them screaming in Greek for the Archangel Michael to come to his aid.

"De Jountuil! *De Jountuil!*" Rainaut hollered, but had no answer. "Aueric de Jountuil!"

From the front of the ship came many, louder cries, and a dozen of the oarsmen slaves strove to pull in their enormous oars before they were broken by the closing pirate ships. The tarida began to wallow as the tiller was released.

"There's no time," said Olivia, leaning close to Rainaut to be heard. "We must go now."

"Yes." He helped her over the rail, making sure she could hold on while he joined her.

A shudder, the first indication of impact, of the rending corvus, passed down the length of the tarida, the wood of the ship just starting to moan with strain.

"Hurry!" yelled Rainaut as he shoved Olivia hard, sending her falling toward the froth of the wake. Then he leaped, arms windmilling, as he plunged into water.

Strange sights and sounds assailed him as he plummeted beneath the surface. The undersides of all three ships hung like enormous fish above him, and the movement of the oars in the water was like watching playful schools of minnows. He looked wildly for Olivia, and was appalled that he could not find her. Finally, his chest hot with lack of air, his arms aching, he broke the surface just as the side of the tarida broke under the onslaught of the beak of the first saettia. He was tossed about as the sea rushed and gurgled at the sudden opening.

Olivia struggled to the surface, her efforts sluggish, feeling the water leech away her strength with every movement. If only it were night, so that she would have some protection from the sun, at least. Her shoes, with their precious lining of Roman earth, were growing wet, the sustaining bond failing. She felt dazed, sickened. Only her dread of lying helpless on the floor of the ocean, deprived of every sense but consciousness, kept her from succumbing to the merciless combination of water and sun. Weakly, but with iron determination, she began to paddle away from the three ships toward the distant outline of the hills of Cyprus.

"Olivia!" Rainaut shouted, knowing he could not be heard over the enormous furor of battle. He thought he could see her a little way off, making scant headway in the churning water. "De Jountuil!" He tried to make out the identities of those he saw fighting on the canted deck of the tarida, but could not. His eyes stung, his face hurt, and the shine of sun on water gave him a ferocious pain through his temples. Reluctantly he started to swim away from the battle. There was nothing he could do, he realized. He had only his short sword with him. The tarida was taking on water fast and it would not be long before those aboard her would have to surrender to the pirates or go into the water. Praying that Olivia truly had got away, that de Jountuil was not trapped aboard the tarida, he started to swim in the direction of Cyprus, pausing now and again to look for other swimmers.

He had covered half the distance from the wreck of the tarida to the shore when he saw someone floundering in the water not far from him. Though he was nearly exhausted himself, he changed direction, determined to give aid. When he saw that the other swimmer was Olivia, he was jolted with renewed strength and purpose. He wasted no breath in calling to her, but increased the reach of his stroke as he tried to reach her.

Behind them, there was a ragged shout from the pirates of the two saettias as the tarida slipped under the waves. Long grappling hooks on heavy lines were broken out and tossed at the sinking ship, securing the wreckage for towing.

Olivia's face was sun-scorched, the skin of her cheeks and forehead beginning to blister, her lips cracked and peeling.

She opened her eyes with difficulty as she felt someone grab her mantel and turn her onto her back. Painful though it was, she did her best to smile. "Valence."

Rainaut could not conceal his shock. "God and the Saints, Olivia."

"Those of my blood . . . sun and water . . ." She swallowed hard, but could not speak again. Her strength, usually greater than others knew, was failing her rapidly.

Rainaut kissed her brow. "I'll help," he said, hoping his sense of futility was not too apparent in his voice. "I'll pull you to land, Olivia."

"If . . ." She coughed. "If the night . . ."

He made no sense of what she said, but replied, "We'll be on the shore by nightfall." As he said it, he consoled himself with the knowledge that they would be on the shore or they would have drowned. Cyprus seemed a long way off. The body of an oarsman slave bobbed in the waves, not far from them. Rainaut saw it with foreboding. He worked to rig a sling improvised from the wide silk-and-leather girdle that she wore; he passed it across her back and under her arms, praying that it would not give way.

"Thank . . . for trying," Olivia said, her voice hardly more than a croak.

Desperately, hopelessly, he pulled the sling over his shoulder and started once again to swim, permitting himself the reward of looking at the distant island once every ten strokes. He made himself move automatically, the way he did when he drilled with sword and battle-axe. He shut out fatigue and pain and exhaustion and kept to the steady, repetitive action, permitting the strain to daze him so that he would not have to feel his body as he pressed it to and beyond its limits.

When he felt his feet scrape on rocks, he thought he had gone mad. Then he banged his hand on another rock and shouted aloud. Slowly he struggled to his feet, the water coming no higher than his waist. "God," he whispered.

Olivia sagged against him, all but unconscious.

His hands were still unwieldy as he tried to untie the girdle that bound them together. He could not bring himself to look at her burned face, but he spoke to her in a rough undervoice as he worked the knots loose. "We're on . . . a spit of land. At low tide, we'd be on the beach. It's still a long way to the shore, but we can walk it now. We don't have to swim anymore. We're safe, Olivia." He paused to bless himself. "I thank God for our deliverance, and I pray to be worthy of His care."

Rainaut's words reached Olivia as if from a great distance, as if called down an echoing well. She was so completely enervated that to lift her hand was a greater effort than she could summon. Her skin hurt as if she had been rubbed all over with nettles and coarse salt, and her face and hands tormented her. She tried to speak, but her throat was parched and her mouth too raw for the words to come.

Half-dragging, half-carrying Olivia, Rainaut made his way along the long, partially submerged spit toward the shore. He was afraid to stop for rest, because he doubted he would be able to move again once he halted. The westering sun glared down on them and made purple shadows on the sides of the Cypriot hills. "Just a little more," he panted. "A little more. The beach is up ahead. A little way. A few more steps." He spoke as much to himself as to her. "Almost there. Look. Almost there." His legs ached, his thighs quivered with each step he took, and he had to concentrate fiercely to keep from stumbling.

Then, miraculously, they were on the beach, in the shade of an outcropping of dark rock. It was cool, out of both sun and wind, and far enough from the water that the sand underfoot was dry.

For a moment, Rainaut strove to help Olivia to lie down with some semblance of comfort; then he collapsed at her side, his eyes closing as he fell.

It was night when he came to his senses, awakened by the litany of pain in his body. He groaned as he started to sit up, his back and shoulders so stiff and filled with hurt that there was no position he could find that brought him ease or relief. A relentless hunger competed with his agony for attention.

"Valence?" Her voice was hardly more than a whisper. "Valence?"

"Olivia." He turned, wincing, toward her. "Are you . . ."

"Over here," she said in the same breathless voice.

"Where?" It was a clear but moonless night and the hours in the full glare of the sun had taken their toll; he could hardly make out the shapes of the large rocks in the starlight—Olivia he could not see at all.

She touched his shoulder. "I'm here." The weakness she heard in her own speech vexed her. "We're . . . alive."

"On Cyprus," he added, hoping it was true. Without thinking, he reached out for her and drew her close. To his surprise, she resisted him. "There is no sin."

"Sin?" She let her head rest on his shoulder. "That means little to me, Sier Valence."

"Then why—" His lips rested against her sunburned forehead, and he kissed her there, not as lightly as he had intended. "Olivia, why?"

It was always difficult, she told herself as she remembered the other times, and the variety of responses she had encountered. "I am not what you think I am," she began at last, her eyes fixed on the middle distance. "I am not like you."

"You're Roman," he added, hoping to make her laugh.

"Yes," she said seriously. "I am Roman." The next would be the test, when she would know absolutely whether he would accept her. She recalled others who had laughed, or upbraided, or were repulsed. "I am Roman in the way the Caesars are."

"Old patrician family," he said, wondering why she was telling him this, and why now.

"Yes," she said slowly, feeling her way. "I cried *Ave* to Claudius and Nero and Galba and Otho and Vitellius and Vespasianus. I . . . I was condemned to death by Vespasianus."

"The sun has addled your wits," Rainaut murmured, pity cooling his passion.

"The sun has hurt me," she corrected him, with some of her asperity returning. "But my wits are fine. I am trying to tell you what . . . what I need of you. I want you to understand why my love is . . . as it is." If only she could still weep, she thought. Tears would excuse so much. But since she had wakened in her tomb, her eyes remained dry.

He adjusted his arms so that he held her more securely. "Rest, Olivia. In the morning—"

"In the morning, my face and arms will blacken and blister, and I will be powerless to move, without your help, your love, tonight." She spoke with deliberate bluntness. "I am wholly at your mercy, Sier Valence. My . . . life is in your hands."

He hushed her with half-words and gentle nudges that were not quite kisses. "It will be better, once we've rested and eaten."

"Yes," she said with strange intensity.

"I will not let you come to harm." He kissed her hair, then rested his scarred cheek on the top of her head. "I will stay with you."

"It will not be enough," she said softly, as much to herself as to him.

Rainaut felt her tremble under his large, square hands. "I have sworn to have no love before the love of God, Olivia. Perdition waits for those who set aside oaths made to God." He wanted, suddenly, to convince her; for the first time the words sounded hollow to him.

"If you will not let me love you, I will be as good as dead by sunset tomorrow." There was nothing of wooing about her. She spoke as if she were discussing mild weather. "You are my salvation, if I am to be saved."

"That's blasphemy," whispered Rainaut, trying to feel shocked without success.

"It is truth." She lifted her face to him, looking up into the hidden blue of his eyes. "Valence, I do not lie, I do not blaspheme."

As part of his mind searched for a rebuke or an argument, his mouth met hers: disputes vanished as their kiss deepened. How was it that he had never realized that she was made for loving him? Why had he never seen how sweetly her body moved and fit with his? Or had he known it and denied it? His arms tightened and he pressed close to her, hating their garments for being between them.

With both arms around him now, Olivia began to feel her surge of desire and she welcomed it, welcomed him. It had been so long since she had experienced the enormity of love that she almost broke away from him.

He ended their kiss but did not release her. "I will be damned for this," he said, wishing he could see her face. Nothing had ever moved him as she did, no woman before had shown him that the entire world was less than a kiss.

Slowly, awed by her, he began to caress her. His hands were tentative, for he knew how badly the sun had burned her. Yet there was more than concern making him hesitate; he had never wanted to know a woman with her body before, had never before sought the soul in the flesh.

"Here," she whispered, loosening her clothes. With Khouri she had been deliberately tantalizing; with Rainaut, she was oddly shy, knowing she was more vulnerable to him because of his deep tenderness for her.

He stopped her. "Let me. Please."

She dropped her hands, palms up, to her sides, to lie on the soft, cool sand. When she trembled, it was not from cold.

Rainaut could not speak as he opened the front of her bliaud. The lacings were not entirely dry, and the chilly damp feel of the narrow silken cords startled him. He gave his full attention to the lacings, taking care not to rip the cloth as he pulled the lacings free. He was breathing a bit faster now, as he opened the front of her bliaud. With a soft sound, partly of protest, partly of expectation, he slid his hands through the opening, searching.

"Wait," she said urgently. "Valence, listen, just a moment." The words came in a rush. "I need something of you, something from you with your love."

"Anything," he said, his fingers making their first discoveries, his ardor increasing. "You have me now. Always."

He was not as skilled a lover as Khouri had been, but there was more fervor in him, more wonder, than Khouri would ever experience. Olivia was shaken with Rainaut's exultation, with the joyous frenzy that changed his caresses from hesitant to eager, that transformed his deference to recklessness. In her weakened state, she could not respond with the full range of passion that stirred at the core of her being, yet she was able to meet his desire with her own, to reach far beyond the increasing rapture of their entwined, united bodies to the melding of their very souls.

What sustenance she took from him as they moved together was as much from their joining as from his blood; the fulfillment they attained nourished them both.

It was some time before either could speak. It was only after a long, leisurely kiss that Rainaut finally said, "You are worth damnation, Olivia," as he stared down into her eyes. "Not all the Hosts of Heaven could keep me from you now."

"All the Hosts of Heaven are formidable opposition," she said, troubled behind her smile.

"You are dearer to me than redemption and—"

She put her fingers on his lips, stopping his words. "Don't. Don't make loving you a contest. You are not a prize to be won by me or by God, you are Valence Rainaut, and Valence Rainaut is my lover and my love."

"Thanks be to God and all the Saints in the calendar," said Rainaut, catching her hand in his and holding her in a suddenly tight embrace.

"No," Olivia said, shaking her head once. "You need thank no one but yourself, and for your own sake."

He laughed aloud. "More blasphemy. Or is that heresy?" His lips were gentler now, and he was willing to let her rouse him, to give over to her the finding of new pleasures and greater joys. Twice he stopped her to work his own magic on her, to seek out the hidden treasures of her body, to revel in the glory of loving her. The feel, the scent, the taste of her filled his being. Nothing he had known before had summoned so much from within him; no woman had shown him a fruition of such ineffable splendor.

Olivia, lying on the length of his body, wished again that she could cry—but this time, for jubilation.

*　　*　　*

A note from the jester Fauvin to Prince John, written in English.

To my most respected and reverend Prince, your unfortunate servant sends greetings and regards to you from the island called Cyprus, upon the occasion of your brother's occupation of it.

From what Reis Richard has said, it is his intention to sell this place to the Poor Knights of the Temple. The Hospitalers have their part of Rhodes, and this way, the Templars will have their own island, too. Reis Richard has not yet mentioned what he intends to do with the money he will acquire from this sale. Doubtless it has not yet crossed his mind.

Princess Barengaria has arrived with your Mother Eleanor, who has declared that she wishes to see the marriage of Reis Richard and his betrothed as soon as it may be arranged. So the day for the Mass and the feast has been set for the twelfth, and already Reis Richard has ordered a grand entertainment for everyone. It is said that the food and drink will be served for three days and nights without stop, that dancers will dance and musicians will play and sing all that time. My feet ache at the very thought. There will be masques and mock battles and everything that a bride could possibly want for her wedding festivities, with one possible exception, and the pages are not going to say anything to the little Spaniard.

In conquering the island, Reis Richard has come upon several bands of pirates. Most of them have been flayed or hanged or had their hands cut off. There are some lepers who have been sent back to their caves to rot away alone. Also there were a few survivors of a recent pirate battle found, one of whom is a Hospitaler and the widow he escorts. Two oarsmen, slaves from Antioch, were also found, as well as one of two cooks. Sadly, he has damaged his arm and the physicians have said that it cannot be saved; he must let them cut it off or be dead in a week. There were also a small group of survivors of one of the winter storms found on the south side of the island, living in a small village and tending goats. Until Isaac accepts surrender, the complete search of Cyprus is not complete and there are certainly more unexpected inhabitants. It is rumored that there is a community of monks at the crest of one of the highest peaks, and that they live in cells and practice a Christian rite so ancient that the Copts know nothing of it. You might find it interesting, my Prince; you are so curious about so many things.

Word has it that the Islamites are preparing to meet our forces in summer. From what I have seen of this place, I am not pleased at the thought. The days already are bright and hot, and it is only May. The people here say that the summer *days are like ovens, and the rocks hum in the heat. Already some of the knights and men-at-arms have suffered various complaints because of the heat. While it is not possible to discard mail before a battle, some of them would like lighter armor than what they must wear. A few have the flux and we have been warned that it will increase as the days get hotter. Flux is never to be taken lightly, but flux in armor is as grisly a thought as putrescent wounds.*

I doubt anyone has mentioned it in regular dispatches, but there have been some difficulties with our men raiding local villages, both for goods and for women. Three knights especially were accused of rape. Reis Richard has excused them of this crime, but there are Cypriots who are displeased with our men, and who have no reason to want to help them. If the Crusade goes poorly, I fear for the safety of our knights at the hands of such villagers. Not that I blame them. Two of the women were still girls, and they are ruined for life. No man on Cyprus will have them, they cannot become nuns because they are no longer virgins, and their families do not have enough to support them the rest of their lives. All that, because three knights were bored and wanted a little sport. These villagers are not their serfs, Cyprus is not their fiefdom; they had no right to take the girls, no matter what Reis Richard has said.

Queen Eleanor has established her small household in as lavish a style as is possible here. She says it is to show Barengaria honor; I suspect it is to keep the Spanish Princess in everyone's mind. As a mother, Queen Eleanor has always indulged her favorite son in whatever he wished, but this time she is adamant.

I have met Barengaria of Navarre. I have performed for her a few times, though I am getting too old for such tricks. She is a lovely, quiet creature, something like a bird trained to sit on the hand. She does not speak much—her command of French is not very good—but she watches everything, and often she prays. Poor Princess, to be dragged away from her family to chase a bridegroom over half the world in the company of his mother. I hope your brother can forget himself long enough to do well by Barengaria. She is fascinated by him, and if he will only be husband to her as well as King, she may be content.

When we leave Cyprus, I will send you word again. As far

*as I can determine, Reis Richard has not incurred more debts
with France since he reached Cyprus, and perhaps the money
from the Templars will be used to reduce what is owed, though
the rumor is that there are other plans for the sum. May God
guide and protect you, my Prince, and give you strength to
persevere.*

Fauvin

*By my own hand, on Cyprus, the 8th of May, the Lord's
Year 1191.*

· 18 ·

Midnight had passed but the roistering continued un-
checked. From galleries and rooftops, banners with the
leopards of England and the Pegasus of the Templars floated
on the warm night breeze. All of Limassol celebrated the
marriage of Richard of England to Barengaria of Navarre.
Musicians and acrobats and jugglers and jesters vied
with one another for the attention and coins of the crowds.
The chapel of Saint George was bright with candles, and the
sounds of chanting could occasionally be heard through the
revelry.

"Templars, Templars," said Rainaut to Olivia as he
looked out the window to the street below. "Gui de
Lusignan is here in company with a good part of the Order,
if the streets are any indication." He stood half in the room's
deep shadow, half in the torchlight from the street which
made the scarlike part of his face seem inflamed. "It
wouldn't be wise for you to go out, not with the Templars
about in such number."

"And you? What of you?" She had been assigned a room
on the other side of the inn from his, but she had not set foot
in it.

"I must go out. Reis Richard has done me the honor of inviting me to watch his mother's musicians perform." He held up a hand to silence her. "One of the pages will come for me soon. It would be unwise for me to refuse. It is bad enough that we were shipwrecked, but to have Sier Aueric missing . . ." His words trailed off to nothing.

"How long do you think this will go on?" Olivia asked, gesturing toward the street.

"All night. Another day as well, perhaps. Richard is out to show everyone how he is in the world; he will not be a vassal of Reis Phillippe." He rubbed his hands together. "I feel as if I ought to put on armor, the way they're all behaving."

"Drunk and capricious, you mean?" Olivia asked in a level tone. "You'd be spoiling for a fight if you did that. Cote and surcote, that's all you need. If there were any way you could leave your sword behind, I'd suggest it."

Rainaut sighed. "Of course." He stared across the dark room at her. "I would rather be here with you."

She smiled but shook her head. "Remember what I told you: what I am, you will become if you continue as my lover. It is hard enough that you have forsworn your oath for me—"

"I did that gladly," Rainaut interrupted her. "From Hell I will thank God for you." He came toward her, reaching out to her. "Olivia, as soon as we may, we'll be gone from here. You and I. The two of us. The rest doesn't matter."

"I hope you never change your mind," she said quietly, feeling his arms close around her.

"Why would I do that, when I have already given up all hope of Heaven and salvation for you?" He kissed her, tantalizing them both with promises. "I have traded one Communion for another," he whispered as they drew apart. He let go of her reluctantly. "I will not be any longer than necessary. I must show myself"—he indicated his family arms—"as the rest will tonight. I will also have to face the Master of the Hospitalers, or whoever is his deputy here on Cyprus. I cannot remain in the Order now." There was a tinge of regret in his voice.

"Must you do so at once?" Olivia asked, sensing again his keen sense of failure.

He nodded. "There is no purpose in delay. I have an obligation to my House and God, as well as to the Order, not to disgrace the Hospitalers." He took the edge of her long sleeve and kissed it. "I wish I could bring you with me safely, but you see what it is like out there. Even the harlots and camp-followers are staying off the streets, for good reason."

Olivia accepted his decision. "As you wish, then." She went to the corner, to the low bed. "I will wait for your return."

Suddenly and unexpectedly he grinned. "I will hurry," he vowed, bowing to her as he left the room.

The streets were as crowded this late night as they were at the height of market day. Everywhere the leopard banner of England flew with the red cross of the Templars above the vast celebration. It was not easy to make progress through the streets because of the constant jostling of the fighting men gathered to witness the wedding of Reis Richard to Barengaria of Navarre. The two names resounded along the narrow streets, occasionally with sly jokes added to the good wishes.

Rainaut had covered half the distance to Richard's headquarters when he came upon a troupe of jugglers performing with trained dogs. There were more than two dozen Templars gathered around the performers, all with the Pegasus badge on their shoulders; eight wore personal arms as well, though three were abated with a bar sinister. Most of the Templars were speaking Spanish, urging the jugglers to toss daggers instead of balls in the air.

"Here's an Angel!" offered one of the Templars, holding up a large gold coin. "Toss my mace, and it's yours."

The juggler pretended not to understand.

"Go ahead," urged another. "Take the money."

Two of the jugglers looked around uneasily, sensing the dangerous mood of their audience.

"For the honor of Sancho of Navarre," said one of the Templars, throwing two silver coins onto the ground. "Do not refuse us."

All four jugglers stopped performing and came together in the center of the circle. One of them spoke hesitantly in French. "We cannot do this. We are not allowed to handle weapons. It is against the law for us to do what you ask." He said this deferentially, his head lowered in respect to the knights, his manner as servile as the lowest slave's.

One of the Templars stepped into the circle. "Here. I say you will take this dagger and you will juggle it, along with three others. I say you will do this while we watch, that way you will not have to worry about breaking the law." He had put one hand on his hip just above the hilt of his dagger; now he drew it and held it out to the juggler, making it a challenge.

The Templars shouted approval, menace as well as encouragement in the sound; two of the jugglers exchanged glances as they watched their circle narrow.

"I say you will do this," the Templar went on, holding out the dagger to the juggler, daring him to take it.

"We are Cypriot, not one of you. We live here," said the senior juggler. "We must obey our laws." He backed away, but not far enough to encounter any of the Templars on the other side of the circle.

"Juggle the daggers, idiot, or you will not juggle anything again," said the Templar implacably.

"Bonsier," began the juggler, trembling now with fear.

"I will cut the tendons in your arms, fellow, if you do not juggle the daggers." There was no humor left in his words. He took a single step forward, eyes as hard as if he faced Islamites in battle.

"Bonsier, for the love of God—" the juggler said, then began to pray in Cypriot Greek.

A few of the Templars laughed, but the others, ready for a fight, were moving to hold the other jugglers.

Rainaut pushed his way through the crowd, drawing his sword as he went. "Good Templars," he said, coming into the center of the circle. "If you hurt these men, you do your Order and Reis Richard no honor." He swung the sword around once, and a few of the Templars stepped back.

"You're no Templar," one of the knights growled.

"Hospitaler," sneered another.

"And as such," said Rainaut, grateful that his voice was strong and confident. The cold in his gut was spreading, feeling massive. "I am mandated to defend those Christians who are under attack. These jugglers are Christians under attack. These jugglers are Christians and you have . . .

212 · *Chelsea Quinn Yarbro*

have tried to do them harm." He was able to meet the eyes of the first Templars. "Leave these jugglers alone. Find other sport."

"One Hospitaler tells twenty of us to leave?" jeered a voice from the crowd.

"Unless you wish to disgrace your badges, yes," Rainaut answered with a calm he did not feel.

A few of the Templars gave derisive laughter in response, but one voice cut through it all. "You are a fine one to speak of disgrace, Sier Valence Rainaut."

At the sound of his name, Rainaut swung around toward the voice, trying to place it. "Who calls me?"

The first row of Templars broke as one of their number pressed through from behind. "Ruiz Ferran Iñigo Foxa," said the Templar, bowing in an exaggerated and insulting way.

"Foxa," said Rainaut, staring at the man.

"We are not in Tyre now, Rainaut." He reached to his sword. "You have yet to answer to me." He gestured around the circle. "My fellow Templars are witness. We have a cause. You are defending these vermin. I am enforcing our request to them. We fight as champions then." He smiled, and a new, livid scar down his cheek puckered.

"Fighting now?" Rainaut asked, wondering how everything had changed for him so quickly. "On the night of Reis Richard's wedding?"

"What better time?" Foxa was proudly insolent. "I said to you in Tyre that we had much to finish."

It was foolish to remain here in such danger, Rainaut knew. It was stupid to fight Foxa in a crowd of half-drunk Templars. Disgraced as he was, it was dishonorable to battle on anyone's behalf. He brought his sword up, drawing a small dagger from his sleeve. Now he wished he had worn his chain mail, though it would have been a terrible insult to Reis Richard. Cote and surcote did not offer much protection from swordcuts.

Foxa indicated the Templars and the jugglers. "They can be our marshals. If that is satisfactory."

Rainaut's mouth was dry as old cotton. Not trusting his voice, he nodded, his whole attention on what Foxa did with his sword.

The senior juggler, terribly confused at the strange altera-tions that had occurred so swiftly, approached Rainaut only to be sharply warned back by two of the nearest Templars. Miserably the juggler got out of the way, muttering to the others in Cypriot Greek.

"I have wanted this," Foxa said.

There was no answer Rainaut could offer. He moved carefully so that there was less torchlight dancing in his eyes, then prepared to block the first, determined swing of Foxa's sword.

Metal rang on metal and the Templars cheered approval. The two swords, still pressed together, arced all the way to the ground; only then did the two combatants stand back, bringing their swords up once more.

"Ready, Foxa," Rainaut made himself call as he began to circle the small area where they fought, hemmed in by the Templars.

Foxa gave two experimental swings to his sword, then brought it in, low and hard, trying to slice into Rainaut's side.

Rainaut's sword slammed the Spanish blade aside, and then he turned, his sword still in motion toward Foxa's shoulder. As the sword struck, Foxa screamed and jumped away.

"You will answer for that," Foxa said, glancing at the spreading dark stain on his surcote. In the torchlight, his blood appeared almost black.

"I did not seek this fight; you did," said Rainaut, striving to get a little distance between himself and Foxa.

"What coward turns away from a true battle?" demanded the Spanish Templar.

"This is no true battle," countered Rainaut, moving cautiously, sensing the anger in his opponent. "This is merely pride." He chose the word knowing it would sting, hoping that the greatest sin would goad Foxa to recklessness and mistakes.

Foxa swore. "And God will roast you on a spit," he added.

"For my sins. As He will you for yours," said Rainaut, trying to calculate how far he could push Foxa. He changed his stance, crouching a little lower, his sword held angled across his upper body as protection.

This time, Foxa's blade ripped down the side of Rainaut's cote, rending the fabric and leaving his arm and side exposed. Foxa tried a second pass, but he missed as Rainaut slid away from the upward cleft of the Spaniard's blade. Foxa moved back a step or two, swinging his sword as a cat might lash its tail.

Rainaut tore away most of the cloth he could reach. He did not want to risk entangling himself in the trailing fabric or slipping on a dangling tatter. He flung the scraps of cloth away, and was surprised to notice that one of the jugglers picked all the cloth up, holding it with care as the fight continued. Rainaut did not want to be distracted, but this single act caught his attention, and for a moment he was lax in his attention.

In that instant, Foxa swung around, his sword moving as inexorably as a scythe, and this time, it left a bloody trail down Rainaut's back.

Rainaut bellowed from the pain, and this time when he faced Foxa there was a cold rage in his heart such as he had never known. In a remote part of his mind, he felt the pain from the swordcut, but it meant little to him beyond mild annoyance. He pressed the attack, his sword moving steadily, driving Foxa back into the living wall of his comrades. With a sound like a howl, Rainaut came after him, lifting his sword as he reached out to grab the front of Foxa's surcote.

Foxa dropped his sword and raised his hands, wrists crossed. His eyes burned at Rainaut. "In the Name of the Cross," he said, repeating the formula that would save him.

"Pax vobiscum," Rainaut responded, lowering his sword in a shaking hand. It was all he could do to keep from striking at Foxa's neck, no matter what the Spaniard invoked. He stepped back, cold and pain hitting him at the same time.

"It was a misunderstanding," one of the older Templars said as he came toward Rainaut. "We were misunderstood."

"How unfortunate," said Rainaut, sheathing his sword and holding out his hand to this Templar; he knew he could not offer the same courtesy to Foxa.

"Certainly it is a good thing no one was seriously hurt," the older Templar went on with pointed determination. He approached Rainaut carefully. "If I may be sure you are not badly hurt?"

"My back is cut; Foxa's shoulder is cut," Rainaut said with no particular emotion. He could feel blood matting what was left of his clothes, but he was not able to associate it with the ache that had taken possession of him.

"I would like to determine this for myself, Sier Hospitaler," said the older Templar, more forcefully than before.

"Yes," Rainaut agreed. "If you must." He took a deep breath, then started to turn.

Foxa, who had been watching this with growing wrath, hissed, "Look at his arm!"

The older Templar glanced once at Foxa. "His back is where you cut him."

"But look at his arm, *his arm,*" urged Foxa, openly staring now. "Christ Fasting! The man's a leper!" He drew back, terror blending with the fury in his eyes.

"What?" Rainaut said, dread and denial warring within him.

"The skin. It's white, there's no hair." Foxa blessed himself and moved further back. "God save us."

Several of the other Templars blessed themselves; the jugglers disappeared into the crowd, leaving nothing behind but a little pile of torn cloth.

"I am not a leper. I have an infirmity that does this. Because of the sun." Rainaut's voice, belligerent and too high, convinced no one.

"Lord Jesus, a leper," muttered another one of the Templars, moving away from Rainaut.

The older Templar looked closely at Rainaut. "There are places on your arm, on your shoulder, that have no hair, where the skin is white as a scar. I must report you as unclean."

"But I'm not," Rainaut insisted, though he was not certain this was true.

"We have to report it," the older Templar said. "We are required to report it." He came a step closer. "There's a place on your cheek as well. I should have noticed it earlier, but I thought it was just a scar."

"I tell you, I am not a leper." He wanted to sound

reasonable, and sensible, but he could hear the stridency and the panic in his words.

The older Templar shook his head. "I'm sorry. Where are you staying?"

"I . . . at the inn, by the Old Market." He paused. "I have been ordered to report to Reis Richard and to my Order. If I do not—"

"I will see word is sent. Foxa knows you; he will—"

Rainaut interrupted. "I am Sier Valence Rainaut from Saint-Prosperus-lo-Boys in Aunis."

"A Hospitaler," added the older Templar. "Very well. I will attend to the matter at once. You need not be worried that your honor is in question. I give you my word." He looked at Rainaut. "Are you alone? Have you a squire or—"

"I am providing escort for a Roman widow. We were shipwrecked and have not been able to . . ." He raised one hand in a gesture of acquiescence. "Not that it matters now."

"You have been in the company of this Roman widow you escort?" the Templar asked.

"Yes," said Rainaut defensively.

"Then I must report her as well—"

"No!" Rainaut protested, starting forward, then checking his movement. "No. She is not concerned in this. She is not to be—"

The older Templar shook his head sadly. "I must report her as well. It isn't a decision I will make; you know that. It is out of your hands and mine now." He looked around at his men, then pointed to Foxa. "You will have to be taken to the infirmary. The Hospitaler has damaged your shoulder. While you are there, you are to say nothing of this to anyone. It is for the Hospitalers, not the Templars, to determine what is to be done with Sier Valence." He paused, giving his men the opportunity to argue. "I will tend to all these things before I retire for the night."

"So soon," Rainaut said flatly. "Very well."

Some of the Templars had already faded into the night; now, at a signal from the older Templar, the rest of them moved on. Three of the Templars went with Foxa, one of them already making jokes about the fight.

"Will you post a guard on me?" Rainaut asked, resigned

now to what he knew would happen. He had broken his oaths, he had given himself to damnation and turned from his salvation, and now he was about to reap the whirlwind, as Scripture assured him he would. He thought about Olivia, and as much as he wanted to blame her, to place all the responsibility on her shoulders, he could not. He had wanted Olivia. Even when he had not sinned with his flesh, he had sinned in his thoughts, in his heart. She had not corrupted him, he had damned himself.

"If you will give me your word there should be no need for a guard yet. It may be that the Hospitalers will require it, or Reis Richard may decide he wants one for the protection of the people." He made a face. "If it were up to me, you would not be under guard at any time."

"Thank you," Rainaut said simply.

*   *   *

Text of a report from the physician Theodates to Ioannes of Rhodes, monitor of the Knights Hospitaler of Saint John, Jerusalem.

To my most reverend superior and valued advisor, the physician Theodates is much saddened to have to give you the following report. My prayers come with it, and my most fervent wish that you will not deal harshly with this afflicted knight, but grant that he be provided the protection of the Order. I am aware that this is an unorthodox request, but I truly believe that if Sier Valence Rainaut must be cast out of the society of Christians in the usual manner, his faith will be lost to him.

As you have surmised, it is apparent that this Hospitaler is unclean. I have examined his body and I have found that there are four distinct areas—the side of the face and onto the neck, the arm, the upper chest and the top of the hip—where the skin is hairless and white. Although there is no indication of the rotting away of fingers and toes, I fear that will come in time. The eyes have an odd cast to them, and Sier Valence complains of great sensitivity to light. While I have not encountered this symptom in lepers before, I fear it may mean his eyes are rotting, which will leave him unclean and blind. Another odd aspect of his affliction is that his urine has changed color, being now a brownish color. What that may bode for Sier Valence I cannot bring myself to consider.

Sier Valence has admitted that he has been aware of these whitened and hairless areas of his body for some time, but because there were no other indications of leprosy, he hoped it was a different condition, for the whitened areas are much more like scars than is usually encountered in lepers. He has also said that he is aware that he had condemned the widow he escorts to share his fate, for they have been close companions for more than three months, which assures that the contagion has gone to her.

She, upon being questioned and superficially examined, declares that she does not have leprosy and will never have it. It is true that on cursory inspection there is no sign of it on her limbs, and I take the word of the female slave Sannah that there are no other signs of it elsewhere. This widow, Bondama Clemens, has insisted that Sier Valence does not have leprosy either, but some other disease that is dangerous to no one but himself. That is the fidelity of a woman speaking, for Sier Valence has already said that he has abjured his oaths for the sake of this woman, and she does not deny it. Perhaps she will provide Sier Valence some consolation before his body ceases to function properly, or hers fails her. For it must fail her, not only for contagion, but for her sin, which is very great.

Let me repeat my petition that Sier Valence be provided some protection through the Order. He has been subjected already to the darkest despair, and I am ashamed to say it, but I cannot deny that it is possible he will, in such a state, take his own life. In order to spare him the occasion for greater sin than he has already brought upon his soul, let me suggest that he not be cast out, that he not be abandoned to the jackals and wolves, as so many others have been. This forsworn Hospitaler has none of the defiance and contempt we often see in such unfortunates.

Also, since he is a vassal of Reis Richard, he is entitled to some protection for as long as the English King is on Crusade. It requires that you release him from the Hospitalers and present him as a common English knight, part of Reis Richard's forces. It is not a gesture the Templars would approve, but in this one instance, I believe it is the greatest charity we can provide to this suffering man.

If you decide that you must cast him out, I would ask you not to make his banishment complete, that he retain some access to the English and French forces. If he is ruled dead, he will be without any protection in this place of war. I beg you to consider his plight and at least keep his name among the living.

In the Name of God and in the hope of His Mercy, I commend myself to you and to the Knights Hospitaler. May you be given victory over the enemies of Christ. May you serve God with a humble heart in triumph.

Theodates, physician
Cyprus

By my own hand, one month after the marriage of Reis Richard and Barengaria of Navarre, the 12th day of June in the Lord's Year 1191.

PART II
Atta Olivia Clemens

Text of the Will and bequests of Sier Valence Rainaut.

Knowing that my days in the company of men are ended and that my name is to be enrolled among the dead, I pray God now to guide my thoughts that I may dispose of my worldly property in a way that will bring honor on my House.

Those possessions I have as one who was a Hospitaler: my armor and my one surviving horse I leave to the Knights Hospitaler, knowing they will find use for them far wiser than any I might name. My weapons I have been given the right to retain, and because of the uncertainties that face me, I have elected to keep them.

That portion of my inheritance of lands and revenues in Saint-Prosperus-lo-Boys I bestow half upon the church of Saint Prosperus, half upon my oldest surviving nephew, Geoffroi, with the admonition that it be kept and passed to his heirs as long as Rainaut is a House.

Those personal possessions I have still in Saint-Prosperus-lo-Boys are to be disposed of in this way: my horses and their tackle are to be given to my two nephews, Geoffroi and Willaume, with the admonition that they are to be used with honor and to fight for the honor of God and Reis Richard. My three wooden chests I leave to my sisters, to be added to their dower, and to be preserved for their daughters. My other property is to be distributed to the poor, with the single exception of the mantel lined with marten fur, which I wish be sent to the family of my comrade-at-arms, Aueric de Jountuil, who drowned off Cyprus during a battle with pirates.

May God pardon my sins and bring me to His Feet on the

Day of Judgment when all the earth will give up its dead and everything will be revealed. Since I am already to be numbered with the dead, I pray that my family will offer Masses for the repose of my soul.

In the knowledge that this will stand as my dying wish and cannot be countermanded, I fix my name and sigil.

Sier Valence Rainaut

By the hand of the scribe Eugenius, on the 9th day of August, in the Lord's Year 1191, at the monastery of Saint George, Cyprus.

· 1 ·

There was a knock on the door that brought Rainaut's head up from where he had rested it on the prayer stand. "Yes?"

"It's Huon," called the youth who had been given the task of serving him as squire this last time.

"So soon," murmured Rainaut as he blessed himself and got to his feet. He was dressed as if for battle, his arms bordered in black on his chest, his mail shined beneath the surcote. "The door is open," he said after a moment of hesitation.

Huon, too, was formally clothed, his surcote blazoned azure, bendwise three scallops argent. At thirteen, he was awkward, shy, and puzzled by what he saw around him. He bowed to Rainaut. "The priests are ready."

Rainaut nodded, picking up his mantel; this one was a simple dark brown with fur trim, for he was no longer entitled to wear the black Maltese Cross of the Hospitalers. He kept his face averted, so that Huon would not have to look at the white patch on his cheek and jaw. "So am I, almost." He looked around the room. "That case, there, is all I am entitled to take with me when the Mass is over."

"Must you leave the armor?" Huon asked, still puzzled.

"Yes. Dead men have no use of armor, being in the hands of God or the Devil." His manner was remote and very polite. "We must not keep them waiting." He slung his mantel around his shoulders.

Huon stood aside in the open door, taking care not to let Rainaut touch him for fear that the leprosy would be passed to him, and he, too, would be cast out of the society of men. "I will see to it that you are—"

"You will see that I have what I am granted, and nothing more, or you will suffer for it needlessly." He looked back at the young squire. "You mean well, but it will not help me and it will hurt you."

"Oh," said Huon in a small voice. He stayed two steps behind Rainaut. "The widow is—"

"God!" Rainaut burst out, then once again mastered himself. "That I brought her to this." He had been filled with despair through the last several days while it was decided how his case was to be handled. During that time he had been kept in a monk's cell, watched over by a confessor and slave to tend to his needs. He had not seen Olivia, nor spoken with her. He had come to fear that she hated him for what he had brought upon her.

"She is to be cast out with you." Huon sighed. "She told the Master that she knew you were not a leper."

A faint, astonished smile plucked at Rainaut's mouth. "Did she?" Perhaps she was not as furious with him as he thought. "What has become of her?"

Huon did not answer. They were almost to the central chapel for the monastery, and here there were monks, their cowls over their faces, the candles they carried dark. He motioned to Rainaut to walk ahead, into the chapel.

As Rainaut genuflected, he was flanked by two monks who led him to the foot of the altar, to stand where his coffin would have been. A moment later two other monks escorted Olivia to his side and joined their hands.

Her hand tightened on his, then relaxed. "I understand we are not to be married," she said lightly, ignoring the outraged scowls that were directed toward her.

"We might as well be," Rainaut responded, taking courage from her. Now that the Order had condemned him, he felt oddly free. For the first time in several days, he smiled, and stretched the scarlike mark on his face.

The Abbot of the monastery approached, his face grave. "You have been entrusted to us by the Master of the Hospitalers, with instructions that as you are unclean, you are no longer one of the company of men, but are beyond the gates of death. The priests are ready." He blessed first Rainaut then Olivia. "Pray God He show you His mercy."

"Since you do not?" Rainaut asked, releasing Olivia's hand.

The Abbot shook his head and turned away, making a signal to the vested priests at the altar.

As the Mass for the Dead began, Olivia found it difficult to concentrate; in her long, long years, she had not been reminded of her own mortality with quite such directness as she was now. She remembered waking in her tomb, and the perilous escape from it, Sanct' Germain using a pry-bar to make a hole in the bricks that sealed her in. She had been condemned to a living death then, as well. How many years had gone by since then—more than a thousand. A sensation that was not quite dizziness passed through her as the Requiem continued.

From time to time, Rainaut sang along with the monks, refusing to surrender himself without protest. His fear which had filled him with ice for days faded away now that the actual moment was upon him. He longed to rage, to throw the candles from the altar, but he could not bring himself to so heinous an act. How strange to be numbered among the dead while there was hot blood in his veins. It was tempting to laugh, but he had enough caution left that he did not want to blaspheme and place himself beyond redemption. Most of all, he wanted to be alone with Olivia—that would come soon enough—to comfort her, to apologize for what he had done.

The priests kept on with their tasks, going mechanically through the celebration of the Mass, paying no heed when Rainaut joined in the responses. All four priests were careful not to touch either Rainaut or Olivia, and kept the capacious sleeves of their habits from brushing against them.

In the dark-draped chapel, the monks grew indistinct as

the afternoon wore on and the hillside fell into shadow. The high stone walls rang with the prayers for the dead.

"It's almost over," Rainaut whispered to Olivia. "They have used the most elaborate form of the Requiem."

The nearest priest glared at him as he pronounced yet another blessing.

"If we were truly dead, it would not matter," said Olivia, knowing that in other circumstances she would find that amusing. She stared at one of the high windows. "Do you think we'll be gone from here before sunset?"

"A little," said Rainaut. He shrugged as he saw the sharp gesture of admonition from another one of the priests.

"Good," said Olivia softly.

"How? So that we will not be more disgraced than we are already?" He had let his words grow a bit louder in defiance, then subsided. "Forgive me, Olivia."

"There is nothing to forgive," she said, turning her fascinating hazel eyes on him. "There are others who might want forgiveness, but you do not need it from me, not for this or for anything else."

The nearest priest glared at both of them, and faltered in his recitation of the familiar words.

"Not much longer. They don't bless us, but they do ask God's mercy on us," said Rainaut, not knowing if Olivia knew the variations on the Mass for the Dead.

"This whole Mass is a curse," Olivia said, an ironic smile crossing her face briefly. "Worse than any disease."

This time the priests did stop, and one of them came as close as he dared. "You are unclean beings, forsworn, and you dare to interrupt holy words."

Olivia regarded the priest with amused contempt. "Ask those who have known me a long time: they will tell you that I dare to interrupt anything." She obliged them by falling silent, her mind roaming over her long memories. She had not encountered so rigid a world in a long time. Regius was atypical for his time, and the Byzantines had been more convoluted in their methods and motives. Two hundred years before, while she was living in the north at Brescia, when much of Italy was the Kingdom of Lombardy, there had been that dreadful year when the local monastery had become convinced that there were demons everywhere, and had set about condemning everyone and everything that frightened them. This travesty of a Mass was the same sort of ritual, she thought, conducted for similar reasons. Perhaps they had been infected with madness, those monks, and it had spread through France and England and Italy, making everyone mad.

"Olivia," Rainaut said, with enough urgency that she suspected he had already spoken to her once.

"I'm listening," she said, looking at Rainaut and ignoring the dark-habited men.

"They want my armor and all articles you have of vanity—mirrors and beauty enhancers and—" He looked away.

She shook her head. "I have been here for a while; they know I do not possess a mirror nor any other . . . vanity they might name." She looked at the priest. "Are you done, or is there more?"

"We have further duties, but you must go. We will then cleanse the chapel of your presence." The priest would not look at either of them as he spoke.

"I have one small sack of belongings," said Olivia as easily as she could. "It has been inspected three times and I will therefore assume that I have your permission to take away everything in it."

Huon, who had watched the celebration from the back of the chapel, now came forward. "I will take you to your cell, Sier Valence, and I—"

"This is no longer Sier Valence," one of the priests admonished. "Sier Valence is dead. This *was* Sier Valence, but now he is only a leper."

"While I serve him," said Huon, his voice cracking with the intensity of his words, "he is Sier Valence, and that would be true had he been in his grave for years." He turned to Rainaut and bowed properly. "I will have to take your armor, Sier Valence, and those objects you have bequeathed to others."

It was all Rainaut could do to stop himself from clapping the squire on his back. "I will go with you, and I will accept your escort to the gate of the monastery when all this is finished."

Olivia could see that some of Rainaut's sense of purpose was returning. "I thank you both," she said. "It will not take me long to be prepared." She started away from the altar and was given a sharp reminder to genuflect.

"I am dead," she reminded the priests sweetly, "and therefore I cannot do as you ask." She walked out of the chapel, half-expecting one or more of the monks to detain her and force her to kneel to the crucifix. Behind her, she heard shocked murmurs, which satisfied her more than she wanted to admit.

While Huon collected the various items he was required to take to the Hospitalers' headquarters on Rhodes, Olivia made certain she had her sandals and her three mantels ready along with the few coins she had been able to salvage from the purse she had carried on the tarida. It was not much, but she knew that she would need every bit of gold and silver she could find if she and Rainaut were to escape from Cyprus. Before she left the little room, she looked around it one last time, sensing it would be some time before she had even the modicum of comforts offered in this visitor's cell.

Huon was standing with Rainaut as Olivia joined them near the side gate of the monastery garden. "It is not supposed to be allowed," said the squire, "but if you must get a message to those . . . those you cannot reach"—he coughed by way of disclaiming—"a note delivered to the English docks, the customs house, will find me."

"Here on Cyprus?" Olivia asked.

"Unless you are able to leave the island, and few ships are willing to carry lepers." He looked down shamefaced at the two long, yellow cowls in his hands. "And you must wear these now. To refuse . . ."

"They stone lepers to death if they're caught without their yellow cowls," said Olivia at her most matter-of-fact. "We'll wear them." She held out her hand to Huon. "Don't worry; this is not your responsibility, and I do not blame you for what has become of us."

Huon tried to smile at her, then looked away, his skin flushing. "I do not mean to offend."

Rainaut seized his cowl and pulled it defiantly over his head. Most of his face was obscured with the hood, and the cope reached almost to his waist. "Worse than what monks wear," he said harshly.

Olivia put her hand on Rainaut's arm. "I will see we get off Cyprus. To remain here is worse than death. If we leave Cyprus, we have a chance. Here, there is only madness and starvation." She tugged her leper's cowl on. "You may tell the priests that we have the cowls and we left wearing them."

Once again the young squire hesitated. "If you leave the island, what will become of you?"

"That depends on where we go," said Olivia. "We must not remain here, that is certain." She studied Huon briefly. "Will you do me one last favor?"

"If it is in my power," said the squire.

"I will provide you with a letter. See that it is carried to Roma." She pulled the rolled and sealed document from her sleeve. "This may gain us a little aid. If you will get it on a ship bound for Roma. It goes to an estate near Roma called Sanza Pare."

Huon nodded. "All right. I'm not supposed to take letters from Sier Valence, but they said nothing about you."

Olivia lowered her head. "Thank you. I am grateful. Perhaps, one day, I will be able to thank you with more than words."

"It isn't necessary," said Huon, suddenly very much embarrassed.

"It is," she countered. "Never mind."

Rainaut had been staring hard at the door in the wall. "I suppose there's no purpose in delay."

"Probably not," said Huon, reluctant to open the gate.

Olivia filled the awkward silence with another question. "Tell me, is there a lesser gate out of the garden?"

Huon looked startled. "There's one by the sheepfold."

"Would it make any difference if you let us out that way?" she asked.

"I suppose not," said Huon, frowning.

"Then let us leave that way." She had already started to walk away from the garden gate toward the livestock pens. "Come, Sier Valence. Humor me in this."

Rainaut shrugged. "Out is still out, Olivia," he reminded her as he trailed after her. He was puzzled by her request but did not want to hear her explanation until they were outside the monastery.

"I have to tell you to leave," said Huon as they reached the sheepfold gate. "I don't want to do this."

"I understand that," said Rainaut. "It is your duty, and you are sworn to uphold your duty. We will go quickly." He took Olivia's free hand in his. "See? We are ready."

The sheep, gathered into their fold not long before, were restless at the intrusion of these unfamiliar beings. They made low sounds of distress, and most of them kept to the side farthest away from the gate, fretting as the three unfamiliar humans lingered there.

Huon gave a sigh of resignation. "I will tell them you have gone." The gate was stout and the hinges stuttered as the squire pulled it open. "God keep you," he said as Olivia and Rainaut went through it into the shadowed twilight.

When the gate was closed and the bolt slid into place, Rainaut turned to Olivia. "Why this gate?"

"Because the lepers are always let out through the other. I have heard that there are those who prey on lepers, who beat and rob them of what little they have. I didn't want us to be among them." She held up the sack she carried. "We have little to lose, and we must guard it carefully or we are lost."

"What fool would attack a leper?" scoffed Rainaut.

"Desperate men have done more dangerous things for a little gain," she warned him. "And we are beyond aid, so long as we wear these cowls." She reached up for the hood of hers.

"You're not going to take it off, are you?" Rainaut demanded, horrified.

"Certainly," Olivia answered in her most sensible voice. "I can tolerate being forced to beg—it has happened to me before now—but I will not make myself a target for those who seek out the helpless."

"But—" Rainaut protested as Olivia removed the yellow cowl. "For God's sake!"

"What has God to do with this?" Olivia said. "Some men have done this, and they are the ones who will answer for it. If you believe you must wear the cowl, as you wore the Hospitalers' mantle, then do so. But I am no leper. Neither are you." She had been walking away from the monastery walls, toward the part of the village that housed the swine-and-sheep market. There were a number of low-slung shelters that during the day stalled animals for sale, and during the night offered minimal shelter to beggars.

"You have said that, but the physicians saw my body, and they have said—" Rainaut began, only to be interrupted.

"I have seen more than your body; I know your blood, your soul. I tell you, you are no leper. The affliction you have is real, but it is not leprosy, though your skin turns white and the hair falls out, and your eyes redden. You will keep all your fingers and toes, and you can harm no one." She had stopped walking to say this, and as she spoke, she heard a stealthy footfall behind them. "Where's your dagger?" she asked in French.

"My belt," he answered, bewildered at her sudden change.

She bent down, forcing him to do the same, and reached for the hilt of the dagger as she did. In one swift movement, she had spun around, rising, the dagger flashing in her hand as she caught the arm of the beggar who had been following them.

The man howled and rolled away, cursing. Behind him was the fading sound of running.

"Keep away from us, or more of the same," Olivia ordered the cowering man in heavily accented Greek. She held the dagger at the ready, prepared for a second attack if it came.

The only response was another, more comprehensive curse, and departing footsteps.

"How could you hear that?" Rainaut asked as she gave him back his dagger. "And where did you learn—"

"You ask a woman who has lived alone for most of her life how she comes to learn to fight?" Olivia asked.

"Very well," Rainaut conceded. "But what man taught you? Who was willing to instruct you in fighting with a dagger? Or is that your only skill?" The last question was almost a joke, a way to keep from making it appear he doubted her.

"I can use a short sword if I must, and one or two other weapons. I have learned at various times in my life, for various reasons." She patted the sack she carried. "I want to be sure we protect ourselves as well as what we have."

Rainaut rubbed his face. "All right. Tell me what you believe I will have to know." They were far enough from the monastery now that the walls appeared to blend with the rise of the hill, indistinguishable from the other buildings in the town. "Where do you think we ought to go tonight?"

"Where we are not expected to go," said Olivia frankly. "Away from here, out of the village, so that we will not be at the mercy of beggars in the morning." She also wanted to find a place where neither of them would have to face the sun at mid-day. "There are caves in the hillside. Some of them are occupied, but many are not. One of them should suffice for a little while."

"You've thought it out," said Rainaut, shocked that Olivia was so prepared.

"What else was there to do for all those days they kept me in that cell? All I had was prayers and rats to occupy me"—she did not add that the rats had been her only sustenance and that she was more famished now than she had been in years—"so it was no hard task to plan for our . . . release."

"I hadn't realized that . . ." He had been so lost in his own misery for all the days he had been examined and questioned that he had not considered her plight. He had missed her, longed for her, but had not thought about what she would have endured during that time.

They were at the walls of the town, though in this quarter they were in poor repair, neglected since the Cypriots had expelled the Byzantines less than a decade ago; it was not difficult to find an opening and scramble through it, emerging in the rocky vinyard that flanked the village.

"Did you mean it?" Rainaut asked, reaching to take her arm. "A cave?"

"For the dead, one hole in the ground is as good as another," she said, wishing his dejection would fade, taking refuge in a bravery that was more assumed than genuine.

"The dead," he said slowly. "We are with the dead."

"According to the good offices of your Church," she said, her lightness tarnishing a little. Her eyes, almost invisible to him in the oncoming night, revealed more than she knew. "And my church as well, as much as I have one." Sadly, tenderly, she kissed him, touching him only with one hand

and her parted lips until he relented and pulled her desperately into his arms. They remained locked together, apart from the world, until a distant plea for alms brought them back to their plight.

Rainaut looked back toward the village walls. "Perhaps it's best to be gone. There is nothing left for us there."

She began once more to walk. "Not any more."

*   *   *

Text of a letter from Ithuriel Dar to Niklos Aulirios.

Greetings to my persistent and impatient friend at Sanza Pare near Roma, who has been more assistance to me than any other I have known in my life.

I have learned that your mistress, the Roman widow Clemens, was indeed on Cyprus at the time of the wedding of Reis Richard and Barengaria. There are three reliable witnesses I have discovered who definitely saw and spoke with her, and who say that she was truly planning to leave for Roma on the first available ship. This is proving to be awkward. Because Reis Richard was here and bound eastward, and with Reis Phillippe also engaged on this Crusade, almost anything that can hold water has been commandeered for the use of the Kings. What they do not take up is given to pilgrims and monks and priests and bishops and all the rest of them. This has grown markedly worse in the last three months, and now that we are nearing the season of bad weather, it is likely that there will be a slight improvement in the situation. Most priests don't like to test God's whim on the sea in storms.

The bergantino I have acquired requires repairs and I will be here for another two or three weeks while the ship is put into proper condition once again. The trouble is not extensive nor is it so severe as to render the ship unseaworthy, but there are several beams that are showing signs of weakening, and I would not want to depend on them during a storm. I have enough money to pay for the repairs and the men doing the work can be trusted. When I put to sea again, the bergantino will be the stoutest ship on the sea.

I was told that the knight who was escorting Bondama Clemens was found to be ill and has been in the care of his Order. I have not been able to see the man, or to talk with him. If only I could reach him, I might be able to find out where Bondama Clemens is now. Be certain that I will continue to try to locate the Hospitaler. One of the Templars still left on Cyprus now that Reis Richard has sold it to them told me that Sier Valence Rainaut was discovered to be a leper. None of the Hospitalers will confirm or deny that—as you would expect. But then, knowing the cordial relationship that exists between these two Orders, I am not surprised that there have been such rumors about Rainaut. I would expect it in any matter of illness.

So far, no one I have spoken to in three of the island's ports remembers such a woman as Bondama Clemens, unless she was traveling in disguise, which you tell me is not impossible. I have still with me ten large crates of Roman earth, and will give them to her as soon as I locate her, as you have instructed me.

Pardon my lack of success in finding your mistress. You have been generous and helpful, and I have not done much to aid you in locating Bondama Clemens. I agree she is a most resourceful woman, but in this world, that may not be sufficient. For that reason, I have contacted those I know in the Islamic world, in case there is word of her there. If she has been taken, I will do all in my power to gain her freedom.

                                                    Ithuriel Dar
By my own hand, on one of the few Feasts both Christians and Jews can share, that of Michael the Archangel, in the Christian year 1191.

Four small boats rode at anchor beyond the breakers, each with a haloed lamb painted roughly on the worn sails. The inlet was named for Saint Spiridion; there was a large Greek crucifix halfway up the cliff, and a ruined tower above that.

"It will take money," said Hilel Alhim. "We are not supposed to take people from the island without the permission of the Templars." By way of comment, he spat. "Ever since they have come, they have made it impossible for simple trading men to make a living. They want our ships—for charity, of course—or they want our goods, also for charity. Why should I take your money?"

"Because all we wish to do is leave. My leman has been badly burned. He is scarred, disfigured. He can no longer fight. You know what that means." Olivia gathered her heaviest mantel around her, for the sun was deceptive, burning without giving warmth, and the wind cut hard.

"I could take the money and then turn you over to the Templars," suggested Alhim, his narrow face looking more predatory than before. "It has happened before."

"And it will again, but not through you," said Olivia. "For if that occurred, your sister's family near Famagusta would meet with misfortune through your greed. Wouldn't they?" Her smile was wide, sweet, and insincere.

Alhim frowned. "I am going to Laodicia—that's what you Romans call it, isn't it—to Tarsus, to Attalia, Rhodes, and Tarentum. That will not be a swift passage, but eventually, you will arrive."

The thought of those long, miserable days at sea made Olivia faintly sick, but she nodded briskly enough. "It is better than languishing here."

"Is it?" Alhim asked without interest. "Among the goats

and the simple people? But you long for Roma, don't you? and the bustle in the streets and the gold."

"I miss my home," said Olivia. "And I intend to return there." She straightened up, her bearing more imposing than before. "I will pay your price, and you will deliver my leman and me to Tarentum. Is that acceptable?"

"Gold is always acceptable," Alhim said, staring up at the sky as if searching for portents there. "Naturally, you will not travel in the open. I have four closed compartments in the hold of my ship. They were originally intended for spices and other rare goods, but recently they have carried battle harness and horse tackle. I suppose they could accommodate two passengers, if you weren't too fussy." He was now regarding the horizon to the south. "They say that the fighting is worse."

"Oh?" She could not permit Alhim to know she was curious.

"Between Caesarea and Jaffa. The Islamites fled Caesarea before the Crusaders got there, so Reis Richard was deprived of a battle. He's hungry for one." He cleared his throat. "His men are suffering."

"That was expected," said Olivia, wondering if she ought to tell Rainaut about the Crusade's progress; he was fretting already and such news might distress him more.

"Fever and the flux are taking a toll." Alhim gave a satisfied nod. "They have salt fish, but nothing else to help them. I have heard that some of the men-at-arms have ordered their families and followers to turn back because of the danger. Not that there is any place to turn back to." He laughed. "The price is gold, Bondama; my cousin told you how much."

"I have a third of it now," said Olivia, reaching into her mantel for her wallet and the hoarded coins. "I will give you another third when we have set sail, and the last when we arrive in Tarentum." She put the six coins into his hand. "Test them if you like."

Alhim chuckled. "You are not going to give me false coin now, not when you need my ship. I will test your coins when you leave my vessel, not before." He indicated the inlet. "Be here, on the beach down there, at sunset day after tomorrow. There will be two small boats to carry you and this scarred leman of yours to my ship. If you are not here by the time the sky is wholly dark, I will sail without you, and be damned to you." He bowed elaborately.

"Of course," said Olivia with equal courtesy. "What must we bring for our passage, other than gold?"

"There are no pallets in the hold rooms, they are simply empty rooms. I have very little space to carry extra goods. If you have much you want to transport, you cannot do it on my ship." He slipped his bag of coins into a pocket in his capacious sleeves. "A pillow or two will make your passage easier."

"I will tend to it," said Olivia bluntly. "Sunset, day after tomorrow."

"You and your leman will honor my craft," said Alhim with a hint of ire. "It's so rare that Roman nobility comes aboard." He started to turn away from her, then stopped. "I expect you and your leman to remain out of sight."

"All right," said Olivia, who knew she would not want to move from her place in the little cabin.

"There are other passengers coming on this voyage, and I want no questions asked." He shook his finger at her. "That means that I expect you to be invisible."

"I will tell my leman," she said, hoping she could convince Rainaut that their safety depended on their discretion. "A man as scarred as he is does not want—"

"I don't want to know about his scars," said Alhim. "The lie will do well enough for most, but I know what your leman is, and as long as he keeps away from the rest of us, I will not require that he continue his deception." Olivia started to protest, but Alhim continued. "Your leman could be without all his fingers and toes, or his nose and ears for all of me. You have paid and I have taken your money. We understand each other."

"If you . . ." She let her words trail away. "We will be here."

"Bring dark colors. I don't want the rest to know who or what is coming aboard." He bowed again and began to make his way down the narrow path that led to the beach.

"Alhim!" Olivia called after him. "If you are not here night after tomorrow, the Templars will learn of it."

"I supposed they might," he called back without turning.

Olivia watched until Alhim was almost to the beach, then she started along the same trail in the opposite direction, toward the ruined tower and the rising stone cliffs beyond. In the bright, enervating sunlight she had to go slowly. At night, or with more of her native earth in the soles of her shoes, she would move quickly and surely along such a path, but with so little protection, she dared not risk any accident or misstep. The last quarter of her walk was the hardest, for she scrambled over tall outcroppings, the crude hand-and-toe-holds cut into the rock tending to crumble from time to time, toward the opening of a cave. She swung around one tall spire-like boulder, and then entered the welcome shadow.

"Olivia?" came Rainaut's voice at once, apprehensive and faintly angry.

"Yes," she answered, going up to him with a tentative smile. "I've done it."

Rainaut turned toward her, his face set under straight brows. The scarlike patch of skin on his face was large and now covered most of the left side of his neck. More of his tawny hair had fallen out, leaving the side of his head above the ear quite bald. "Commendable," he said, doing his best to keep in the deepest shadows.

Her step faltered; she heard wrath in that word, and she came toward him, her hands out to him. "Why are you angry with me?"

"Not you," he said, shying away from her, standing so that she could not see his face. "I am angry with myself." He put his hands over disfigurement. "How could I, as I am? Who would speak with me, as I am?"

Olivia could not respond at once; an emotion compounded of grief, love, and something else, perhaps impatience, perhaps fear, stopped the words in her throat. "That's why I went," she reminded him carefully. "We decided it was best."

"Yes," he said abruptly. "And I haven't changed my mind. But that it should come to this, that I must hide in a cave, like some hunted creature, while you, who I am sworn to protect, must go alone to meet a smuggler—" He slammed the palms of his hands against the walls of the cave, watching his blood stain the stone.

Olivia reached out and stopped him, taking his hands in hers and forcing him to look at her. "It does not matter, Valence," she said. "I have done far worse in the years I've lived, and I have survived. So will you."

"All my hair will fall out, won't it," he said, unwilling to meet her eyes.

"Probably," she said. "And your eyes will redden and you will become more sensitive to light. Most of your skin will be like a scar, white and stretched-looking." She recited these horrors without revulsion. "But I do not love you for your skin, or your hair."

"Why not?" He tried to break free of her without success.

"Beauty is fleeting, if all you see is the skin. Beauty can last all life long if what you see is the soul," Olivia said quietly, thinking that even a life, from her perspective, was fleeting.

"Fine sentiments," he scoffed, his voice breaking.

"No, simply the pragmatic truth." Reluctantly she let go of him. "I wish you would believe me."

Rainaut held his hands across his waist as if he had taken a sword thrust into his vitals. "I am *hideous,*" he howled at her.

"Not to me," she said. "Your face is not handsome now, which is unfortunate. You suffer, which causes me great pain. But that does not change my love for you." She laughed once, sadly. "It also doesn't stop me from wanting to throttle you when you fall into these sulky states."

He was so shocked that he rounded on her. "Sulky? Me?"

"Yes," she said serenely. "From time to time you are sulky." Her hazel eyes warmed. "And when you are, I would be delighted to belabor you with the flat of your sword."

"You would." He sat down, almost at the mouth of the cave, and stared down the slopes toward the distant sea. "Melancholy is one of the cardinal sins."

"Oh how charming," said Olivia ironically. "You've been collecting sins today, is that it?"

"I am a great sinner," he said, the little jollity he had shown fading quickly.

"I think you're showing more stubbornness than anything else. You are determined to be a great sinner, and you will magnify anything you think or do in order to accomplish that goal. It's foolish, Valence." She sat down beside him, letting her feet dangle, her skirts pulled up as far as her knees. "I have known men who were true sinners, and you are not like them."

Rainaut was gazing at the distant horizon, shielding his aching eyes with his hand. "You can leave me, if you like."

"What?" Olivia demanded, truly shocked at his offer. "What do you mean by that?"

"You can seek out another protector, who is whole and clean and who will be able to aid you in your return to Roma. I am more of a liability than anything else. In very little time, I will be nothing less than a noose for you." His blue eyes were somber, his voice steady and low.

Olivia regarded him incredulously. "Is this a noble renunciation or a run for cover?"

Rainaut squinted as he stared out, away from her. "I am not fit company any more. Say what you will, no man can look on me without horror."

"Certainly you were more comely when your skin was as other men's, but what of it? I have known men who were deformed, who were born with stubs in place of arms, with three legs instead of two. I have known men with joints as gnarled as the roots of trees, who have lost legs and arms and ears and faces to war." She thought back to Regius' son, his chest still bleeding sluggishly as he accepted her blood to save him, and his father's wrath. "You are not my lover because you are well-formed and whole, but because you are Rainaut. How often must I tell you that before you believe me?"

He was looking away from her now. "I am not safe to know."

At this Olivia laughed aloud. "Valence Rainaut, *I* am not safe to know." She put her hands on his shoulders and forced him around to look at her. "Did you believe what I told you, a few days ago, about when and where I was born?"

Rainaut shrugged, squirming a little under her hands, and made a deprecating joke, not answering her question. "It doesn't matter, Olivia."

"Yes, it does, because it is the truth. You know how I love you, and that for me, your blood is you, and your love." She smoothed his sparse hair back from his brow. "Why should a vampire like me be put off because you have an ugly disease?"

"Don't," he snapped.

"What?" she asked, refusing to release him.

"Say you are a vampire." He directed his stare at her. "It could bring you trouble, to say such things."

"It has certainly done so in the past," said Olivia, sensing his attempts to seal himself off from her. With a sigh she let go of his shoulders. "But the fact remains, I am a vampire, and have been since I woke in my tomb more than a millennium and a century ago." She once again looked out to sea.

"I know what you're doing," Rainaut said after a while.

"Do you?"

"You are trying to keep me from melancholy, to turn my thoughts away from my sins. You have this fable so that I will not dwell on what has become of me." He tried to smile, but the white skin distorted his efforts to a rictus.

"It's not a fable," said Olivia, beginning to feel very tired. "Why do you think . . . why do you think I taste your blood when we lie together?"

"To ensure you will not be with child, of course," said Rainaut.

"To what?" Olivia asked, taken aback at his answer. "How would taking blood stop—? Never mind." She tucked her legs under her and leaned against his arm. "I had a child, once, long ago, but it died."

Rainaut glanced over at her. "Truly?"

"Truly," she said, remembering the peculiar expression in Justus' eyes when the infant was made ready for burial. "There was just the one, no others."

"But since you are a widow, a child now—" Rainaut persisted.

"That's not possible," said Olivia. "I taste your blood for love of you, and no other reason. There is nourishment in love, Valence, little as you may believe it." She hesitated, then went on. "When we come together, we partake of one another. To taste your blood is part of that. For those like me, it is our only sustenance."

His expression grew bitter. "With such hunger, I suppose that any source will do."

"No." He had started to move away from her, but she held his arm. "No, that is not so, and you will not think it is."

"But you said—" he began only to be interrupted.

"I said that there is nourishment in love. Do you think that any man will give that? Oh, yes, there are ways to rouse a man to dreams of passion, but that is . . . makeshift. It is fodder, little else. What I need, what I yearn for, is love that gives of itself. You have given me so much, Valence. You have opened your heart to me, and have made a gift of it." She lifted his hand and kissed it.

"Never mind that all this brings dishonor on us both," he said, mocking himself as well as her.

"What dishonor?" Olivia asked sharply. "Where is the dishonor in receiving a heartfelt gift? Where is the dishonor in acknowledging love? If your honor will not tolerate that, it is nothing to seek." She scrambled to her feet and went back into the cave. "Without you, I would be . . . not dead, but something far worse. By now, I would be lying, unmoving and desiccated, by the sea, assuming I could reach the shore at all after the tarida went down."

"Of course," he said, not believing what she said.

"Or I would be on the floor of the ocean, living but immobile, condemned to remain there, knowing everything, capable of nothing, until the sea and its creatures destroyed my flesh. Without you, without your love, I would be lost." It was easier to say these words with a little distance between them. Olivia hated his sense of resistance; this way she did not have to experience it. "Rainaut, believe me, if you had no love for me, I would know it, and nothing you or I did would make any difference."

Rainaut shook his head slowly several times. "You are a persuasive devil, I'll allow that. You are filled with the deadliest honey." He got up, moving once more into the deep shadows. "Tell me again how my disease is not leprosy, though my skin is white as milk. Tell me again that I am clean, though my eyes turn red and my hair falls out. Tell me, Olivia."

"You taunt me," she said quietly. "But that does not change your love. Nor mine."

Rainaut remained silent for some little time. When he spoke again, it was in a gentler voice. "Will you miss me?"

It was all Olivia could do to keep her voice even. "Yes."

"I hope so," he said wistfully. "There will be few who do." He moved a little closer to her. "If only I had honor left. I think I could endure all the rest of it if I still had my honor."

"You have it," said Olivia softly but with great feeling. "It isn't something that can be taken away. You have done nothing to cast off your honor." She gathered her courage and went to him. "You are as much a man of honor now as when you wore the black Maltese Cross, as when you gave your vassal's oath to . . . it would be Henry, wouldn't it?"

"Yes," said Rainaut. "Yes, it was the King's Grace, Henry of England, by that name the Second." He recited this dreamily. "He was a stern man, haunted and powerful. It was late when he came to Saint-Prosperus-lo-Boys, but he would hear nothing of sleep until he had received his oaths of fealty."

It was on the tip of Olivia's tongue to ask why it was so important, but she managed not to ask. "And you have been for England since that day."

"Yes; before that, through my father." The glistening track of one tear marked his scarred cheek. "When I saw the leopards of England, while they were preparing for the wedding, I knew such abiding pride. God has shown me the fallacy of that." He smeared the wet away. "I am not worthy to weep for England, or for Reis Richard."

Olivia took his wrists, bringing his arms around her waist and pressing his hands together in the small of her back. "You are worthy of the greatest achievements, Valence."

"If that were so, I would not be a leper," he said, trying halfheartedly to get away from her.

"You are *not* a leper," she said for what seemed like the thousandth time. "Even if you were, the disease would not make you less than you are." As she rested her head in the curve of his neck, she whispered, "I ache for you."

"You seek my damnation," he muttered.

"No, nor your salvation. I seek only your love." Releasing his wrists, she brought her hands round and began to unfasten his loosely tied girdle. "If either one of us is damned, I am. It does not stop me loving you." She dropped the plaited leather thongs to the floor of the cave. "Once we are on the sea, we will not be able to be together"—and, she added to herself, she would feel far too sick to seek him out—"or pass the time in love-games. Before we leave, let us have one more time for loving."

"You are afraid you will not find blood enough on the ship?" Rainaut asked in a tone intended to hurt.

Olivia took a step back. "There would be more than enough blood on the ship, if that was what I wanted." She wanted to box his ears, but sensed that he was determined to egg her on so that they would not have to face the more dangerous issues of their longing and need. "I have survived on rats, and worse."

Rainaut could not laugh. "So you tell me; so you tell me."

"If matters are bad, I will show you while we are on the ship," she said, watching him. "Rainaut, you came to me, you sought me out, though you knew to do so was a risk for you. At that time, you gave little thought to what might be between us, because it never occurred to you that I would desire you. You believed everything in the songs and tales, you thought that there was a code for love, for the way of men with women. You have tried to make me one of those vicious Wooing Ladies in the troubadors' songs, but I do not strive to waken desire where it does not exist, and I am not like your Adored One, always unreachable, always ideal, elevated and pure. I am a woman as you are a man, and my love is like yours. You and I are more the same than we are different: I am not a tool of the Devil, bent on turning you from Grace, and I am not an instrument of Grace, to save you from the Devil; I am your lover, as men are your friends."

"Sophistry," he scoffed without success.

"It isn't," she said, helplessness growing in her. "You don't believe me."

Rainaut slid his long, blunt hands up her body, finally holding her face. "I believe you mean what you say," he said, his lips close to hers. "But how can you bear my embrace, knowing what I am?"

"You bear mine well enough," she pointed out. "And you know what I am."

He pressed his mouth on hers in a long, languorous kiss. His tongue found hers in sweet, forbidden pleasure. When he moved back from her, he was breathing more deeply. "That's only a start of what I wish I could have with you."

"Let me have the rest," said Olivia, her hazel eyes brilliant in the dark of the cave.

"Of this?" He indicated his body.

"Of you," she said steadily, loosening her lacings. "Now, here."

"And when you shudder and draw away?" he inquired with elaborate courtesy. "What then?"

"It will not happen," she said, starting to shed her garments.

Rainaut watched her, caught by the challenge he sensed in her manner. "Once we begin, I won't stop."

"Good God, I hope not," said Olivia with conviction. She was almost naked, her fawn-brown hair providing more coverage than the rail that covered her loins.

With an incoherent vow, Rainaut reached for her, dragging her into his arms, his blue eyes hot as metal in a forge. "No one has loved you as I do, Olivia," he growled to her as he wrestled out of his clothes and explored her body. "When you come to despise me, leave me."

She closed her eyes, feeling light-headed. Her fingers moved blindly, restlessly, over his body, discovering sensations he had never encountered before, that she had not been aware he possessed until then. It was piercingly sweet to reach the limen of love, to pursue their brief unity with olamic fervor, since both knew, and could not bring themselves to admit, that this was the last time they would join their bodies in order to share their souls.

*   *   *

A letter from the squire Huon to the Master of the Knights Hospitaler of Saint John, Jerusalem, on Rhodes.

To my most revered and respected Master, the blessings and greetings of this esquire from England, with many thanks to you for all that has been given me through the Hospitalers, which must include my coming into the Holy Land, for without the cause of the Holy Sepulcher and the aid of the Order, I would never have known that my vocation lies not with the Hospitalers, but with the monks of Saint George of the Latins, here on Cyprus. I have asked for admission as a novice, and have been welcomed.

It is true that once a man has given oath, he is dishonored if he abjures it. No one can deny that, and I make no excuse for what I have done, but that I was called of God: for it is also true that the fealty given to God is before all other fealties. I humbly beg you will not hold me in disgrace, nor cast shame upon my House for what I have done. I had been as one blind until God willed otherwise. Now that I see, I must seek, that I may find, as is promised by God in Scripture.

My eyes were turned to God when I saw how much God had changed the life of that excellent knight, Sier Valence Rainaut, who has been cast out of the world because of his uncleanness. He, like Job, was blameless, and those sins that were on him were the sins of living men. He strove to fulfill his oaths, to honor his Order and to defend our faith, and yet he became a leper, and the Requiem was sung for him. Until then, I had not thought how it would be to have to answer God for all I have done when I was not prepared. I thought that as one who would become a Hospitaler, there would be no disgrace that could touch me but the pain of sin. Wounds taken for the Glory of Christ were welcome to me, and I longed for the day I would face an Islamite for that great test.

Now I know that there is a greater mystery, one that is much more than a question of courage or honor or any other simple thing. Nothing in men's lives is so great as God, and yet, nothing is so far from understanding. God is an enigma to me, and only through a life dedicated to prayer and the contemplation of God can I hope to know what God is, and what I must do. Without that peace, there is no peace for me, and without that victory, I will be nothing more than a soldier fallen in battle. I pray for the Hospitalers and for all Christian knights and men-at-arms in the Holy Land defend-

ing the sacred places of our faith, but there are others I pray for as well, and I know that as a Hospitaler, I would not be doing the work God has shown me must be done.

I ask you, for charity, to inform my family what has become of me, for the monks here will not permit me to write to them. This is the only letter I am allowed to write and send, and so you will know that I place much faith in your honor and good will. There are many I might wish to write to, but my trust is greatest in you.

May God grant you gain dominion of Rhodes before the Crusade is a greater struggle than now. You have obtained a needed foothold, but now that the Templars have Cyprus, you must be aware of how great the necessity is in possessing the place without question or dispute. Having part of the island is a salvation, but possessing the whole would be a triumph not only for the Hospitalers, but for all Christians.

With my thanks and the vow of my prayers for as long as there is breath in my body, I surrender to you my name and my arms, both of which I can no longer own.

Huon
his device: azure, bendwise
three scallops argent

By my own hand on the feast day of Saint Dionis of Paris, in the Lord's Year 1191. In sempaeternum amen.

· 3 ·

By afternoon the blustery wind had forced Alhim to order the sails lowered and half the oars shipped. The dozen official passengers confined themselves to their box-like cabins on the central deck. All cargo was tied down, the hatches secured, and there were two men assigned to the rudder, both of them tied to the stoutest part of the aft railing.

Deep in the hold, Olivia shifted in her coffin-sized quarters, her whole body wracked and miserable. She had learned long ago to be stoic about the discomforts of sea travel, but this was more than she wanted to endure. She longed for escape; deliberately she set herself to remembering—taking care to skip those recollections that were bound up with the sea—the most compelling places in her past. Roma and Ravenna and Alexandria, Aquileia, Skopje, Sinope, Phasis, Gaza, Carthago Nova . . . so many places, so many years. Chersones and Tiflisi, Bizerta and Tunis. And Roma, Roma always and inevitably. Homesickness seized her more than the wretchedness of crossing water. She longed for Roma as she sought love, as she searched for egalitarian justice, as she missed Sanct' Germain. She gave a soft, protesting cry, bringing her hand to cover her mouth as she did.

"Olivia!" Rainaut tapped on her door, just loudly enough to be heard over the racket from the sea and the groaning of the ship.

She made her voice steady and even. "Yes?"

"Are you well?" he demanded.

"I am no worse than I usually am crossing water," she answered indirectly. No matter what he did, there was nothing he could do to change this for her unless he could procure a barrel of Roman earth to ease her distress.

"Do you need anything?" he asked through the rough planking that served as a door.

"Dry land underfoot," she answered brusquely. "I will manage."

There was a pause, then Rainaut said, "I am going to get the food Alhim has for us. Do you want any?"

"No," she answered, trying not to sound too impatient. "Have my portion, if you wish." Her last meal had been consumed more than a thousand years before, in a cell, while she awaited immurement.

"You're sure?" He had pried her door open a little. "I could bring some water."

"Nothing, thank you," she said, beginning to lose her temper, though it was no fault of his that she was so tormented. "Leave me; I have this trouble crossing water— you know about it. You've seen it before." She was pleased by his concern for her, yet the thought of his company aggravated her beyond words; she had reached a point where she most wanted to be alone. "Go on; get your food, but take care. The ship is tossing and it might not be easy to move about. Alhim won't protect us if we're discovered." She hoped that this reminder would sharpen his wits.

"Don't worry," he said. "Everyone's in their rooms, even that monk. He was out on deck before mid-day, speaking with one of the sailors." He leaned his forehead against the splinters of her door. "Olivia?"

"Yes?" She heard the plaintive note as he spoke her name and was able to keep her irritation out of her response.

"I never intended that you should be subjected to . . . any of this." His voice was low and hard to hear, but the poignance in his apology was so apparent that Olivia was startled. "You deserved better than I have given you."

It was fortunate that he could not see her faint, ironic smile. "There are those who would disagree," she said, huddling into a fetal ball. "You didn't intend this to happen," she went on, more loudly. "I've told you that before."

"If you decide you must leave me, then do—"

She interrupted him. "Oh, go get your food and leave me alone. I will not abandon you, Valence; your blood is in me, and I cannot. How many times must I tell you that?"

Whatever he answered was little more than a mumble as he moved away from her door and started down the very narrow walkway toward the center of the ship. He was troubled by Olivia's outburst, but more, he was fighting the melancholy that continued to strengthen its hold on him, no matter what he did. He reached up to one of the beams as the ship lurched to the side at the blow of a wave striking the bow deck. As the vessel steadied, Rainaut continued along the walkway, always taking care to be ready to grasp the beam again.

In the cook's quarters, three sailors huddled around an Egyptian-style drum-stove, all of them soaked, all of them seeking a little warmth before venturing back into the squall. As Rainaut came through the narrow door, none of the sailors looked at him.

"Your trencher's there, and the lady's," said the cook, addressing the stove. "More in the morning."

One of the sailors made a sour remark in a language Rainaut did not know; the other two laughed unpleasantly, and the cook brandished a long-bladed cleaver at them, saying to the ceiling, "Pay them no mind, Bonsier. They are ignorant sailors."

Rainaut picked up the two trenchers, making no comment on the spartan and tasteless fare and trying to find a way to balance them both in the crook of one arm. He kept his face turned away from the men. "It's nothing to me," he said, stepping back through the narrow door, puzzled by the cook's words. He whispered a quick prayer of thanks for the cook and the food, then started to make his way back toward the hidden compartments in the forward hold.

He had gone less than half the distance when he saw a man—an Islamite, judging by his clothes—hurry down the hold ladder and slip into the shadows. The careful and covert manner of the Islamite caught Rainaut's attention, and he sought cover behind a stack of bales containing dried herbs. Some of the thin sauce covering the beans and scraps of chicken slopped onto his arm, and he took a few moments to brace himself against the bales.

When Rainaut looked up, another man was just slipping down beside the Islamite, both of them in deep shadow.

". . . and I will say I lost it in this storm," the newcomer was saying to the Islamite. "Take it and"—Rainaut could not hear the next few words—". . . wouldn't believe me? I am an honest monk, everyone knows that."

"Surely Allah will reward you handsomely in Paradise," said the Islamite. "As will our great Saladin when he learns of this."

"It is for the triumph of Islam I do this," said the man who had called himself a monk. "Only Allah is great."

"Allah is great," echoed the Islamite. "But tell me how you"—again the storm drowned the words—". . . you entrusted?"

The self-proclaimed monk moved slightly and Rainaut could see he was tonsured. "I have other documents with me, but I will have to deliver at least two of them, or there will be suspicion. With the progress I have made, I can't take that risk." He looked around suddenly. "Did you hear something?"

"How can you tell with this storm?" asked the Islamite calmly. "There are rats in the hold; there are always rats."

Rainaut held his breath and willed himself part of the shadows.

The monk waited, his whole stance watchful, alert to every sound. "What's that smell?"

"Herbs," said the Islamite. "That whole side of the ship is filled with bales of them."

". . . no . . ." The monk frowned. "Something else."

As the ship wallowed and pitched there was a sudden crash from the cook's quarters.

"Ah," said the monk. "Doubtless something has spilled." He gave his attention to his Islamite companion once more. "I think I will be able to carry one more set of documents before I am questioned too closely. The Christians are in such disarray that only Phillippe of France has reliable heralds to carry his messages." He made a gesture of resignation. "So, this will tell you of what Leopold of Austria is planning to do with his forces, and what support the Templars are pledged to provide. This"—he offered a second, smaller document—"is a list of the noble pilgrims who are supposed to visit Jerusalem by Epiphany. All would demand a handsome price from their families. Some might come to the True Faith, given instruction." He chuckled. "Praise be to Allah, if there were a noble Crusader brought to Islam."

The Islamite nodded vigorously. "Praise Allah in all things." His voice had risen, and now he looked about nervously, as if his outburst might have been overheard.

"There is no God but Allah," said the monk just above a whisper but with such fervor that the words were carried by his emotion.

"Are there any other considerations now?" the Islamite asked after a brief silence. "Do you have anything more for me?"

"I have maps in my quarters, if you have need of them," said the monk.

"No," answered the Islamite. "These documents should

be sufficient for our work." He glanced around. "We had best not remain much longer. One of the sailors inspects the holds from time to time, to be sure the cargo has not shifted."

The monk took a step back onto the walkway. "We are supposed to land tomorrow. I will be at the Palms Inn near the south gate of the city; it's used by pilgrims and merchants, if you need to speak to me again."

"It should not be necessary," said the Islamite. "You will carry documents again in the spring?"

"Yes. I think it will be safe. But I will want to . . . disappear after I deliver what I have." He paused. "With desertion so high in the ranks of the Crusaders, who will notice the loss of a single Hieronomite?"

"It will be noticed," said the Islamite with a certain grim humor, "when their men are ambushed and their ranks destroyed."

The monk made a motion to the Islamite, urging him to silence. "Later. We will speak later," he said, starting for the hold ladder.

"Fraire Eleus," the Islamite called softly after him, "if you have played us false, remember that the arm of the Sons of the Prophet is very long, and we will find you wherever you go."

"If I play you false," Fraire Eleus said from halfway up the ladder, "then you may burn out my eyes and fry my testicles for me to eat. On the sacred pages of the Koran, I do not play you false."

The Islamite bowed deeply as Fraire Eleus disappeared up the ladder.

Rainaut waited until the food in the trenchers he carried was almost cold before he dared to move from his hiding place. Then he slipped to his forward compartment, his mind jubilant for the first time since the Requiem had declared him officially dead. As he sat and ate the unappetizing contents of the trenchers, his thoughts ran feverishly, searching for ways to warn the Crusaders of what he had overheard. Long after the last of the pasty gravy had been licked from his fingers, Rainaut continued to ponder, hoping to find some means of notifying someone—anyone— who was of high enough rank that he would be believed.

Finally, as the squall began to blow itself out not long after nightfall, Rainaut steeled himself to speak with Olivia.

"What now?" she asked as she heard him tap on her door.

Briefly he told her about the Islamite and Fraire Eleus, and his own deep concern. "I know of it now, and I have an obligation to——"

"Do the dead have obligations?" she asked, knowing her own answer. "You are forbidden contact with Christians."

"I know," he whispered. "But if this Fraire Eleus is a spy, what then? Men will die because of him, and if I cannot stop him, the sin is mine."

All of Olivia's body hurt as if she had been dragged behind a swift chariot over rough ground. She bit back a sharp retort and attempted to answer sensibly. "If you are dead to them, you have no means to reach them. They have cast you out, you have not left on your own." She rubbed her hands together slowly, trying to ease the soreness.

"But my fealty . . ." he began, then stopped and tried once more. "I took a vow, as vassal of Reis Henry and now of Reis Richard, and I am bound by that vow." He waited for her to speak, and when she was silent, he continued. "I have a House and for that, I am under obligation. You understand that, don't you? Olivia?"

Olivia was staring at the cinnamon-scented wood little more than an arm's-length above her. "Valence, they cast you out. They have declared you dead. How can you be bound to them now, when they have said they will not have you?" Even as she spoke, she knew it was useless. "Who would accept a message from you?"

"My esquire, Huon," he said uncertainly. "There must be others . . ." His confidence faded as he considered his comrades. "They will have to listen. They will die otherwise."

"They may die in any case, have you thought of that?" She turned carefully onto her side. "There's not much room, but enter, Valence."

Awkwardly he pulled back the door. "I've lost more hair," he warned her. "And more of my skin is white."

"I don't mind," she said, saddened by his lost demeanor. "Sit. If you draw your knees up, there's room enough." She had raised herself to a half-sitting position, bracing her elbow against the sack she had carried since they were given their yellow cowls and cast out. "Does the light hurt your eyes more?"

He hesitated, then nodded. "The torchlight isn't too bad, but the sun—"

Olivia nodded in sympathy. "Yes."

"It's like needles in my eyes," he said as he did his best to hunker into the small space available for him. "When we land at Tarsus, I must try to reach someone," he said, taking up his argument once more.

"Do you think it will be permitted?" she asked, curious in spite of herself; she admired his loyalty almost as much as she was puzzled by it. "How can you gain access to anyone if they will not allow you to approach them? There is no Sier Valence Rainaut any longer for them."

"I have to find a way," he said, his expression hard to read now that half his face was white as marble. "If I do not, then my death—the death they have forced on me—is truly in vain."

Olivia made a second attempt at finding a less painful position, without success. "It was their decision to cast you out; why do you owe them anything more now that you are among the dead?"

"For my oath," he explained as if she were a ten-year-old child. "Until I am in my grave, I am not released from my oath, no matter what happens. That is the way it must be, or fealty is nothing." He drew his knees almost to his chin, crossed his arms atop them and rested his chin on his arm. "It isn't your way, Olivia, I understand that. But I am still a sworn knight."

"And you are determined to tell someone that there is a monk who is giving documents to an unknown Islamite," she said in resignation. "Even if you could reach someone of rank, what then? What can you tell them? That there is a monk who has been giving some sort of documents to an unknown Islamite? How can that warn them, and of what?"

Rainaut turned his ruined face toward her. "I have to do something. If I do not, I am worse than damned." He reached out to her, just touching her hand with his fingers. "I know that you do not understand why I must do this. I'm . . . sorry."

Olivia did not answer at once, and when she did, her mind was far away. "When I was young, my house had running water, hot and cold, and the water came from pure aqueducts. There were no fireplaces or hearths in the house because it was heated by the holocaust and a series of vents under the floor. There were special underground chambers where we kept ice year round, even in the heat of the summer. I bathed every day in hot, scented water—everyone, even the slaves did. I rode in open chariots, and I knew how to drive them. I owned land, in my own name, in my own right. Had my circumstances been different, I would have sued my husband in open court for how he handled my goods and monies. When it was learned what he had done, the Emperor had him executed—not as Imperial whim, but as part of the law. You have no notion how far we have fallen from that time. And all along the way, I have tried to keep a little of what I had then, some of the good things that you have lost." She caught his hand in hers. "So perhaps I do understand, in my own way, what you feel. But listen to me, Valence; you are at risk."

"It sounds as if you grew up in the kingdom of Prester John," said Rainaut with a short laugh. "Houses heated by vents under the floor." He shook his head, trying not to smile.

"I told you you could not imagine what has been lost," she said remotely as she pulled her hand away from his.

"And did you hear Our Lord speak, as well?" he asked, daring her to say she had.

"No. He was dead before I was born—not that I would have known about him, in any case." A memory rose, unbidden, and she told him, "But there was a feast one night . . . Nero gave a feast in the Golden House. There were Messianic Jews to be punished, and he had them executed during the festivities." She remembered finding Sanct' Germain in the laurel grove, and how he had sheltered her while human torches were lit in the enormous garden.

"Nero was a tool of the Devil, sent to destroy all true Christians," said Rainaut, not at all sure he believed what she was telling him.

"Nero was a spoiled boy who didn't know the difference

between a Farsi and a Jew, and didn't care," said Olivia bluntly. "The Jews were rebelling against the Roman garrison, and for that they were condemned to death, as were all rebels." She cocked her head to the side and regarded Rainaut with curiosity. "Do you doubt me?"

"Of course not," he lied unconvincingly.

She shook her head. "Of course you do," she corrected him. With a sudden motion of her hands, she shook off her reverie. "If you must reach someone with the Crusades, will you let me approach someone for you? You are identified as a leper—"

"So are you," he reminded her.

"—and one who has been a Hospitaler. More are apt to know about you and refuse to see you." In spite of the pain, she pulled herself upright. "Don't say no yet. Think over what you have said. If it is so important to you that the warning be given, let me help you."

Rainaut sighed. "If there is no other way, very well. Otherwise, you are to keep clear of what I do. They stone lepers who touch those who are not unclean."

"Just to make sure the leper is truly dead?" Olivia asked with a sardonic lilt to her words. "How providential."

* * *

Text of a letter from the Venetian Giozzetto Camarmarr to the Benedictine scholar Ulrico Fionder.

To my esteemed and learned cousin, whose name is praised everywhere, and who is known for his learning and piety, your less worthy cousin Giozzetto sends heartfelt greetings, and a small donation in thanks for your many prayers.

In the last six months, our ships have carried many more Crusaders and pilgrims to the Holy Land than we have carried sacks of grain or jars of wine. Truly this Holy War is a Godsend for the families of Camarmarr and Fionder. Our profits have trebled in the last year, and there is no reason to assume that our good fortune will not continue.

It is true that three of our ships have been lost to pirates in the last two years, but we have not only replaced them, we have added more ships to our fleet, and now we have a total of eleven ships wholly and completely owned by our two families, for which we thank God in His goodness. Even our dealings with the Islamites have increased as the pilgrims coming back from Jerusalem have wished for silks and spices and brassware that is found only in the Holy Land. One of our tarida bastardas brought back a full hold of ginger, pepper, Egyptian cotton and Damascus cloth: we have yet to reckon the extent of the profit we have gained from that single ship.

Therefore, we are now at pains to ensure our continued markets. We have dispatched negotiators—most of them Venetian Jews, so that the Islamites will not be offended—to make contracts with mercers and spice merchants—so that when the Crusade is over, we will not have to scramble for a place in the market, if you understand this.

Of course, I realize these considerations are of little interest to a great and holy scholar like you, but we are now in a position to aid you in your studies, for in such places as Jerusalem and Jaffa and Ascalon there are many texts that will be of interest to you and which you may wish to peruse. You have only to tell me what they are, and you have my assurance that every effort will be made to secure those writings for you, as a donation to your Order for the great good works you do in the Name of Christ. It will be my personal joy to present these to you on my return from my next venture into the Holy Land. Think, good cousin, of the treasures to be found, writings from the days of Jesus Himself, writings that might even have been taken down when He was preaching. Many cities boast rare texts from that time, and are treasured for their ancient worth.

We have decided not to purchase wood from what we have been told was the True Cross. It may be quite genuine, but a ship's carpenter has told me that he does not believe the wood we are being offered is more than a century old. Since we do not wish to perpetrate fraud, or to offer spurious relics— although there are many and many who are not so scrupulous

—we have refused the offer, and will be content to find manuscripts for great scholars, which will ultimately have greater worth than any of the toys of less honest men.

May God reward you for your devotion and your prayers, may He guide you in study and sanctity. May Maria bless you with wisdom and mercy.

       Your most affectionate and respectful cousin
       Giozzetto Camarmarr
By my own hand on the eve of the Feast of All Saints, in the 1191st year of Our Lord.

· 4 ·

His long yellow cowl obscured his face as Rainaut pushed his way through the crowded streets of Tarsus toward the Church of Saint John where the Hospitalers had their chapter house. He had little hope that he would be received there; still, the attempt was necessary, he told himself.

When he reached the door of the church, a sarjeant blocked the way. "The hospice of Saint Lazarus is outside the eastern gate, leper. You must go there. You cannot be admitted here."

Rainaut resisted the urge to walk away. "I was a Hospitaler, before I became unclean. I have urgent information for the Master of the Order in Tarsus." Just for such defiance he knew the sarjeant could beat him with a cudgel if he decided to.

"Dead men know nothing," said the sarjeant with rough pity. "Leave, before both of us have to answer for you."

"But there is a betrayer—" Rainaut began, only to have his words cut short by the sharp blow of the sarjeant's long staff on his shoulder.

"I told you: the hospice of Saint Lazarus will take you.

Only the living may enter here." He had moved to block the entryway completely, his stance determined and menacing.

"There is a betrayer," Rainaut repeated in an undertone as he walked away from the church, making sure that he remained in the sarjeant's sight for some little while. Only when he was certain that the sarjeant had ceased to watch him did he duck into a narrow alley, taking up a position like hundreds of other beggars along the way.

What Rainaut had thought was a heap of discarded rags suddenly erupted into life, and a man—grizzled, stick-thin, his face scarred, his eyes empty pits—shambled out of the tangled cloths on his knees. "Who's there?" he demanded in a querulous voice.

"I am," said Rainaut, staring at the man in hideous fascination.

The beggar groped toward him. "I won't have others here. This is my place."

"I'm not begging," said Rainaut in what he hoped was a soothing tone. "I don't want your place."

"That's what they all say," the beggar answered at once, reaching for a short dagger in the filthy ruins of the acton he wore. "But I'm too clever for you. I'm blind, but I'm no fool." As he said this, he crawled toward Rainaut.

"You're a fool if you fight me," said Rainaut. "I have both eyes, I have been a belted knight, and I stand on both feet."

The beggar stopped. "What of it? I've kept my place here for almost a year. I won't give it up to a French-speaking bastard who seeks to gull me." He inched closer to Rainaut. "I got both my hands yet."

Rainaut moved back two steps. "I am not a beggar. I do not want this place," he repeated, thinking that the man was scarred in his mind as well as his body. "I want to find a way to get a message to the Hospitalers, that's all."

"Hospitalers!" The beggar spat. "Every one of them is a liverless coward. They've no stomach for battle and no blood for glory." He dropped back, resting on his useless lower legs. "What man wishes to address a Hospitaler, I'd like to know."

"One who has been one," said Rainaut, suddenly much too tired to fight about it.

"Oh?" The beggar considered this as he played with the hilt of his dagger. "And what are you now?"

"No one. Nothing." Until that moment, the enormity of his exile had not struck Rainaut; now it went through him like a cauterizing blade.

"Why's that? You deserted?" The beggar cackled. "Half the men-at-arms have deserted, and enough of the knights that none of the kings want to talk about it." He directed his empty eyes toward Rainaut. "Which is it with you?"

"None of those," said Rainaut wearily.

"Dishonored, then? They caught you with booty?" He tossed his head back and laughed. "Good thing if you got a little of your own."

"No; they say I am unclean." The words were vile in his mouth; it contaminated him to say them, and he spoke with greater feeling than he thought he possessed.

"A leper, are you?" If the beggar was distressed he showed no sign of it.

"So they tell me." Rainaut sagged back against the uneven stones of the wall. "I have to get word to the Hospitalers, or to Reis Richard. They will not admit me—"

"Small wonder," said the beggar. "You're a walking dead man. If you think they'll heed you, you're badly mistaken, young fool." He started to slip back. "I'm hamstrung," he explained. "As if I needed that along with the rest."

Rainaut, who had recognized the beggar's accent, asked, "How does an Englishman end up a beggar in Tarsus?"

"The same way a Frenchman ends up a leper here," came the answer without rancor. "The damned Crusade, of course. I came as a man-at-arms. I heard all the tales of glory they told, and when they said Gui de Lusignan needed men to support him, well, that was better than being a weaver in Kent, wasn't it?" He laughed once more. "The Templars aren't very nice in their requirements, and I knew enough about arms to qualify for their support men. It wasn't much money, but it gave me a praiseworthy reason to leave England, and excused me from paying absentee rents on my cottage. I had a harridan of a wife and two sons with no more understanding than a turnip between them. It was a greater temptation than I could resist to take up the Cross.

My name's Bynum." This last was an afterthought. "Who were you before they buried you?"

"Valence Rainaut, from Saint-Prosperus-lo-Boys, in Aunis." It was only after he spoke that Rainaut realized he had not used his title.

"Another one of Reis Richard's vassals," said Bynum. He wagged his fingers in Rainaut's direction in an admonitory way. "Why do you want to seek out Reis Richard or the Hospitalers?" He was playing with his dagger again, but this time without any implied intent.

"To warn them. I have to warn them." Rainaut could see the disbelief in Bynum's expression, and he went on, "I have learned of a spy, a monk who is really an Islamite, who has documents that could—"

Bynum cut off this earnest description. "Why bother about that? What possesses you? You owe them nothing more than what they have already had of you—your life."

"I have my oath as a knight and as a Hospitaler," said Rainaut somewhat stiffly. The avowal had a hollow ring now, and he heard it with shock.

"Listen to me, Valence Rainaut: all that is behind you. Let it go." Bynum sat back once more and occupied himself tossing his dagger from hand to hand; in spite of his blindness, he rarely missed his catch.

Rainaut shook his head. "I cannot." He gazed away from Bynum toward the distant steps of Saint John's, wishing he knew a secret for gaining entry there. "The men who are in danger are my comrades-at-arms. If they are in danger, I must aid them if I can, even if they despise my aid."

Bynum laughed outright. "Straight out of a troubador's song, and better for the lack of a tune," he jeered.

"Think of how the Islamites have treated you, and consider what you may spare your fellow Christians," said Rainaut with feeling.

"Islamites have always treated me very well," said Bynum with a frown. "If it weren't for the Islamites, I would have starved last winter."

Rainaut was aghast. "How can you say that? Look at all they've done to you."

"Oh, you thought that *Islamites* did this to me, did you?" His laughter was so derisive that it sounded like a hail of arrows striking stone walls. "Oh, no, no, no, Valence Rainaut. No, no. It was good, pious *Christians* who did this to me, sincere and righteous men from Greece who feared that the Templars intended to capture half of Byzantium, and therefore sought a confession from me and two others. They—the other two—are in their graves. I am . . . as I am." He flung his dagger with sudden fury, and it was embedded in the wooden frame of the doorway where he sat. "You owe nothing to Christ and to God. You owe nothing to kings or Orders or any of the rest of it. They've tossed you out, my lad, and they won't be pleased to hear from you again, no matter what you have to tell them."

"No," said Rainaut, starting to back away. "You are—"

"Heretical?" Bynum ventured with tremendous good humor. "Blasphemous? Anything you like." He laughed again. "Give yourself a year as a leper and see how you feel."

"I pray it will never come to that." Rainaut spoke distantly as he stared at Bynum, who had been an English weaver, with a wife and two sons, and was now blind, scarred and crippled, living on alms in this side street of Tarsus.

"We all do that at first, lad. We promise we won't forget our purpose, our vows. Oho, how we struggle to pretend we are still men among men." He hooted twice. "It won't last: believe me, Rainaut, it won't last."

"With aid and guidance—" Rainaut began, remembering all the admonitions he had received as a child.

"Aid and guidance." Bynum shook his head many times as he went on speaking. "Not for the likes of you or me. We're beyond it all now. We're less than the mules that pull the wagons, we're less than the onions in their soup." He paused. "You say that you want to warn the Hospitalers. Have you tried?"

"Yes," Rainaut admitted.

"You wear a yellow cowl, don't you? They won't let you into a house or a church or anyplace but the hospice of Saint Lazarus. That's worse than a bear-pit; have care." He began to feel along the doorsill, searching for his dagger. "No one speaks to those in yellow cowls."

"Do they speak to beggars?" Rainaut asked with a contempt that shamed him.

"When they notice me, sometimes they say a word or two, as if I were simpleminded. They *pity* me." He said this last with venom.

A year ago, Rainaut would not have understood why Bynum loathed pity, but now he shared the feeling. He straightened his shoulders. "I have a few pieces of silver. They're yours if you'll help me."

"Help you do what?" Bynum asked, immediately suspicious.

"Help me reach the Hospitalers," Rainaut said simply. "You may be right, but if I do not make some attempt, it will be a greater burden than my soul can bear."

"What nonsense!" scoffed Bynum. He laughed once more. "You are determined to have your cross, aren't you? You'll even hold the nails for them." Saying this, he scuttled closer to Rainaut. "What makes you think—even if you reach them—that they will be saved?"

"I must try," Rainaut persisted stubbornly.

Bynum turned his head heavenward, as if rolling his eyes. "What a fool you are." He paused. "You want me to help you, don't you?"

"If you will," said Rainaut quietly.

"To reach one of the Hospitalers or English knights, is that correct?" He rubbed at his jaw. "You wish that?"

"Yes," said Rainaut emphatically.

There was a silence between them while Bynum considered what Rainaut said. "I know only two men associated with the Hospitalers. The knights don't bother with such derelicts as I am. I know a page and a herald. If they will speak to me, I will try to get them to hear you." He fingered his dagger. "Not that it will do any good."

Rainaut was at once relieved and apprehensive. "Why do you say that?"

"Your yellow cowl. It means nothing to me, but it will distress them, you have my word on it." He made a sudden swipe at the air with his dagger. "Take care that they do not do for you when they find what you are."

"They won't," said Rainaut with faltering conviction. "I was one of them."

"So was I," said Bynum. He moved away and reclaimed his position in the doorway. "No one's talked to me in . . . oh, most of a year now. They said a few words from time to time, and all the rest of it, but you talk to me." He considered this. "You're not planning to put a knife in my back, are you?"

This sudden change back to suspicion baffled Rainaut. "Why should I do that?"

"For my place. It's a good place. You get alms here. They don't beat you very often and you won't starve. There've been others who tried." He touched his dagger. "I'm still here."

"I don't want your place. They wouldn't let me keep it, even if I had it," Rainaut said, desolation coming over him more deeply than before.

"True; true." He fell silent, and Rainaut wondered if he had been forgot or dismissed. Then Bynum spoke again. "I hear that Reis Richard is leading the Crusade. Is that true?"

"Yes, they say so," Rainaut answered.

"Even if they take it, they won't keep it. Jerusalem's too far from France and England. They'll lose it if they take it." He nodded his head several times, keeping cadence with his words. "They want it for the Glory of God, or so they say. But it's a rotten place, and it will consume everyone who comes there."

"Jerusalem?" Rainaut asked, not certain of Bynum's meaning.

"Jerusalem, Ascalon, Jaffa, Sidon, Tyre, all the forts and towns and monasteries. It's this *place,* do you see? It ruins us. We weren't made to be here, and when we come, it poisons us. Look what happened to me. To you." He chuckled angrily. "Still, if you want me to speak to those I know, I will. For honor, if you like. Can you read or write?"

"A little. Enough," said Rainaut.

"I never learned letters, but the Brothers taught me to count and to compute. I know my numbers well enough." His jaw came up defensively. "Not everyone who knows such things is a noble or cleric."

"You were fortunate to have teachers," agreed Rainaut once he decided what was best to say. "For a weaver, the skill must have been useful."

"It helped," Bynum allowed. "I have nothing to write with, nor anything to write on. Do you?"

"No," said Rainaut. "I can try to get them at Saint Lazarus. They may have no room for me, but they might do that much." He wondered if there were writing materials in Olivia's sack that she took such pains to keep by her. "If they will not, I will find it elsewhere."

"What you do is describe what you know. You do that, and I will try to arrange a chance for you to speak with the page or the herald. They aren't much, but—"

"They are more than I could have done alone," said Rainaut in a sudden rush of gratitude. "May God bless you for—"

Bynum held up his hand. "Oh, no. No, no, no. I've had all the blessings I can stand for a lifetime." He leaned back and directed his empty sockets squarely at Rainaut. "Come back tomorrow, after morning Mass, and meet me here."

"Why after morning Mass?" Rainaut wondered aloud.

"Because I often receive alms after Mass. They might even give you a coin or two, though most people won't go near lepers." He gave another sudden burst of laughter. "Back in Kent, I was always cold. England is like that, summer and winter. I felt that the cold had got into my bones. I thought that here I would flourish, like a plant in the sun. But now, I know that this is not the summer I longed for, it is a grill, and I have been left to parch and char on it."

"You could get passage back," Rainaut suggested to him uncertainly. "You fought as man-at-arms with the Templars; you are entitled to be carried home now that you can no longer fight."

"To do what?" Bynum asked in soft ferocity. "Weave? My wife was a shrew when I left, and I was a whole man. What would marriage be like now that I have no eyes and I cannot walk?" There was no trace of self-pity in him. "I am dead to them, and so I will remain."

"In fact, we're both dead men?" Rainaut said, trying to achieve some of the same mordant amusement Bynum had.

"Only I know it, and you deny it," said Bynum. He rubbed at the enormous calluses on his knees. "Bring me the writing, and I will do what I can."

Rainaut hesitated. "Why?"

"For something to do. Because you spoke to me. Because I

know it's futile. Because I want to make amends before I die. For caprice, or honor, or vengeance. One of those may be the reason." His laughter was low and crooning. "And perhaps I am mad as well as blind, and nothing I have said is true." He grinned in Rainaut's direction. "You won't know that until tomorrow."

"I—" Rainaut began, then stopped. "I will be here after the first Mass. If you are, I will have messages for the page and the herald. You can take them or not, as you wish." He suddenly wanted to be gone from that narrow, hot alley. The walls seemed to press in upon him and his head rang with pain from his reddened eyes. He backed away from where Bynum sat, and almost fell as he reached the main street, which was a step higher than the alley.

Angry voices shouted at him to keep his distance, and one woman screamed.

Belatedly Rainaut remembered to call out: "Unclean! I am unclean!" In the next instant he had to dodge a blow from a quarterstaff and a small volley of stones and pebbles. He cringed as curses were yelled at him. Scuttling like a beetle he retreated along the wall of the fortified house that fronted the street until he found another churchyard. With a sob, he rushed through the iron gate into the peace of graves and headstones. Shading his eyes, he looked for the most protected part of the cemetery, and when he found it, he moved cautiously toward it, knowing that not even those who tended the graves would impede him. He would be able to wait until sundown to leave the city and rejoin Olivia outside Tarsus' gates. In the meantime, this was respite. Here, among the dead, he would be safe.

*   *   *

Text of a letter from the Chatelaine Fealatie Bueveld to the Abbot of Sante-Estien-in-Gorze.

To the revered Abbot, my deliverer and my mentor in trial, I fulfill my continuing obligation to you by informing you of what has transpired in my pilgrimage. I fear that this letter will be long in reaching you, for circumstances are such that all the world seems in constant upheaval and no one can think himself safe.

There has been a great battle of Crusaders and Islamites. If half the tales one hears are true, all the coastal towns are now hip-deep in blood. I have spoken with knights who took part in the siege of Acre in July, and they are confident that by this time next year, Jerusalem will once again be in Christian hands. Reis Richard has made Acre his headquarters, although he is often in the field. In September, Reis Richard had another great victory over the Islamites at Arsuf. I have been told variously that he conquered Ascalon as well, but the most prevalent story is that the Islamites themselves destroyed the city to keep it from falling into Christian hands. What the truth of these tales is I hope to determine before reaching Jerusalem itself, which I pray God will be after Christian forces have reclaimed it.

We are currently at Tour Rouge, which is like a keep. We have been denied escort south for at least two weeks until more is known about the actual progress and disposition of the Crusades. If Ascalon is truly in Christian hands, then the door to Jerusalem and Egypt stands open, and those who battle for the Glory of God will sweep the Islamites before them. If Ascalon was destroyed, then the course of the Crusade is uncertain, for without that city, only Jaffa is close enough to supply it from the sea, and it has no access to Egypt. I have yet to learn why the Egyptian access is as crucial as is said, but in time it will be explained to me, and I will pass the information to you. It puzzles me that the Islamites would willingly destroy their own city, but they bow to a fallacious deity, and possibly they are being misled because of it.

We have made application to the French, the English, and the Austrians for permission to enter Jerusalem, but so far this has been denied. It might still be possible to join with some of the other pilgrims and enter the city on foot and unarmed, but the terms of my pilgrimage would not then be fulfilled, and my husband would be well within his rights to declare me no longer his wife for the offense I have given the Comes de Reissac. Therefore I will remain here with my small company and await the time when we may join with Christian chivalry in entering those holy gates in full harness.

Two of our mules have foundered and I have purchased new ones to carry our goods. The expense was much greater than I had anticipated, and that now means that our return must be overland, since we will not then have sufficient funds to ship all our horses, our gear, and ourselves. Passage on ships is hard to obtain in any case, and the cost is high.

In following the conditions of this pilgrimage, I have prayed at every church and shrine along the way from Franconia to the Holy Land. More and more often, this has brought me distress, for I have seen for myself those cast-offs from the fighting—men who have lost hands and arms and legs to battle—men whose minds are no longer wholesome—families driven to the greatest extremities of poverty and misfortune. And there is disease everywhere. This is a pestilent land, where infection lurks in the very air we breathe. Luckily we have thus far been spared the flux, which has claimed so many others. The Bailiff here has informed me that in August alone, one hundred twenty-two men died here from nothing more than bloody flux. I pray God that no such catastrophe will befall those on Crusade, and that those men-at-arms who accompany me will be spared that deadly fate. There are risks enough, what with bandits and slavers and other scoundrels preying on those who have come here for their soul's salvation.

I ask you to speak with my husband on my behalf. Tell him what you think is best from the letter. It is my fondest hope *that he will accept my expiation and will restore me to my place, and that the dishonor I have brought upon him will be forgot in light of what I have done. If he cannot do this, I will be guided by you in my actions, although I must warn you that I have no religious vocation and would not be suited to a cloistered life. Since I was trained to stand in the place of my husband, to protect and defend my holdings, I find that I cannot set that aside entirely. Whatever disposition is made, I beg you will hold in your deliberations the nature of my temperament.*

For your guidance and prayers, you have my continued and abiding gratitude. For your wise counsel, you have my most profound respect. With the aid of God, His Son, and Holy Maria, you will be alive and hale when I return, that I may have the opportunity to acknowledge your righteousness and merciful judgment before God and our community.

> *Fealatie Bueveld*
> *Chatelaine of Gui de*
> *Fraizmarch*

By my own hand and under the seal of Castel Fraizmarch, on the feast of Saint Theodore the Studite, who is venerated here in the Greek tradition, on November 9th, in the Lord's Year 1191.

· 5 ·

There was no doubt that the herald was nervous; he coughed and shuffled from one foot to the other, all the while plucking nervously at the cote-of-arms he wore. "I'm not supposed to be here," he said as soon as Bynum appeared. "If it's ever learned, I'll—"

"I won't mention it. You had the note I sent to you." He had propped himself up on the third step of the narrow

staircase. "The fellow is determined to speak with someone."

"I shouldn't listen," Aimeri said miserably. "This is
wrong." He took several steps away from Bynum, then came
back. "This monk who is a spy? What of it?" Before Bynum
answered, he went on, "It's preposterous. No monk would
spy for the Islamites. It's unthinkable."

Bynum's ruined face was expressionless. "But perhaps
you still ought to listen to the fellow, in case he has learned
something."

The herald swore under his breath as he fretted. "A leper.
He ought to be at Saint Lazarus."

"He tells me he used to be a Hospitaler. Like you."
Bynum made his grimace of a smile. "That's what he says.
Of course, all he is now is a leper."

"Oh, God," Aimeri murmured, blessing himself. "I can't
do this. I want no part of this. I must not listen to someone
who is unclean." He had turned on his heel and was about to
walk away from the concealed meeting place when he saw a
cowled figure at the far end of the narrow court. "Holy
Christ and the Angels."

Rainaut moved to the edge of the shadows but avoided
the open sunlight. "I must speak with you," he said, keeping
his hands at his sides though he wanted to reach out and
restrain the herald. He sensed the fear the herald felt, and he
did his best to mollify it. "For the sake of all the Knights of
Saint John."

"I shouldn't be here." Aimeri paced; he strove to avoid
Rainaut, at the south end, and Bynum, at the north end of
the narrow court. "Well, what is it? I can't promise anything,
you understand. There's probably nothing I can do. I
mustn't reveal how I have obtained this . . . information."

"Coming here on a ship not long ago—" Rainaut began
only to be interrupted.

"How could a leper come on a ship?" The herald almost
shrieked the question. "No leper is welcome on a ship."

"Through bribery and concealment," said Rainaut in a
level tone. "There is no other way."

Aimeri blanched. "Oh, God."

Rainaut chose to ignore this outburst. "During a squall at

sea, while I was in the hold, I chanced to overhear the meeting of an Islamite and a man in the habit of the Hieronomites, who passed information to the Islamite, and who gave his word to continue his spying. There could be no mistaking his intent. He was not drawing out the Islamite for the benefit of Christians, he was betraying Christians to the enemy. This Hieronomite gave documents to the Islamite, one of plans of the agreements between the Templars and Leopold of Austria, one of the names of pilgrims who would command ransom if taken. This monk encouraged the Islamite to act, and gave praise to the Islamite Allah. He is a traitor to his King and his God, and for his ill work, the lives of Hospitalers and many other worthy Christians are in danger." It was difficult for Rainaut to contain his emotions; his voice grew ragged as he spoke.

"What did this supposed spy give to the Islamite? Was there anything specific, or do you have only this . . . this fable to offer me?" Aimeri was taking refuge in disbelief and bravado now, replacing his earlier dread with scorn. "What ship was this? What Islamite took the documents? Or don't you know?"

"No, I don't know," said Rainaut, knowing he had been defeated. "And I could not identify either man if I saw him now, for the light in the hold was very low and the two of them kept to the shadows, as spies do." He crossed his arms. "You will not help me."

Aimeri blustered. "Well, with so little, and so much doubt, I cannot see how there is anything to help with." He waved one hand as if banishing a noxious odor. "The world is filled with spies, they say. There are always rumors."

"This is no rumor," Rainaut said quietly.

"And in a war, half the world seems to change sides," the herald continued as if Rainaut had not spoken. "There is no reason to think that even if a monk gave documents to an Islamite—which I question—that they were genuine. Most likely the monk was offering the Islamite faulty information, to lead the Islamites into error." He turned on Bynum, approaching him with subdued fury. "Why did you tell me to come here? Why did you want me to listen to this? There is trouble enough in the world without such intrusion."

"I asked him to bring me you," Rainaut said, stung to

anger on Bynum's behalf. "I thought that you might have sense."

Aimeri continued to upbraid Bynum. "You are a disgrace! You have almost caused me to make a fool of myself. I will not forget this. Lepers! Monks!" With that, he pushed past Bynum and hastened away up the narrow stairs.

"I did warn you," Bynum said after a short silence.

"Yes," Rainaut agreed.

"A pity you did not listen," he said complacently. "But you understand now?"

Rainaut was staring down at his white knuckles where his long, blunt hands locked together. "Someone must listen. There must be someone who will listen."

Bynum's strident laughter echoed around the little court. "You don't understand yet, but you will, my friend." He rocked back, bouncing on his heels. "They don't want to hear you, they don't want to be told of apostate monks and spies. All they want is the assurance that they can still take Jerusalem. The fools haven't yet realized that they lost Jerusalem when Saladin ordered Ascalon razed."

"There will be men killed and held captive." Rainaut said this with dire certainty. "I must—"

Bynum's patience was nearly exhausted. "You've tried, Rainaut. You made the attempt. That's all anyone requires of you, king or God. You can confess with a pure heart now." Once again he laughed. "Take me back to my doorway."

Rainaut obeyed, picking Bynum up in his arms and starting down the long, vaulted alley, feeling how pathetically thin the man was. As they went, he asked, "Does it bother you that you are touching a leper?"

"Saint George defend us! No. No, no. What can leprosy do to me that has not already been done? My toes might as well rot off for all the good they are to me, and how much more disfigured can I become?" He paused, then went on more seriously, "If I had not lost my eyes, it might be different, but since I can't see, what difference would it make?"

They were almost to the far end of the alley, and Rainaut took care to be certain no one had occupied Bynum's doorway. "I am in your debt."

"There is no debt, leper," said Bynum indifferently. "You have now discharged your duty. For the sake of the peace of your soul, let it go." He twisted in Rainaut's hold. "If you try again, it will be worse. They will end with stoning you." By Rainaut's silence, Bynum knew he was not convinced. "You were fortunate this time—Aimeri is only a herald. If you approach a knight, or a sarjeant, it could go badly."

"What is it to you if it does go badly?" Rainaut asked as they reached the doorway where Bynum lived.

"Nothing at all," said Bynum. He steadied himself with a hand on the doorframe as Rainaut put him down. "There are hospices for afflicted knights outside of the city. Find one and take what comfort you can there."

Rainaut had the oddest sensation that Bynum's empty eyes could actually see him. "And if I cannot do that?"

"You're already a living dead man." He pulled his dagger out, snicking it at Rainaut. "That should be cross enough to bear."

There was some justice in what Bynum said, Rainaut allowed. He straightened up. "Remember me in your prayers, Bynum, as I will remember you in mine."

"The only thing I pray for is death," said Bynum, and faced away from Rainaut with as much finality as if he had dropped a portcullis between them. "If you were wise, you would do the same." With a sharp gesture, he motioned Rainaut away from him.

The words of thanks Rainaut had wanted to speak would not come; he knew that Bynum had done with him. Feeling suddenly very clumsy and inept, Rainaut stumbled out of the alley into the busy street, remembering at the last moment to cry: "Unclean! I am unclean!" It still appalled him to see the repugnance and loathing in people around him. As several shoved and jostled to get away from him, he wanted to call out to them that he could not harm them, that he had no wish to make others unclean.

A shard of brick glanced off his forehead, then half a dozen pebbles struck his back. He heard a rock bounce off the wall behind him, and not far away, someone was shouting to bring stones. They would not kill me, Rainaut told himself. Not long ago he might have been able to convince himself; now he ran, arms raised and locked above his head to shield him and to protect his eyes from the sun. The cold, numbing fear that had shamed him so many times in the past settled just below his ribs, spreading out through his vitals as he ran for the nearest city gate.

Beyond the walls of Tarsus there were storage sheds and inns; beyond those, there were chapels and farmsteads. And beyond those, at the edge of the enormous wastes, there were hovels where the beggars and the afflicted took shelter. In one of those noisome three-sided huts, Olivia welcomed Rainaut back from his futile errand.

"You look tired," she said as she moved the long palm fronds from the entrance. It was hot inside, but not with the blind implacability of direct sunlight. "Be careful; I found three scorpions in the wall chinks this morning."

Rainaut hesitated before dropping onto his knees. "I think I would welcome scorpions after today," he said in a low voice. "Perhaps I'll look for them later."

As she adjusted the three woven mats that served as a floor, Olivia remarked, "There's a cut on your brow. Did anything happen?" She did not sound upset or even particularly curious; Rainaut had no idea the effort it cost her to do this.

"They tried to stone me as I left the city," he said, exhaustion in every aspect of his body. "After I saw the herald. That was useless." He dropped his clenched fist onto the mat. "No one cares, or they don't care enough to listen to a leper. If I could find a way to approach someone who is whole who would believe me and help me." He stopped; the futility of his predicament now felt overwhelming. "You've heard me say all this before, haven't you? Not that it has made any difference."

"It's to your credit that you still care for your comrades no matter how they have treated you," Olivia said in the same studied way. "The maimed one? Your English friend? Bynum? Will he not help you again?"

"No," said Rainaut softly, staring down at his hand. "The skin is changing. My hands are starting to turn white, too. And there's no hair left on my arms." He rubbed his forehead, wincing as he touched the cut left by the brick that had struck him. "I thought leprosy would kill the hurt, that I would be numb where it touched me. That's what I've been told. Everyone knows about—"

"If you were a leper, you would be," said Olivia, wanting to yell at him. The only indication of her feelings was the very precise way she pronounced each word. "Since you are not, there is no respite."

"Oh, yes," he said with weary sarcasm. "That fancy of yours. You know more of disease than anyone living, I suppose, and you know that I am not a leper. What is destroying me only appears to be leprosy and is actually something else, which is not a dangerous disease at all." He leaned back, his eyes closed. "Olivia, I treasure you, and I thank God night and day for your fidelity, but you need not maintain your lie for me, not now. I know what I am."

"No," she said with great determination. "You know what others want you to believe and you haven't the courage to trust me." Her hazel eyes snapped. "Not that it matters now. We have lost our place on Alhim's ship and it will be some time before I can find us other passage." She tossed five gold coins onto the mat beside him. "At least you need not starve while we wait."

He stared at the coins as if they glowed. "Where did you get these?"

"I earned them," she said bluntly.

He was very still. "How?" He motioned her into silence as soon as he asked the question; he stared at the coins so he would not have to look at her. "They're Persian," he said, making his identification an accusation.

"So they are," Olivia agreed. "I have enough to purchase us passage again—or I will have in a short while—if there is a ship that will take us."

"Us? Us? There are ships that will take you," he said, closing his eyes again. "That's what should concern you, Olivia, not how much you can bribe a captain to put me aboard."

She did not trust herself to speak at once. "What absurdity is this now? I thought we agreed."

Rainaut swallowed hard, but still the tears came. "You can leave. You ought to leave. Here I can do nothing for you but cause you more misery than I have brought you already." He rolled onto his side. "If God were merciful, He would let me die."

As she listened to this outburst, Olivia tried not to rebuke him, for she knew how much it pained him to make his confession. She waited until Rainaut was silent, then knelt beside him and took his hand. "I don't want to leave you. But I promise you this—if we find those who can offer you better care than I can give you, and are willing, I will see you are established with such aid. Otherwise, I cannot abandon you. Don't bring up your arguments again: we have said it all before now and nothing has changed. Your blood is still part of me, and that's the end of it."

Rainaut listened to her without moving. "I will hold you to your word," he said when she was finished.

"Certainly," she said, unable to keep the aggravation out of her tone. "And if," she went on after faltering, "you think to force me into turning away from you, you will have to find other means. I am bound by blood, as you are by your vows." She reached out and took his hand in hers. "Whatever was in the documents, surely has happened already. You can't undo the damage and you give yourself needless pain."

He pulled his hand away. "I must reach someone. I have to find someone who will listen. Until I do, I will have to remain here. That should not hamper you. Find another ship and return to Roma, where you belong. You don't need to tell them about the Requiem. You are clean, that's apparent enough."

Olivia sighed. "There's no point in argument. We do not and will not agree. Here. I have cheese and fruit for you," she said, refusing to be drawn into the dispute that had almost become a habit for them.

"I don't want them." His hunger was sharper, more demanding as soon as he spoke his denial.

"But you do, you know." She offered him a small, firm, hard-skinned apple. "And there is water, which you also need."

"And you don't," he challenged.

She refused to be goaded. "No."

He took the apple and sniffed it. "Where did you get

this?" He did not like the reproach he heard in his voice, and he was ashamed of the anger he felt, seeing her whole. The smudge of dirt on the edge of her jaw did not detract from her loveliness, and her fawn-brown hair, tied back as simply as a farmer's, was shiny and clean. "And where did you wash your hair?"

"At the same place," she said. "There is an inn, catering to those who are not pilgrims, not far from—"

"I know the place," he said condemningly.

"I've gone there to serve as translator. The owner pays me, allows me to use the baths, gives me food. Those I translate for pay me . . . whatever fee we agree upon. I have Persian and three different forms of Egyptian, two forms of Greek—which was what I was using today—Roman, Latin, Frankish, French, both Norman and Parisian, a little German, Armenian—"

"You are a most remarkable and accomplished lady," Rainaut said, cutting her recitation short. "A treasure for the innkeeper, no doubt, who has plans for you."

"He does not," said Olivia with a slight smile. "If I were fourteen, a golden-haired Venetian, and a boy, he might change his mind."

Without thinking Rainaut blessed himself. "What creatures live in this part of the world! How does such perversity flourish? What does the heat do to them, that they are disposed to such usage?" He felt his own outburst with astonishment, amazed at the shock and disgust he heard.

"Perhaps that is why your Reis Richard came here?" Olivia suggested gently.

Rainaut held up his hand. "I cry you mercy," he said, nodding to her. "I do not know why I . . . It is a sin, a very great sin, but there are those who are ruled by it, as others are ruled by gluttony or wrath. Only God is incapable of sin."

"On that you and the Islamites agree," said Olivia, once again moving the food nearer to him.

He did not answer at once while he munched on the apple. When he did, some of the animation which had been gone from his eyes had returned. "Do you think that any of these guests at the inn would be willing to carry a message, in exchange for your service as a translator?" He no longer had eyebrows, but the expanse of silvery skin above his eyes moved as if he had lifted them. "And would you be willing to try it?"

Olivia poured out a cup of water and offered it to Rainaut as much to give her a little time to think as from any sense of courtesy. "Urgently?"

"If at all possible." He had finished the apple and set the core neatly aside.

She watched him, and knew she could not refuse. "All right, but I cannot assure you that the message will be carried or received." How much she wanted to touch him, to hold him for consolation and kindness and love, yet she did not dare, not while he dreamed of his final expiation. "What shall I tell whomever will carry the message?"

He sat a bit straighter and took a long drink from the cup. "That it must reach as high as possible among the Hospitalers, so that I need not trouble myself with pages and heralds any more."

"Very well," she said. "Tell me what you want the message to say, and I will write it."

Rainaut began on the cheese. "If we don't succeed now, then God has willed that I not succeed. But I know someone will pay attention, and then that false Hieronomite will be caught and shown for the traitor he is, to his country and his God." He chewed steadily, persistently. "In all my prayers I thank you, Olivia." Then his manner softened. "I've been a poor bargain, haven't I?"

"I've made worse ones," she said candidly.

"So much travail and so little joy," he said distantly, his blue eyes focused on something far away from that hovel by the desert road. "You should have remained in Tyre."

Olivia laughed bitterly. "That would not have answered."

"Still," he said. "You deserve more than this. I am no protector for you, nor lover now. I apologize, Olivia."

"There is no reason; you know that." She cleared away the scraps from his meal, humming occasionally, while Rainaut knelt in prayer. Only when he blessed himself and turned did she speak to him again. "Tell me: what shall I say in this note?"

Text of an unofficial letter from the secretary of the Metropolitan of Hagia Sophia to the Abbot of the Benedictine monastery on Rhodes.

To my reverend and most pious fellow-Christian, I take pen in hand again to share my thoughts with you and to hope that your prayers will aid me in this troublesome time, for all of us face a great test, and I fear greatly that we are failing in that test. Information has reached me that Reis Phillippe is in poor health and speaks of returning to France. Reis Richard wastes time at Jaffa and speaks of rebuilding a city the Islamites themselves destroyed: Ascalon. It is Jerusalem that is the goal, and all else is as nothing before it.

I would not say this to others, and I write to you in confidence, but this supposed treaty that has been discussed between Reis Richard and the vile Saladin has greatly shocked me, and I am filled with trepidation at the suggestion. How is it that so great a warrior as Richard Coer de Leon can be misled by this Saladin? Of all the Christian Kings who have come to the defense of Our Lord, none has been as diligent as Reis Richard, and none has brought such accomplishments on the field of battle as he. Now the rumors are that he is willing to hold back, with Jerusalem almost in sight. How can such a thing happen? Reis Richard has got near the most sacred walls, and now is content to retreat? What demon has entered his mind that he should consider such a thing at this time? Has not the sand run red with French and English blood that now cries out with that most sacred blood of Jesus for vengeance?

We of the Eastern Rite have been critizised for our lack of zeal in not joining the Crusades, and there are some for whom such condemnation is well-deserved. But many of our number have looked to you as our salvation, and we see that when faith must be most burning, most enduring, it is little more than a travesty. Where is the ardor that marked the beginning? Where is that eternal torch of sacred duty? Have the men of the Crusade quenched it with riotous living and plunder, or did they never have it at all?

Pray forgive this outburst, but I have such great feeling within me that I must speak out or succumb. The great fighting men of Christendom have been the wonder of all, and to hear that they are unwilling to press forward is more distressing than words can tell you.

We have seen some of those who have fought and paid the price—not the dead, but the injured, the maimed. Surely they have earned the respect of Christians everywhere. That many now live as beggars is a reproach to all of us, especially to those Kings who have brought their men to this distant place and then refused them succor when their usefulness is gone. Here at Hagia Sophia we offer prayers for those fallen in battle every day, and those who come for alms we make a daily donation of bread.

What may I do to aid you in bringing renewed purpose to the Crusaders? How can I evoke the stern glory of reclaiming Jerusalem if the knights and men-at-arms can do nothing themselves? Victory is being taken from us at the very hour it might be in our hands. I beseech you to exhort the Crusaders to extend themselves, to press onward into the very heart of the foe in order to gain the most precious triumph. Never has our need been greater than at this time, when our purpose is forgot or uncertain. Zeal will strengthen the might of the Crusade, and I beg God and you, good Abbot, to kindle it in the hearts of all Christian warriors for the struggle to come. For those who have fallen and will fall, be sure my prayers and the prayers of the faithful at Hagia Sophia are with you, and will be a sweet anthem when the Last Judgment comes. Be sure that in that hour, those who fought for Our Lord will be among those refulgent in glory, just as those who deserted Our Lord at His hour of need and neglect will be first amongst those cast forever into the burning abyss.

With the assurance that my devotion to your cause, which is also the cause of Our Lord, remains foremost in my prayers

and meditations, and that my castigations are from an excess
of dedication rather than the carping of a frightened servant.
The victory of Christians over the might of Islam is my sole
concern, and worthy of all sacrifice in that cause.

Alexios from Salinika

With the consent of my master, by my own hand and under
seal, six days before the Most Holy Mass of Christ in the
Lord's Year 1191.

· 6 ·

Niklos' arm swept brushes, styluses, inkpots, and parchments onto the floor. "What do you mean, you *lost* her?" he demanded as he swung around to face his visitor.

"That's what I've been trying to tell you," Ithuriel Dar protested as he came into the study. "You wouldn't let me finish."

Loose slates rattled on the roof, making an eerie tattoo for their conversation. At the back of his mind, Niklos knew he would have to order repairs as soon as the rain slacked off. "As you wish," he said, trying to be patient and reasonable. "Tell me what happened."

Ithuriel Dar had a new scar on the bridge of his hooked nose and he was missing the little finger of his left hand. He paced down the study, then spoke to Niklos. "I told you about what happened on Cyprus."

"It's ridiculous. Olivia's no leper." He said that with such unemphatic conviction that Dar was almost convinced. "So you have completed a search of the island."

"For all the good it does, yes," Dar admitted. "I did get to speak to one of those apprentice monks at the monastery of Saint George of the Latins. He saw Rainaut and Bondama Clemens turned out." It was not possible to look at Niklos now. "He said that they . . . well, she took a few things with them. Apparently she must have kept some money, because she bribed a local sea captain—the fellow's known to be a smuggler—to take them off Cyprus."

"What!" Niklos surged to his feet and in four long strides had seized Dar's shoulders. "Repeat that."

"She . . . she and the Hospitaler . . . the leper . . . they were smuggled off Cyprus." Seeing the expression in Niklos' ruddy-brown eyes, Dar babbled on, as if words were the only thing that would hold him at bay. "It was . . . just a small ship. It . . . is seaworthy . . . nothing to look at . . . not very fast . . . but Bondama Clemens was safe while she was aboard her. I vouch for that." He tried to lift his hands without success. "You frighten me, Aulirios."

Niklos snorted. "With reason." He released Dar and stepped back. "It's not your doing, I suppose," he went on more calmly. "No one knows better than I what Olivia can get up to. Bribed a smuggler, did she?"

"Yes, . . . Magister," said Dar, when he had decided on an important enough title for Niklos.

"Magister?" Niklos made a gesture of dismissal. "I'm a bondsman, Captain Dar," he reminded his guest. "Where was the smuggling ship bound?"

"One of the men working with me found the captain—a rascal named Alhim—in Rhodes. He said that Bondama Clemens and her leman had gone ashore at Tarsus and never returned. It may be true."

"Yes, and it may not," said Niklos heavily. "Is this rascal of a captain known for slaving?"

"No," said Dar, visibly relieved to say it. "He is too small a dealer for that, and has too little money. Smuggling and some theft—"

"And piracy?" suggested Niklos.

"Not in that ship," Dar said with a quick smile. "You couldn't bring down a lily pad in a duck pond with Alhim's ship. But I wouldn't leave goods unguarded on the wharf when he's about."

Niklos nodded, sharing some of the amusement Dar felt. "Then you think she did go ashore?"

"Yes, and possibly at Tarsus. The captain had no reason to

lie about it." He folded his arms as if facing into the wind. "I am prepared to leave for Tarsus as soon as the weather clears. You have only to order it."

"Tarsus," mused Niklos. "And by the time you get there, she will have joined a caravan or a troupe of mummers or stolen a horse and gone to Antioch or . . . anywhere." He pinched his nose between his thumb and forefinger. "Agh. I can't think about it. But I must."

"She is a . . . an intrepid woman," Dar offered, unsure how to respond to what Niklos said.

"Intrepid." He considered it. "She is that." The first flicker of lightning tweaked the sky, and shortly afterward a rumble of thunder. Niklos went to the window and stared out at the clouds. "At last. It's been threatening since yesterday."

"It'll last two days at most," said Dar. "This time of year, we'll have a little time between storms. I could set out for Rhodes and . . . backtrack from there."

"But backtrack to where?" Niklos wondered. "Try Tarsus first; see if you can find out where she is, or where she's been. Someone *must* have seen her, leper or no." His breath on the windowglass blocked out the storm beyond.

"Magister," said Dar, who had to use some sort of title for Niklos, "most people do not see lepers. Lepers are dead. They are . . . invisible."

Niklos nodded, blowing on the pane again. "It costs a royal ransom, but it's worth it when it rains," he said, tapping the glass lightly. "Invisible," he went on, indicating he had been listening. "Possibly. But people notice Olivia."

"She is a memorable woman," said Dar, recalling the way she handled the loose stallion on the docks at Tyre.

"Someone will have seen her, will have talked to her, and they will remember." He was more energetic now, and his attitude was decisive. "All right, let's try it this way: you go to Tarsus, and find out if that Captain Alhim really landed there. That's first. If he did, then try to discover if anyone has seen either Sier Valence Rainaut or her. Be careful. There are those who would embroider any fable if they thought it would gain them a sequin or two. If she is still there, find her. If she has gone elsewhere, find out where and follow her. I have letters here, somewhere . . ." He looked at the pile of parchment strewn on the floor. "Yes, well, I'll have to find them for you. The point is, I have them, and they are travel permits that will get her aboard the first available vessel bound for any port in Italy. You'll have them before you leave, two sets, in case you need them."

"Who authorized them?" asked Dar, astonished to hear that such plans had been made.

"A . . . a highly placed churchman," said Niklos with slight confusion.

"A friend of the Clemens family?" Dar pursued, both curious and apprehensive.

"Something like that," said Niklos as he sorted through the scattered sheets. "You will have them, and a safe-passage for both of you. That's in case you are detained anywhere. The wording is vague enough that it will cover most circumstances." He held up two folded vellum sheets. "The safe-conducts. That's a start."

Dar watched Niklos at his task, his canny features puzzled. "One of the slaves could do this, Magister."

"I will attend to it," said Niklos distantly. He had righted the inkpots and had used the corner of his cote to blot the worst of the stain. "But you put me in mind of another matter. My mistress owns several ships—"

"Owns?" Dar repeated incredulously.

"Yes," Niklos said evenly. "She owns several ships. She bought them and she owns them, though the law makes this difficult, and it is arranged through a number of . . . ruses." He gave Dar a thoughtful smile. "She would be very annoyed if she discovered I've told you this."

"I will say nothing." Dar was certain no one would believe him if he were foolish enough to reveal Niklos' information.

"You will need proper authorization to take over one or any of her ships and use them to bring her home. I'll have to draw that up and send it to . . . the churchman for signatures, sigils, and seals." He stood up, dusting off the folds of his cote.

Dar coughed delicately. "Is it so simple a thing to command a favor of a churchman?"

"For Olivia," said Niklos obscurely. "I will have that for

you, and a list of the ships and captains. They will honor the authorization if they can read it, and I'll make sure it is in four or five languages at least."

"French, Latin, and Greek," Dar recommended for a start.

"Yes, yes," Niklos said, his mind already on other things. "You'll need gold as well, and"—his voice became suddenly very soft, very quiet—"you will need to carry several chests with you."

"Chests?" Dar echoed. "What is this? Perhaps you should speak to the smuggler and be done with it." From time to time Dar sensed something alarming about Niklos Aulirios, though he could never quite identify what it was. Now he felt more alarm than he had before, though he still could not explain it.

"You will carry them," said Niklos. "For Olivia."

Dar hid his unease in brashness. "Filled with jewels and clothes, no doubt. So that she can—"

"The chests contain earth," Niklos interrupted. "Roman earth."

This time Dar had the sense to keep his notions to himself. "With the Crusaders commandeering ships still, there might be difficulties securing even one of her own." It was a safe thing to speak of, and a legitimate concern.

"The churchman will take care of it." He found the other documents and tucked them into his sleeve. "Very well. I will tend to these matters this evening. For now, I want you to come here." He had gone to a tall, wide chest at the end of the study. There were maps of all kinds inside, suspended from wooden hangers to keep them flat. Most were recent, but a few were ancient, their ports identified by alphabets Ithuriel Dar had never seen.

"This is a treasure," Dar marveled as he looked at a frayed sheet of papyrus showing the Dardanelles and the Black Sea beyond.

"Olivia thinks so," said Niklos, handling the map with great care. "There's another one—she doesn't like to unfold it because it might fall apart—from well before Christ. Her friend Sanct' Germain Franciscus gave it to her, years ago. If you wish to see it, she will show it to you when she returns." As he spoke he selected a map on heavy parchment, with

Latin names in fading ink. "This should be the best." He pulled the hanger from its rack and carried the map to a trestle table where they could work standing up.

Lightning scampered overhead, pursued by heavy-footed thunder.

Four beeswax candles were lit, and while Dar was amazed at this extravagance, Niklos bent over the map. "Now then," he murmured as he traced the outline of Cyprus, his finger not quite touching the parchment or ink, "we know she left from here, is that right?" He had indicated the town of Famagusta.

Dar shook his head slightly. "Not there properly. There's a cove, on the southern arm, named for Saint Spiridion. That's where Alhim brings his ship. I'm assuming they left from there."

"Why?" Niklos inquired. "Why that place? If Alhim is known to smuggle and to use that cove, why not choose another place?"

Dar shrugged. "It's easiest in waters you know," he suggested. "And there are many caves in the cliffs there."

"A good place to hide, you mean?" Niklos ventured.

"Smugglers have reasons to hide many things. And lepers—"

"And lepers live in them," Niklos finished for him. "Yes, you're right about that."

"We'll suppose they left from there," Niklos decided. "Bound where? Tarsus is to the north. You would think a man with a small ship would go east, to Tyre or Tripoli or upriver to Antioch. There's better trading to be done, and a shorter voyage." He tapped the table beside the parchment.

Dar, who had been staring at the names on the map, frowned. "What are these places? I know Sidon and Tyre and Caesarea, but see here?"—he pointed to a place between Jerusalem and Gaza—"Castrum?" He pulled at his belt. "With a number. And this, something about a red eagle?"

"This is a very old map. Some of the names have changed since it was made." The disinterest in Niklos' demeanor did not encourage more questions from Dar. "Why Tarsus first?"

"Possibly not Tarsus first," Dar allowed, riveting his attention to the problem once again. "But Tarsus is not so far from Antioch. Antioch and then Tarsus, perhaps, working west." He cocked his head to study the map more closely. "Tarsus to Rhodes, with perhaps a stop in between." He started to rasp his thumb over his short-trimmed beard. "Alhim's ship does not carry much in the way of supplies. They will have to put to shore every five days at the most."

"So what does that suggest to you?" Niklos asked.

"Tarsus first; we're set on that." He looked squarely at the map, his dark eyes extremely blank. "She's going against the tide. We must make allowances for that."

"And what does that mean?" Niklos had stepped aside so that Dar would have a better view of the old map.

Lightning and immediately thunder.

Dar looked up, a bit dazed. "The storm?"

"It's rambunctious," said Niklos. "Tell me about going against the tide."

Dar scraped at his beard once more. "Everyone is bound for the Holy Land. As yet, not many are coming back. It is more difficult to move away from there than to arrive there."

"Indeed," said Niklos, a world of implication in the word.

"So she will not be able to move as quickly. We must remember this while we search for her." He had once again achieved the vacant stare of utter concentration. "We are assuming she is going to come by ship, though we both know she is a poor sailor. Might she decide to use the land route?"

"It's possible," said Niklos after brief reflection, "but not likely. It would take much more time, wouldn't it? And it would require her to pass through Constantinople."

"That's not necessary," Dar protested. "She could cross to Gallipoli, take the road to Durazzo, then cross to Bari or—"

"Another Crusaders' route," said Niklos. "Beset with the same problems."

Dar made a gesture of helplessness. "Unless she travels through Africa, I can think of no way to bring her from Tarsus to Roma that does not use Crusaders' routes part of the way." He held his hand over the map. "See for yourself."

"I see," said Niklos, barely glancing at the old parchment. He had studied the map before, and was always drawn back to the same conclusions. "All right, Tarsus, and then along the coast toward Rhodes. She is traveling with a man who has been cast out as a leper. Therefore they will not be able to stay in the usual accommodations, and that makes your work more difficult. The man was a Hospitaler, and they may have some record of him."

"Not a leper; a leper is a dead man," Dar said. "Magister—"

"Stop that," Niklos said mildly.

"Bonsier, then. Only God remembers the dead," Dar reminded him. "There will be no records."

Lightning; thunder; rain so heavy that Dar thought a wave had washed over the villa.

"Someone will know," Niklos insisted with quiet intensity. "Someone will remember, and we'll find them. Her."

Dar hesitated, then blurted out: "If she's a leper, too?"

Niklos growled out a laugh. "Olivia a leper. Never."

"The Hospitaler is," Dar said carefully. "It is an affliction that—"

"Olivia is not a leper," said Niklos.

"There are other things, terrible things," Dar said, feeling wretched, but convinced that the worst had to be faced.

"You mean that she could be dead?" Niklos asked, and for an instant, in the lightning flash, his handsome features were almost demonic. "She is not dead. I would know if she were."

"You . . . might not hear . . . there might be . . . no one would know." The eruption of thunder was welcome in the silence.

"I tell you," Niklos said conversationally, "I would know if Olivia were truly dead."

Dar swore comprehensively, and when he was through, he said, "Tarsus first, then west along the coast."

Niklos smiled more with his teeth than his eyes. "Reports at every stop. I will see that you have a scribe with you. Don't worry, we'll find one who isn't a crabbed weakling. You'll have gold to pay for the transport of letters."

"You have paid me a great deal already," Dar pointed out.

"And I will pay you a great deal more if that's necessary." He tapped the trestle table again. "You're worried that if you don't find her, or find her dead, that I will demand compensation of some kind from you. I won't. Neither will Olivia."

"You have spent—"

"A great deal of money?" Niklos finished for him. "Yes. I am empowered to do that. She will not blame you for anything I have done." He paused to listen. "It's starting to slack off. That's something. All but the old roads are thigh-deep in mud. Tomorrow I'll see you and your goods get to the Via Flaminia; you should find it less difficult to go from there."

Dar bowed, more confused than ever. "When I arrived, I feared you would seize my ships and be rid of me." It was not an easy admission for him, and his voice caught once as he spoke. He looked at the windows instead of Niklos.

"As the kings of old used to kill the bearers of bad news? What I want from you is your honest effort and the truth of who and what you find. I don't hold you to blame for anything Olivia does." He hooked his thumbs in his wide leather girdle. "Why do I frighten you, Dar?"

"Because," —he swallowed hard— "because you are not as other men and your mistress is not—"

"Olivia's unique," Niklos agreed.

The lightning was distant, barely a twinge of the eye.

"Both of you—" said Dar. He tried again. "You are not like anyone else."

Thunder lumbered into the hills.

Niklos nodded once, nearly imperceptibly, his eyes fixed on a place on the inlaid floor where the stones formed a rosette. "She has given me . . . everything I am. Not because we are the same—we're not—but because . . . of my bond." Now he looked at Ithuriel Dar. "Find her."

Dar was deeply moved by Niklos' inadvertent eloquence. "I will search," he promised. "If she is there, I will find her."

"I know," said Niklos, then his head rolled back and he glared at the ceiling. "I hate not knowing. I hate waiting. If I could go with you in safety I would. But she insisted I come here, that I prepare her household and remain here, and that is what I must do."

There was nothing Dar could think of to say. He bowed deeply, showing far more respect to Niklos than any bondsman was entitled to have. "I will be ready to leave in the morning."

"If there's no rain. If it's raining, we'll prepare everything for your departure, and then you will be free to find what amusement you may here. There's new wine in the cellarhouse, but they tell me it's undrinkable." He made a sweep of his arm to indicate the whole villa. "We're poor on entertainment, but perhaps something can be arranged."

Dar had backed most of the way to the door. "It hardly matters," he said. "For a man like me, a day spent lying about is treat enough."

"As you wish," said Niklos, and addressed the last to a closing door: "The servants will carry out your instructions." He stood by himself in the center of the study for some little while, doing his best to quiet the anxiety that possessed him. Olivia was lost. The acceptance of that was the greatest self-condemnation he had ever known. She was without resources, without friends, without her native earth. Only the night was her friend now, and there was little blood to sustain her. He knew Olivia, her courage and her loyalty; she would never desert her Sier Valence, no matter what became of him. More than anything in his life Niklos longed to aid her, and felt helpless as he listened to the last stutters of thunder.

*   *   *

Text of a note from Valence Rainaut to Orval, Sier de Monfroy, Deputy Master of the Knights Hospitaler of Saint John, Jerusalem, at Tarsus.

To the most respected Master of the Knights Hospitaler of Saint John in the hospice at Tarsus, I, who was a Hospitaler, send urgent warning. If the danger were not so great, I would not commit the sin of addressing you now that I am a leper.

I know of a man who claims to be a monk and is thought to be pious. He is giving documents to the Islamites, and through his perfidy, we are deprived of our goal. I beg you to meet with me and listen to what I have to say. I will not touch you, or come nearer to you than five paces. I will wear my cowl and not face you, if that is your preference, but I must tell you what I have learned so that others will not be lost for my laxness.

I am in the company of she who was my leman and is now my agapeta. She will be with me, and if you find you cannot address me, you may speak with her, and she will speak with me.

Once you learn of what transpired, I am certain you will act in order to contain the damage done by this false monk. I pray that God will show me Grace and let me see the day that Jerusalem is once again in Christian hands. While I was still in the company of men, I swore to give my life for that day, and if we achieve our victory, then I will have fulfilled my duty.

a leper
who was Sier Valence Rainaut

By the hand of my agapeta, under seal, on the Feast of Saint Anastasius the Persian, in the Lord's Year 1192.

· 7 ·

On the north side the chapel wall had nearly crumbled, but the rest of the small, domed box was reasonably intact, though the doors had long since been hacked up for firewood. An incised stone at the back of the altar indicated that the chapel had been dedicated to Hagia Irene three hundred years before.

"It's Greek," said Orval de Monfroy as he stepped over the threshold, kicking the worst of the rubble out of his way.

From the shadows, Rainaut said, "Yes. No one comes here now but beggars."

"Well, they're—the monks—are supposed to offer charity, aren't they?" de Monfroy asked casually as he looked around, hardly moving, while his eyes darted and probed.

"You're here because of my note," said Rainaut, and it was almost a question.

"I am here because I received a note; I don't know that it was from you. Since you are here, I suppose it was yours." He had a jeering way about him that grated on Rainaut. If it was possible to saunter in chain mail, he did. "I admit I am curious. That's often the best course. I'm not prepared to take needless risks, and so, if there is an apostate monk giving our secrets to the forces of Islam, then it must be stopped, the monk must be apprehended and punished." He came one step nearer the altar. "I am here as I said I would be. I am here on your terms. It is sundown. I have only two short swords, and the quillons are bound." He held out his empty hands, his harness creaking and ringing softly. "I am here in good faith, leper. Alone."

Rainaut came carefully out of the shadows to the right of the altar, his cowl drawn down over his face so that his features could not be seen. "My agapeta is with me. Only she. No one else." He did not look directly at de Monfroy, but noticed that the man was lean, and even in armor, he moved gracefully.

"Where is she?"

From behind him, Olivia said, "I am here." She had thrown her cowl back, and left her hair unveiled, confined only with a wide ribbon. As she approached de Monfroy, she was relieved that law required the distance of five paces be kept between them, for there was a light in his eyes that was ravenous and possessive. She drew her mantel more closely around herself. She realized de Monfroy could be more dangerous than an entire Order of renegade monks. "Neither of us is armed."

De Monfroy laughed. "Oh, surely for a while yet?" He met her blank stare with a cold smile. "Armed? Lepers? Fingers and toes fall off." He laughed once more, defiantly. "What are you determined to tell me?"

There was no trace of humor in her. "It is Valence who is determined to speak. He was willing to risk punishment—"

"Death, in fact," said de Monfroy.

"Yes," Olivia said, refusing to be moved from her purpose. "He is willing to risk death in order to warn you. He believes he is honor-bound to tell you." She wished now she had worn her cowl up, but she did not want to hamper her vision.

"You're easily the most interesting herald I've encountered in the last year," de Monfroy said speculatively. "And in the company of a leper."

"He was my leman," Olivia said, an edge in her voice.

"A pity." He looked from Olivia to Rainaut and back again. "More and more fascinating," he went on, just this side of insolent. "Notes from leprous Hospitalers, meetings in ruined Orthodox chapels! An agapeta who was a leman. I must tell my troubadors about this. And my jesters." He found a section of wall that was relatively intact and leaned back against it. "What do you intend I should know?"

Rainaut was shocked at the attitude de Monfroy displayed. "You wear the Maltese Cross and you talk like a Prince's crony." He pointed to the de Monfroy arms blazoned on his cote: sable, a pale ermine engrailed. "That . . . that places you under obligation."

"Valence—" Olivia cautioned.

De Monfroy chuckled. "For your homily I rode out into this desolation."

"I have no homily," Rainaut all but shouted. "I have a warning." He was shaking visibly and if it were not for his pride, Olivia would have gone to his assistance.

"A warning. What soldier in the Holy Land has not had a warning? In fact, you have nothing," sneered de Monfroy.

"Tell him, Valence," Olivia said, hoping to lessen the hurt of de Monfroy's behavior.

"By all means tell me," de Monfroy agreed. He made no attempt to conceal a yawn. "What made you send that note? I could have you stoned for it. Or burned. Both of you." The prospect seemed boring, judging from his manner.

Rainaut steeled himself. "Coming here, not very long ago, aboard a small ship from Cyprus, I overheard a monk, a Hieronomite named Eleus, tell an Islamite that he had documents for him, indicating troop movements, I think. Our troops. He offered the Islamite maps as well."

"Very fine reporting, former Hospitaler. You haven't forgot how to do it." He pursed his lips. "Who was the Islamite?"

"I'm not certain. The light was very poor and the weather was rough. We . . . we were traveling in the hold." Rainaut glanced once at Olivia, then looked out toward the distant, crenelated walls of Tarsus, fading to blend with other twilight shadows.

"I should think so," de Monfroy said. "A Hieronomite named Eleus. Not a common name, but not uncommon either. You wouldn't happen to know what country he's from? Or how old he is? Or what he looks like?"

"I . . . no. He spoke Norman French." As he listened to himself, Rainaut wondered if Olivia had been right, and he had, after all, nothing of importance to tell the Hospitaler.

"So do I, so do you. So does your very beautiful agapeta." De Monfroy left his place by the wall and strolled toward Rainaut. "And half the Islamites in the Holy Land speak it."

"He is a danger," Rainaut insisted. "For the sake of lives that could be lost, stop Fraire Eleus."

"If you want to find a way to save lives, then find a way to stop the flux," de Monfroy responded. "That would be of use to us. Reliable guides, wholesome wells, food without vermin, all those would be of more use than stopping a spy. The whole world is alive with spies. Lord God and the Virgin's Tits! what's one monk, when our soldiers are too weak from flux to lift a sword, when we have hundreds of men deserting every month?" He kicked at some of the rubble on the floor, the long rowel of his spur buzzing as he did.

"He has betrayed his faith." Rainaut started forward, then held his place for fear of coming too near to de Monfroy. "He has—"

"Become an Islamite himself?" de Monfroy asked. "So have others. Monks are the worst of the lot. And perhaps he is still a Christian and still a monk and faithful to his vows, working now to deceive the Islamites." He tapped the end of his nose with one mailed finger. "There are a few foolhardy souls who will do that. We found one of them last week." He wagged his head in disapproval. "They'd spitted him and turned him over the fire. The men didn't like that; they wanted to even the score for him. So we gathered up a few Islamites and roasted their hands and feet off. So you see:

one monk more or less isn't going to change that, no matter who he's working for."

Rainaut had been prepared for denial or argument but not for cynicism. He could think of nothing to say to de Monfroy, not even an apology for this fool's errand. Shaking his head slowly in disbelief, he moved toward the fallen wall of the chapel. "God save you for hearing me," he said without emotion.

"Amen to that," said de Monfroy with feigned geniality. "If there is nothing more?"

"No," Rainaut whispered. "Nothing."

"Then pax vobiscum." He started away, then looked once again at Olivia. "If the time comes that I may be of service, it would be my . . . pleasure to—"

Olivia's chin raised. "Thank you," she said icily. "Since I am a leper, I doubt it would be possible."

"Perhaps," he said, making the word lascivious. Then he strode away toward his tethered horse. As he swung into the saddle, he began to whistle tunelessly through his teeth.

Rainaut had flung back his cowl and braced his arms on the altar and was staring down into a darkness greater than anything night could conjure. His skin was white as marble in the pallid light of the waning moon. All his tawny hair was gone, from every part of his body, and his features were beginning to droop as his skin lost its suppleness. "How can he be a Hospitaler?" he asked eventually. "His oath of fealty to his King—Phillippe or Richard, it doesn't matter—should require better of him than this. I've never seen anything—"

"De Jountuil had similar views," Olivia reminded him gently. "Yet he was a good knight."

"He always spoke in jest. It was his way," said Rainaut. "De Jountuil would never—" He broke off, unable to find words condemning enough for what he felt for Orval, Sier de Monfroy.

"Not all men serve honor as you do," Olivia said, unwilling to debate the question.

"He is worse than the monk!" He punctuated the last by slapping his hands onto the altar, jarring himself in his outrage. "Will you write another letter for me? Someone must listen. There has to be someone who is willing to help me." He gave a single dry sob like a cough.

Olivia had come to his side, and she put her head on his shoulder. "No, I won't write another letter for you."

He rounded on her at once. "How dare—"

"I will not see you endure this again," she said, standing her ground and ignoring his clenched fists. "You are dissatisfied with the Hospitaler who answered your summons this time. You are insulted by his manner."

"And you are not?" Rainaut bellowed at her. "That I should have to stand and hear such things said to you! If I were not unclean—"

Olivia refused to be drawn into that battle again. "What if the next one you try is not worldly, like de Monfroy, but a zealot, who would have you burned or stoned or drowned?" She waited while he considered her question. "What then, my love?"

This time Rainaut did not answer at once, but lapsed into a distressing silence. "They'll die."

"So do we all in time, I'm told," she said, thinking of the countless times those she cherished had been lost to her.

"Through treachery," he added.

"The treachery, Valence, is not yours." Her manner changed subtly. "You have done all your oath ever required of you and more. No one could hold you"—she stopped, recalling other times, and amended—"no reasonable man could hold you accountable for Fraire Eleus' betrayal now. You have given your warning to an officer of your Order, though you are no longer part of it. What occurs now is in the hands of de Monfroy." She looked out through the crumbled wall. "It is night, and we can travel now. I will be strong, your eyes will not ache, and by morning, we can be gone from here."

"Without a guide, we'd die in the desert." His shoulders had slumped, his attitude enervated.

"There are guides to be had. I have spoken to a man at the inn, and he has agreed to take us, if we will meet him before midnight." She said this with a show of enthusiasm in the hope that he would give up the oppression that seemed to overwhelm him.

"A guide. More likely a thief." He held out his hands so that the moonlight struck them. "They don't look so bad at night, like this. You can't see how white they are."

"He is a guide, the innkeeper and two of the travelers vouch for him. He is expensive but he is reliable. And he asks no questions we cannot answer in good faith." It was difficult for her not to touch him. She wanted to take him in her arms and offer her nearness as comfort if nothing else. But Rainaut no longer wanted that, and when he felt her come near, he cringed, as if she were burning.

To cover his reaction, he said, "You say it is expensive."

Olivia was not fooled, but she said, "I have enough to pay him," not going into the price she had agreed to pay.

"I have no money." He drew his cowl over his head once more. "It is not fitting that you should pay."

"Since I have money and you do not, it's the only sensible arrangement, however." She knew he wanted to draw her into an argument, to provoke her into leaving him.

He shook his head vehemently. "I refuse."

At last her patience snapped. "Oh? And what are we to do, then? Remain here begging for alms until someone decides to stone you or you starve? Is that demanded by your oath as well?" Her hazel eyes were very bright, clear as water in the moonlight. "You behave as if you were guilty of a terrible crime, not that you are the victim of ignorance."

"God does not visit leprosy on—" he began only to be cut off.

"Diseases are not punishments for sins! Diseases are misfortunes. They are not the result of sorcery or spells or Heavenly vengeance, they come from impure water and foods, from miasmas and intolerances of the body; they come from wounds and congestion of the blood." She folded her arms. "I will tell you this again, since you seem unwilling to hear me: I know your blood and I know your disease, hideous as it is, is not leprosy. And you did not get it through an act of celestial pique." She stepped back from him. "If we are to meet the guide, we should leave here now."

Rainaut blessed himself. "God give me good counsel," he murmured to the Greek cross drawn on the wall.

"I have already given you good counsel," Olivia countered, "and you will not hear it."

"I am praying," he muttered.

"Quickly," Olivia advised him. "We have some distance to go." She walked away from him to the empty door. "I have warned the guide that we must travel at night." She gathered her courage and went on. "For we must travel at night, Valence. Your skin and eyes cannot take the sun; nor my nature. Without my . . . protections, the sun is very dangerous for me. And I have no . . . sustenance to revivify me."

Rainaut winced at that. "Olivia, it is not fitting—"

"I am a vampire, Valence, and I live through the taking of blood. I can get by on the blood of animals for a time, but it is less than bread and water. You have said you will not be my lover: I do not go where I am not wanted. There is no savor, no virtue, in blood that is given without love, without shared flesh. Therefore, I must now take precautions. And so must you, not because of me but because of what is happening to your eyes."

At last he blessed himself and raised his head. "How do you mean?"

"You tell me the sun hurts your eyes," Olivia said, coming closer to him. "The whites of your eyes have been almost red for some time, and the blue is . . . mottled with brown." She thought how much she had loved the deep, clear blue of his eyes and she ached for him. "Every time you are in the sun it is worse. So we will travel at night, and spare your eyes."

He put his hand to his forehead. "I thought the pain was just—"

"There is real damage being done," Olivia said firmly but with kindness. "I'm sorry."

"A leper and blind," he mused. "What a fitting end for a knight who is a coward in his heart." He bowed his head. "Very well, if we must leave, let it be now." He went on more lightly, "Does this guide have any idea where we are going?"

"For the moment, it is enough to be going west," she said. "If we go to Smyrna, we can cross to Thessalonika. I know a merchant in Smyrna who would carry us." She did not add that she had been in partnership with that family for over a century.

"I have no wish to leave the Holy Land," said Rainaut dreamily. "What is there for me in Europe, now I am unclean and made dead? It would be best if I went to the hospice of Saint Lazarus—"

"And starve with hundreds of others?" Olivia asked bluntly.

"Then a monastery—" He cut the word off. "No. They wouldn't have me." He shook himself. "For the time being, we'll go west."

Relief made Olivia brusque. "Very sensible. Now come quickly. The guide will not wait." She led the way out of the ruined chapel and to an old, unused road. "This is the most direct way to the inn, but watch how you go, for some of the road is worn away now."

He fell into step beside her, walking at a good pace but not rushed. They went with only the sounds of the night around them under the hard glint of the stars and the ghostly wash of moonlight. They were more than halfway to the inn when Rainaut spoke. "I wish you would not do that."

Olivia was so startled that she had to keep herself from stumbling. "Not do what?" she asked when she was back in stride with him.

"Call yourself a vampire."

"But I am." She wondered what had triggered that request.

"No, you're not. Not in the way we're told vampires are. You do not tear out throats and devour unbaptized children. You do not wear bloody cerements—"

"I should hope not," she interjected.

"—and smell of the charnel house. You do not turn into dust or smoke at the touch of the Cross or the Host." He was indignant.

"Yes?" she prompted.

"But that's what vampires are supposed to do," he said with a trace of exasperation. "My nurse and my confessor told me stories—"

"They were wrong. I explained that to you, remember?"

She had taken care to tell Rainaut about what she was and the risks her love posed before he was in any danger from her. "And I am burned by sunlight—you've seen it. Water is torture for me, running water the worst; I am immobilized by it. I do need my native earth. The blood you know about for yourself."

There was a silence before he responded. "Yes. Nothing was ever like it." He slowed for a few steps. "Olivia, you said that if we loved too often, too deeply, that I would become as you are when I die."

"It was not often enough," she told him in a carefully neutral tone.

"Oh." He increased his pace once more. "If we had, if I had died and not died, would I still be a leper?"

This time she did not correct him. "We are as we are when we die. I'm sorry."

"Um," he said. "Then perhaps it's just as well."

This remark stung, and it was a short while before Olivia trusted herself to answer in the same musing tone, "Why? Since you are counted among the dead already?"

But in the few heartbeats before she spoke, Rainaut had once again retreated into melancholy. "I would be damned twice."

*   *   *

Text of a letter from the Deputy Master of the Poor Knights of the Temple, Jerusalem, in Acre to the Chatelaine Fealatie Bueveld.

To the worthy chatelaine of Gui de Fraizmarch, I have seen your request for armed escort to Jerusalem for purposes of penance, along with the letters from your husband and from the Comes de Reissac, which makes it more difficult than it might be to have to refuse you.

The current progress against the Islamite Saladin has reached a critical point, and we are warning all pilgrims, even those who are religious and going on foot, to wait until the city is once again in Christian hands. As matters stand, we cannot assume anyone safe, either within the walls of the city or on any route approaching it. Sadly, there is as much danger from Christian chivalry as from Islamite, for there are sallies and skirmishes which cannot be anticipated.

You say you are with escort, which is to your advantage, but four armed knights are not much protection from a company of Islamites. Not long ago a small party of pilgrims from Navarre were caught between a company of Templars with French chivalry and a raiding party of Islamite soldiers. Unhappily, all the pilgrims were killed during the fighting. Though you are more protected, it is most likely you would have suffered the same fate as the Navarrese pilgrims.

I will do as you request, and pass all your petitions along to higher authority, but I must tell you that both Reis Richard and Reis Phillippe will refuse it. The Austrians and Germans might plead your case, but they have no bearing in this instance. The Templars, being engaged in active fighting, cannot give you escort at this time, and as you have re- marked, the Hospitalers have not time to accommodate you until late in the year, which is a considerable time.

Of course, you may take your chances and enter Jerusalem with other pilgrims to pray at the Holy Sepulcher or other Christian shrines, but to do so you will have to put off your harness and weapons and come on foot. The terms of the penance set for you would not be fulfilled, but your soul might benefit in any case.

We hope to have advanced the lines to the gates of Jerusalem by June, for to be candid, sickness among our troops increases in the heat of summer, and we must use care in our campaigns then. Once we have secured the city, you and your domestic chivalry will be as welcome as other Christians in Jerusalem. Until that time, you must wait for our victory or enter the city unarmed. I will provide you with documents for your husband, the Abbot of Sante-Estien-in- Gorze, the Comes de Reissac and any others you require, explaining the impossibility of your fulfilling the terms of the penance, but with the assurance that you did enter Jerusalem, if that is what you decide. I cannot answer for any other, but for myself, such a letter, with proof of the visit and the prayers indicated, would be sufficient, and I would consider the penance accomplished.

There may be other acts of expiation that would also be acceptable. If you have no confessor with you, then I recommend you seek out one of the Bishops on Crusade, and ask for other terms of the penance more accommodating to the circumstances as they stand at this time. The ruling of a Bishop ought to be acceptable to all concerned. A Bishop from Troyes is currently with his troops in Acre, and unless the fighting grows worse, they will be there for a short while. He will review your penance and advise you if you can reach him before he joins the rush to Jerusalem.

Believe me, Chatelaine Fraizmarch, I hope you have good fortune in your quest; as the disowned younger son of a younger son, I know for myself that the demands of honor are rigorous and unforgiving. God speed your just cause.

> *Renet, once d'Ilenvair*
> *Deputy Master of the Poor Knights*
> *of the Temple, Jerusalem*

By the hand of the scribe Fraire Pythias, under the seal of the Templars, on the Feast of Saint Nicephorus of Antioch, whom the Orthodox Rite celebrates tomorrow, in the Lord's Year 1192.

· 8 ·

Jamil had supplied mules to carry them through the mountains; squat, strengthy beasts that moved at a long, steady walk but obstinately refused to go any faster. Jamil himself, a jovial fellow with an eyepatch and a crocodile grin, admitted cheerfully that the charges he made were ruinous, but that he was the best guide and the least corruptible.

"For it is true," he told Olivia some time after midnight as they made their way up a long slope, the mules carrying their heads low and snorting, "that others will agree to guide and then sell their charges into slavery, or lead them into traps, or other terrible things. I do none of this." He held up his right hand. "I would swear by my balls, but I haven't any." His laughter, like his voice, was high as a boy's.

Rainaut had said nothing since they had mounted their mules at the back of the field behind the inn. He was lost in gloomy reverie, refusing to respond to any comment or question addressed to him. Once, when a small fox broke cover ahead of them, he glanced up, but otherwise he might have been baggage instead of a man.

"I was told you are honest," said Olivia. She had dressed in men's clothing—over Rainaut's sullen objections—so they could move more quickly and at less risk. "For what you were paid, you had better be."

"You see, that is another reason for all the money," Jamil informed her with an expansive gesture. "If I charge too little, everyone will be afraid that I will harm them or sell them. If I charge a great deal, then you know you are safe." He indicated the rising mountains off to their right. "I know some trails that would frighten a mountain goat up there.

The mules will take them well enough. Watch out when you dismount, by the way, Bondama: Atlas there likes to bite."

"I'll remember," said Olivia, making a face no one could see. She had noticed earlier that Atlas tended to nip.

"Atlas and Achilles. I name them for heros. It encourages them. The Bonsier is on Hector. I have more of them, for larger numbers. Everyone must be willing to ride. No carts on these trails, that's what I tell everyone. No carts and no horses. If a horse is frightened, it bolts. Not these mules, they keep walking." He pointed up ahead. "At that boulder, the one that looks like the prow of a ship, the trail turns sharply to the left and down. Be ready." He considered. "The Bonsier?"

"I trust he heard you. Hector will follow in any case, won't he?" Olivia said, aware that it was useless to attempt to break the shell of Rainaut's self-imposed isolation.

"Through the fires of Hell, if necessary," said Jamil with pride. "Nothing will stop Hector."

"I hope not," said Olivia. The night was anodyne for her and she felt at peace in the darkness. If only she had a sackful of Roman earth, she would be easy in her mind. As it was, she already dreaded the coming of morning and the vitiating power of the sun. "How long until we reach the main road to Smyrna?"

"Four days, Bondama, if all goes well. Since you require that we travel at night—not that I object or question this—it may take a little longer. If there are delays, well, who can tell?" Jamil waved his hand toward the distant crags. "If you had no guide, you would be lost in this wilderness, prey to beasts and brigands. With me, you know you will be taken to the road and put on your way. That is why my price is high." He patted Achilles on his neck. "They're good-hearted, in their way."

Olivia had bred horses and mules in the past, and was familiar with them. "Mules are sensible creatures," she said, though she missed her horses. "In the mountains no animal is better."

"I knew from the first you were a canny one," Jamil declared as he clapped his hands in approval. "Last year there was a knight, he'd lost an arm at one of the fortresses—I forget which—and was insulted because I told him he would have to ride a mule. He was bound for one of old Barbarossa's cities. In the end, he had to go another way, for he would not ride a mule. He was a foolish knight."

"Yes he was," Olivia agreed.

"He had two destriers with him; great hulking warhorses, with big hooves and the appetites of hungry lions. How were they to cross these mountains on trails like this one? It was useless." His indignation was more for dramatic effect than from lingering offense. "I told him that the destriers were fine if we were going to charge fortifications, but they would not do well on these mountains. He swore at me and called me many unkind and unchristian things. I was told that he went to Constantinople."

Olivia, who had been to Constantinople, shuddered. "He might have done better to keep fighting here."

"That was what I thought," Jamil said, clapping his hands again, shifting in the saddle as Achilles made the steep turn he had warned Olivia and Rainaut about. "There," he called back over his shoulder. "You see? It is as I described it."

"So it is," said Olivia. She followed his example and clung to the mule with her calves. "Valence," she raised her voice, hoping he would listen, "take care here."

"He is a strange companion, Bondama," Jamil said as the mules tromped down the narrow defile.

"His illness makes him so," said Olivia, knowing it was true and heartbroken for it.

"Maladies are terrible things. In my day I have seen many and many struck down." He made three gestures to ward off the Evil Eye. "My brother was stunted. He never grew to a greater size than an eight-year-old child. It was brought upon us by the ill-wishes of our enemies."

"That is unfortunate," said Olivia, carefully questioning nothing that Jamil said. "Was your brother older or younger than you?"

"Older. A pleasant enough fellow, and most able. He was good at fixing things, especially things in the house. Thanks to him we never had a fire in the kitchen." He fell uncharacteristically silent.

"What became of him?" Olivia asked.

"I don't know," Jamil admitted. "When he reached

twenty, and it was apparent he would grow no more, our father sold him to a troupe of Frankish mummers. I was nine then, the youngest." He slapped his thigh. "But that was long ago, Bondama, and the world is a different place."

"We're being followed," Rainaut said suddenly.

Jamil and Olivia turned in their saddles to stare at him. Jamil spoke first. "Are you certain, Bonsier?"

"Yes. There are six or seven of them, on foot." He was sitting straighter, more alert than he had been in hours. "I doubted at first, but then I heard them signal."

"Prophets of God," said Jamil, making more signs to ward off the Evil Eye.

"What is it?" Olivia asked sharply.

Jamil sighed extravagantly. "It is . . . They have seen the Bonsier's cowl. They know he is a leper." He raised his head to the night sky. "There are lepers in these mountains, and they prey on other lepers. They are outcasts and they know no laws, for they are beyond the laws." He felt for his sword. "You are armed, Bondama?"

"Both of us are," Olivia answered. "Why?"

"Because there is a place ahead, not very far, where the trail passes through a gap between two crags. The way is steep and dangerous, and it is an ideal ambush." He pulled Achilles to a stop. "We must be prepared. If we are being stalked, it is by those lepers, for only they hunt these regions. All other brigands and robbers keep away, for fear of them."

"They are moving closer," Rainaut warned. As Hector stopped, he reached for his sword. "I will fight if you permit me," he offered.

"Why would I refuse?" Jamil asked in astonishment.

"No knight would accept me as a comrade-at-arms now," Rainaut said in flat anger.

Jamil stared in disbelief. "What an absurd notion." He drew a dagger and his sword. "I am not so nice as they—I want all the help I can have."

Olivia had drawn her sword. "Do not worry; I know how to use it."

Jamil set Achilles in motion again. "Take care. I will tell you just before we enter the gap, so you may be prepared. It is a little way along this trail."

"And you had best go on talking, or they will know we are

on guard," Olivia advised, bracing herself in the uncomfortable saddle.

Rainaut was silent again, but this time, it was the silence of anticipation.

"Yes," said Jamil, speaking more loudly than before. "My poor brother. My father was certain that he was cursed in the womb, and his size proved it. He killed two of the sons of his enemies in retribution, and they in turn murdered his brothers and their children. When my father sold my brother, he said that he hoped the evil would leave with the son."

"Poor son, to have so much hurt." Olivia had once owned a midget, a lad from Egypt who had been part of her household when she lived in Alexandria, and she had learned much from that tiny, bitter scholar.

"He was a good sort. I liked him better than some of the others." Jamil swung his sword experimentally. "My father died the year after he sold my brother; he took the sweating sickness and nothing could save him."

"And you?" Olivia asked lightly as she listened to the sounds in the night around them. She could feel the weight of eyes on her, and her body grew taut in preparation.

"Oh, our enemies had caught me already, and gelded me. My father had no son worthy of the name outlive him. He was most miserable." He pointed toward a looming mass of rock. "We're approaching the place, Bondama, Bonsier."

Olivia drew her sword and angled the dagger in her belt. "I am ready. Sier Valence?" she called over her shoulder.

"Ready." He sounded almost as he had before he had been cast out of the Hospitalers and the society of men. "It is not fitting to fight from the back of a mule."

"Better than standing on the ground," Olivia pointed out as the mules plodded into the gap. "How many steps?"

"A dozen, a little more," said Jamil. "Be prepared."

The attack came suddenly. Five men in stinking rags dropped down on them from the high rocks, howling like demons. Most of them carried knives and hatchets.

Jamil was knocked off Achilles and carried to the ground in the first rush. He screamed a curse as one of the hatchets sank into muscle and bone at his shoulder.

Achilles plodded on three or four steps, then stopped.

One man had landed on Achilles' rump and was trying to knock Olivia out of the saddle. She swung around, drawing her dagger and slamming it home in the same movement. As the brigand took the blow, he fell heavily against her, trying to grab her with bandaged hands while he died.

Rainaut had his sword ready, and the leper who grabbed him was dead before he reached his goal. The second attacker swung aside in time, but landed heavily on the rocky ground, screaming as his leg gave under him. Rainaut dragged on Hector's reins but the mule refused to move from the trail.

Jamil had knocked one of the leper outlaws off him and had struggled to his knees. Half of his cotehardie was turning black in the moonlight as blood pumped from his wound. He struck out with his sword but did little more than slap at his attackers.

"Behind you!" Olivia shouted as she saw another of the outlaws coming toward Jamil, a maul raised to batter.

Jamil turned, but he was too slow, and the maul struck him on the side of the head. With little more than a whimper he collapsed and was still.

Another leper was grabbing for Olivia's saddle. She kicked him in the jaw, using the metal stirrup to increase the damage. There was a crack of breaking bone and a shriek.

"On the left!" Rainaut cried out, and Olivia scythed her sword, feeling cloth shred as her attacker jumped clear.

Rainaut had another leper on him, this one holding onto Hector's reins and trying to hack at the mule's throat with a wide-headed battle-axe. Rainaut was too close to the rock to have room to use his sword, but he slipped his hand to the quillons and coshed the leper with the hilt; the leper took one last swing at the mule as he stumbled away, but it was enough.

With a grunt, Hector dropped to his knees, then fell to his side, all but trapping Rainaut beneath him. His legs kicked twice, and then he died.

Rainaut struggled to pull his leg free of the body; one of the attackers shouted incoherently and ran toward him, a long dagger poised to strike. Before he could reach the pinned Rainaut, Olivia's sword bit deep in his side, casting him back against the rock.

"To me!" Olivia shouted to Rainaut. "To me!"

Cloth and leather were rent as Rainaut dragged himself out from under the mule. He narrowly avoided the vicious hack of a hatchet, then reeled under the glancing blow of a mace. Half walking, half crawling, he covered the distance between Hector and Atlas.

"Up behind me," Olivia ordered while she kept two of the leper brigands at bay with quick swings of her sword. "Hurry."

Aching, his body shaking with pain and effort, he clambered onto Atlas' rump, wrapping one arm around her waist.

"Hold tight," she said, then dug her heels and the pommel of her sword into Atlas' flanks.

The mule brayed in protest and for the first time in his life lurched into a ragged canter. Down the steep trail he went, jolting and rocking, eyes rolling, long ears flat back against his neck. Sparks flew from the rocks where his hooves struck, and he brayed defiance at the night. Olivia jolted in the saddle, hanging on with her legs as the mule careened down the mountain. She could feel Rainaut bounce and slide in an effort to stay on.

"Damnation!" Rainaut shouted as the mule's violent turn caused him to drop his sword.

Olivia did not bother to respond. Her arms were starting to ache from the strain of holding Atlas' head. She tried to listen for sounds of pursuit but could not distinguish anything over the racket of their own precipitous flight.

Atlas came to a stop quite suddenly. One instant he was cantering, the next he had come to a stop. He lowered his head and panted.

"Do you think they followed us?" Rainaut asked, looking back up the trail.

"I don't think so. I don't hear anything." Olivia patted the mule's neck. "We came out of there—"

"It was fast," Rainaut said. "They killed Jamil."

"Yes," she said. "And they would have killed us."

"They were lepers," Rainaut said, as if he were just learning new words. "Lepers who prey on lepers."

Olivia lifted her head to gaze up at the night sky. "It's safe, don't you see? Lepers are dead men, and they attack others who have been made dead men, and no one will stop them."

She made a gesture to the forbidding crags rising above them. "Who would want to pursue them in any case? Where would you go to find them?"

"I am ashamed that there should be lepers who could do this to those as afflicted as they are." He tugged at his yellow cowl. "It is terrible enough to be a leper."

"When I was much younger," Olivia said, "there was a time when Christians were still a very minor religion, but growing stronger. That was when many Christian men were going to the desert, to live apart from the rest of mankind, which they said they hated for sin, and to devote their days to meditation and the renunciation of the flesh. They all made a point of that, giving up the flesh and its damning pleasures. And all of them were haunted by dreams and desires that tormented them with all the sins of the flesh until some of them were quite mad. These lepers are similar men."

Rainaut hugged her and then released her. "You always try to find ways to ease my anguish, don't you?"

"That wasn't my purpose," she said, wishing she did not feel as defeated as she did.

"But you . . . Olivia, I do not deserve your kindness." He took hold of the high cantle of the saddle rather than put his arm around her as Atlas moved off once more.

"Was I being kind?" she asked, her tone sharp.

"You have always been kind to me." He wanted to touch her hair, to make her stop the mule so that he could lose himself in her arms and her kisses. But that was no longer possible. He repeated his denial to himself as Atlas plodded on, making it his litany so that he would not succumb to temptation. As a leper he was not entitled to pleasure or comfort or gratification, much as he might long for them.

Olivia felt his withdrawal, the cruel discipline that erected barriers between them. She wished she could make him listen to her, that she could convince him that his honor was not destroyed because he had a disease that turned his skin white and caused his hair to fall out. But she knew there was nothing she could say that he would accept now; he had moved himself beyond her. Her thoughts were heavy as the mule followed the narrow trail deeper into the mountains as the night wheeled on toward morning.

Shortly before dawn, Atlas brought them to a sheltered meadow that was little more than a declivity in the side of the mountain. There was grass and a little stream, and the remnants of a shepherd's hut.

"We won't find better," Olivia said. "Jamil said that there are no inns on this side of the crest."

"That shelter looks as if it would fall over if the wind blew," Rainaut said as he slid off Atlas' back.

"It's better than lying in the open." She was exhausted, and knew she could not risk exposing herself to sunlight. "For one day . . ."

He shrugged. "For one day, I suppose it will do." He had gone to the stream and examined the banks. "I think it's pure enough. There are no skeletons around it." He had seen his share of tainted wells in the desert and now he took precautions automatically.

As Olivia dismounted, she said, "I'm going to make hobbles for the mule, and a grazing line. That way he will not go too far while we rest." Under other circumstances she would have permitted herself the slight restoration of a cup of the mule's blood, but Rainaut would be outraged if she did. Another day or two of her particular hunger would be difficult but not intolerable, she decided. She began to unwind the long rawhide braid from where it was tied to the saddle.

"Do you think the lepers will follow us?" Rainaut asked, more repugnance in his words than he knew.

"I doubt it. We've come a long way."

"But we're on a trail. All they have to do is take the same road." He was becoming apprehensive now, looking about the little meadow as if it were the bait for a trap.

"They don't know where we've gone. The way we rode off, how could they? Besides, you saw how they were bandaged. I don't think they can travel very far, not with their feet rotting." She did her best to speak evenly, without obvious emotion of any kind, but there was an expression in her hazel eyes that Rainaut did not miss.

"You despised them. You loathed them." It was more a confirmation than an accusation, but he grabbed her arm in so sudden and painful a grip that she drew back from him in shock.

"For attacking us," she said. "Not for being lepers. For that I am more saddened than you can know."

He laughed nastily. "They disgusted you." He released her. "I disgust you."

She finished taking the rawhide line from the saddle. "You know how I feel. I have told you." As she secured the line between two trees, she went on, "You want me to turn away from you, to leave you to your suffering. That isn't possible. You know why, whether you believe it or not."

Rainaut unsaddled the mule. "Do you think we will find our way to the road to Smyrna?"

"The mule has traveled it enough. I suppose we'll have to rely on him to get us there." She secured the reins loosely to the tieline. "It's almost dawn. Listen to the birds."

Both of them were quiet, the first rustlings and piping calls of morning holding their attention. Atlas, freed from the burden of saddle and rider, lowered his head to the grasses and began to eat. Along the eastern bastion of mountains the vastness of night was fading toward brightness.

"We need to rest," Olivia said, looking at Rainaut. "Come."

He hesitated. "Do you wish to sleep alone?"

"No, Valence," she said. "Neither do you."

"There is great temptation," he said as he came toward her. The last touches of winter had left the mountains sere, but there was a scent on the wind that promised the richness of spring.

"Only if you are willing," she reminded him. "Since you are not—" She looked over at Atlas grazing. "You're probably as hungry as he is. We'll find you something to eat after sunset."

"And you?" he asked, letting himself fall into step beside her.

A shrug was her only answer.

*   *   *

Text of a letter from Ithuriel Dar to Niklos Aulirios.

To my Roman friend with the Greek name, greetings from Tarsus, where I landed day before yesterday. It is a busy place, this city, with much of the trade that would usually go to Caesarea and Sidon and Ascalon and Tyre being moved here instead to avoid the calamities of the Crusades. Many of the merchants coming from the East, some of them from lands beyond the sway of Islam, have chosen to come to market here rather than seek out those in disputed territory.

I have, as we discussed, made inquiry at many places in an attempt to discover if anyone has seen Bondama Clemens or the knight who had been her escort. The difficulty is that since the knight has been declared dead, those who might have seen him will not admit to it because it is not proper to conduct any business with lepers. There are one or two people I have encountered here who might have information if I can find a way to ask for it that does not imply that they have done anything wrong in dealing with Valence Rainaut or any companion of his. How easy this will be I do not know.

Someone has suggested that I speak with some of the beggars of the city, for they see and hear more than anyone, and where such unfortunates as lepers and other outcasts are concerned the beggars are more likely to know about them and to admit that they know than others who are worried about the implications of such dealings. With patience I might be able to find someone in the next two weeks with reliable information. I must have care, for there are those who will tell you anything if they think you will pay them for whatever they say.

I have spoken to a merchant from Tyre who informs me that the house of Bondama Clemens has been occupied by vassals of one of the Hungarian nobles. They have their pages and other servants as well as a half-dozen slaves to maintain their household. It was rumored that they did not pay for the property because of being Crusaders and therefore excused from such costs, which means that the sums that the Court of Bourgesses are supposed to send to you on Bondama Clemens' behalf will not be forthcoming.

If Bondama Clemens has been here recently, and if she has not left by sea, she will have to have crossed the mountains, for the coast roads have been designated as military and therefore proper documents are required for those not part of the Crusade to use them. These documents are not readily obtained and cost a great deal for those who are permitted to have them at all. It seems reasonable to assume that she has found a way to cross the mountains. From what you have said, she would rather travel that way than by sea. I will make the appropriate inquiries and, with any good fortune at all, I will have something more to report to you very soon.

Food here has become expensive since much of the food-stuffs stored in warehouses and held for winter consumption has been confiscated for the use of the soldiers going to the Holy Land. There are many merchants and artisans here who have objected to the practice of turning so much over to the Crusaders just because they have a cross on their sleeves. It is true that many of these soldiers have added to their wealth by selling the various foodstuffs back to the populace at very high prices. If this means that they are abusing their place as Crusaders, no one has yet to reprove them for it except the merchants and artisans. No one in the Church has said that the practice must stop, and so I assume that it will not, at least not for a while.

Yesterday there was a ship arrived from Jaffa carrying some of the English and French wounded. Ever since Reis Phillippe left the Crusade last autumn, there have been more casualties among the French knights, and the French vassals of England. They praise Reis Richard, but they also say that he is not protecting his men as he ought. Word is that the fighting has not gone well and that some of the knights are suffering from the sweating fever, as Reis Phillippe has been rumored to have. One of the smaller fortresses was all but wiped out from the sweating fever. Between that and the bloody flux, there are more Crusaders dying from maladies than there are dying from wounds, although I have heard that the wounds are worse than you might expect because they so often mortify.

I will persevere in my search for your mistress. Someone in this city must know where she has gone if she has been here, and I will find that person and learn all that I can. Rely on me to complete this task for you. I pray that I will have better news for you shortly.

Ithuriel Dar

By the hand of the scribe Iakkobus on the Feast Day of Blessed Chrodegang the Frank, in the Christian Year 1192.

· 9 ·

At the outskirts of Acre there was a settlement of hovels and tents where many of those who had lived within the walls had taken refuge when the Crusaders had reached the city. Families who had owned fine houses the year before were now huddling in flimsy shelters, hoarding what few belongings they had been able to salvage from the battles.

"The bishop will be within the city," said Giralt Esanne to Fealatie Bueveld as they made their way through the pathetic remnants of the people of Acre.

"I wonder he can bear to ride to battle with this all around him," Fealatie said, motioning her three mounted companions to keep close together.

At the gate there were Templars in full harness and surcotes, supervising the movement of people in and out of Acre.

"You are?" the Templar asked as Fealatie reined in.

"The Chatelaine de Fraizmarch," she said, making sure that the device on her shield was visible.

"And those?" He indicated the other men with her.

"Domestic chivalry, sent with me for my penance," she

said, finding the words still galled her. "We're here to speak to the Bishop—"

"He's not here," said the Templar. "There's a Papal legate staying at the moment. Will he do?"

Fealatie nodded as much as her chain mail would permit. "Yes. He would be most acceptable." She did not yet know if she felt apprehensive or relieved at this news. There had been so many promising beginnings that had led to so many deep disappointments.

"I'll make sure you have escort." He glanced once at the three men with her. "Domestic chivalry. You sure you don't want to become Templars? We would be pleased to have you with us."

Giralt answered for himself and the other two. "If we joined, it would be the Hospitalers, since we are entitled to be in their number." It was a calculated insult and he waited for the Templar to show offense.

"There's nothing to being a Hospitaler; any coward can wear a Maltese Cross and say he is defending Jerusalem, but it takes a man of courage to be a Templar," the Templar informed him with ill-concealed mockery.

"Stop this bickering," Fealatie said to Giralt. "I want to see the Papal legate and I hope he will receive me. If we must await his summons, is there a place we may stay, or must we find accommodations outside the gate?" She was a bit lightheaded from fatigue and the constant irritation of wearing armor in this climate. "We are all in need of rest."

The Templar shrugged. "There are a few houses that might be willing to give you accommodation. Ask the Bishop if he will say which you are to use; if not, there are beds in the houses of the Genovese." He stood aside so that the little party could ride past into Acre.

The city looked more like an enormous barracks, with almost every person on the street a man in armor or a man-at-arms. There were farriers and armorers as well, and a few women, most of them the wives and followers of the soldiers occupying Acre. Almost every large house was adorned with banners. They flapped from windows and rooftops and hung above doorways, the leopards of England being the most frequently displayed. Since Reis Phillippe had left the Holy Land, few of his men flew either his household banner of bees or the Oriflamme of Saint Denis, substituting their personal devices instead. A fanciful menagerie flourished on the banners: the caboshed boar of Janos of Hungary, the naiant dolphin of a Sicilian Norman, the salient-countersalient white stags of Conrad's men, and everywhere the Templars' Pegasus.

"Where is this Papal legate?" asked Giralt, addressing Sigfroit de Plessien, who was vassal to Fealatie's father.

"Wherever the banner of the Tiara is, I suppose," he said, staring in fascination at the richness of the display that could not hide the marks of battle scarring the buildings.

A small procession of Cistercian monks came around the corner, proceeding in double file directly toward Fealatie and her three knights. They chanted for the dead as they escorted five figures in yellow cowls toward the gates of the city.

At Fealatie's signal the men moved aside and lowered their eyes in respect and fear. Only when the monks had passed them did Fealatie speak again. "One of the churches will direct us to the Papal legate," she told them. "Giralt, you take the Hospitalers; Sigfroit, you take the Hieronomites and the Benedictines. Gace, see if there are Ambrosians here, and speak to them if there are. I am going to try to find the funda, to see if any of the Bourgesses are here to aid us."

"If they see you, they'll tax you," warned Gace. He was an imposing figure in the saddle; dismounted as he was now, he limped on an inward-turning foot.

"We are here for reasons of penance and cannot be taxed unless the Church permits," Fealatie reminded him. "Come, find out where the Papal legate is. I will await you at the funda." She went forward, leading her horse, watching to see that her men did as she ordered. Try as she might, she could not rid herself of the belief that her penance would not be completed and that her husband would disown her with the approval and sanctions of the Church because of her failure. The thought horrified her, and she tried to banish it from her mind, but without success. She followed the widest streets toward the merchants' quarter of the city where the funda stood.

A number of camels were being unloaded in the center of

the courtyard of the funda, and clerks from the Court of Bourgesses inspected the cargo, making notations and haggling with the men from the caravan. Their disputes were carried on in competitive shouts and screams with extravagant gestures and posturing. Two Bourgesses stood in the middle of this confusion, gravely observing the transactions.

Fealatie secured her horse to the knights' rail, then started through the crowd toward the Bourgesses, taking care not to become involved in any of the arguments around her. As soon as she was close enough to be able to be heard, she bowed to the Bourgesses—an unusual courtesy—and said, "Worthy Bourgesses, I pray you will direct me to the lodgings of the Papal legate."

Both Bourgesses turned to stare at her. "Did you speak?" the older of the two asked after he had stared at Fealatie for a short time.

"I did," she answered, that sinking feeling taking hold of her again.

"A woman in battle harness," the younger Bourgess mused. "It is not correct."

"I am a chatelaine, and in that capacity, I have undertaken a penance which must be accomplished in harness." She had become used to the thoughtful pause her answer brought about, and the measuring looks. "I must speak with the Papal legate."

"It is not proper for a woman to approach the Papal legate in such garb," the younger Bourgess said in condemning accents. "In fact, it is not proper for a woman to approach the Papal legate at all. Who are you planning to speak for you?"

The older Bourgess nodded ponderously. "And traveling alone. Worse than a harlot. What explanation can you give for your conduct? It is against the law for a noblewoman to travel alone, no matter how dressed. It does not bode well."

"I am in the company of three knights, my domestic chivalry. They have been with me all the way from France to escort me and to testify to my penance. I have documents to vouch for this."

"Are they invisible, that you stand here apparently by yourself?" The younger Bourgess laughed at his own wit. "How can we question them if we cannot see them?"

Fealatie's throat was dry and her voice cracked. "They are praying." It was not quite the truth but it was an acceptable reason they were not with her. "They are to meet me here," she added, standing a bit straighter, one hand on the hilt of her sword.

"When will that be?" asked the younger Bourgess. "These merchants have brought goods that must be taxed, and it is our duty to inspect their goods and assess the value." He spoke carefully, as if he thought Fealatie could not understand.

"I will wait," said Fealatie with what she hoped was resolution rather than obstinacy. "When my men join me, then you will be good enough to tell me where the Papal legate is staying." She took three steps back and found herself a convenient niche near the animals' water troughs.

Both Bourgesses were relieved not to have to deal with the importunate woman in armor, and returned to their tasks with vigor and determination. Occasionally one or the other would glance over to see if Fealatie was still waiting, and each time was troubled to see that she was.

"There you are." Gace was the first to find her, coming up to her with his halting walk. "The Papal legate is staying at the church of the Premonstratensians, and his retinue is being housed by the Pisans; some of the merchants are still living in their houses, it seems." He looked around the funda. "The caravans come no matter what."

"Where is this Premonstratensian church?" Fealatie asked, unconcerned for the caravans. "How large is it?"

"Good-sized, old-fashioned, from what I could see of it. One of those round tower churches. It was probably here at the First Crusade." He wiped his brow with the hem of his cote. "I looked for an inn, but they all seem to have knights in them."

"We'll find something," said Fealatie. She pointed to the far side of the funda. "There's Giralt." She raised her hand to enable him to locate her, remarking to Gace as she did, "We may have to separate, but so long as one of you is with me, the terms of the penance are fulfilled."

"If it were up to me, Bondama," said Gace uncomfortably, "I would swear that you had been to Jerusalem, and that you had fulfilled the terms of the penance, so that we could all return home." He leaned against the edge of the trough to take some of the weight off his misshapen foot.

"That would be . . . dishonorable. I would abjure my oath. Any benefit that came to me for such a betrayal would condemn me more than my failure would." She could not conceal a degree of wistfulness. "If it were possible . . ."

Gace slapped his thigh with a mail-gloved hand. "You're as true a knight as any man, Bondama, I'll give you that."

"The Papal legate—" Giralt said as he made his way through the stacked crates and chests.

"Is at the church of the Premonstratensians," Fealatie finished for him. "Gace has just told me. All we must do is gain admittance to him and present our petition." She said it quickly so that she would not have to consider the enormity of such an undertaking.

"We will address him for you. Otherwise it could take months before you were permitted to speak, even here. There is no saying that the legate will still be here in a week, let alone a month." He pointed to another entrance to the funda. "Sigfroit."

The third knight came to join them, his face set. "You know where the Papal legate is, no doubt." He was disgusted, irritation shown in every line of his body. "He does not want to take any petitions before the capture of Jerusalem, or so I was told."

"What?" asked Giralt as Fealatie turned pale.

"That's what I was told. All petitions are being refused until Jerusalem is in Christian hands once again." Sigfroit made an emphatic gesture. "He is not willing to consider anything less important than the reclamation of Jerusalem. No knight wishes the liberation of Jerusalem more than I do, but for a Papal legate not to receive petitions from good Christians—"

Giralt cleared his throat. "How can we approach him? There must be a way."

"Conquer Jerusalem," suggested Sigfroit in a tone that was made rough with contempt.

Fealatie tried to resist the sense of defeat that was threatening to overwhelm her. "Is there another way?"

"There must be," said Giralt. "I will find some way to

speak to him." He regarded Fealatie with concern. "What do you want us to do?"

She sighed. "It's been so long, and there have been so many delays. I want to complete my penance so that neither my husband nor my family will be shamed by me any longer. Since I cannot enter Jerusalem in armor now, I suppose I must speak with this Papal legate. The alternative is to chase after bishops and kings, and since Reis Phillippe is no longer Crusading—" The frustrations of the past months made her want to scream and weep, but neither was proper while she was in harness.

"We will get the attention of the Papal legate," said Giralt, his eyes including the other two knights. "We may be only domestic chivalry but we are not wholly unconnected."

"Take care that the Papal legate does not try to turn us into Crusaders," warned Gace. "They've lost a great many men and they need more."

"We're witnesses to the penance," Sigfroit reminded them. "They cannot order us to abandon that charge."

Fealatie made an impatient gesture. "Find out first if the man will speak with us. If he will not, then there must be some alternative." She looked at the banners hanging from the gallery of the funda. "With so much of the nobility of France and Austria and England here, surely there is someone who can aid us."

Sigfroit exchanged doubtful glances with Gace, but Giralt spoke with confidence. "We will find you that aid, Bondama."

"The question is, where to start," said Sigfroit, adding, "If we must hunt down bishops and the like, I will need a meal first."

"Of course; you're all hungry," said Fealatie, and realized that she was ravenous. "There must be some place we can buy food." She was acutely aware of the dwindling supply of coins left to them. "We need beds for the night and stalls for our horses."

Gace said, "I think I can make arrangements for the horses. I saw a device I know on one of the banners; we're cousins and that should count for something." He motioned to where their horses were tied. "We might learn something about lodging from him as well. He's with a group of Reis Phillippe's knights, over in the Pisan quarter."

"What bearing? What's his device?" asked Sigfroit, so they would know what to look for.

"Sable guttee de larmes," he said, indicating his own device which was argent guttee de sang. "There are five variations in the family. It started with our great-great-grandfather." During their travels, Gace had regaled them with stories of his great-great-grandfather, and this newest information was met with knowing looks.

"Find us this cousin," said Fealatie. "The sooner we establish ourselves, the greater the chance we have of gaining the Papal legate's ear."

They got their horses, then started toward the Genovese quarter of the town. On the way they saw more signs of fierce battles, including two large houses that were almost entirely destroyed. There were more armed men than merchants on the street, and places where the people would usually hold market were occupied only by men-at-arms and their families.

"They say that another attack is being planned," Sigfroit remarked when they had walked some distance in silence.

"It's safe to say that; as long as Jerusalem is in Islamite hands, an attack will be planned." Fealatie stopped at the sluggish well where four streets came together. "Which way?"

"To the left. It isn't far." Gace let his horse drink before leading him on. "Is it a sin to want a bath, I wonder?"

"If it is," said Giralt with determination, "then I will confess it. Afterward."

They all laughed.

"There it is," said Gace, indicating a formidable house with huge, stout doors of thick wood. From one of the upper windows, a black banner sprinkled with tear-shaped silver drops flapped erratically in the wind.

"How do we get in?" Fealatie asked, her eyes on the door.

Gace found the bell-rope and tugged on it twice, nodding as he heard clanging within the walls. "They'll send someone."

The man who opened the doors was an imposing figure,

the veteran of many campaigns with the scars to prove it. His grizzled hair and creased face made him forty at least; he carried a maul slung across his back. "Who comes and why?"

Gace motioned the others to silence. "You house a cousin of mine, Sier Quesnes de Thurotte. Pray tell him that Sier Gace de Heaulmiere is here and begs his assistance." He bowed to the man-at-arms, although courtesy did not require him to do this.

"And the others?" the man-at-arms asked with suspicion.

"I will explain all to my cousin." He made this statement a dismissal. "We will wait in your courtyard."

"I cannot permit it," said the man-at-arms. "If Sier Quesnes invites you in, that is another matter." His expression indicated he doubted there would be any such offer.

"Then we will stand at your door," said Fealatie bluntly.

The man-at-arms stared at her as he closed the door.

"What do you think?" Sigfroit asked when the man-at-arms had been gone for some time.

"I think my cousin is hard to find," said Gace, unwilling to be discouraged. "And I think that the man-at-arms likes making us wait."

The others muttered agreement.

Giralt was saying, "If we find nothing here, we must look for other—" when the man-at-arms again opened the door, not quite as grudgingly as before. "Sier Gace, your cousin Sier Quesnes awaits your company in the courtyard." He stood aside so that the four could enter, leading their horses. "The courtyard is through the passage to your left. There are grooms to tend to your mounts."

"Well, that's something," said Fealatie in an undervoice. She held out her reins to a man whose ears and nose had been cut off, and who wore the badge of Pisa on his shoulder.

The others turned over their horses to other grooms and then fell into step with Gace.

Sier Quesnes was dressed in barbaresque fashion, in a bournous of cendal shot with gold thread. His hair was concealed by a damask turban, and his beard was perfumed in the manner of the Islamites. He looked toward the newcomers and held out his arm to Gace. "Sweet cousin," he called. "Have you come to be corrupted by the temptations of the East?"

"I've come for your help," Gace said, going to embrace his cousin.

"Best not," said Sier Quesnes. "Your mail will ruin my silk." He leaned forward and kissed Gace on the cheek. "That will do: you're not a peach-faced boy, after all." He looked at the others. "So martial."

"We need lodging and food," said Gace, taken aback by what he saw.

"That can be arranged, if you don't mind close quarters." He turned this into a lascivious promise.

"There is a problem," Gace said flatly, and introduced Fealatie, outlining her predicament.

"It is very awkward," said Sier Quesnes when he had heard him out. "However, it would be worse if I turned you away. We're all vassals of France, aren't we? There are obligations." He twiddled the ends of the lorins around his waist. "Oh, very well. Since this is a manner of penance and honor, it would not be proper to send you away. For the time being you may stay here. We'll arrange it somehow. As to the Papal legate, that may be more difficult, but something will be done." He bowed in the Islamite manner. "You are welcome here. Take care, though. The place is alive with thieves." He grinned. "We cut their eyelids off and take them out into the desert." Then he clapped his hands, summoning slaves to tend to his guests.

*   *   *

Text of a letter from Hilel Alhim to Orval, Sier de Monfroy.

To the most illustrious knight, Orval, Sier de Monfroy, the humble shipowner Alhim sends greetings, with profound thanks for the generous sum paid for your requested informa-

tion. It is rare for those in my position to attain so great favor, and with so little effort required. May Heaven reward you for your charitable nature and your good works.

To answer your inquiry as best as I am able: yes, the Bondama Clemens traveled on my ship from Cyprus, in the company of one who had been a knight. She said that he had been disfigured, but I feared that the man was a leper and had been cast out from his knightly company. Nothing was ever mentioned of that, but I saw his face once, without hair and white as spume. She insisted that they travel concealed, so I had not much opportunity to speak with him or to learn what their plans were.

Originally she arranged their passage to take them all the way to Italy. She gave sufficient money for such a journey, and spoke of returning to Roma. Yet at Tarsus she and her companion left the ship and did not return. You claim to have seen them near there, and certainly it is possible that they decided to go overland, for Bondama Clemens was not comfortable on my ship. There are those who cannot be at ease on a moving vessel, and it appears that Bondama Clemens was one such.

Where she came from before Cyprus I am not certain. She is not a Cypriot. The knight in her company referred several times to the Hospitalers, and if he had been once of their number, it might explain why he was with her, for if he had been part of her escort, he could remain with her. That is conjecture on my part, but since you are a Hospitaler as well, it may be that you can discover much in the records of your Order. Such a knight with such an affliction must be recorded somewhere.

Doubtless your inquiries are for the benefit of Bondama Clemens, for if they were not, I would be at fault in answering you. But since you are a sworn knight, it is not possible that you would intend anything dishonorable for the Roman widow. So I respond to you in good conscience and with the knowledge that you will show true chivalry to Bondama Clemens. If her companion is truly a leper, it is unfortunate that such an affliction should be visited upon so lovely and gracious a lady. I pray that you will find it in your heart to protect her.

There can be no question of your motives in this case;

surely you are demonstrating again the charity that caused you to pay me so well. For that, may Heaven bless you.
Hilel Alhim
By the hand of the scribe Fraire Basilios on the 17th day of March in the Lord's Year 1192.

· 10 ·

A distant bell roused Olivia from her stupor; she lay back in the covered nest of pine-boughs and listened to the tolling that accompanied sunset. Beside her, Rainaut shuddered and moaned, captured in a dream. She moved closer to him, her brow lined with worry; in the last week, he had grown worse. A sense of futility washed through her, and she put her hand on his shoulder, having nothing else she could do to help him.

Atlas grazed on a long tether, his ribs starting to show from the labor of carrying a double load through the mountains. His long ears moved at the sound of the bell, and he raised his head.

"It won't hurt you," Olivia said softly as she worked her way out of the makeshift shelter of leaves and branches. Some of them were still damp from the rain the night before and she felt the moisture in her clothes. Her ears rang as she moved and she realized she would have to take nourishment soon or be overcome with hunger. Memories of other frenzied feedings sickened her, and she resolved to catch a rabbit or a fox before the night was over.

Rainaut murmured incoherently, his legs thrashing through the boughs. He rolled onto his back and struck out with his right arm, then dropped back into deeper sleep.

He would need food, too, thought Olivia. The disease had its hooks into him irremediably, but she could alleviate the hunger for him, for a while. She picked up the sack that contained their remaining coins and few possessions and carried it with her to where the mule's saddle lay. Using one of the smaller knives, she went to Atlas and began to clean out his hooves, taking care to check the shoes, to be sure they were still fastened securely to the hooves. They could not afford a cast shoe while lost in the mountains.

For they were lost. She grudgingly admitted it the night before, when the trail they were following eventually faded and disappeared, leaving them on the side of a rising shoulder with no building or other road in sight. She had tried to keep going north and west, since the road to Smyrna lay in that direction, but they had covered little ground, and so slowly that Olivia had begun to wonder whether it would be best to backtrack and try to find the main route again.

Rainaut awoke with a shout, sitting up, his hands out to protect himself. He looked about wildly, panting, his red-tinted eyes glazed with fear.

Olivia looked up. "Valence," she said as if he had done nothing unusual. "I was about to wake you."

He rounded on her, his scar-like countenance no longer capable of expression. "I was dreaming."

"So I thought," she said, continuing to tend to Atlas' feet. "Something unpleasant, I thought."

He flinched at that. "Unpleasant," he repeated. "It will be dark soon."

"Yes," she said, approaching him now that her task was finished. "Will you be ready to leave?"

"I can leave at any time," he said defiantly. "I am your servant, Bondama." This last was a fury, and it impelled him, bringing him to his feet.

"You were my lover, my leman, Valence, not my servant." She kept her voice steady, but it was an effort; his condemnation was more painful to her than she could admit to anyone but herself.

"But I served you, Bondama. And for that God has made me suffer." He kicked away the branches at his feet and ran his white hands over his clothes to rid them of twigs and leaves.

It was useless to argue with him when he was in such a state, and so Olivia busied herself with saddling the mule, her mind deliberately on other matters. "There may be a church or a monastery near," she said when she could trust herself to speak evenly. "Perhaps we can get some food."

"And one of the monks will oblige you by opening a vein?" he challenged.

"Stop that," Olivia told him without heat. "It is your disease that speaks, not you. I have no wish to listen."

"Then leave me," he said, and suddenly his eyes were bright with tears. "Olivia, my most-loved, please leave me. Before I become worse than—"

She stood still, the saddle girth dropping out of her fingers. "Don't ask that," she said.

"Please. *Please.*" He put his hands to his face as he wept.

"You know I can't," she said, deliberately returning to her work. "If you are safe and protected, if you are not in want or in danger, then if you wish it, I will go, but you are blood of my blood, and I cannot abandon you." She tested the girth for tautness and then began to reel in the plaited tether. She worked automatically, not looking at him.

"It is agony for me, Olivia." His words were soft and thick. "Look at what I have become. Look what I have made you."

"Don't dwell on it," she said, at last able to meet his eyes. "It doesn't matter."

He turned away from her, his back hunched, his head lowered. He remained that way while she adjusted her bamburges so that her legs were protected, then he drew on his solers, securing them with wide thongs around the ankle. "It is torment," he said when he turned back to her.

"I'm sorry," she said.

Again the distant bell sounded, this time joined by a second, higher bell, the two of them conducting a kind of dialogue, the higher bell answering the lower.

"Shall we try there?" Olivia asked, hoping she would be able to follow the sound of the bells; in the mountains sound was often misleading and confused.

"There is no reason for a monastery to offer charity to a leper," said Rainaut. "But why not?"

Secretly Olivia was relieved by his response. He had been sunk in despondency for three days, in a humor so dark that she had been afraid to speak to him. If he were willing to seek out assistance of any kind, she saw this as an improvement. "Come," she said. "The mule's ready." She tightened the girths a second time, then swung up into the saddle, gathering in the reins and bringing Atlas around to Rainaut. "Give me your hand," she said, reaching down to him.

Without speaking, Rainaut grasped her hand and came up behind her, settling down against the cantle, one arm around her waist. He looked up at the sky where the first stars shone. "I pray there is a haven for those like me. Is that sin, do you think?"

"No," said Olivia, and started the mule on his way.

It was midnight before they heard the sound of the bells again, this time much nearer. The ringing continued for a while, long enough for Olivia to get a good sense of where the bells were. As they reached a narrow roadway, she cocked her head and listened.

"It's to the left, down the slope," said Rainaut.

"Yes, I think so," Olivia agreed. "Come." She nudged the mule into motion. "I wish I knew what we were looking for," she added when they had gone a short way along the road. Although it was night, her eyes had no difficulty in making out the brush and trees that lined the roadway.

"You said a monastery," Rainaut reminded her.

"What else would be out in so isolated a place?" The question was more apprehensive than rhetorical. "What if it is a stronghold for robbers?" It was not impossible, she knew, for robbers and bandits to employ such a ruse to trap unwary travelers.

"You'll probably triumph over them," said Rainaut. "You did before."

She waited before responding. "It would be better to run and hope we're not followed."

"Why? What danger are you in?" He chuckled, and his arm around her tightened.

"A great deal of danger," she said with asperity. "I am not wholly immortal and I am not invulnerable. If my head is struck off or battered, I would be as dead as you would. And wounds that do not kill me are painful and incapacitating for a time. I do not want to risk so much."

He reached up with his free hand and ruffled her hair. "You make light of your powers."

"I don't, you know." She could sense his elation as she had sensed his despair. Both troubled her; she had realized months ago that the alterations of temperament were part of his disease, and as they became more extreme, she knew his affliction was growing more severe.

"Think about it," he went on heedlessly. "You could make yourself invaluable to Reis Richard or Reis Phillippe. You could pass on your gifts to them, and at the same time protect them from their enemies. You would be stronger than any king in the world, if you did that."

"No," said Olivia with force. "It would make me the object of hatred and curiosity. No one who is . . . what I am can endure such attention. There would be prison or the stake for me, and in the end I would die the true death, and the king I served would fall with me." She paused, hoping he was listening. "I do not love for power, Valence."

"But you have it," he said, catching some of her hair in his hand and pulling it. "You are life and death to me."

"If you had allowed it, I would have been life only," she said.

The road turned, and ahead was a small compound, a belfry rising atop the tallest of the buildings inside the walls. Over the barred gate a single lamp burned, and beside it hung a length of rope.

"What sort of place is this?" Rainaut asked.

"There is a chapel of some sort," Olivia said, indicating the cross atop the belfry. She studied the burning lamp. "Why do they do that, do you think?"

"In honor of God," said Rainaut shortly. "Are you going to ring?"

Olivia got off the mule and handed the reins to Rainaut. "Wouldn't you?" she asked before she walked to the gate and reached for the rope.

"Wait!" Rainaut called.

"Why?"

"It might bring misfortune." He drew his sword. "If you must do that, at least I will be prepared."

"You won't need a sword here," Olivia said, hoping she was correct.

"You can't be certain." He kicked Atlas to get the mule to move closer to the gate.

"No," said Olivia. "But I'm willing to take a chance." Before he could protest again, she reached up and rang the visitors' bell. Knowing how late the hour was, she did not assume her summons would be answered quickly, and for that reason was more surprised when the small side-door, hidden in an angle of the wall, opened almost at once.

A woman of middle years and austerely simple dress raised her hand in greeting. "God bless and keep you, travelers."

Olivia looked at the woman more closely. "And God bless and keep you," she said, crossing herself as she did.

"You are on the road very late," she said. "Have you a place to sleep for the night, or are you without shelter?"

"Who are you?" Rainaut demanded before Olivia could answer.

"I am Kalere Navrentos; my brother and I keep this place for those in need of aid." She smiled, looking from Olivia to Rainaut. "Whoever you are, you are welcome here."

Rainaut got Atlas to move a few steps closer. "No doors are open to me. My cowl is yellow. I am a leper."

"Sier Valence," Olivia said, hoping he would not damn himself more than he already had.

"This door is closed to no one," said Kalere Navrentos. "You are welcome to enter. We offer simple fare and simple comforts." She regarded Olivia. "Would you like to enter?"

"Yes," Olivia said. "My companion is very hungry, and I have need of . . ." She faltered, knowing how many Christian communities forbade bathing as a sign of vanity. "If it is permitted, I would like a bath."

"There is a small bathhouse that you may use," said Kalere. "It is available to all those who wish it. The water is cold, just as God gives it to us." She indicated the main gate. "I will open for you." With that she stepped back and closed the little side door.

"It may be a trap," warned Rainaut as soon as the door was shut.

"For whom? And why?" Olivia asked. "You need food—"

"So do you," he said with a hint of malice.

"All right, so do I. There is shelter here, and respite. Whether you desire it or not, I do." She went to the gate as it swung open.

Once again Kalere made a greeting that was also a blessing. "In the name of the Christ, come in and be welcome in His Name."

"And the mule?" Rainaut asked, deliberately rude.

"Certainly. There is a barn with stalls and hay. If you are too tired to tend to him, I will take care of him." Kalere bowed her head, saying, "We turn no creature away."

"I'll tend to Atlas," said Olivia, anticipating another outburst from Rainaut. "You have a meal, and thank God that our steps were guided here."

"You mean that you had ears sharp enough to follow the bells," Rainaut corrected her.

"That is why we ring them," said Kalere, still smiling pleasantly. "We pray that we will bring those in need of our aid to our door."

"How many are there in your community?" Olivia asked, trying to make the question sound disinterested.

"My brother and I built this place. There are twenty-three travelers with us, if I count the two of you. Some have remained with us for quite a while, some leave the day after they arrive. We thank God they have been here, however long they stay." She stood aside as Atlas grudgingly came through the gate, and then she took a moment to secure it again. "We wish we could leave the gates open all day and all night, but there are desperate men living in these mountains, and for the protection of the travelers who come here, we must bar the gates at night. It is sad that it must be so." She made a gesture that took in the whole of the compound. "The chapel is at the center, as you see, where it belongs. There is an infirmary, a refectory, dormitories for men, for women, and a few rooms for those who are married, or families with their children." She smiled. "We have a room for you to share, if that is what you want. It is simple, but—"

"We are not married," said Rainaut.

If Kalere found this distressing she gave no sign of it. "If you are united in God's eyes," she went on, "you have reason to want such a room."

Rainaut glared, then looked away. "Lepers are not entitled to such charity."

"Everyone is entitled to such charity," Kalere corrected

334 · *Chelsea Quinn Yarbro*

him gently. "No one comes who is not welcome. We have
had thieves and murderers and madmen here, and all have
been welcome; no one has ever harmed us, nor will they."
She smiled at Olivia. "Everyone, whoever they are, whatever they have done, is welcome here."

Olivia had the strangest sensation; Kalere knew her for
what she was. It was so unlikely a possibility that she had to
resist the urge to laugh: there had been times in the past
when she had experienced similar sensations, most of them
more from her own fear than genuine intuition. Now she
watched Kalere speculatively. "How do you mean that?"

"No one need be afraid once they are here. Our Lord
taught that if we are to love, we must accept and embrace
everyone; my brother and I have striven to do this. Anyone
who comes to so remote a place as this one cannot be here by
accident." She looked from Olivia to Rainaut. "Your beast is
weary and you are exhausted. Both of you will be fed." She
started to walk away from the gate, then looked back at
Olivia. "The bathhouse is there"—she pointed to a small
stone building beyond the chapel—"and there are provisions for bathing there."

"You are most kind," said Olivia, puzzled by Kalere and
her apparent perspicacity.

"I? No. I am only doing as the Christ bade all of us who
believe in His Word." She indicated the mule. "There is a
stablehand in the barn, if you need him. Wake him and tell
him what your animal requires."

"And he will be pleased to accommodate me?" Olivia
asked, smiling in spite of herself.

"Certainly. The stablehand came here four years ago, a
man hunted by brigands and soldiers alike, a man who
declared himself the enemy of man and God, who was
friend to no one. He wanted a place to hide, and thought we
were stupid enough to protect him as long as it suited his
purpose. Well, years have gone by, and we still protect him.
He no longer thinks it stupid of us, and he is no longer an
enemy to man or God." She gave a trill of happy laughter.
"He tended animals at first because he thought they would
hide him. Now he does it for the love of them, and for love
of the Christ." She looked at Rainaut. "You do not believe

me? Speak to the man tomorrow and ask him to tell you his story."

Rainaut hitched his shoulders. "It matters little to me either way. If I speak to him, it will not change my mind about anything."

Olivia wanted to shake him for his callous behavior, but Kalere motioned her to silence. "Your food will be ready shortly. In the meantime, your room will be made ready." She gestured to Olivia. "And your bath awaits you. I see there is a sack tied to the saddle. It will be taken to your room."

"By a brigand?" Rainaut asked in patent disbelief.

"By one who was a brigand. As you were once a soldier." She paid no attention to the shocked expression in his eyes. "I will attend to your needs at once."

"Do you wish to know who we are?" Olivia called as Kalere started to walk away from them toward the building where the rooms for married couples and families waited.

"Only if you wish to tell me. You need not if you would rather not." She looked directly at Olivia.

"I am Atta Olivia Clemens. I am a Roman widow. I have been trying to reach Roma for some time. Until recently, I lived for some time in Tyre." As she said this, she could see Kalere's face change slightly. "Before that, I lived some years in Alexandria."

"And the knight?" Kalere inquired. "You need not tell me if you would rather not."

"The knight," said Rainaut heavily, "is a dead man. I was once Sier Valence Rainaut, vassal to Reis Richard of England and Knight of the Hospital of Saint John, Jerusalem. But that was before I was a leper."

"You are welcome here, Sier Valence," said Kalere, undisturbed by Rainaut's announcement. "If you will come with me, you will have food."

He pulled his yellow cowl back off his head. "Look at me!" he ordered Kalere. "Look at what I am."

She stopped and did as he insisted. "Yes. It is most unfortunate that you have been disfigured, but there are many who suffer so, from leprosy and other causes. I pray

God will send you tranquility in your suffering."

"What the Devil is the matter with you?" Rainaut demanded as Kalere continued on her way to the buildings close to the chapel.

"Nothing," she said to him. "Come. You will feel better once you have dined. And you, Bondama Clemens. You have needs as well."

Olivia resisted the urge to offer a flippant and dishonest response to her observation. "I thank you."

"We'll talk when you have finished your bath. You, Sier Valence, must have food before anything else." She indicated a door a dozen paces ahead. "Enter there. I will see that your mule is cared for."

"The man who was a robber?" Olivia ventured.

"Certainly." Kalere looked at the mule. "It's a good thing you did not have to ride him much farther. He's all in, poor fellow."

Olivia smiled and bowed her head in resignation. "Tell me what you wish me to do, and I will do my best to comply."

"Do whatever suits you," said Kalere, and then added, "You may wish to start with your bath. Open that door, and speak to the woman who will attend you."

For once, Olivia was happy to capitulate.

* * *

Text of a letter from the Papal legate at Acre to Fealatie Bueveld, Chatelaine Fraizmarch.

To the worthy Chatelaine of Baron Gui de Fraizmarch, the blessings of God on you, and His care in this time of testing and trial.

I have reviewed the documents your escort has presented to me, and listen to their accounts of your pilgrimage here, and your attempts to fulfill the terms of your penance. You have been dutiful and devout in your compliance, and in these matters I will notify your husband that you have been most faithful to your vows. That you were willing to undertake a penance that I will say is an extreme one shows how great your desire to restore the honor of your House is, and I am convinced that your efforts are worthy.

Had I been approached at the first, I would have recommended that there be alternate penances offered in case Jerusalem were still in Islamite hands—which is, most lamentably, the case. It is not possible for you to enter that city in harness, no matter what your husband or your confessor may wish. If I were to be consulted, I would have several modifications to propose. Because of the distance between you and your home, I will see that a copy of this letter is sent to your husband and to the Abbot at Sante-Estien-in-Gorze for their consideration. It is fitting that they should be given the opportunity to assess these proposals and to meditate on them, so that both religion and honor might be accommodated by your actions.

It is my duty to tell you that you must persevere in your attempt to reach Jerusalem, or you must be willing to seek the higher prize: the only penance that I can offer in place of the prayers in Jerusalem is for you to seek and find the Holy Grail. Only that is of greater religious merit, and only that would be acceptable to the Church and to the honor of your husband and your father. Those who seek the Grail are dedicated to so great a degree that their purpose does much to erase sin and error from their lives. It is said that God does not permit the Grail to be attained by any who are not pure in heart. Surely if you cannot find expiation in Jerusalem, your search for the Grail will impart the same blessings as those you already seek.

It is not my desire to overrule the wisdom of your father, your husband, the Comes de Brissac, and the Abbot of Sante-Estien-in-Gorze. All these men have knowledge and care beyond what I can achieve in your case. However, as Papal legate, I do know some of the desires of the Pope and of the Church in regard to penance, and for that reason, I suggest that if you cannot, after all attempts, gain entrance to Jerusalem in harness, you must consider the good of your soul and the merits of penance, and decide then if your oath and duty are better served by a lack of fulfillment of the terms of penance, or if you might ameliorate the burden of sin through undertaking a task more severe but capable of completion.

I pray that it will be acceptable to your husband and your father that your entrance to Jerusalem, unarmed and on foot, will suffice. If this is not deemed sufficient, and if you are obliged to keep to the original conditions, then I earnestly beseech you to search for the Grail and thereby purge yourself of sin. The great error you have made requires a great sacrifice to show yourself worthy of redemption. You must recognize the enormity of your shame, and be willing to continue your efforts to make amends.

Your escort is willing to continue with you, and for that reason if no other I encourage you to persevere, to dedicate yourself to the Grail and to accept the aid they offer in that most sacred hunt. If you were unable to find escort, or if you had been mandated to accomplish your penance alone, I would not recommend a task so severe. However, since your domestic chivalry is able to accompany you, I trust you will not disdain their support. It is as much for the good of their souls as for yours, and in choosing the harder road, you also choose the greater victory.

My prayers for your forgiveness come with this letter.

Fazio Cavalignano
Papal legate at Acre

By the hand of the scribe Fraire Luccio, under Papal seal, on the Feast of Saint Burgundofara, foundress of the Faremoutiers, in the Year of Our Lord 1192.

· 11 ·

Rainaut was awake when Olivia returned to their room. "You have fed," he accused her.

"Yes," she said, coming to the side of the bed they shared.

"Who was fortunate enough to earn your favor?" He

threw the words at her as if they were weapons, and watched
for the hurt they inflicted.

"One who slept and dreamed," she said, fatigue all but
overwhelming her. "In the morning, he will know only
that—a dream."

"Be damned to you, woman," Rainaut muttered, drawing
the simple blankets around him.

"Valence," she said, sitting on the edge of the bed, "we
have been here almost two weeks. I have limited myself to
rats and rabbits until tonight, for your sake. But that is less
to me than bread and water is to you. To visit a man with a
dream is fare as simple as what Kalere and Rafi offer at their
table, yet I am content with it, for your sake. What more do
you want of me? I cannot starve, but I can madden with
hunger. Neither you nor I wish for that." She reached out to
touch him only to have her hand batted away.

"No." He stared up at the whitewashed ceiling. "Why
would you want to touch me? I'm more of a monster than
you are." There was no self-pity in his voice, only a colorless
hatred.

Olivia bit back the retort she wanted to give. When she
could trust herself, she said, "You have no reason to be
jealous."

"Jealous," he scoffed. "Of a dream?"

She rose and walked away from him. "There was a time
when I could have helped you, if you had let me. When we
first met, if you had not forbade me to love you, some of this
might have been avoided. But that time has passed, and we
are what we are."

He looked at her, his eyes following her as she moved
about the dark room. "I loved you then, to distraction."

"Yes. You did love me then, but it has changed."

"I have changed," Rainaut said.

Olivia came back to the side of the bed and gazed down at
him. "You have changed—I have not. It is my nature,
Valence. Where I have given love I can never deny it. That
you do not want love of me any more is more anguish to me
than you can know, or will ever know, since you will not be
as I am when your life is over." Her voice was distant and
intimate at once. "When you first sought me, so much
against your will, I was filled with joy. You awakened me

from years of isolation, when I was more a sleepwalker than a living woman—for whatever else I am, I am a living woman—and restored my passion. I had set aside longing and desire and ardor because they were dangerous. You gave them back to me. Your love has been the most cherished treasure to me."

"And through it you have lost everything," he added, his tone hard and unforgiving.

"I have lost everything before and survived it," she told him. "And who can say if I would have been able to keep anything if I had not loved you? Can you understand how much you have given me, how much you have done for me? Without you, without the love you offered me, I would not have been drawn back to the love of life. It was not the delight of your body—or not only the delight of your body—that roused me, it was the fervor of your soul."

"It was lust." He glared at her. "Lust."

"Frenzy," she corrected softly. "For both of us, I think. Lust would have burned itself out in a day or a week. Even now, if you were healed, you would not refuse me."

His eyes were bright with tears but he spoke with contempt. "If I were healed, we would not be here."

"No," she said. "I would probably be back in Roma and you would have returned to the Holy Land, with the Hospitalers as escort once more." Her smile was faint and wistful. "Who knows, you might have taken the gift I offered you, and come to my life when you died."

"It is better I am unclean," he said, deliberately harsh.

"Is it? Is it better to turn away from love, too, as you have withdrawn from life?" Her hazel eyes softened. "Oh, Valence, I love you. I could pile words, one on top of the other, to try to tell you how much, but I could not. I love you: that is the most I can say without cheapening the worth of loving. To say anything beyond that would limit it, no matter what eloquence I used. I love you and I will love you all my life."

Rainaut attempted to laugh; it became a cough.

"All my life, Valence." She bent and kissed his forehead, then, more swiftly, his mouth.

He moved back from her as if burned; he wiped his face with the back of his hand.

She saw the gesture, as he intended she should, and her heart sank. "Tell me," she said more conversationally, as if there was no conflict between them, "why do you fear me now?"

"You seek to turn me from God and salvation," he blurted out, startled and taken aback by her question.

"How? By loving you?" She drew a long, uneven breath. "If you think that love is finite, to be meted out in calculated parcels—so much for the family, so much for the Crown, so much for lovers, so much for God—then I suppose you could have reason to fear, because you were afraid you would run out of it. Love isn't like that." She moved away from him, her body trembling. "I wish you could believe me."

For a moment he relented and tenderness came back into his voice. "So do I, Olivia."

She was incapable of tears, but there was a gnawing pain in her chest and throat which was as close as she could come to weeping. This was not the time, she thought, doing her best to stifle the dry sounds of her grief. She steadied herself against the whitewashed walls, unable to bring herself to turn and look at him.

There was a sound of movement from his side of the room, the whisper of blankets tossed aside, and then he was behind her, his arms around her, his white cheek against her hair. "Olivia," he whispered, holding her tightly. "No. Don't turn. Don't look at me. For God's sake, do not look at me."

"But it doesn't matter—"

He cut her off. "It matters to me. I want you to think of me as I was, the way I looked when I first saw you, when I first touched you. Do you remember?"

"Yes," she breathed, seeking for the ghost of their rapture as he spoke.

"You were like no woman I had ever known. You are like no other woman. Not my wife, not the courtesans I've employed. You were like a lamp in the night, the end of darkness. If not for you, I would never have known desire that grows with fulfillment. I would never have known gratification that increases the capacity to be gratified. I

would never have known what it is to discover myself
through losing myself. You gave all that to me, unstintingly.
I should despise myself for allowing you—"

"No," she protested.

"—to carry me so far from my sworn purpose. I ought to
have put you behind me the first time I saw you. You turned
me from every oath I ever swore. It was my duty to spurn
you, and I was not strong enough for that." He kissed her
hair and the edge of her jaw. "Yet no matter what punishment is visited on me, I cannot deny you, not in my heart."

"Valence." Her hands closed over his.

Suddenly he released her and shoved her across the room.
"God protect me, I am a leper and even that is not enough! I
am still in your thrall."

She closed her eyes against his renewed harshness. "You
were never my slave or my victim."

"Then I am my own, which is worse." His voice broke.
"Do not keep me, Olivia. I have nothing for you and can
take nothing from you."

Her voice was steady. "Do you wish me to leave?"

"It is wrong of me," he answered obliquely. "I am sworn
to protect you."

"Then you do wish it," she pursued. Now that she had
asked, it was easier to press him for his answer.

"I wish to be left to myself, so that I can try to make peace
with God before I am called to pay for all my sins." He
blessed himself. "How can I do that if you are with me? You
are the soul of my idolatry. I cannot search for God when I
can reach for you."

She nodded. "All right. I will speak to Kalere or her
brother and see what I can arrange. If you like, I will ask for
other quarters."

Rainaut started to answer, then laughed. "I ask you to go
from here, but I do not want you away from me while you
are here. I am a foolish and vain man, Olivia. Forgive me for
that."

"There is nothing to forgive," she said quietly. "It will not
be easy to stay with you, not for you or me."

He made an equivocal gesture. "If you are within these
walls, I would spend all night listening for sounds of you,
wanting to catch a glimpse of you. If you are here with me, at

least I will be spared that. When you are gone, then I will know that I cannot hear you or see you, no matter how much I look. If you are still here, I will have to clap my hands over my ears to keep from listening for your step, your voice. Stay with me, if you can bear with my inexcusable treatment."

"And if you cannot bear it?" she asked, her manner kind.

"I will think of something then. You and I will deal with that if we must. But if you are leaving, then let me have your company." He reached out his hand to her. "Olivia."

She faltered, not knowing how much she could endure of his erratic temperament. She was aware that his illness had created some of the extremity of feeling in him, but some of it was inherent in the man. Her frown deepened as she considered his state of mind. "I do not want to refuse you," she said at last.

"Then you'll stay." He smiled. "Here, with me."

"For the time being," she said carefully. "If it becomes too difficult, then I will ask Kalere to make other arrangements for me until I leave."

"You will go back to Roma, I suppose?" Rainaut asked with false cheer.

"It is my home," she replied.

"And what is there to keep you away?" His attempt at a smile was more a grimace of pain.

"If it were up to me, I would bring you with me," she said. "But you will not have it." She glanced at the bed. "It is very late. I need rest, and sunrise is coming."

"After a night of love, you are doubtless tired," he said, then went on before she could speak, "Pay no heed to me. I think perhaps you were right after all and I am jealous, because I can no longer love you myself."

"I would take no harm from you, nor you from me," she reminded him, as she had many times already, knowing it was useless.

"So you say," he chided. "You also say I am not a leper and that my disease cannot be caught from me. How can I trust anything you tell me, when you are trying to comfort me with such lies."

"They are not lies," she said wearily.

"Then why is—" He stopped. "No. There's no point in going through this again, is there? You need rest and I . . . I ought to go to the chapel, to pray." He held his hands up, palms toward her. "I was in error. I should not have started this again. I didn't mean to cause you more hurt."

"It's not important," she said. "If you believed me, it would be, but since you don't, it isn't." For a little time they stood, silently staring at one another. "Go to your prayers, Valence. Let me sleep."

He bowed. "As you wish, Bondama."

When he had left the room, she went to the bed and began to take off her muslin bliaud. She undressed automatically, folding her garments and setting them on the floor beside the bed. Then she climbed between the rough sheets, wishing there were a mattress filled with good Roman earth under her instead of the hempen cords and a mixture of horsehair and straw.

Her sleep was deep, almost to the point of dreamlessness, but when she woke, an hour before sunset, she was not much restored. She knew she was mourning Rainaut, and she could not reveal it to him. As she dragged her ivory comb through her hair, she forced herself to go on to more practical considerations. If she left this refuge, she would have to travel disguised. Did she want to travel alone? She had the yellow cowl that would make her prey to none but the leper bands—the recollection made her shudder—but would deny her any charity along the road. It was not a sensible choice, she decided, and weighed the possibility of wearing men's clothes and claiming she was a eunuch. If she dressed like a merchant or a Greek religious, she might get away with it, but the risks if she were discovered were enormous; not only were there harsh laws for such conduct, she had no one who might aid her if she were apprehended, which would mean imprisonment at best. And prison meant esurient hunger and its madness.

"You're awake," said Rainaut as he came through the door. He looked haggard, and he rubbed at his reddened eyes. "You are expected in the chapel after sunset. Brother and sister want to speak with you."

"What did you tell them?" she asked almost without feeling.

"That I have decided you and I must separate." He made the statement bluntly, his face averted.

"And what was their response?" If she were going to meet with argument or resistance, she wanted to be prepared.

"They claim they understand." He gestured toward the door. "They have offered to . . . to assist you." Once again he rubbed his eyes. "They ache. At the back."

At another time, she would have been able to offer him draughts to ease the hurt; in her house in Tyre she had kept medicinal herbs and ointments, substances and tinctures that would take the worst of his pain away. She wished she could offer him pansy and willow, or syrup of poppies. "I'm sorry," she said, that being all she could give him now.

"Will this blind me, do you think?" He might have been asking about the weave of a cloth for all the emotion he showed.

"Eventually," she admitted. "And your skin will not be able to endure sunlight—it will make you ill if you walk in the sun." She decided to take the chance. "I have seen this malady before; I've told you. Very well. Listen to what will become of you, and believe me or not as you wish. Your eyes are not going to be able to stand the light of day for much longer. The red you see in them is from damage from the sun. For a time, if you are careful, you will be able to see at night."

"The way you do?" he asked with faint contempt.

"No, but it doesn't matter." She hesitated and went on. "Your skin will puff and swell if you stay in the sun, and so you will not do that. You will become a creature of the night. Not as I am, but a creature of the night nonetheless. Your liver and kidneys will grow weak and in time will fail you, which will mean your death. You may have moments of . . . delusions, hallucinations; visions, if you will." She started toward him, and then stopped. "You don't want me to stay, do you?"

"No," he said.

She nodded her acceptance. "I will make arrangements." As she went to the door, she paused, staring at him. "Whether I am here or elsewhere, you are part of me now, in your blood and soul, and I will never be wholly free of you."

"Benedictus qui venit in nomine Domini," he recited. "Here is my blood which is shed for thee." He grabbed her arm. "Go. Go. While I have the courage to let you."

Olivia could not speak as she left the room and crossed the compound to the chapel where Kalere and her brother Rafi waited for her. She made herself notice the minutest of details about the buildings, the pebbles of the walkway, the dampness and weeds around the well, so that she would not think of Rainaut.

Kalere was kneeling at the altar, her head bowed. Beside her, her brother read from an ancient manuscript in a language Olivia had not heard for more than five centuries. Rafi stopped reading as Olivia crossed the threshold.

"God give you His gifts," he said.

"And you," Olivia responded automatically. "You wished to speak with me?"

"It is necessary," said Kalere, turning to face her. "It is apparent that he is not improving."

"No, he's not," said Olivia, coming toward the altar. Without meaning to, she asked, "Where did you learn Asian Greek?"

"You recognized it?" Rafi asked in some surprise. He had a fine voice, deep and musical; it seemed mismatched with his rough-hewn features.

"Yes." Olivia waited for more questions or a challenge: when none came, she said, "He wishes me to leave. He's said so before, but this time . . . this time he wants me gone."

"He does not want you to see him fail more than he has already," Kalere said. "It is his duty to release you from your promises to him. He should have done this before he was cast out, but he was unable to order you—"

"He had been my escort for some time. It wouldn't have mattered if he sent me away, I still would have shared his fate without his presence." Olivia looked from sister to brother. "You will care for him? He is going to get worse. If he would let me remain with him, I would do it."

"That would be cruel," said Kalere gently.

"I know." Olivia stared down at her hands. "He is no leper, Bondama, and neither am I."

It was Rafi who responded. "He is afflicted and you are not—not in the way he is. There are other ways for one to be cursed." He looked down at the manuscript and read out several tolling lines. "If you know the language?"

" 'Knock on the door that is you yourself and walk on the road that is you yourself, for that door will open to your soul and the road will lead you only to your soul. Open the door that you may know yourself, and open it that your self may truly be yours. Tread the road of yourself that you may arrive at the self that is truly yours.' " Olivia translated. "What text is that?"

"A very old one," said Kalere.

"If it is in that tongue, it must be," Olivia said.

"There is a group of pilgrims due here in two days," said Rafi as if continuing their discussion rather than changing it. "We will arrange for you to travel with them, if that is satisfactory to you. They are not inclined to ask questions."

Olivia hesitated. "It is . . . best if I travel at night." Without her Roman earth and with little blood to sustain her, she dreaded the sun.

Kalere glanced at her brother. "They would accept a scout to go ahead of them. Night travel would be acceptable, though a little unusual."

"I will consider it," said Olivia, already certain that she would refuse.

"You are welcome to stay here," Rafi told her.

"No," Olivia said at once. "I could not do that with Rainaut here as well. It . . . it isn't possible for me to be near him and not . . . I could not stay away from him."

Neither brother nor sister questioned this. "Where will you go?" Rafi asked. "You need not give us an answer."

"To Roma. I have a villa to the northeast of the city. It is called Sanza Pare. There are those who would hold a letter for me even now." She put a hand to her brow. "I would . . . want to know . . . when—" It was more awkward than she thought possible to speak of Rainaut's death.

"We will send word, Bondama," said Kalere.

Olivia nodded. "Thank you. If there is anything—"

"We will see he is tended." Kalere's eyes softened. "Do not judge yourself too harshly, Bondama. He has shut himself away because he can bear naught else. It is not to your discredit that he does this. If he cared nothing for you, he would accept your aid without a thought. It is his love that does this."

"I have . . . an obligation to him. There is a bond." She hoped that there would be no need to explain anything more.

Ravi shook his head. "He would fail in his oath as a knight to permit you to remain with him." He laid his hand on a page of the ancient manuscript. "Listen: 'Those who seek salvation through martyrdom thinking that the suffering is the salvation do not know the Living Christ. Those who believe that joy is meted out as reward for pain know nothing of the promise of salvation. Those who seek out torment in the name of God have cast the Father in the role of tormentor. Those who seek glory will not spurn the pain, but those who seek pain will not find the glory.'" He met Olivia's eyes. "Let him learn to find the glory. While you are here, he will know only pain—his own and yours."

Olivia was very still; finally she nodded.

*   *   *

Text of a letter from Gui de Fraizmarch to the Abbot of Sante-Estien-in-Gorze.

To the most reverend and worthy Abbot Eustache of Sante-Estien, my greetings and prayers for the benefit of your aid and understanding.

I have your letter written on the 11th day of March in which you describe what you choose to call the plight of my wife in her attempts to fulfill her penance in the Holy Land. You have described her efforts and the reasons she claims to have been unable to accomplish what has been required of her. You advise me to be willing to permit a change in the requirements so that she may act in accordance with prevailing conditions and enter Jerusalem on foot and unarmed in order to pray at the Holy Sepulcher.

The alternative, as you have set forth, is that she and her retinue must remain in the Holy Land until Jerusalem is once again in Christian hands and she would therefore be allowed to enter the city in harness and armed, her horse in bard and her escort similarly armed. The dishonor she has brought upon me and my House is such that I can permit no alteration of the terms of her penance, and if that means she is—as you have chosen to term it—in exile until Jerusalem is once again in Christian hands, then so be it, she is in exile, and may think herself fortunate that that is the worst to have befallen her.

This woman has disgraced me. Nothing else can be considered but the dishonor she has brought on me. While it is claimed that the disgrace was not intended and that she was under duress as my chatelaine, bound to protect my holdings during my absence, there can be no circumstances that would excuse her actions. To have sustained the siege of the Comes de Reissac was lamentable but still tolerable, though she took it upon herself to defend Castel Fraizmarch without consulting others as to her responsibility in this case. Much embarrassment might have been avoided if she had been willing then to seek some assistance so that a truce could be negotiated. That she mounted the attack and conquered the Comes in open combat is wholly unpardonable. She has abjured my oath of fealty and has compromised my House. Her actions, which she claims were only to preserve Castel Fraizmarch, were of so grievous consequence that you know I would be well within my rights to imprison her or consign her to a nunnery for the rest of her days.

You and the Comes himself were willing to permit this penance, and little though I approved, I did not want more ill will between myself and the Comes de Reissac. Now you ask that the severity of her penance be lessened, that she be allowed to modify the terms of her acts, and I tell you, after what she has done, after the inexcusable way she has conducted herself, it is not possible or desirable that she be excused one item of her terms of penance. When she left here for the Holy Land, it was with the understanding that she would enter Jerusalem in harness, garbed for war and ready to fight, as she fought de Reissac. Nothing else will expiate her sins against the honor of this House, against her father's House and against the King. If she is forsworn in church, which she would be if she did less than she vowed before God to do, then she is worse than a heretic and deserving of all the torments and suffering that can be meted out to human flesh in this life. You may be sure that if she attempts to return with her penance incomplete, she will learn more than she wishes to know of those torments.

You say that you have addressed the Comes de Reissac on behalf of my wife and he is willing to have her accomplish her penance in these lessened terms. This is inconceivable, and I question the motives of this man, unless he is liverless. If that is the case, then I can well understand why he would be willing to mitigate my wife's penance. No wonder he was beaten in battle by a woman—he is no better than a woman himself. If the Comes has forgot himself so far that he is willing to deny his oaths, that is upon his honor and his soul. I am not so lacking in my purpose and I will defend his honor when he will not. Inform my wife that she is bound by the terms of her oath which she made before me, you, and God. If that is not acceptable to her, she will face worse than my wrath if she is reckless enough to return to France. You will tell her that my terms stand, and what will happen to her if she abrogates her duty in any particular whatsoever.

I hope you will look into your heart once again, good Abbot, and see how you have traduced God's purpose with your lax notions. If other religious were as spineless as you, we would have the Islamites hollering their curses from the rooftops of Roma. Pray for a return of faith and dedication, for it is clear that you have lost your zeal. My wife will suffer the pains of Hell if she is allowed to forget her obligations in this world.

Gui de Fraizmarch

By the hand of the scribe Jean-Colin, on the Feast of Saint George of Cappodocia, patron of soldiers, in the Lord's Year 1192.

On the evening Olivia left, Rainaut refused to talk to her. He barred the door to the room they had shared, and when she called her farewells to him, he was silent.

"I am sorry," said Rafi as he went to the gates of the compound. "It may be the only way he can let you go at all."

"I hope that's all his reason," said Olivia, trying to maintain her composure. She had decided earlier that she would not be upset by anything Rainaut did to her on the eve of her departure, but she was finding it difficult to accept being closed out of Rainaut's life.

"If there are others, he and God know of them, and he and God will know of them at another time." He looked at the little sack tied to the saddle. "Your belongings only, no provisions; are you sure you will not change your mind?"

"No provisions," she said, repeating what she had told them already. "I will manage as I go."

Rafi sighed. "We can give you water, at least. The well here is pure and sweet."

"Thank you, no." Olivia, dressed in men's clothing, her hair drawn back and tucked into a Greek iron cap, looked little enough like herself. She had deliberately smudged charcoal along her jaw and darkened her brows with it, so that a quick glance in the night would not betray her.

"We will tend to him, Bondama, and we will pray for you," said Rafi. "We read and write in Greek. Kalere knows some French, as well, so we will send word to the villa in Roma. If there is any word to send."

"I am grateful," said Olivia. "I will remember you, and when I am home again, I will see that a donation is sent to you."

"There is no need," Rafi assured her.

352 · *Chelsea Quinn Yarbro*

"But it is a thing I wish to do." Olivia spoke with purpose but without giving offense.

"We will be glad of it, if you send it, and will not be disappointed or cast aspersions on you if you do not. We do not offer this sanctuary for any earthly reward, but for the chance of coming to know with enlightened minds. We provide the haven for those who seek it, for those who find it. We gain understanding, which is enough." He blessed himself and her, then, as an afterthought, Atlas as well. "He may be a dumb beast, and an unnatural one, but he does the work he was made to do, and he goes in the world to accomplish his tasks, which is more than many others do."

Olivia patted the mule's neck. "He is a reliable creature," she said, gathering up the reins. "I will let you know I have arrived at Roma, and my thanks will come with that notification."

"As you wish. My sister and I will remember you, whatever the case." He started back toward the doors of his compound, standing open, as always. "If ever you have need of us again, Bondama, we will be here."

"That is very kind," said Olivia, hoping that she would never again be caught in these mountains. She got into the saddle and tugged Atlas around so that he was facing to the north. "If he will listen, tell Rainaut that though I leave him I do not stop loving him."

"We will, when he will listen." He raised his hand. "Go now. Stay on the east side of the stream and you will find the pilgrims' road in a night or two. There are stations for rest all along it."

"I'll remember," Olivia said, clapping her heels to Atlas' sides and resigning herself to his steady walk. She looked back to the compound only once, when the bend in the road put it directly to her right. She saw the outline of the chapel and the roofs of two of the larger buildings, but otherwise the place was sunk in dusk, almost indistinguishable from the rocks around it.

That night Olivia pressed on as relentlessly as she could, permitting Atlas to stop for water only three times, and to graze only once. She considered taking a cup of blood from him, to give her some little stamina, but in the end decided that the mule had greater need than she.

Morning found her not far from a mountain sheepfold, and she paused long enough for a taste of blood from three of the sheep, not enough to weaken any of the animals, but enough to sustain her through the next day and night. She slept under a fallen tree, Atlas grazing on his tether line nearby. Her sleep was filled with dreams, often dark and frightening, and she was not much refreshed when she woke shortly after sunset.

That night she covered more ground, arriving at the pilgrims' road toward the end of the night. She could not see any of the stations where pilgrims could sleep and prepare simple meals, but there were crosses hammered into the trunks of trees, and crude signs in Latin, French, and Greek identified the wide, dusty track as leading from Iconium to Tyana. Olivia gave a tight smile and turned Atlas toward Iconium, hoping that she would find a protected resting spot before the sun was up.

Not long before dawn, she saw one of the stations for pilgrims, a small, square building with a tiny chapel attached. The station had only three high windows and a narrow door, which was firmly shut and bolted. Refuse lay strewn on the west side of the building, and a short distance away, a stone well supplied water and overflowed into a long, narrow trough. There was a donkey tied up outside the station near the trough and it started to bray as it caught the scent of Atlas.

Immediately the mule set up its own raucous greeting, and Olivia jobbed at the bit to try to quiet him. He stopped the noise but began his own version of bucking in protest, and Olivia had her hands full for a little while, until she and her mount were safely past the station and the attendant donkey. The nearness of pilgrims and the risk of discovery made Olivia a little nervous, and she took the precaution of leaving the pilgrims' road, looking for her shelter at a slight distance from the curious eyes of those traveling to or from the Holy Land.

She came upon the ruins of a fort, one abandoned for centuries, judging by the tumbledown walls and the deep sands that filled half of the place. Olivia found one end of the fort where the walls were more intact and the sands had not yet filled in the structure. She took the time to gather fodder for Atlas, for she did not want him loose on a tether line, alerting others to her presence. She improvised a pen for him as the sky was glowing pink at the eastern horizon, then took refuge in a narrow room that was still intact, under the tallest wall. From the scent of the place, it had been used to store fruits and wine. Olivia wrapped herself in a dark mantel and fell once more into sleep as the rest of the world awoke.

That night she traveled again, moving westward along the road, taking care to read all the signs she came upon. She felt her strength waning, and at last she took a chance, taking a cup of blood from Atlas. As she drank, she hoped she would find more sustaining nourishment before many more nights went by. It had been several hundred years since she had had to exist wholly on the power of blood; she had abhorred it then and loathed it now. "Don't worry," she said as she patted Atlas' shoulder. "It will be just this once." Little as she wished to recognize it, she was in need of humanity, of rapture, of intimacy, for nothing else would truly preserve her.

By the end of the night, she had passed through a village and was, according to the signs, nearing Iconium. She decided not to attempt to reach the town, but chose to find yet another secluded place to pass the day, hidden from the sun and all prying eyes.

Finding such a haven was not as simple a task as it had been before, and she had to look in several places before she was satisfied with her selection: there was a rough hut, abandoned for at least a year, with the Plague symbol fading on the door. A byre, also deserted, was next to the house, and it was here, in the musty hay, with spiders and rats for company, that Olivia decided to sleep. She found sweet grass for Atlas and brought it to the broken manger, and once the mule was eating, Olivia spread out her mantel in the loft, where she would be protected from the sun and from anyone venturing to this forgotten farmstead.

Shortly after sunset, she wakened to Atlas' warning bray. She was instantly alert, her night-seeing eyes searching for the cause of Atlas' disturbance. Her sword, shorter than many carried by men-at-arms, was balanced for her hand,

and the dagger she slipped out of her belt was thin and sharp. She eased herself to the edge of the loft and stared down.

Two scruffy boys in beggars' rags had sneaked into the byre, one of them clearly intent on stealing the mule, the other more cautious.

Atlas laid his long ears back and kicked out with his front feet.

The darker of the two boys laughed, but the other was growing more frightened, gesturing and speaking in whispers, as if he were afraid of more than the mule.

"Don't be an idiot," the darker boy chided, reaching for a long board and holding it in front of him for protection. "We can sell the animal and get away from that warehouse."

The other boy spoke so low that Olivia could not make out what he was saying. He blessed himself twice, and at last burst out, "There's been plague here. You know what that means."

"No one has seen a single ghost here," the darker boy mocked.

"No one has been here in more than a year," protested his companion.

In the loft, Olivia smiled and silently began to spread out her mantel.

"If you'd help me, we could catch the damned beast," the darker boy said with an angry gesture to the other. "You take one side of his head and I'll take the other."

"But—"

"Look," the darker boy said in exasperation, "someone brought him here and left him here. That means—"

"That means something happened to whoever brought him here," said the more cautious boy.

"Ten thousand devils!" the darker one swore, making another sally toward Atlas without success.

"He'll kick your head in," warned the more cautious boy.

"Not before I beat him between the ears," vowed his more reckless companion.

The careful boy tried to pull the darker boy back and was rewarded with a slap on the side of his head. "Why'd you do that?"

"You don't try to stop me, Ismael. If you're too cowardly to help me, then keep back." The darker boy started toward Atlas a third time, carrying his improvised cudgel higher, his expression as intent as a cat at a mousehole.

"A-a-a-a-a-a-hhhhhh!" Olivia moaned as she rose in the loft, her mantel spread out beyond her shoulders, held in place by her sword. She quivered, making the dust-colored cloth shake, and her moaning became a screech.

Atlas gave a high scream and lashed out more furiously with his front feet.

Ismael stood transfixed by the sight, but the other boy, who up until that moment had been the more adventure-some, flung the board he held aside and bolted for the door, his rags flapping around him as he yelled in terror, "Ghosts! Ghosts! The place is haunted! Plague ghosts!"

Olivia let her howls die away to silence, though she continued to make her mantel tremble.

Ismael blessed himself and very slowly backed out of the byre. "We didn't mean any harm," he called out in a voice that broke into childish treble as he got through the door. Unlike his companion, he did not run, but walked quickly and purposefully away.

Atlas demolished most of what had been unbroken of the manger. He snorted and squealed one more time.

"They're gone," said Olivia to calm him. "Steady there, Atlas." She tucked her dagger back into her belt and slid her sword into its scabbard. As she gathered up her mantel, she added, "I think Ismael might talk of this. We had better not be here if he decides to come back."

The mule kicked out with his hind legs and put a hole in the wall.

More than anything, Olivia longed for a bath. Her skin itched and she could feel grime on her legs and the back of her neck. She was certain that more than charcoal dirtied her face now, and she was afraid to try to put her comb through her hair, knowing that there would be snarls and knots. Before she pulled her mantel over her shoulders she took time to shake it out and to brush off the straw and twigs that clung to it. She wondered if she ought to have a tale of escape from bandits to account for her appearance.

This turned out not to be necessary. Only one gate to Iconium was open after sundown, and it was manned by two men-at-arms of the Hospitalers, both of them clearly suffering from the ravages of bloody flux. They glanced over Olivia, accepted her assurance that she was a eunuch, and told her that accommodations for Christian travelers were to be found in the Greek quarter of the city, which was immediately south of the sheep-and-lamb market.

Olivia thanked them, and considered her few remaining coins; three of silver and a dozen of copper. Luckily, she thought as she made her way through the narrow streets, she did not have to purchase food as well as lodgings. She saw two hostels for knights, grander than most of what the town had to offer in the way of accommodations: one bore the badge of the Templars, the other the three leopards of Reis Richard. Near these two were the humbler inns for merchants and pilgrims of means. It was one of these that Olivia decided to try, approaching the building by way of the passage between its stable and kitchen; she had seen a light and hoped to find some of the staff still awake.

A cook was sitting in the open larder door, a bucket of hot water between his knees and a half-plucked chicken in his hands. He looked up at the sound of Atlas' hooves on the paving stones and brought a large cleaver into the light. "Who is it?"

"A eunuch," said Olivia. "I arrived late in Iconium and I'd rather not sleep in the street."

The cook laughed guardedly. "They'd rob you of more than your missing eggs before morning." He raised one of the two oil lamps and tried to get a better look at Olivia.

She turned her face so that the light fell on one side only, disguising her more than the cook realized. "I have money," she said, making a show of reaching for her coins. "Not a great deal, but enough to pay for a place to sleep."

"A place to sleep, is it?" The cook chuckled. "Not as easily had as it was once." He pulled another handful of singed feathers from the chicken he held and dropped them into the bucket of hot water.

"Why is that?" Olivia asked, the scent of blood making her a bit giddy.

"The pilgrims, of course." He gestured to the open kitchen door. "Every hostel and inn is crowded, and it will not slack off for quite a while, is my guess."

"Pilgrims?" Olivia repeated, trying not to look at the chicken. Her need was for more than blood; looking at the bird was a sharper reminder than she wished to experience. "Have the Crusaders stormed Jerusalem, then?"

The cook chuckled once more, this time with a hint of malice in the sound. "Not exactly. Stormed Jerusalem? Last year, they might have done it, but not now. They are losing ground. Not only in regard to Jerusalem. Ascalon is not the bastion Reis Richard wants it to be, and there are few who are willing to help him make it stronger. It was bad enough when Reis Phillippe had to return to France, but now, with troops killed in ambushes and illness thinning the ranks and many of the soldiers having second thoughts and deserting, there aren't enough Crusaders left to give Saladin much more than a few days' amusement." He went on plucking the chicken. "Most of the pilgrims are going home, taking a lesson from the Crusaders, I suppose."

"Is there danger?"

The cook shrugged hugely. "Where is there no danger, other than the grave? What place can anyone go where malign fate cannot pursue him?"

Olivia remained still, considering what the cook had told her. "The Crusade—is it a rout?"

"Nothing so clear and final," said the cook. "There are those who are saying that this is only a setback. A setback! Say rather a death-knell. Reis Richard and the Templars have both asked for more men and supplies." He yawned suddenly, then continued. "But Reis Phillippe isn't the only ruler who is unwilling to spend any more money on defeating the Islamites." He pointed with his jaw toward the street. "There's a contingent of Hospitalers staying here, returning to France. Most of the men are sick or wounded and they are under escort from their Order, to ensure they are not taken for ransom or robbed."

"The Hospitalers are everywhere," said Olivia, more to herself than to the cook.

"Christian soldiers are everywhere, some of them where you'd least expect them." He sneered knowingly. "They get a taste for silk and debauchery. They aren't made for the land, for the heat and the starkness of it, and it ruins them, one way or another." He was almost finished with the chicken. "I have three more of these to do. After that, I can make a place for you behind the larder. There's a small room, with a cot. The landlord has no more beds available, but this room will take you if you're not too fussy."

"That's satisfactory to me," said Olivia, her mind filled with doubt. She was afraid that the cook might take it into his head to watch her, and then she would not be safe. "I am bound to Smyrna; is there any chance, do you think, to arrange to travel with any of the pilgrims going that way?"

"It's not for me to say," the cook answered. "The Hospitalers or the Templars will have to give you permission if you seek to go with pilgrims. Still, I can't think why you would not be welcome. I'll speak with the landlord and tell you what he says. Or you can speak with him yourself if you'd rather."

"Whatever you suggest," she said, hoping that she would not have to face too many people in Iconium, for each encounter was a potential denouncement. "In the meantime, is there room for me to stable my mule?"

"There are pens at the back of the stable. A few of them are empty; choose one." He was concentrating on his work again, no longer much interested in speaking with this newcomer. "Water troughs run through the pens. There's hay piled up in the last stall. You may put your saddle and bridle on one of the racks in the middle of the stable. No one will take them."

"God send you His blessings," said Olivia, dismounting at last.

"Come to the kitchen when you're through and I'll see that you have something to eat. I can't offer very much." The cook held up the plucked chicken. "Scrawny, but better than some I've seen. I was able to buy ducks last year, but this year they all went to soldiers before Lent."

Olivia hesitated. "I do not want to place you in any difficulty with the landlord, if food is so hard come by." She paused to let the cook think a short while. "I will fend for myself if it would be less of a demand on you. I am already in your debt for a place to sleep."

"It will cost you three copper coins, providing they weigh enough." He reached down for another chicken. "Take care of the mule. We'll talk when you've finished."

"You are generous," said Olivia with a slight bow.

"Oh, not that, exactly," said the cook. "But slaves like me know what it is to be in need." With this obscure reassurance, he waved Olivia away and went back to his task.

Olivia led Atlas through the stable and out into the yard of enclosed pens. As the cook had told her, there were three still vacant, all of them small, none of them clean. She secured the mule with his tether line and set about unsaddling him and giving him a cursory grooming. When she was finished, she turned him into the largest of the three pens and carried the saddle bridle back into the stable, setting the saddle on the far end of the rack with the bridle tied to the pommel rings. She rubbed her brow, trying to ease the ache there before she went back to the cook, her single sack of belongings tucked under her arm.

"There you are," said the cook as Olivia approached him. "Ready for prayers and sleep? Or do you want a bite to eat?"

Esurience flared in her, and despair. "I had better rest first," she said, her voice sounding husky in her own ears. "Later, perhaps, if it is convenient."

The cook chuckled, the sound like the snap of banners in the wind. "If there is anything left after all the pilgrims have eaten, it is yours."

Olivia murmured a few appropriate phrases while she resigned herself to one more night of animal blood for sustenance.

Text of a confidential letter to Robert de Sable, Grand Master of the Poor Knights of the Temple, Jerusalem, from the secretary of the Metropolitan of Hagia Sophia.

To the most worthy and Christian knight, the Grand Master Robert de Sable, greetings and continuing prayers to you, not only in my own devotions, but as part of the continuing devotions of that most holy of Metropolitans, my master of Hagia Sophia.

We have lately heard of the many reverses suffered by all Christian men-at-arms and chivalry currently sworn to up-hold the honor of Our Lord in the Holy Land. My master has been much shocked to have news indicating that after so splendid a start, the forces of our faith are no longer in the advance, but have fallen back on almost all fronts, and now are in the position of vanquished foemen and the target of all manner of Islamic treachery. Most shocking was the informa-tion that many of the Crusaders had been led by guides to that part of the desert where neither pure water nor relief from heat is available. It was to our sorrow that we were appraised of the death of so many valiant Christian soldiers, and we have once again petitioned Heaven to come to the aid of Our Lord's defenders, protecting them from further misfortune and disgrace.

You of the Templars have always set the example for all other Christian warriors to follow, and your continuing devotion to the cause of the liberation of the Holy Sepulcher can never be called into question by anyone. Your sacrifices and your endless zeal are commended by every leader in the Christian world. That we of Byzantion have no such fighters is forever a blot on our military men. Your constant struggle to uphold the glory of Christ and God is the very culmination of true Christian faith. All other soldiers are lessened when compared to your pure and faultless fidelity, which always shines with the luster of hosts of angels.

With so much of excellence about you, and in so glorious a cause, how can it be that you would consider turning away from the protection and glory of Our Lord, to retreat from the most crucial test of faith that ever Christian was privileged to have? How can you, of all soldiers, be content to leave Jerusalem in the hands of Islamites and defenseless to the predations of these despicable men? Had God given such an opportunity to me, I would have embraced it with the passion of one vouchsafed a welcome in Paradise. Yet you, who have seen on the field of battle the ramparts of Jerusalem, have been willing to withdraw from that most sacred city and to waste what is left of your numbers in the most trivial of conflicts, answering more to the beck of kings than to the clarion of God's cause and your soul's salvation.

If you have lost sight of your most exalted goal, then let me have the office of bringing you to the full realization of your purpose as the Grand Master of your Order. You are the Marshall of God on earth, as the Archangel Michael is the Marshall of the Hosts of Heaven. It was the Archangel Michael who battled Satan himself and sent him tumbling to his prison in Hell. If God so empowered His Archangel, He will likewise give might to you in the name of the most holy city and the honor of the Holy Sepulcher. What earthly honor, what king's reward can compare to the freeing of the Holy Sepulcher? You have it within your grasp to turn back the Islamites as Archangel Michael turned back the rebellious angels who put in their lot with Satan and serve now as the devils in Hell. What could be more worthy of your strength of arms and your life's-blood than the banishing of those hellish Islamites who have so greedily spread through the lands where the Christ has reigned?

Persevere, I beseech you, not only in the name of Our Lord and His city Jerusalem, but in the name of the vows of your Order, which call you to the greatest of contests ever offered men of honor. Speak to the Christian kings who have shown so little faith of late. Urge Reis Phillippe not to forget his obligation to all those in Frankish cities throughout the Holy Land, if he cannot be persuaded to recall his oaths to God.

Spur Reis Richard on to the victories that first marked his arrival in the Holy Land. Forget the petty rivalries which have clouded the sense of righteousness for so many soldiers. Bring accord to the men who came with Barbarossa and have not found a leader to satisfy them. You and your companions in the Hospitalers are all the hope left to Christendom. If you fail now, the honor of God will be tarnished and the glory of your Order forever tainted.

My prayers and the prayers of all in the Greek rite are with you; as we prayed for your victories, we now pray for a return of purpose for you as well. May God open His way to you, that you may again be worthy to be His champions in battle.

Alexios from Salinika
secretary to the Metropolitan of
Hagia Sophia, Konstantinoupolis
By my own hand with the approval of my master, under seal, on the Feast of Saint Athanasius, the 2nd day of May, in the Lord's Year 1192.

· 13 ·

Against her own exhaustion and need, Olivia rose not long after mid-day and sought out the cook. She made a point of thanking him where his minions could hear her, praising him for the aid and advice he had given her. "Be good enough," she added, wishing she felt less debilitated than she did, and knowing that her weakness would exact a price, "to tell me where I must go to apply for passage to Smyrna."

"You could leave the way you came," said the cook as he supervised the turning of four enormous and heavily laden spits, "alone on your mule. That way you need have no one's permission."

"That way there is danger, as well." Olivia put her hand

on the hilt of her sword. "And this way, someone knows if I do not reach my destination."

"An excellent point," agreed the cook. "Well, it must be the Templars or the Hospitalers. I'd go to the Hospitalers, if I were you. These days the Templars are only interested in other fighting men, which clearly you are not, in spite of that metal cap of yours." He made a gesture with a greasy ladle intended to take in the others in the kitchen. "Fair enough for a eunuch, isn't he? But not likely to be a knight."

Several of the scullery slaves laughed, none of them kindly. One, a lad of no more than fifteen or sixteen with the fixed but unfocused stare of the simple-minded, threw his head back and crowed heartily.

"You're very helpful," said Olivia, trying to conceal her irony.

The cook responded candidly. "Probably not, but in these times, help is not easily come by. Go to the Hospitalers. Tell them where you wish to go and ask if any of them will be escorting pilgrims that far. It will be easier to come to an agreement with two knights than with an entire party of pilgrims, no matter who they are." He swiped the back of his hand across his sweating forehead. "Stop by here when you return. I'll hold that room for you until you have passage out of Iconium."

Olivia bowed. "You are most gracious."

The cook laughed again and urged one of the scullery slaves to work harder. "It will be the same charge each night. I am not one of those landlords who is forever increasing his rates."

Olivia gave the usual polite answers as she made her way out of the kitchen. She was amused and troubled at once, for she sensed the cook's attraction—to a fresh-faced eunuch, not to a disguised woman—and was not eager to be accused of her particular deception. At the same time she felt a deeper anxiety, and she knew it sprang from her need to apply once again to the Knights Hospitaler. If she had not left Rainaut so short a time ago, it would be less worrying to apply to them. Or so she argued with herself. When she had left Tyre in the escort of two Hospitalers, she had wealth, rank, and Roman earth to protect her. Now she was without all three and the prospect of putting herself in the hands of the Hospitalers once again was not wholly welcome. She briefly considered the cook's sarcastic advice and wondered if she dared to leave Iconium on her own, without any escort or companions. The dangers of such an enterprise more than outweighed the temptation it offered.

When she reached the chapter house of the Hospitalers, she saw that she was far from the first to petition them: a large gathering of men waited at the door of the chapter house, all of them standing in the heat of the sun since there was no shade here at this time of day.

Impulsively, she entered the Hospitaler chapel and approached the altar, kneeling when she was four steps away from it. She raised her folded hands to her face and tried to puzzle out the best way to proceed.

A little later, while her debate with herself continued to rage, she heard footsteps behind her. She knew better than to turn, for that might be regarded as irreligious. Keeping her hands raised, she looked covertly around the chapel as much as the movement of her eyes would permit, but could not see the other supplicant without moving her head. She continued her apparent prayers, wincing as she heard a second man, this one with ringing spurs on his heels, come into the chapel. At least, she insisted to herself, she was no longer in the sun, which was one genuine improvement.

Two priests came into the chapel and began preparations for their mid-afternoon Mass. One of them gave Olivia a long, critical stare, but said nothing, and in a short time continued about the tasks of preparing for worship.

More men entered the chapel; the air was close and quite warm. In an hour it would be stiflingly hot. Candles and incense were lit, their smoke contributing to the smell of the place. Gradually knights and pilgrims found places near Olivia, and in a short while the chapel was crowded; the odor of unbathed flesh and unwashed clothing grew oppressive.

At last the Mass began, the priests intoning the liturgy in high, nasal voices while the responses were deep and uneven. Olivia kept her voice low, so that she would not attract any more unwanted attention than she already had. Over the centuries she had learned many versions of the Mass, noting now with impatience that the greatest alteration she had seen in all that time was a tendency for the service to become longer. There was a time when Christian worship required little more than a communal supper and a bishop to pronounce "Ita Missa est" before bread was broken. Those days were far in the past, in the remote time before Niklos Aulirios had become her bondsman. She bit her lip to keep from crying out at his memory, and in the next breath cursed herself for the direct stare she had attracted from one of the two officiating priests. For the rest of the Mass, she tried to shut out the pressure of so many people around her and to follow the ritual in an exemplary manner.

She was just getting to her feet after the Mass was finished when the priest who had stared at her two times came up to her. She lowered her head respectfully and wished there were fewer people in the chapel so that she could make her escape. "Good Pere," she said when the priest made a gesture to detain her. "What do you wish of me?"

"I could not help but be struck by your zeal and devotion," he said, his voice still high and nasal. "It is not often that eunuchs show such piety."

Olivia cursed herself in amusement. The very thing she had hoped to avoid through the appearance of devotion had been enhanced by it. "Perhaps it is that not many eunuchs are welcome in worship." She knew of churches which expressly forbade eunuchs to participate in services when women were present; she assumed the priest knew about them as well.

"A lack in some of our faith, I fear," said the priest. "After the ferocity I have seen in battle and the torture endured by Christians, I no longer see the shame in being without the means of generation." He put his hand to the large, jeweled crucifix hanging from the massive gold collar he wore. "You came into the chapel early, doubtless to prepare yourself for the Mass. But I wondered if there might be another cause as well."

Olivia did her best to conceal her confusion. "Good Pere, I am not worthy of such . . . assistance."

The priest persisted. "All who serve God are worthy of aid

from His servants," he corrected. "What was troubling you? You showed yourself to be worried even while revealing your piety."

It was obvious that evasion would lead to more, not fewer questions. "I am returning from the Holy Land, going to Roma," said Olivia, secretly pleased that what she said was the truth. "I have . . . lost my companions through misfortune, and I seek those who are willing to permit me to travel with them. But, as you have remarked already, not all pilgrims welcome one . . . such as I am."

"True enough," said the priest, his eyes hardening. "How many were in your company when you left the Holy Land?"

"Three. We took ship bound for Roma, with many goods and other belongings, but it was attacked by pirates off the coast of Cyprus. Most of those on the ship drowned, and all the goods were lost; a few of us reached shore." She looked away from the priest. "It has taken me some time to get this far."

"A terrible story," said the priest, his sincerity giving him a sternness that Olivia found disquieting. "And all for your faith in God."

"I doubt my faith is as strong as that," said Olivia, fighting a sudden and catastrophic urge to laugh. The unsteadiness of her voice was misinterpreted by the priest, whose mouth set in a grim line.

"There is many another Christian who would benefit from your humility," he told her, his hold on the crucifix tightening. "Have you applied for escort yet?"

"No. I have very little money." She was curious now, but also growing wary. "If I reach Smyrna, I will be able to find passage on a ship bound for Barletta or Ancona or Ravenna, and from there I can travel on foot to Roma."

"You are on foot now?" inquired the priest, looking at the high solers she wore.

"I have a mule," she explained. "Without him, I would not have found a way through the mountains."

The priest nodded. "They are worthy beasts for all they are unnatural." He focused his eyes on a point two or three strides behind her head. "You can be sure of my help," he said at last, as if he had read a message or instructions.

"Pere, that is not necessary," Olivia responded at once, feeling a rush of panic.

"But it is," the priest declared purposefully. "It is not right that one who has already endured pain and privation for the sake of his faith should be caused greater suffering. You have long since been forgiven your sins, whatever they are, and the agony given to those like you is more than acceptable in Heaven's eyes. Suffering expiates all sins. Leave such cruelty beyond all Christian reparation to the Islamites." He motioned to Olivia. "Come with me, good eunuch." At that he stopped and regarded her with narrowed eyes. When he asked, his voice was harsh. "What is your name?"

Olivia had prepared herself to answer. "Olivier," she said. It was a name she had used before, one that she knew she would not forget to answer to.

"Olivier. A hero's name," said the priest as if this confirmed some private impression.

"A name, good Pere, that is all. If a hero had borne it in the past, then it falls on me to maintain the high esteem the name has commanded from the past." She might have smiled, but she feared that it might give her away, and so her expression remained stern. "It is my duty to show the name to advantage."

"There is much worthiness in what you say," the priest promised her. He indicated the entrance to the chapel. "Come with me. I will see that you find company for your travels that merits your attendance."

Olivia bowed her head. "You are most capable, good priest. I am in your debt, now and in the future."

The priest once again blessed her. "Good eunuch Olivier, you are one of those who is most worthy of the praise of Christians and of those who are in Orders. Let me make you known to those who wear the Maltese Cross of the Hospitalers, so that you will be aided by their numbers as you cross the country toward the port of Smyrna." He started toward the door. "Come with me, good eunuch, and I will see to it that you are placed in the most respected company for the duration of your journey."

Olivia listened to him and tried to think of a proper way to answer him. "What is your name, good Pere? So that I may number you among the other Christian travelers in my prayers?"

"I am Pere Savaric, from Gascony, as it is called by those who live there. In this world I am vassal to Reis Richard." He made a gesture of blessing and once again indicated the entryway. "You must come with me so that I may speak with the Hospitalers on your behalf." He straightened himself and started toward the door. "Accompany me, good eunuch, and we will make certain that you are on your way to Smyrna. It is not a port that Crusaders prefer, but you are not one with other Crusaders, are you?"

"Not truly, no," said Olivia, trying to hold on to some little control of the situation which was suddenly out of her hands. "I am not a Crusader in the sense of one who has done battle, either."

"There are many who might reveal that, if they were honest in their souls and their confessions," said Pere Savaric. "You have demonstrated exemplary candor in what you have revealed of yourself. There are others who are less entitled to glory who have seized it for themselves. You are not of their company, but are part of those who bow to God in the company of Saints."

Olivia was so puzzled that she could think of nothing to say; she lowered her head and blessed herself, saying to Pere Savaric, "For your esteem, I thank God most heartily." At the same time, she wondered how long it would take her to break free of the priest and return to the kitchen in the hostel.

"So, be guided by me, Olivier, and come. We will speak at once to the Hospitalers, and if they are not willing to help you, then we must approach the Templars." He rubbed his hands together. "You will find that these men, though they are God's warriors, are also filled with devotion and will recognize your worthiness." He was already moving through the door, motioning to the men gathered there to get out of the way. "I will take you directly to the Master here in Iconium and you can be certain I will not let them refuse you."

Olivia followed after, a sinking feeling in her heart. She had intended to make herself unnoticed, as invisible as she could. Now this priest was making an exception of her, and was determined to bring her into much closer contact than she wished to have with the authorities of the Hospitalers. She tried to think of a reasonable objection, one that Pere Savaric would endorse, but nothing occurred to her. There was always the most desperate action—admitting that she was not a eunuch—but that would bring about greater dangers than she already faced.

"Down this corridor," said Pere Savaric as he opened a side-door in the courtyard. "You see that there are dormitories on your left. The third door on the right is that of the Master of the Order. He always reads after worship in the afternoon. He will give us a little time." He prodded Olivia along with the encouraging grasp on her arm, his determination so palpable that it was almost as if his hand were a manacle.

"Is it wise to disturb him while he reads?" Olivia wondered, trusting that this might lessen Pere Savaric's purpose.

"For some it would not be, but I am his priest and he often seeks me for advice. There is no reason I would come to him in this way unless the cause was urgent." He reached the door and knocked. "Magister Vergier," called the priest. "I must speak with you."

There was an incomprehensible reaction from the other side of the door.

"It is urgent, Magister Vergier. You are one of the few who can resolve the problem." He knocked again, this time with more force. "Magister Vergier."

"A moment, Pere Savaric," said Magister Vergier, his footsteps indicating he was coming to open the door.

"You see?" Pere Savaric asked of Olivia, and she had the fleeting notion that he was showing off, making his position clear to her in a way he would not be able to do with most other pilgrims and petitioners.

"You have his ear: a great honor." Olivia hung back as the door opened.

"Well, Pere Savaric?" Magister Vergier asked, his fringe of graying hair in disarray, his cote hastily thrown on and not yet belted. "What is this urgent matter?"

Pere Savaric was not the least embarrassed to discover Magister Vergier in this disorder; he bowed slightly and said,

"I have learned that this eunuch, Olivier, wishes to join a party of pilgrims for his protection for his travel to Smyrna where he plans to take ship, bound for Ancona or similar port so that he can reach Roma." He cleared his throat. "There are those who are not pleased to have eunuchs in their number, but that is foolishness."

Magister Vergier had been able to follow this explanation without too much confusion. He frowned as he listened. "You," he said, glancing toward Olivia. "You're bound for Roma, are you?"

"Yes. I have a home there. I have been in Tyre. Pere Savaric has heard my story and has taken pity on me." There were few things Olivia liked less than being pitied, and some of her rancor echoed in her tone of voice.

"Bound for Roma and home." He rubbed his stubbled chin. "I have a party of wounded Hospitalers going from Tarsus to Smyrna. Most of them are able to ride, but a few need assistance. Do you know anything about tending the injured, eunuch?"

"I have some knowledge of medicaments," she said, trying to keep her attitude humble. "It would be an honor to aid those who have fought for the glory of Our Lord." She hoped that she had not overstated her attitude, for that might awaken suspicions. Her face grew slightly flushed, which Pere Savaric took as a good sign.

"There. A true servant of the servants of God. This fellow will be worth having along, I'm convinced of it. If you doubt it, then say so now, that I may take him to the Templars and see what they have to say." Pere Savaric shook a finger at Magister Vergier. "You know the Templars. You cannot trust them to use a eunuch honorably. They will see his beardless cheeks and will want him to do service as a girl. It would be an error for us to expose Olivier to that."

"Not that it probably hasn't happened before and will again, considering," said Magister Vergier with a resigned look. "I will speak to the escort. Doubtless another pilgrim with some skill with tending wounds would not be too much of an imposition." He raked his fingers through his hair in an effort to neaten it. "I will have an answer tomorrow before afternoon worship. Whatever the escort decides must be accepted." He folded his arms as he glared at Pere Savaric. "And you are not to search out this escort and plead this fellow's case. Leave that to me."

"I will pray, and repose my trust in God and you," said Pere Savaric, blessing Magister Vergier and beaming at him. "I am sure that you will recognize the wisdom of what I've suggested. You are sensible and steadfast in your faith."

Olivia wished there were a way to convince the priest to be less emphatic. "I will do whatever is required of me so long as it does not require me to take the life of a fellow-Christian," she said, knowing that the Crusaders were not above rampaging through local villages when the urge was on them.

"You see?" Pere Savaric said to Magister Vergier. "He's everything you could want for those wounded knights. All that would be better would be a dozen capable whores, but that would bring sin on their souls, so this eunuch is of more use." He put his hand on Olivia's shoulder again. "You will thank God for Olivier before you reach home."

Magister Vergier turned his eyes upward in silent and irritated petition. "I've said I'll speak to the escort. I can do nothing more. The rest is in the escort's hands." He stepped back, then added, "And Heaven's, of course."

As soon as the door was closed and the bolt firmly and noisily put into place, Pere Savaric beamed at Olivia. "You see? It is not so difficult. You will have your passage home, and the men will be grateful for the service you can render them." The light of fanaticism illumed his face. "You will bring relief to suffering, which is a cardinal charity, and you will do it in the service of those who are soldiers of God, which will add to your acts. God will look on you with favor."

"And upon you, for bringing it about," said Olivia, shrewdly guessing what Pere Savaric wanted to achieve.

"That is nothing," he said, though his wide, tight smile belied his denial. "There will be healing and God will be served. Thank Him every day for the opportunity and He will never deny you blessing."

"I will remember, good priest." She wished she had reason to leave now.

"Come with me to the chapel and we will thank God together for the blessings manifest and the blessings to come." He took her by the wrist and all but dragged her down the hall behind him.

As Olivia hurried after Pere Savaric, she consoled herself with the thought that in the chapel she would not be exposed to the phthartic touch of the sun.

*   *   *

Text of a letter from Niklos Aulirios to Ragoczy Sanct' Germain Franciscus.

To the most extraordinary associate of my mistress, Niklos Aulirios sends greetings from Roma and hopes that if this place called Lo-Yang truly exists that Ragoczy Sanct' Germain has found a haven there.

Your letter, which was sent to Alexandria, has only just been brought here, and that more by accident than anything else: vassals of Henry, the Holy Roman Emperor, returning from the Crusade, had the letter which was given to them at Ascalon by a monk coming from Alexandria. Because they were bound for Roma and one was literate, the monk entrusted your letter to them, and now it is in my hands, held for the arrival of Olivia.

It is true that she has not yet come here. I have men searching for her, so far without success. That alone causes me concern, for although I know how resourceful Olivia is, and how determined she can be, I am also aware that these are unsettled times in the Holy Land, and she might find more hazards than even she can manage.

Why I tell you this I do not quite know. In that Lo-Yang place, you are hardly in a position to help me search for her. And by the time this reaches you—if it does reach you—I will doubtless have found her. Still, you are the one who is her most treasured friend, and it lessens my fear for her to write to you on her behalf. Certainly if you were anywhere in Europe I would have sent for you before now.

If it were possible, I would leave the estate I have purchased for her and go looking for her myself. However, the law now requires a legally appointed factotum to be present or the villa is liable to seizure. Now that the land is producing well and there are foals in the pastures, many of the local landlords are searching for an excuse to claim this place as their own. One of the local monasteries has informed me that half the grapes in the vinyard are theirs by right. There are others who feel the same way but have not the cloak of religion to conceal their avarice. Olivia has ordered me to establish a home for her, and that I have done. I am not going to risk this place when I have other means of searching for her; not yet, in any case. If the men who are trying to find her are not successful by the end of summer, then I will have to make some arrangements for here and look for her myself, in spite of her orders and in spite of the laws here. There are many times when I wish that were possible now.

How have you fared in this city-that-may-not-be-there? Have you been permitted to live more in the way you would like? Do the people of that land tolerate you better than those in this country do? What of Rogerian? Is he still with you? Doubtless the links he has forged with you are as durable as mine with Olivia. I know he and I are the same sort, and it would take more than a Crusade to break my tie to her.

Always it comes back to Olivia, doesn't it? Not necessarily for you, but for me. She is more than family ever was, or it may be that my family was lost to me so long ago that my bond with Olivia is stronger than memory. Is it the nature of what you've made me, or is there something intrinsic to her? I do not expect you to answer that question. I am musing more for my benefit than for yours, and to quiet my alarms.

When she returns I will see she reads your letter at once—if she doesn't ask for it before I mention it—and I will hope she has the means to get word to you that she has returned to Roma in safety. It is hard to endure separation, and if that is so for me with her, what must it be for her with you? I hope that you will be able to send her word again, for she has been worried about you ever since those comrades of yours were burned in that barn. If she knows that you are well, it will hearten her more than any news I might give her about crops and the repairs of the roof.

I am so much a creature of my own time and place that I will tell you I will pray for you, though that is not precisely what I mean, nor is it quite what I intend to do. Perhaps it is best if I put it in these terms: I trust you are restored and once again part of the world; those times of despair, as Olivia has shown me, are the greatest burden for those whose lives are so very, very long.

This letter is being carried by a monk who is bound for Armenia. He has promised to find a caravan traveling the Old Silk Road and will entrust it to the leader of the caravan, with the request that it be handed on until it has reached Lo-Yang, or whatever place you are. A scholar of your capacity, and your foreignness, should not be impossible to locate even in mythical places. If all goes well, it should take no more than two or three years to reach you, if it is to reach you at all, and if you have not gone to yet another city in the Silken Empire, or the Kingdom of Prester John. By then Olivia will be here and the travail of the last two years will be memory. Or so I hope with all my soul.

Niklos Aulirios
bondsman to Atta Olivia Clemens
By my own hand and under seal on the 22nd day of May in the Christian year 1192.

· 14 ·

Sigfroit and Giralt emerged from the Genovese church Santissima Annunciata in ill-concealed fury. They crossed the wide street in long, heedless strides. "They won't help us," said Giralt before Sigfroit could speak. "Since the Papal legate has made his decision, only a Cardinal or the Pope himself will be allowed to overrule him, or so says this bishop as the priests have advised us he would."

Gace made an impatient gesture and growled an obscenity. "Where do we go from here, then?"

"We have been to most of the coastal cities," said Giralt in an attempt to soften the blow this news was to Fealatie. "That may count for something. We have seen almost every bishop and Catholic Siegnier between Ascalon and Antioch. What more can we do?"

With deep fatigue Fealatie answered, "I suppose we can wait for the conquest of Jerusalem." She squeezed her eyes shut so that she could not weep. "Not that it's likely to happen soon."

"No," agreed Giralt sadly. "Not the way things stand now."

"They say that Saladin will accept a truce," said Sigfroit. "There are those who want the fighting to be over, Islamite as well as Christian. Too many men are dead or missing, and there are not enough coming to replace them."

The entrance of the funda of Scandalion was narrow; the arrival of a company of men-at-arms wearing the badge of the Holy Roman Emperor forced Fealatie and her men to give them room. They jostled their way into the central courtyard and found a corner that was fairly quiet.

"So what is to be done?" asked Gace when they were settled. "Do we go on to another city or fortification? Or another church, in the hope of finding a Cardinal in residence?"

"Be quiet, Gace," said Sigfroit without heat.

"I'm willing, if that is what you"—Gace bowed toward Fealatie—"decide must be done. I am sworn to you and to your cause, or so I have been told. But I doubt you will find anyone who will modify your penance. It is Jerusalem in harness or nothing. They are determined. Your husband is the most determined of all."

Giralt held up his hand. "You're affronting her. It's hard enough to have the priests speak against her; it is intolerable when you do." Anger flared in his eyes, then he deliberately calmed himself. "We will have to decide what to do."

Gace laughed. "We can wait forever, or we can leave and not go home."

"Will you stop that?" Sigfroit demanded. "It is bad enough that we must endure these slights and insults from the Church and that the terms of her penance condemn all of us, but to have you continually urging sedition is more—"

Once again Giralt motioned for silence. "There is no point to haggling over what we cannot change."

"Well," said Gace when they had said nothing for several heartbeats, "there is always the Grail."

"Enough!" Giralt protested. "What possesses you?"

Gace shrugged. "I am tired of heat and dust and sand and bad food and poisoned wells. I am tired of sleeping in straw, of burning like a loaf in the oven, of bowing to every religious as if they all were kings. I'm tired of being an outcast because my chatelaine won a victory. She should be honored, not shamed. And we should share her honor."

"And as it is, you are—" Fealatie could not go on. She turned away from her three men, one hand to her eyes.

"Gace, you're despicable," Giralt hissed at him.

"I'm only saying what every one of us is thinking," he said sullenly.

"Even if that's so," Sigfroit cut in, determined to stop the hostility that flared among them, "we have vowed to escort Fealatie, and escort her we will, while there is breath in our bodies and blood in our veins."

"A fine thing for you to say," Gace muttered, but much of his pugnacity had faded. "If not Jerusalem and not the Grail, what?"

Fealatie forced herself to face her men. "This impasse was not part of our pact. None of us thought we would be stopped from entering Jerusalem. I am willing to release you and to stipulate that your obligations to me are discharged."

Gace stared at her, the beginnings of delight in his eyes. Sigfroit looked shocked. Fealatie's expression did not change. Giralt was grief-stricken. It was Sigfroit who spoke first. "You . . . cannot mean this."

She stood straighter, her voice was stronger as her conviction grew. "I do mean it. I give you full release and my word that no one can accuse you of abrogating your oaths, either to Fraizmarch or to the Church." Now that the words were out and there was no abjuration possible, she felt as if her bones were made of sand. What if Sigfroit and Giralt wanted release as well? Desperate as her plight had been with three armed knights for escort it would be a hundred times worse if she were alone. It pleased her that she did not speak of her fears but continued resolute.

"You can't stay here alone," said Giralt, as if he had sensed her dread. "Bondama, you must not say—"

Gace interrupted him. "I want a release, written by you and witnessed by a monk or priest, so that there can be no question of desertion. The terms will not be conditional or detracting from the honor of my House. And I want some proof to offer your husband when I report to him. He is not a forgiving master."

"What sort of knight leaves a chatelaine in a foreign land without escort?" Sigfroit scoffed. "What sort of man abandons a woman in a place like this?"

"She is a chatelaine, not a woman." Gace glared at Sigfroit. "Isn't that what brought us all on this fruitless journey? Just as well if she suffered a woman's fate and remembered what she is. Let her get her belly big and her dugs full, and then—"

"Enough," said Giralt, dangerously quiet.

"This knight knows what women are for," Gace said defiantly. "And so would both of you if the sun had not baked your brains." He looked at Fealatie with narrowed eyes. "You'll stand by your offer? You will not change your mind by nightfall? Or play some trick that will keep me in this hellish place?"

"It would be better if you changed your request," said Giralt, glancing from Gace to Fealatie.

"No, I will not change. If you are not willing to serve me, I will provide you with the release you want. I want no unwilling men at my side. I will be certain you are absolved of obligation; you're right about my husband." This last did not come out well, but she went on, "It will be witnessed as you ask, and Sigfroit and Giralt"—she stopped as both men objected, then overrode them—"Sigfroit and Giralt will witness the release as well, so that there is no hint of clandestine dealings."

"Sensible," said Gace, starting to smile.

"And necessary, if you are not to be questioned." She

regarded Gace for a long moment. "When . . . when do you wish to leave?"

"As soon as possible. At once. Tomorrow, if you can arrange it." He ignored the condemning oaths of his fellow knights, saying, "I can be ready to depart in the morning."

"I'll try. I'll have to find a churchman who will help draw up the release." She turned to Giralt. "Will you find a priest to do this?"

"No," said Giralt, looking at her with steady, worried eyes. "I will do nothing that puts you in more danger than you are now." His voice grew stern. "I pray you, don't ask that of me, Bondama."

"All right; Sigfroit?" She waited for his answer.

"If Gace wants this release, he should be willing to find his own cleric for the task," he said, unwilling to look at Gace any longer. "Let him muck out his own stall."

"I'll attend to it," Gace said promptly, with a meaningless smile. "I ought to have suggested it myself."

Giralt started to speak, then fell silent.

"It's decided, then," said Fealatie. "Gace is to leave us without dishonor, and we . . . we will have to decide how to proceed." She put her hands on her wide belt, attempting to assume the confidence that had been wearing away over the months of indecision and delay. "In the meantime," she went on with a feigned cheerfulness, "let us have a meal. It's more than past time for—"

"Oh, no. I do not break bread with him," said Sigfroit, indicating Gace as if he were a minor servant.

Gace's face darkened and one hand went to the poignard in his belt. "Do you dare—"

"Certainly not; you are the daring one. I would not take any gauntlet of yours." The insult was deadly, and all of them knew it.

"Sigfroit, for Our Lord's sake—" Fealatie began.

"I will help in obtaining his release, I will endorse your signature, but I will not share food with him, or take his challenge," Sigfroit said, stepping away from them.

Fealatie could not argue with him. "Giralt?"

"If you insist," he said quietly, meeting her eyes. "If it is your wish, I will do it, for your sake; else not for my hope of salvation."

"Fine words," Gace jeered. He cocked his head toward Sigfroit. "At least he's honest."

Giralt made mallets of his hands, preparing to fight. Fealatie stopped him, stepping between him and Gace. "No," she ordered. "No. There will be no more divisiveness."

"Tell *him,*" Giralt muttered, his eyes growing flinty as he stared at Gace. "He is the one who is leaving."

Fealatie took a step closer to Giralt. "Please. *Please* do not do this. It is painful enough to have him go; to have such anger at his leaving is worse than any condemnation from my husband. Giralt. For your oath, if not for me."

It was Sigfroit who answered for Giralt and himself. "We are your men, Bondama Fealatie, and what you ask we will do."

"Is it settled?" Gace asked when Giralt had opened his hands and taken several steps back. "Food, and then I will find a priest. The Bourgesses must be able to recommend one."

"Yes," said Giralt with bitterness. "Best speak with the Bourgesses. It is less disgraceful than going to one of the churches for absolution."

"No more," Fealatie insisted. At least she would have Giralt and Sigfroit, she told herself. She would not be alone, and likely to suffer the penalties women endured if they disguised themselves as men. In the company of her knights, her battle harness was not a disguise; alone it became the means of her condemnation.

Once again no one spoke.

When the silence had been stretched out as much as any of them could endure, Sigfroit said, "I am going back to the inn."

"Good," Fealatie concurred, looking to Giralt for support. "Will you come?"

"Yes." He had positioned himself between Fealatie and Gace, and now made it all but impossible for Gace to speak directly to the chatelaine. "Let me accompany you."

Fealatie wanted no more abrasions, and she was terrified of being alone. "All right." She knew that there was no reason for her to speak with Gace again, but she had enough sympathy for him that she wanted to find a word or a phrase that would mend the rift he had created. "It is a fine thing to long for home."

As Gace bowed to her, Giralt took her arm to move her away. "He is not worthy of being the dust under your feet, Bondama."

True to his word, Gace found the needed cleric, a Cistercian monk, who was willing to write a formal release and witness it.

"By mid-day tomorrow it will all be over and you can congratulate yourselves on your valor while I make arrangements to return to France." He was full of bravado and would have swaggered if his malformed foot permitted it.

Sigfroit refused to speak; he stared at the ceiling of the common room of the inn, his jaw set. Giralt made a point of speaking only to Fealatie. "I have a notion, Bondama, and I hope you will consider it. Since we have yet to receive permission to approach Jerusalem."

She answered listlessly. "What is it?"

"You said yourself that only a Cardinal or the Pope could determine if you have met the conditions of your penance, or could impose new terms on the penance. If that is the case, then it might be our best course to go to Roma and find a Cardinal who will listen to you and who will decide what is to be done." The words came out quickly, more from nervousness than from enthusiasm. "It is a satisfactory solution to the problem, isn't it?"

Fealatie sat a little straighter on the hard bench. For the first time in months her thoughts quickened without fear. "It might be one means," she said, not letting herself hope.

"It could be the *only* means," said Giralt. "And it is one that . . . that your husband cannot cavil with." He took care not to appear to speak with Gace, or to seek his advice. "We could be here another year without getting nearer Jerusalem, no matter whose aid we solicit. If we go to Roma, it could be that we will not have to return here, or if we do, it will be with the means to fulfill the terms of penance."

Sigfroit, who had been ignoring the whole, began to listen attentively. "If a Cardinal declares your penance done, there is no one in France who could question you." He hesitated. "Your husband is a . . . stern man, and without such—"

"My husband is a good Christian," said Fealatie, trying to

keep from hating Gui de Fraizmarch who had treated her with such unforgiving harshness.

Giralt spoke carefully. "It is fitting that a Cardinal determine the matter. Not just for your husband, Bondama, but for the Comes de Reissac, who requires expiation. Since de Reissac endorsed your penance, he must approve the mitigation from a Prince of the Church. We are witness to your many attempts and can address a Cardinal or your husband on your behalf."

Neither Giralt nor Sigfroit was willing to speak against Gui de Fraizmarch, although both had long since decided that the man was overly severe in his punishment of his wife. Sigfroit heard Giralt out, and added, "We are honor-bound to see that your penance is fulfilled; if there is a Cardinal who will endorse what you have done already or will set an acceptable goal, it will satisfy me and my oath entirely."

"And it is so much safer in Roma than here," added Gace, and grinned sourly when the others refused to speak to him.

"I will see if there is passage," Giralt volunteered. "If there is not, then I will try to get safe-conducts for the road. One way or another, we will get to Roma."

"And then?" Fealatie asked of the air.

"You will persevere and that will bring vindication," said Giralt with feeling, his hands almost touching her. "What reasonable man would refuse to assist you? It is for the benefit of your soul as well as to regain the honor of your House and your husband's House." He wished she would smile, or that she would show more animation. All through their long ordeal she had been encouraging and brave. Now, with the first hint of hope, she was languishing. "Fealatie, you will achieve your victory."

"I've had a victory already," she said softly, "and look at what I have reaped."

Only Gace laughed at this, and he slapped his thigh and stamped his feet, making a greater show of hilarity than what he actually felt. "Bondama, you are a treasure."

She turned and stared coldly at Gace. "What have I done to deserve such a compliment?"

Gace laughed more determinedly. "A treasure."

"Of what worth?" She rose from her place and went to

stand directly in front of Gace. "Tell me, Gace, of what worth?"

His laughter stopped as suddenly as a thunderclap. "Great worth," he said emotionlessly.

"Why should I believe that? Why should I not challenge you for the insult you have offered my House through your derision? Or would you refuse my challenge? And why?" She was poised and steely, unflinching in her arrogation, aware that she had gone beyond proper limits, that she was doing herself what she had forbade her knights to do. "Would you face me, Gace?"

He had gone white around the mouth. "No."

"And why not?" she asked relentlessly.

"It would . . . dishonor my oath. Which you may possibly understand." This last was defiant and truculent.

"Certainly," she said, taking one step back. "And before you speak again, I pray you will consider your honor and mine." With that she signaled to Sigfroit and Giralt and left the room.

The following morning, Gace was subdued, addressing Fealatie respectfully and directly at all times, for the first time treating her as he would have treated her husband.

"We will meet shortly with the monk. He has said that the release has been drafted and needs only your approval before it is prepared for signatures and witnesses." He was not dressed in his mail now but in a cotehardie and mantel, for traveling. "I will leave my harness with you, if you require it."

"No; take it with you," said Fealatie. "It is one less thing for us to carry."

He bowed again. "Thank you, gracious Bondama."

"How soon will you depart?" Sigfroit asked, as if inquiring about the hour or the weather.

"With the Bondama's permission, I will leave before sunset. You will not see me again until . . . until we meet in France." He said this unsteadily. "When you return to France, it will be my honor to visit you."

"Spare me that honor," said Sigfroit caustically. "You have favored me with enough of your presence. Once we return to France, there is no reason any of us should meet again." He did not offer any formal farewell.

"Where is this monk of yours?" Giralt inquired.

"He will be here," said Gace with a nervous cough.

"Shortly?" Giralt would have needled Gace more, but a warning look from Fealatie silenced him.

"I am sorry that we cannot offer you food for your journey," said Fealatie with more politeness than truth, "but it must be reserved for those continuing on in my company. You are a knight; you understand."

"Of course," said Gace a bit too eagerly.

She folded her arms, her mail squeeking where she bent it. "When you return to France, do me the service of notifying my husband what I have decided to do, and inform him that he will receive word from me after I have reached Roma."

"Yes, Bondama." He bowed again, taking care to include Sigfroit and Giralt. "And the Abbot of Sante-Estien-in-Gorze. Certainly he must know of your actions as well."

He was spared further embarrassment by the arrival of the monk, a square-faced, tonsured man of middle years tending toward a ruddy complexion and portliness. He carried three sheets of vellum with him along with a small box containing his ink and writing instruments. As soon as he had delivered a cursory blessing, he took a place at the long dining table and spread out his work. "Do any of you read?"

"I do," Fealatie said at once.

"A little," said Giralt.

"No," said Sigfroit. "Not much."

"Well enough," the monk declared, holding up one of the vellum sheets to show the writing on it. "I have indicated that it is agreed that this knight has completed his escort and is released without further duties."

"Yes," said Fealatie, reading over the monk's shoulder.

"Further, there is no fault attached to his departure and no dishonor to his House. His conduct is not to be impugned, nor his departure condemned. In addition, no argument exists between any of you and this knight, nor any blame fixes to him." He paused to look at Fealatie. "I have reason to believe that this is a most . . . unusual penance, and its completion has been rendered virtually impossible. Your husband and the Church demand that you fulfill what cannot be accomplished. Is that essentially correct?"

"Essentially," said Fealatie, resting her hand on the hilt of her sword.

"Since you are aware that the fulfillment of the terms of penance are not possible, this knight is exonerated from the task of assisting you to carry it out." He looked up at Fealatie, tangled brows raised in speculation. "Have I surmised correctly?"

Fealatie nodded once. "That is one way of looking at it."

The monk's lips twitched at the corner in a failed smile. "Very well then. If these items are sufficient, I will make a full and correct copy, and you will sign to show your acceptance and agreement." He was fussy in his movements, forever brushing his fingers over the vellum as if to rid it of dust and lint. "You may stipulate that the knight is being released at his request, if you like."

"I would want that included," Fealatie said firmly. "Yes, include that, if you will."

"Gladly," said the monk as he set to work.

Fealatie read the words as they appeared on the vellum sheet as if they were writ in fire and gave her into the power of Satan himself.

*   *   *

Text of a report on the questioning of Fraire Eleus, made by the Hieronomite monk Folgore d'Orbicciani.

Our Order having been apprised of the possible tergiversation of one of our number by a Master of the Knights Hospitaler of Saint John, Jerusalem, our Senior Abbot has given orders that the monk in question, one Fraire Eleus, is to be questioned. I swear on the Cross that this is a full and accurate recording of all that the apostate Eleus said during the tortures that were applied to him to obtain his true confession on the third and final day of his ordeal.

"*God, God, God, not that again. Oh, God.*"

The secular officer then put the screw on the thumb of Eleus' left hand and tightened it somewhat.

"*I've told you I—ah, no—I have done nothing!*"

The secular officer increased the tightness so that the nail was livid where it could be seen.

After screaming oaths, Fraire Eleus declared again, "*I have done nothing, nothing.*"

At the next turn, the skin of his thumb split and the nail burst in half. Fraire Eleus swooned and was revived with vinegar. When asked again what his deeds were, he answered, "*I am falsely accused. I have committed no sin.*"

Of the three participating in the examination, Fraire Conon was the one who spoke the questions this day, as Fraire Alain did previously. He asked, "*How is it that you were observed speaking with Islamites?*"

"*I swear by the Cross I have never spoken with Islamites.*"

"*Then why has an honorable knight declared that you have?*"

"*He was mistaken.*"

The thumbscrew was tightened for the last time, and Fraire Eleus was again revived with vinegar.

Due to his obstinacy, the secular officer brought in the boot and explained how it was used to crush bone so that the marrow spurted out with the blood. Fraire Eleus was transfixed at what he heard, and had to be held by three secular officers while the boot was placed on his leg.

"*Why does an honorable knight denounce you if you have done no wrong?*" *Fraire Conon asked as the secular officer placed the first wedge at the top of the boot.*

"*It is a mistake,*" *Fraire Eleus replied.* "*God, no, don't.*"

At a signal from Fraire Conon the secular officer struck the wedge two blows.

When Fraire Eleus stopped screaming, Fraire Conon recommenced questioning. "*What reason would such a knight have for denouncing you if you are innocent?*"

"*A mistake, a mistake,*" *answered Fraire Eleus.*

The secular officer struck the wedge three times; the third time there was the sound of a breaking bone.

Fraire Eleus swooned a third time.

"Why are you accused of aiding the Islamites?" Fraire Conon asked when Fraire Eleus opened his eyes.

"No. No. Stop. No." There was more of the same; Fraire Eleus did not seem to hear the question. Vinegar was poured over his head.

"For what reason would you be accused if you were not guilty?" Fraire Conon asked.

"Not guilty. Stop."

"Tell us why you are accused."

"Not. Not. No. No. No."

The secular officer struck the wedge three times again, and this time Fraire Eleus did not open his eyes for longer than it would take to recite four Salutations to the Virgin. When he did open his eyes he was not wholly in his right senses.

"For what reason are you accused?"

An indistinguishable answer.

"For what reason are you accused?"

Fraire Eleus shouted a terrible oath.

"Why are you accused?"

"Not! Not!"

The secular officer struck the wedge three more times; blood and shards of bone spilled out the sides of the boot. Fraire Eleus shook with palsy, during which time his tongue was bitten through, and the questioning was discontinued due to his inability to answer.

Submitted for the examination of members of our Hieronomite Order and for the benefit of those making inquiries of a similar nature, I swear before God that this is a true record of the interview.

Fraire Folgore d'Orbicciani
Hieronomite monk

By my own hand and under seal, on the anniversary of the founding of the Premonstratensians by the Blessed Norbert, the 6th day of June, in Our Lord's Year 1192.

Sier Amis de Meun was camped outside of Iconium, his pavilion larger and less vermin-infested than most available rooms in the town. The black Maltese Cross of the Hospitalers flew above his personal device: argent, a fess azure, radiant, indicating that Sier Amis was in his pavilion and not within the town walls.

"He has agreed to speak with you," said Magister Vergier to Olivia as they approached the pavilion. "He is taking over the escort of the wounded men here, and if it is suitable he will be willing to have you join his company."

"And why would it not be suitable?" Olivia asked, pleased that it was late in the day and the summer sun had declined far in the west.

"That is for Sier Amis to determine," said Magister Vergier stiffly. "He has been here for almost a week; he must know the needs of his company by now."

"What of the escort from Tarsus?" Olivia asked.

"They are continuing to Attalia, to take ship for Rhodes," said Magister Vergier. He gestured to some of the other pavilions erected behind Sier Amis'. "Most of them are staying outside the town."

Olivia wanted to say how sensible she thought they were but feared that would lose her the help Magister Vergier had been coerced into providing her. "How large was the escort?"

"Just three," said Magister Vergier. "Since the wounded men are all Hospitalers themselves, more were not deemed necessary." He paused. "We are a little short of men."

"I suppose it is because of all the fighting," Olivia said carefully.

"Yes. There has been much fighting." He stopped at the

closed flap to the pavilion. "Let me speak with him; then you may."

Olivia bowed. "You are gracious, Magister Vergier."

"Pere Savaric is the one who deserves your thanks, Olivier. He has done this, not I." Magister Vergier's mouth puckered in distaste. "I am merely his tool." He lifted the flap of the pavilion. "Sier Amis," he called.

"Magister Vergier," came the response. "A moment and I will be pleased to receive you." There was an exchange in lowered voices.

"If there are others with you—" Magister Vergier began and was interrupted.

"Nothing significant," Sier Amis responded. "The escort from Tarsus. He has brought documents to me." There was another sotto voce exchange, and then Sier Amis raised his voice. "You are welcome to enter."

Magister Vergier nodded to Olivia once before he entered the pavilion. "God give you good evening, Sier Amis," he said.

"Thrice welcome, Magister Vergier," was Sier Amis' prompt greeting. "Be seated."

Outside the pavilion, Olivia waited, watching the shadows grow longer and less distinct as the day waned. She was torn, wanting to listen and fearing to hear any refusal, so she paced along the front of the pavilion, her shadow for company.

Finally Magister Vergier opened the flap once more. "Olivier. Come here, lad. Sier Amis wants to speak with you."

There was no reading his face, and Olivia wondered if she would be given permission to travel with the Hospitalers or not. She made herself smile as she bowed to Sier Amis. "God give you good evening and a pleasant night."

"And to you, good eunuch," said Sier Amis. He was younger than Olivia expected, no more than twenty-one or -two, yet his russet hair was turning white. There were hard lines around his mouth and his faded blue eyes were framed in a permanent squint. "Magister Vergier tells me that you wish to accompany us to Smyrna and from there take ship to Ancona or other Italian port." He indicated a low-backed chair like the one in which he sat.

"Yes," said Olivia. "If you will accept me I will do all that is in my power to show my gratitude."

Sier Amis apparently had decided to reserve his judgment. He said, "I am told you have some skill with medicines."

"Yes, some," she answered carefully.

Magister Vergier bowed to them both. "With your permission, I will leave you now. Whatever your decision, Sier Amis, send me word of it, I pray you."

"Yes, yes, certainly," said Sier Amis, irritated at the interruption. He waved Magister Vergier away and gave his attention once again to Olivia. "Tell me what you know of medicines."

Olivia sighed. "I have some skill with herbs, I know how to bandage wounds and how to set bones, if I must. I can make a salve for burns if I can get woolfat and aromatic oils. I can make a poultice for putrescent wounds with little more than old bread and water." She decided to stop at that, though her skill was far greater than what she described.

"Useful," Sier Amis said when he had considered what she told him. "Can you tend those who have lost arms and legs?"

"If it is required," she said, then looked up sharply as she heard a clang of metal from another part of the pavilion.

"Pay no heed; it is the other escort leader. He is sharpening his dagger," Sier Amis said, his gesture indicating that Olivia need not be concerned. "What of those who suffer from the bloody flux? It has killed more men than Islamite spears have."

Olivia did not answer at once. "It depends in large part on how serious the flux is," she said when she had considered her answers and chosen what she hoped was a prudent answer. "When the flux is prolonged and the sufferer loses flesh and the skin becomes yellowed, then there is little I or anyone can do but pray. If the flux is not so advanced, salt fish and millet porridge will sometimes help ease the condition. There are a few who sicken with the flux who must be kept from eating anything until the flux has abated. When the flux is watery, it can be more dangerous than blood, for it means that the body is parched and the thirst cannot be slaked." She paused. "Those with the flux ought not to be in harness, but—"

"But if there is fighting we have little choice," said Sier Amis harshly. "True enough. Tell me how you would treat a continuing cough."

"That would depend on its cause," said Olivia. "A cough that is part of a fever is a different matter than those who cough for dust or blooming roses." She rested the tips of her fingers together. "Those with fever must rest, especially if there is a flutter in the chest or much wheezing for breath. When that is the malady, then sleep is more useful than half the potions in the world, but there are a few which lessen the coughing, such as mead with oil of cloves. Where the coughing is from other causes, then the treatment must change. Arabian spirits of gum will sometimes help coughs."

"Yes," said Sier Amis. "What of congested humors?"

Olivia made a self-deprecating gesture. "I would need to see an individual case. Often there are diverse causes for congested humors."

"Of course," said Sier Amis in a tone of voice that told her she had successfully avoided a trap. "How would you treat carbuncles?"

"By cutting and cauterizing, if possible," she answered at once, then went on less certainly. "I would always boil my tools with astringent herbs." Boiling tools was a radical notion now, but when Olivia had been young, it was standard proceedure for all physicians. "It is not done much, but I believe that it lessens contagion."

Sier Amis listened with interest. "Where did you learn that?"

Olivia answered honestly, "I had an instructor when I was . . . younger, who had trained as a physician in Egypt. He told me that boiling tools with astringent herbs improved the tools. I have followed his teaching." It was so long ago that Sanct' Germain had shown her how to care for patients.

"An Egyptian? An Islamite?" This was very nearly an accusation.

"No," she said quickly with a faint smile. "This teacher was not an Islamite."

"A Christian?" The question cracked like a mailed fist.

"Not at first; later." She considered Sier Amis. "Is it important? I was taught long ago."

"Long ago?" taunted Sier Amis. "You are ancient, then?"

"You know how it is with eunuchs; we do not show our age. I am no stripling." She heard someone moving behind the hanging and resisted the urge to look. "I am," she said, choosing a believable age, "about thirty-one."

"You are uncertain." Sier Amis favored her with a grin, no longer as tense as he had been.

"Yes." What would he do if she told him the truth, she wondered, that she was the child of Roman patricians and had died during the reign of Vespasianus? The notion brought a glint of laughter to her hazel eyes.

"Being unsure of your birth is amusing?" Sier Amis asked, his tone too light for criticism.

She covered her lapse well. "One of the few advantages of not knowing the circumstances of my birth is that I am free to invent whatever pleases me. I have met many another who would have been glad to trade places with me."

Now Sier Amis laughed out loud. "You are a funny fellow, Olivier. And your wit has truth. By Satan's Brass Balls—begging your pardon—I have known men who would have preferred an honest serf for a parent to a dishonored knight." He threw back his head. "And you can have both, or neither, as it suits you."

Olivia did not join in the laughter, afraid that the timbre might give her away; she did smile broadly. "Or anything and anyone else."

His laughter tapered off, and he clapped his hands. "Wine. Bring wine!"

As a slave came from behind the hanging, Olivia said, "I do not drink wine. I haven't the head for it."

"I will have some," said Sier Amis with sudden and unexpected belligerence. He got up from his low-backed chair and began to pace. "Travel will be difficult. Many of the men I am to escort are badly hurt, some are ill. Most would not be able to travel if they had no help. It means that anyone attending them would have little rest."

"I do not sleep much," she said, not entirely truthfully. "I . . . I am one of those who is more awake at night than in the day." She hitched her shoulders, and looked toward the hanging as someone approached. "Your slave bringing wine," she said.

"Actually not," said a voice she had heard before. "The escort from Tarsus," said Orval, Sier de Monfroy, as he strolled into the front compartment of the pavilion.

Olivia half-rose from her chair; Sier Amis went to him and clapped him on the shoulder. "Well, you come in good time, de Monfroy. A cup of wine would be welcome, would it not?"

"Certainly," said de Monfroy, looking directly at Olivia. "By all means, let us drink."

There was no way that Olivia could withdraw from the pavilion now without causing suspicion, yet she was frightened of remaining. De Monfroy was too acute, too intent in his scrutiny and there was something about the expression in his face that increased her apprehension. "If you are to discuss matters private to your Order, perhaps I should not stay."

"Why not?" asked de Monfroy sardonically. "What could the two of us say that would embarrass or compromise a eunuch?"

Olivia lowered her eyes. "You are most generous."

Sier Amis slapped de Monfroy's shoulder. "You should have had this fellow with you, de Monfroy. By the sound of it he's worth half the physicians in the world. You would have made better time with Olivier along."

"Olivier?" he said with a speculative lift to the eyebrows. "Olivier. No other name?"

"No," she said quietly.

De Monfroy came and stood beside her chair. "Not even Clemens?"

Sier Amis chuckled. "The poor fellow doesn't know his parents—he told me so himself."

"The *fellow,*" said de Monfroy with heavy emphasis, "the fellow is . . . most enterprising, most ingenious."

"If he's as good with medication as he claims, no doubt you're right, de Monfroy. Strange, though. He's had some odd teaching, not that it appears to have damaged him. But he was taught to boil his tools with herbs. Have you ever heard of so curious a practice?" Sier Amis laughed again, and swung around to meet the slave bringing wine. "Ah! At last."

"There are many curious things about this Olivier, I suspect," said de Monfroy, observing Olivia's discomfort with angry humor. He addressed Sier Amis. "Resourceful, I warrant: this fellow."

"You choose to make mockery of me, good Sier," she said, keeping her voice low. "For what reason do I offend you? In what manner? How is it that you speak to me in this way?" It was a dangerous challenge, but she made it with strong inner satisfaction.

"I will tell you directly, Olivier," said de Monfroy, deliberately slurring the end of the name so that it sounded like her own. "Let me come to it in my singular way."

Sier Amis was busy pouring wine into the two silver cups. He had a generous hand; when he held the first cup out to de Monfroy, a little of the red liquid sloshed onto his hand and ran like blood. Olivia stared at it and yearned for an end to her hunger. If only the man seeking her had not been Orval, Sier de Monfroy. "You are most mysterious, de Monfroy. I hope you will tell me what your great secret is."

"It isn't *my* secret," said de Monfroy smoothly. "But perhaps, in time, I will." He waited until Sier Amis had poured his own wine, then lifted his cup. "To his Grace, Reis Phillippe of France, the Champion of Christendom."

"Reis Phillippe," agreed Sier Amis as he drank. "God, that is good. No wonder we drink it for Communion." He reached for the winejar and topped off his cup. "It is sweet to be drunk, isn't it? It is sweet to forget this hideous place, the terrible fights, and the hardships and suffering."

"Other things are sweeter," said de Monfroy, looking at Olivia with hot eyes. "Taking, *demanding* surrender. That is far sweeter than any wine, and more—so much more intoxicating."

Why did it have to be de Monfroy who found her? Olivia asked herself in well-concealed desperation. She sought a willing lover, a lover who would welcome her and share the most profound touching with her, the touching of souls; instead she was in the hands of one whose lust was more for conquest and subjugation than touching or pleasure. With de Monfroy, there would be no shared delirium, no mutual joy, no exultation, no communion. She shuddered, remembering Justus; a millennium away and his memory could still shake her. She pressed her lips together and tried to keep her fright from showing in her eyes.

"You are silent, Olivier," said de Monfroy, leaning down to speak in her ear. "How is it that one such as you are so frightened?"

"You're provoking the fellow," said Sier Amis. "Leave him alone, de Monfroy. You're miffed because you could not have him to help you when you brought the men this far, and you're jealous because I'll have him to help me all the way to Smyrna." He had tossed off all the wine in his cup and had refilled it. "Drink, de Monfroy, drink. Here, have more. I'll tell the slave to bring us another jar of wine when this one's empty."

De Monfroy bent lower still, so that his face was almost on a level with Olivia's. He whispered to her, "You are not going to Smyrna, Bondama. I have other plans for you. You do not escape me so easily. You are coming to Attalia with me. You have been most unwise, taking off your leper's cowl and putting on this eunuch's disguise. You can be stoned for taking off the cowl; you can be . . . oh, there are a great many punishments you can suffer for your disguise."

Olivia's face grew hot; she could hardly resist the urge to take his winecup and fling the contents in his face. Had she not been certain that he would denounce her, she would have done it and welcomed their combat, where her unnatural strength would give her a formidable advantage. As it was, she kept still, her hands clutching the arms of the chair as if to grind the wood to powder.

"Here. More wine." Sier Amis refilled de Monfroy's cup and gave a stuttering chuckle. "I didn't know you were one for eunuchs, de Monfroy."

"I'm not," said de Monfroy with contempt. "This . . . fellow . . . interests me."

"I said you were jealous. Jealous, jealous, jealous," Sier Amis said in sing-song cadence. "It's because you're too sober, too ambitious." He clapped his hands. "Bring another jar of wine," he shouted. "Bring two jars. Now!"

De Monfroy stood up and moved a short distance away from Olivia. "No doubt you're right, Sier Amis. I have not tasted good wine for days, and now—"

"You behave as if you despise my wine," said Sier Amis, sulking.

"Never that," de Monfroy assured him. "It is the result of the journey. My body aches and my eyes are dry as old nuts in my head. Wine, by all means. Wine and more wine, and we will let Olivier here tend to us when we are swinish." He accepted the last of the wine from the first jar. "You're a good host, Sier Amis. Generous, libacious. A good host." He lifted his cup in ironic salute to Olivia.

Sier Amis' good humor was restored in an instant. "You're the best of company, de Monfroy. You have a barbed tongue, but you're stout-hearted." He wrapped an arm around his shoulder, only partly to steady himself. "If more of the Hospitalers were like you, we'd have a better Order. Too many men in the Knights Hospitaler are faint-hearted, taking refuge in being defenders to hide their cowardice. Not you. Not I. We're the credit to the Order. That's why we serve as Masters." He beamed at de Monfroy. "To the Masters of the Hospitalers." He lifted his cup only to discover it was empty. "Where is the wine!"

Almost at once a slave came around the hanging, two large wine jars on a tray. "Good Master, your pardon."

Sier Amis kicked out at the slave, missed, and had to cling to de Monfroy to keep from falling. "Open them and leave them. Do you hear me?"

The slave bowed deeply and hastened to carry out Sier Amis' orders. He had the wine jars ready to open.

"The wine is sweet, de Monfroy, but not so sweet that we must turn from it for the good of our souls." He shook his head and looked from his slaves to de Monfroy. "Tell me that you understand what has been asked of you, Sier de Monfroy, and I will approve the supplications that have been addressed to you. The summons of all Christian knights to account at the bar—"

The slave decanted the wine and bowed deeply. "Your drink is ready, Bonsier."

"Then leave us," Sier Amis said. He filled his cup sloppily and drank.

De Monfroy watched Sier Amis with a condemning eye. "Your head will not be fond of you if you drink much more." He drank the last of the wine in his cup and set it down.

"Drink with me, de Monfroy," said Sier Amis, his face flushing from choler and wine.

"I have drunk with you," said de Monfroy. "Now I am going to leave you so I can sleep."

"Wine eases sleep," said Sier Amis. "It soothes dreams and it softens memories." He had almost finished the cup. "Have more."

"Not this evening; another time." He looked to Olivia. "I am going to ask this fellow to come with me. I have some questions to put to him."

Coldness filled Olivia. She had hoped that de Monfroy would fuddle his wits with drink so that she could escape. When he had refused more wine, she knew she would not be so fortunate. "I will answer them here," she said.

"Not what I plan to ask. Your answers would trouble Sier Amis. Wouldn't they?" His mouth widened.

"Don't be silly," Sier Amis protested. "He's an amusing fellow. I'd like to hear what he has to say." He made a sweeping gesture. "Speak, Olivier."

"I . . . I do not know what to say," she responded.

Sier Amis laughed heartily. "Such an amusing wit," he said as he wiped his eyes with his sleeve. He sloshed more wine into his cup and all but poured it down his throat. "A good fellow. Good fellow."

De Monfroy bowed to Sier Amis. "I am going back to my pavilion. And Olivier will come with me." He laid his hand on her shoulder, deliberately making it a heavy weight.

"Oh, if you must," said Sier Amis uncertainly. He waved them both toward the flap. "Leave. Leave leave leave."

"Come, Olivier," said de Monfroy, his hand tightening.

Reluctantly she rose and went with him.

*   *   *

Text of a letter from the Venetian merchant Giozzetto Camarmarr to the Benedictine scholar Ulrico Fionder.

*To my most reverend cousin and esteemed teacher, my
loving greetings and thankful prayers that you have recovered
from your illness. Fever has been very bad this summer, and it
has come earlier than usual. There are many who say that the
Islamites have poisoned the water, but I do not believe they
are so foolish, for then the fever would take them as well.*

*I was saddened to learn of the death of your father. My
uncle was a most worthy man, whose impeccable reputation
was well earned and whose accomplishments were distinguished. I have arranged for Masses to be said for his soul
every day for the year of mourning. My thoughts are with you
in your grief, and I pray for my uncle's welcome in Heaven.*

*Three of our ships have been sunk, probably by pirates.
They were commandeered by the Crusaders and have been
used for the transportation of materiel from Venice to the
Holy Land. They have brought the wounded and ill back to
Venice, those who were not able to travel overland. Such ships
acquire strange reputations, so it may be for the best that they
are at the bottom of the sea.*

*However, this means that our resources have been lessened,
and for that reason, I am considering accepting the offer
made to us by a Greek factotum on behalf of his patron. I have
had some contact with him in the past, and I know that he is a
man of honest dealings and that his patron has wealth and
good sense. I am willing to establish a partnership with them
and use their investment to build up our ships once more.
This is in accordance with the offer that has been made,
which is most generous.*

*I ask that you take some time from your studies to review
the copy of the agreement I am sending to you. I can see*

nothing amiss in its terms; it is fair to all parties, or so it seems to me. You, with your learning and your wisdom, will surely be able to detect any possible flaws or disadvantages that I have not been able to detect. If you agree that this is a most exemplary proposal, then I will enter into the partnership at once. With the Crusade losing ground, we will soon have our ships in our own hands once more, and from what I have seen, we will be able to increase our trade with the Holy Land, for many of the pilgrims and Crusaders have developed a taste for things oriental and will be eager to bring them home.

It is possible that after so long a time of uneven fortunes we will at last have true prosperity. While I know that this is of little consequence to one whose treasures are the riches of the mind and the glory of Heaven, nevertheless I pray that God will grant us our trade and our riches. I have daughters to dower, and sons to establish in the world. With this proposed partnership, all that becomes possible. At the same time, Aulirios and his patron will have equal profit with us, so we will not be depriving them with our success. I do not look to grow rich at the expense of others.

My prayers and my thanks are with you at all times, and I know you will give me good counsel on the terms of this proposal. May God give you solace in the loss of your father and may your health remain robust now that you are recovered.

Your most affectionate cousin
Giozzetto Camarmarr
On the Feast of Barnabas the Apostle in the 1192nd year of Our Lord.

· 16 ·

From Iconium de Monfroy went south and west, six Hospitalers and Olivia for company. They traveled as fast as they could, rising at dawn and going steadily until after sunset.

After four days, Olivia was weak and ill, her body so exhausted, so famished that she moved like a sleepwalker and fretted all night long. The one consolation was that de Monfroy had allowed her to continue her pose of eunuch; he took a malign delight in watching her with the men he commanded, and mocked them for blind fools when he had a few moments alone with Olivia.

"I will be happy when we reach Attalia," he said to her as they paused to let their mounts drink at a stream. "Things will be different in Attalia."

"That remains to be seen," Olivia said, her head ringing and her skin parched.

"They will be. Or it will be learned that you have been a leper in the company of lepers. The penalty for taking off your cowl and living in the society of men is stoning." He turned to watch her. "Surely I am preferable to that."

She said nothing, thinking how ironic it was that when she was almost at the limit of her endurance and had the greatest need for a lover, someone as intolerable as Orval, Sier de Monfroy should pursue her. If she were not in such despair, she might have found her predicament sardonically amusing; as it was, the realization only increased her hopelessness.

"You are at my mercy, Bondama Clemens," said de Monfroy, his eyes gloating.

"Mercy is a strange word, de Monfroy," she said without much feeling. She pulled Atlas' head up and absently patted his neck. "He needs to have his hooves trimmed."

"At Attalia you will be rid of the beast," said de Monfroy.

"If his hooves aren't trimmed he might not reach Attalia," she said, hoping to control the queasiness that would lead to useless retching.

"Tonight, perhaps. I will ask Arnaldos to attend to it; he has farrier's tools with him." He was disinterested. Negligently he fiddled with his whip. "It can kiss and it can flay," he said, watching her out of the tail of his eye.

Olivia said nothing; her lips were set.

"Well, Olivier," said de Monfroy a bit louder for the benefit of the Hospitalers around them, "how would you like to come all the way to Rhodes with us? The Hospitalers own part of the island, and there we are masters."

One of the other men laughed angrily. "We should have the whole island, as the Templars have Cyprus."

"Have, but cannot keep," the Roman knight said. "The tale is that they are going to sell it."

"They have only just bought it," said de Monfroy. "Have they tired of it so soon?"

"It's said that de Lusignan will buy it," the Spaniard Aroldos added.

"Why not? He has money enough." Again there was laughter that cracked with anger.

"What does de Lusignan want with Cyprus? Or is he afraid he won't get Jerusalem back, after all?" de Monfroy asked, and before any of the rest could speak, he signaled them to move on.

By the time they stopped for the night, Olivia knew she would have to visit one of the knights as he slept. She had learned long ago how to induce rapturous dreams that would bring her what she needed. If she had to ride another day in the sun, she would have to have blood. She began to study the knights more closely, for she knew the danger of embracing a dreamer who loved not for tenderness but ferocity—such as Orval, Sier de Monfroy.

At last she settled on Cino Forese, because he was the most gentle of this rough lot, and because he came from Roma. She was careful not to appear too curious about any of the Hospitalers, for she knew that de Monfroy was keeping near her, on guard against any attempt to escape or ploy to get help.

As they made camp for the night, Olivia was left with the usual chore of tending to the horses while two of the knights, who were more trusted than she, gathered fodder. Since Forese was one of the knights given that task, she had a brief chance to speak with him as he brought an armload of parched grasses for the horses and mule to eat.

"Do you miss Roma?" she asked.

"Sometimes," he admitted. "On nights like this, yes."

"I, too." It was all she dared say. She went on with securing leads to the tether line, and put hobbles on three of the horses who were known to wander.

"Two more days, Olivia. Three at the most," de Monfroy said as she prepared to enter the small tent that had been pitched between two pavilions. "Then we will be in Attalia and many things will change."

She looked at him, knowing how great his satisfaction was when she showed fear. "I have no desire for you."

"What does that matter? Resistance can be exciting. It adds spice." He put his hand on her neck, his palm against the nape, his thumb chafing at the edge of her iron cap. "Think about escape if it makes the time pass more pleasantly. Then remember that it is only a dream. There is no escape."

Olivia said, "But there will be more wounded for you to escort. You will have your duty to rescue me."

"Not I," he countered. "I have done my escorting for a time. One of these others will be given the work. I have done it twice, and so I am entitled to a rest." The last word became obscene as he spoke it.

Knowing that she would have sustenance that night made Olivia bolder than she had been before. "Take care, de Monfroy, that I do not reveal myself. Here. Now. You will not be able to convince your knights that I am an outcast leper, not until you reach Rhodes where your records are kept. They will think you have me here for your own purposes, you, a sworn Hospitaler, with a mistress disguised as a eunuch."

"You would not. You're not that foolish. Now you have a little protection. If you did that you would have none—not from me, not from these men, not from the Church, and not from the law." He enjoyed telling her this, reminding her of how she was in his power. "Perhaps I ought to do that. Perhaps I ought to tell the knights about you, and let them make their own punishment for you. When they were done, you would be grateful for anything I might give you. But then I would not have you." He stepped back from her. "Goodnight, eunuch. Dream whatever it is that eunuchs dream."

"God reward you for your wishes, de Monfroy," she told him.

"He will, He will," said de Monfroy, and sauntered off to his pavilion, whistling.

Olivia went into her tent and prepared to wait for the others to sleep. Only when she could lie still and extend her senses, testing to be certain every one of the Hospitalers was sleeping, did she move again, this time with silent grace that was as beautiful as it was uncannily swift.

Cino Forese lay on an unrolled padded mat; he had set his mail harness aside but was still wearing his acton. His one blanket was pulled halfway up his chest.

Olivia knelt beside him and began, very, very softly, to speak. "You are asleep, so asleep, and happy to be asleep. You are glad to be asleep, free of every care. You are so happy to sleep, to be at ease. You rest with a glad heart."

His half-smile made Cino appear absurdly young. He tugged the blanket a little higher up his chest.

"You are resting, sleeping, and you are happy. You are full of joy." She spoke just above a whisper and in a sing-song that had no stresses or emphasis. When Sanct' Germain had taught her to do this, a thousand years ago, the tones without stress had been the most difficult skill to master. "You are deeply asleep and dreaming of love, of the joys of love, of the endless pleasures of love. It pleases you to dream of this. You are very happy to be asleep. While you dream of the pleasures of love you have no wish to wake. You desire only to sleep and dream. You dream of love. You dream of embraces and kisses, of all the ways you touch in love. How happy you are to be asleep and have this wonderful dream, this dream of love and the delights of love." She risked touching him lightly on the chest, so that she could be nearer to him. "All the sweetness of love is in your dream, and your dream is the most pleasurable, the most passionate dream—

you are filled with joy at this dream. Your dream is so rapturous, so passionate, that you know it is real. You feel the touch of hands on your body, the caresses and embraces you know in your dream." She moved closer to him still, rousing him with her hands as she continued to woo him.

Forese sighed, in the subtle web she had invoked. He was becoming aroused as his dream grew stronger.

"All of your desires are within reach. Fulfillment is yours for the asking. There is nothing that does not bring you joy and love, nothing that does not add to your pleasure. You have never had so sweet a dream; you have never known a dream like this one." She felt his passion in his flesh, sensed his desire take hold of him. Her sensuous litany continued. "You are surrounded with pleasure and you are filled with love. There has never been so much love, so great a passion in you. You want to exult, you are so wholly given to love. You and your passion are united in your love, and you surrender yourself to rapture. Your mouth is filled with love, your heart burns with love, your flesh trembles for love." With a pressure so light a feather would do more, Olivia kissed him.

He quivered at her kiss, and his head rolled back as his excitement mounted.

"You are joyous, you are ardent, your body and soul are bonded in love, and the love you seek is seeking you, seeking you with kisses and caresses, that your joy may be greater and greater." She lay beside him now, from lips to feet, her hands moving lightly as shadows. "You are so happy, so gloriously happy, so completely happy."

He moved again, this time languorously, as she rested her hand on his thigh.

"Your passion is wonderful. Your ardor is—" She felt him strain for release.

"Joy is yours." Her lips moved from his mouth to the curve of his neck as he gave a short, laughing cry and spasmed.

"Your rest is sweet, your dreams are happy, your love burns more brightly for your dream. Your sleep is a haven, your fulfillment a strength." She moved back from him, already experiencing the beginning of annealing power. As she adjusted the blanket around him, she smiled fondly down at him, regretting that she would never know more of him than this.

"Did you sleep well, Olivier?" de Monfroy asked sarcastically when they met the next morning as the sun was staining the eastern sky the red of rising wind.

"Why?" Olivia asked him, not wanting to have to speak to him at all.

"You seem more rested," he said, adding in an undervoice, "Good. You will need to be rested when I have you."

She continued to fasten the saddlegirths and asked, "Have Atlas' hooves been tended?"

"I don't know," de Monfroy said, for the first time letting his irritation become apparent. "If they haven't, you can keep up on foot for all of me."

Olivia lifted one eyebrow. "Are you willing to risk that?"

"Who could you turn to for help, if I did?" he snapped, unwisely.

"Someone like Pere Savaric or Sier Amis, perhaps," she said, her face thoughtful. "Someone will help." Being on foot in these mountains, she knew, would be more than she could manage on her strength, even traveling by night. None of this showed in her features.

"Or unmask you?" de Monfroy asked. He snapped his fingers and Aroldos came to saddle his horse.

As he mounted, Cino Forese gave Olivia a swift, covert glance with puzzled eyes.

"Where do you want me to ride?" Olivia asked as she mounted. Her iron cap felt tight around her head, and her solers were hot on her feet. She flexed her hands, satisfied that she would make it through the day.

De Monfroy came and took hold of Atlas' bridle. "Ride in front of me today. Behind Aroldos, where I can give you my attention." He let go of the bridle. "We ride fast today. So we will get to Attalia earlier."

"Not if my mule's hooves break," she said.

"If your mule fails you, you'll ride behind one of us." He glared at her. "Behind me."

"Quite a precaution," said Olivia, urging Atlas to fall in

behind Aroldos. She wondered what de Monfroy's plan was that could make Atlas move faster than a rapid walk.

By nightfall, Olivia was once again consumed with weakness, and her body was beginning to ache. De Monfroy had been as good as his word and had moved his little party as quickly as prudence allowed. On the flat stretches of road, he ordered the men to go at a trot, and to force the mule to cooperate, he had two leads tied to the bridle so that Atlas was all but dragged to the faster pace. Olivia, jolted by the rough gait, found herself wishing for one of her own horses or an old-fashioned Roman chariot instead of the saddle.

During the heat of the afternoon, de Monfroy permitted everyone to drop back to a walk, but rest periods were few and brief, and they were not ordered to make camp until the world was so sunk into twilight that they could no longer easily see the road.

By the next afternoon, they were within sight of Attalia; evening brought them through the gates to the hospice of the Hospitalers. De Monfroy took Olivia with him when he went to report to the Master of the chapter house.

"You won't be permitted in his chambers," said de Monfroy as he pulled her by her arm along the hallways. "But I do not want you roaming about on your own. That may have been your plan, but I will not allow it." He indicated two armed men standing before a large door. "Those who must be examined have to wait there. You will wait there. You cannot leave, not with those men to stop you."

"Is anyone else in that room?" asked Olivia.

"Who knows?" He nodded to the guards and pulled open the door. "Three men in armor," he said as he looked at the trio waiting at the far end of the room. "Surely you are not frightened by them?"

"I am not frightened," Olivia lied.

De Monfroy shoved her away from him. "Stay here until I come back for you." He was halfway through the door when he turned back. "If you make any attempt to leave it will be the worse for you. Do you understand me?"

"Yes," she said quietly, loathing the sound of the closing door. She sank down onto one of the short benches that were placed about the room, dejection engulfing her. She stared at the floor, as if she wanted it to open and swallow her up.

"Your pardon," said a voice at her shoulder. "I do not mean to intrude, but there seems to be some trouble here."

Reluctantly Olivia looked up and saw that one of the three harnessed men had come to her side. "Why do you ask?"

The man shifted from one foot to the other, awkward as a boy. "I . . . I know something of de Monfroy. It occurred to me that he is much the same as he was ten years ago."

"If you mean coercive and belligerent, then you are correct." Olivia knew it was unwise to speak this way to a stranger, but she no longer cared. "If you mean otherwise, I ask your pardon if I have given offense."

"And cruel as well," the stranger added grimly. "I am Sigfroit de Plessien, escort of the Chatelaine Fealatie Bueveld." He indicated the other two.

"Chatelaine?" Olivia repeated, looking from Sigfroit to his companions.

"I am Fealatie Bueveld, Chatelaine of Gui de Fraizmarch," she said, offering a bow. "You are?"

"Not a eunuch," said Olivia. "I am Atta Olivia Clemens, a widow from Roma." She indicated the male clothes she wore. "In good company, it would appear." She paused. "Why are you here?"

"We are attempting to find passage to Roma," said Sigfroit. "We require the decision of a Cardinal to modify the terms of a penance." He indicated the third member. "Giralt and I are the protection and escort for Fealatie." At that he stopped. "It isn't correct to speak of her by her name, but we have been together for so long, and comrades—"

Olivia nodded. "Comrades alone do not speak in titles, do they?"

"There was a third, but . . . he has returned to France." Sigfroit glanced at Giralt as if he expected him to break out in more imprecations. "We disagreed."

"I see," said Olivia, who inferred that the disagreement had been divisive. "But you go to Roma." She hesitated. "I have been trying to return to Roma for . . . for years. Or at least it seems that way."

"With de Monfroy?" asked Sigfroit, clearly shocked.

"No," said Olivia. "Not with de Monfroy."

"I don't wish to alarm you, but he is a dangerous enemy," said Sigfroit.

"So am I," said Olivia, adding, "But until I get away from him, he will try to—"

"I know his reputation," said Sigfroit. "It is best not to remain where he can find you."

The optimism that had bloomed for Olivia faded as quickly. "In Roma I would have . . . power. Here, there is nothing I can do. Here I am alone and . . . weak."

"No," said Fealatie. "You are not alone and you are no longer weak." She motioned to Giralt. "Come. The Bondama can aid us in Roma; we can aid her here."

Olivia looked at Fealatie, her thoughts uncertain. "Why would you do this? And what will you do?"

"Let us determine what you need. Then we will decide what we will do." She smiled with merry pugnacity. "I have been hoping for a worthy fight."

"Are you certain this is one?" Olivia asked, liking Fealatie in spite of her own inner doubts.

Fealatie clapped her hands. "If it defends honor, how can it be unworthy?" Then her face darkened. "There are no oaths of fealty here that can compromise the cause, are there? You are not a vassal of the King of France, or widow of his vassal, are you?"

"No," said Olivia, her curiosity increasing.

"Then it is worthy," said Fealatie in a tone that could not be challenged.

*   *   *

Text of a letter from Ithuriel Dar to Niklos Aulirios.

To my Roman Greek friend, greetings and a thousand curses. I am a man of the sea, a man of ships and water, not some mountain goat to go scrambling up cliffs and through passes on the backs of beasts. But I have done all these things chasing Bondama Clemens, and remarkable as it may be, I finally have something—though not a great deal—to report.

I have reached a sanctuary, a strange compound in the middle of the mountains, run by a brother and sister, Rafi and Kalere Navrentos. They are part of an odd religious group, Christians, but a sort I have never encountered. I mention this because it explains a little what they have done.

Sier Valence Rainaut is here. He came here with Bondama Clemens. I have seen him and tried to talk with him, but it has done little good. I am informed that he rarely speaks, that he is far gone in melancholy, and that most of the time he sits rocking and staring. He is greatly disfigured. Had I not been told who he was and been shown proof of it, I would not have known him. His skin is now entirely white, like skin that has been burned and healed badly. He has no hair on his body and his eyes are a muddy color. I understand that his sight is failing and that he can see out of one eye only. I have tried to learn from him what happened, but I can learn little.

Of the brother and sister, I can tell you more. They have opened their doors to everyone who comes here, and they will turn no one away. They have said that if a man came here, armed, angry and dripping with pox, they would not refuse him entry. That they have taken in a leper tells you of their sincerity. They speak fondly of Bondama Clemens and have informed me that she left here bound for Iconium and Smyrna to take a ship to Roma, one way or another.

According to what they have said, she went on a mule and had disguised herself as a eunuch.

So I will leave this place and go to Iconium. And to Smyrna. Who knows, by the time this arrives in Roma, Bondama Clemens herself may be there to read it. I know no one in Iconium, but I have plenty of gold, and a man with gold is a man with friends. The four men-at-arms I have hired are reliable and sensible men, and I do not fear they will forget themselves or me in our travels.

I have left three gold pieces at this sanctuary to care for Rainaut. Certainly Rafi and Kalere Navrentos would care for him well if he were a pauper, but I did not want them to have to do so much without recognition and reward. They say that to render service in the name of salvation and the Savior is sufficient, and while I do not doubt them, I wished to be sure they would not be wanting on his account.

I will send word to you when I reach Iconium, if I discover anything. Then on to Smyrna, if there is nothing more to learn at Iconium. I would prefer to travel on the deck of my own ship; however, a good horse is the only possibility in these mountains.

Everywhere I have gone I have heard that the Crusaders will not succeed in taking Jerusalem, that there are not enough men left to carry on the fight and that many of them are no longer willing to continue the battle. Between disease and desertion, the ranks have been decimated—in the old Roman sense of the word, except that instead of one in ten being killed, one in ten remains to fight. If a truce is offered, it is probable that the Christian forces will accept the terms if they are not too severe. Even Reis Richard is not so thirsty for blood as he used to be, or if he is, he no longer hankers for Islamite blood. One day soon, we may have an end to the killing and the waste.

You may rely on me to do everything I can to find Bondama Clemens, Crusade or no Crusade.

Ithuriel Dar

By my own hand on MidSummer Eve, in the Christian Year 1192.

"What do you think of my chambers?" de Monfroy asked with specious courtesy.

Olivia gave a cursory glance to the room. "Where do you intend me to stay?"

"You *are* to the point, Olivia. I give you that." He touched her shoulder, the gesture a token of possession. "You will remain in this room. It has the smaller windows and the door can be locked from the outside, if that's necessary."

"It may become so," she said, her words bleak. It would be a matter of a week, perhaps ten days before her hunger would drive her to madness, and then she would have to be confined. She hoped that she could find some relief before then, for the thought of tasting such blood as de Monfroy's, even by accident, was repugnant to her.

"Desperate, are you?" soothed de Monfroy. "You will learn to accommodate me." He touched her again, less gently. "In time you will prefer what I do."

Olivia swallowed hard against the disgust she felt. Justus had told her the same thing, as an excuse for his debauchery, and had blamed her when she refused to bring increasingly violent lovers to her bed. She could sense the same cravings in de Monfroy, the same fascination with degradation, a need to instill fear, to humiliate and hurt. She moved away from him. "I am very tired," she said, and it was no more than the truth.

"I had other thoughts," de Monfroy said, almost crooning. "You are mine now, Olivia. You are as much mine as if you were my slave. I am entitled to use you in any way I want."

Olivia gathered her hands into fists but kept them at her sides. "I am tired," she repeated. "I need sleep."

"You will have sleep. All in good time." He indicated the bed with its heavy curtains. "Rest, if you want. A short rest. Then I will have what I have wanted for so long." He had taken off his leather gage and was slapping it onto his open palm. "I will wake you in a while, as soon as it is dark, so that we will not be disturbed."

"What house is this?" she asked suddenly. "Where have you brought me?"

"This is the house of a Pisan merchant. He allows me the use of this wing. In return, I occasionally let him know of cloth and spices to be had for a low price. It works well for both of us." He indicated the hangings of the bed. "Silk, Olivia."

Her courage all but failed her. How would Sigfroit or Giralt find the wing of a house owned by a Pisan merchant? They had had so little time to plan, and their scheme had been little more than a sketch. If they could not find her, she had no idea how to find them, for they had not yet known what quarters would be allotted to them, or where. If she managed to get out, where could she go? She looked at the silken draperies. "They are still bars on a cage, de Monfroy."

"Don't be ungrateful," he warned her, his satisfaction showing in the way he moved to open the bed hangings. "This, at least, is pleasant. There are cellars here that serve well as dungeons, as you might find out if you are not more reasonable."

She strolled around the room. "Where have you put my weapons? You took my sword and dagger and my iron cap. And you've taken the few coins I had left. Where are they?"

"You have no need to know," he said, weighting his words. "But since you ask me, I'll tell you. I've given them away."

"Given what? My sword and my dagger? You gave them away? By what right? To whom?" Her voice rose with each question.

"To the merchant's son, if you wish to know. He's very pleased with them; fourteen years old and just learning to swagger." He knew that such a donation was an insult to her, and he smiled as he told her. "Think of that boy with your weapons. Think, Olivia. Oh, and the coins are gone, as coins so often are. You have no need of them, in any case."

Her anger was not as great as it appeared, since this information was the only hope he had given her. If the merchant's fourteen-year-old son wore her weapons, Sigfroit or Giralt might see them and recognize their distinctive design. There was a chance—very small but a chance—that they would find her through her weapons. "You had no right to give my weapons away."

"I have a right to do whatever I choose. I am a Master of the Hospitalers. You gave up any rights when you donned men's clothing and undertook your deception. What woman is entitled to weapons, in any case? You are not a Chatelaine. You have no husband to declare you his deputy. You should not have any weapons at all. If you possess them you are breaking the law." He watched her, his satisfaction growing.

"Every fishwife has a dagger," Olivia scoffed. "No one claims them. No one suggests that she should be without one. No law takes it from her."

"You are not a fishwife, you are a rich man's widow, which is another matter entirely." He came up to her and took her face between his hands, holding her so that she could not escape his kiss. "You must learn to be more responsive. You must return my passion, or fight me with hatred. You are not to have your lips so like a slice of liver."

"Was that what I did?" Olivia asked. "I wasn't aware of it." She reached up and took hold of his wrists. "If you continue to touch me, I will be sick." It was a meaningless threat, but it had its effect; de Monfroy released her, scowling at her. "And I wish to rest. You said something about rest when you brought me here."

"I said you had better be rested when I come to you this evening. I will not be put off, Olivia. You will receive me, and you will do all that I demand of you." His tongue flicked over his lips. "You will do everything."

"Or what?" she said.

It was obvious he took delight in telling her. "Or you will be denounced, you will be stoned. It is a shame that one as young and lovely as you are should die so uselessly."

"How sweetly you pay court," marveled Olivia. "Queen Eleanor would be proud of you."

"The Queen of England is a harlot," said de Monfroy with ire. "She is a disgrace. Her life has been a constant insult to the honor of England and France. Nothing she has said has worth. Her rebellion against Henry proves how despicable she is." He strode to the door, each step ringing from his long-roweled spurs. He paused and offered her a casual bow. "Very well, Bondama. It shall be as you wish. You invoke the conduct of a troubador, and you will have it, for a while. You will have time to rest. But I will have you when night falls, and I will have you for as long and in as many ways as I like." He opened the door, then left the room, taking care that Olivia should hear him slam the bolt into place.

She put her hand to her throbbing head and strove to marshal her thoughts. Now that she was alone, she was determined to put what few hours she had to good use, and find the means to escape. At least she would have the night to aid her, if nothing else. She took perverse amusement in her situation. It had been so very long since she had been so wholly without resources. Esurience and the sun had taken their toll of her, and the preternatural strength that she would have possessed if she were rested and fed and walked on her native earth had deserted her. Now she was no more powerful than any grown woman who had not slept enough for over a month. She sat on the edge of the bed and looked down at her clothes. Her cotehardie was in tatters and her solers were scuffed and dusty. She longed for a bath and sweet oils to take away the grime and stench of travel. At that moment she yearned for soap and hot water almost as much as she desired intimacy and blood. That was not part of de Monfroy's plan. Olivia made a face. How could any man consider lying with a woman while he was filthy? She had seen it many, many times but it continued to baffle her. Even the most brutal arena fighters her husband had forced upon her had been bathed, massaged, and perfumed before they came to her. But cleanliness was thought to be a sign of vanity now, a sure indication of sin. She braced her elbows on her knees and dropped her chin into her palms. There had to be a way to get out of this Pisan merchant's house. If what de Monfroy had told her about the house was the truth. And she was not certain he was telling her the truth. Her eyes stung with absent tears.

"I'll manage," she said aloud, hoping the sound of her own voice would hearten her. She coughed once and repeated, "I'll manage," this time more firmly. She was not wholly satisfied with the sound of it. "I will find a way." That was better, she decided.

She took off her cotehardie and tossed it into a heap. She had only a cottelle and her Norman trews on now, and though the day had been hot and the room she occupied was oppressively warm, she decided to leave herself half-dressed. There was no reason to give de Monfroy any assistance. She put her solers near the bed, where she could pull them on quickly. As she lay back on the bed, she whispered to herself, striving to gather as much strength as she could before de Monfroy returned. How odd to abhor the coming of the night! She, who had been so much of the night, now hoped to delay its coming. For with it would come de Monfroy.

At the sound of the Angelus bell, Olivia opened her eyes, her mind alert although her body moved slowly, as if she were under water. She blinked, adjusting to the soft light of sunset filtering in through the high, small windows. If only the legends were true, she thought, and vampires were truly able to change shape in the night: she would metamorphose into a bat and flap into the sky, or become a wolf or tiger—at one time or another she had heard that vampires were capable of becoming both those animals—and fight de Monfroy as he deserved to be fought.

She took care to lie still, to give the appearance of being yet asleep, in the hope that her dissembling would give her a slight advantage when de Monfroy came. She made herself close her eyes and rely on her other, heightened senses, anticipating his arrival.

At last, with the room all but dark, there was the sound of the bolt being drawn back and the raising of wards in the lock. She resisted the urge to rush to the attack, guessing that de Monfroy would be armed and suspicious.

He carried an oil lamp and his unsheathed sword. He closed the door softly, with great care, and he crossed the room on bare feet, at pains to make as little noise as possible. He had shed his mail and was now in a cote of samite that rustled when he moved, like autumn leaves driven by the wind. He held the lamp so that its feeble light did not fall directly on the bed, but let him move with safety across the room. As he approached the bed, Olivia could see that he had a short whip thrust through his belt. He paused beside the bed, staring down greedily. "The hour has come, Bondama."

Olivia pretended to be about to waken. She stirred, turning onto her side. She wanted to lash out with her feet, to kick him and knock him over or injure him. If he had been one step closer she might have taken the chance, but as it was, he was just far enough away that she could not be sure of striking him; attempting such a ploy without success would be more danger than remaining inactive, no matter how terrible the waiting became.

De Monfroy reached out at last, holding the oil lamp up so that he could see her features clearly. "I know you are awake. Olivia. You are awake."

She opened her eyes. "I hoped it was part of my dream," she said.

He smiled at her. "Did you? I will remind you of that before the night is over." He placed the lamp in a hanging support. "You are rested?"

"A little," she said, hoping he would keep back from her a bit longer, while she had a chance to evaluate his state of mind. She was worried because he was armed—that boded ill—and because he had brought a whip. She was aware of his need for violence, but she had not anticipated he would begin with it.

"You will be worn out before I am finished with you. And tonight it is only a beginning." He reached down and took her jaw between thumb and fingers, pressing hard so that he felt the bone more than the skin. "You will be completely mine."

"Never," Olivia said very quietly, and revealed far more defiance than shouting protest would.

"Say that again tomorrow," de Monfroy goaded her. "You won't." He pulled the whip from his belt and rubbed the handle along her face. "This is the easy one, only braided leather thongs. I have others, with barbs at the ends of the thongs, and those with lashes of wire. This is gentle, soft." The end of the handle was under her chin and he forced her head back with it, studying her face for a sign of fear. "It will come," he said to himself, musingly, as he bent over her. "The fear will come."

Olivia held the insides of her cheeks with her teeth to keep silent. Orval, Sier de Monfroy brought back too many memories, too many recollections of nights in Roma, long ago, with Justus watching from his hidden room, and then, when that no longer satisfied him, his participation. De Monfroy was too much like Justus; her loathing increased as he spoke to her.

"Women like you. Women like you. You want everyone to believe that you are independent as men. You flaunt yourselves, masquerading as eunuchs and pretending to be men. You go against every ordinance of God and all laws of men, and you take pride in your unnatural state." He leaned ever closer to her as he went on. "You must learn. You must learn what you are. You have to be brought back to the role God made for you. You are to submit to men, to depend on us as you depend on God. Anything else is devilish, damnable." His face was little more than a hand's-breadth away from hers. "It is not for you to defy God and what God has made you. It is for you to adore without question, to be meek, as God intended you to be."

Olivia spat in his face.

He straightened up, the handle of his whip cracking against the side of her face, leaving a bleeding welt. "Whore! Whore! You unnatural slut!"

"Better that than what you are," she said, and launched herself at de Monfroy, reaching for the whip and his sword.

She careened into him, knocking him off-balance. His sword dropped to the floor. He swayed, reaching out for the bedpost to keep from falling as Olivia stretched one hand toward his eyes, the thumb hooking inward. "Back, harlot!" he bellowed, lashing at her with his whip. She got one foot behind his knee and jerked, trying to pull him off his feet.

He staggered, then stood upright. He had his whip hand up, and he brought the thongs down across her back repeatedly, cursing with every blow, until at last Olivia released him and dropped to her knees. De Monfroy continued to strike at her, his curses now a steady muttering, like a prayer.

Olivia scuttled back, searching for the sword he had dropped. The pain in her shoulders and back was a huge weight, as if an enormous animal with tremendous fangs and claws had fixed itself on her. She could feel her weakness increasing, and a dangerous, seductive lassitude that could rob her of purpose.

De Monfroy's expression had changed; there was a vile sensuality mixed with his wrath now, a treacherous pleasure that robbed him of both pity and shame. His curses were more breathless as he pursued her, his mouth shining.

It took Olivia longer than she imagined was possible to get out of range of his whip. She had almost backed herself against the wall, which was more dangerous than almost anything else she could do. Feeling with one hand, she moved beside the wall, hoping she had enough distance before she reached a corner of the room, to break away from de Monfroy's pursuit. She could feel blood on her arms now, and starting to spread down her back, making the rent strips of her cottelle stick to her. It was an agonizing effort to remain silent, but she dared not make any sound beyond that of moving; her silence was essential, for once she screamed, she was not sure she could stop, and she knew with cold certainty that screams or sobs would serve only to incite de Monfroy to greater frenzy.

As de Monfroy lashed out at Olivia, a few of the thongs caught in the lamp hanging. The power of his wrenching attempt to get his whip free broke off two of the braided thongs and brought the lamp hanging crashing to the floor.

In the two or three heartbeats that afforded her, Olivia bolted across the room, throwing herself forward so that she could slide under the bed, for that would not only protect her a bit longer, she had seen a glint from de Monfroy's sword beneath the hangings.

"You are monstrous! *Monstrous!*" shrieked de Monfroy as he flung himself at her. His free hand closed around her ankle, tight as the jaw of a jackal.

Olivia kicked out, her heel smashing into his face and against his hand, but to no avail. She grabbed for the bed to keep from being dragged back to de Monfroy. Her fingers slipped as de Monfroy began relentlessly to drag her toward him.

And then she touched the sword.

At the utmost limits of her pain-wracked body, Olivia

strained to pull the sword close enough that she could take hold of it. Her fingers slipped on the blade, then closed around it. She knew that her hands were cut from the blade, but that did not matter. Olivia took heart from the steel as she dragged it nearer.

De Monfroy had his hand on her knee now, and was using his whip on her belly and flanks; his eyes were as glazed as those of a man wholly in the throes of passion.

Olivia grasped the quillons, then the hilt. She swung the blade horizontally, a hair's-breadth above the floor, shouting once as she did. The impact was so jolting that it was all she could do to hold onto the sword as the steel bit deep into de Monfroy's side.

He roared in agony and rage; he battered at her with the whip as his blood gouted across the room. Then the whip fell from his hands and a paroxysm shuddered through him. He coughed, blood running from his mouth.

Olivia slid away from him, hardly daring to breathe. She lay on the floor near the bed while de Monfroy thrashed once, twice, buckled as if in a seizure, then twitched and was still. The odor of dying filled the room.

Where had she struck him? Olivia wondered as she got to her knees. What blow could be that mortal? She moved a little to the side and saw that the sword had almost taken de Monfroy's right arm off from underneath, sliding up the ribs to the shoulder. She swallowed convulsively, her thoughts suddenly in disorder.

Forcing herself to act, she got to her feet. Her legs seemed as hot and brittle as charring wood. "I must leave," she said to herself in a voice she could not recognize. "I must leave."

Taking care not to look at de Monfroy's body, she made her way across the room. She was about to open the door when she realized that to leave the room was reckless and dangerous. "No," she muttered. "Not that way." Those hoarse, croaking words were oddly reassuring, and she listened to them as if they came from someone else. "Find a mantel," she told herself. "Cover the blood."

She opened the door that led to de Monfroy's chamber, and after a swift inspection, she went through, searching for his chest that carried his clothes. Once she found it, she rummaged in it for something she could wear. Trying not to giggle, she drew out his black-and-white Hospitaler's mantel and pulled it around her shoulders, securing it correctly.

There were four tall windows in the room, one overlooking the courtyard of the house, the other above the stable. "Not the courtyard," she ordered. "The stable. Who will notice? And there's bound to be a gate." She nodded, saying to her own remark, "You're right."

With as much care as she could muster, she opened the window over the stable and climbed out to the narrow ledge. Then, the Hospitaler's mantel flying behind her like wings, she dropped onto the stable roof.

*   *   *

Text of a letter from Gui de Fraizmarch to Sier Gace de Heaulmiere.

To that most worthy knight, Sier Gace de Heaulmiere, the gratitude and obligations of Gui de Fraizmarch are officially acknowledged. The many chivalric deeds Sier Gace has done in the name of that most dishonored Chatelaine Fealatie Bueveld have been revealed, and the devotion which has marked all of Sier Gace's dealings is shown for all to see.

How lamentable that Sier Gace was not able to persuade the disgraced Fealatie Bueveld to abandon her unworthy pursuit of a lessening of the terms of her penance. In returning to give report of her actions, he has demonstrated the meaning of loyalty and the nature of knightly oaths. It was not to the said Fealatie that Sier Gace gave his word, but to her offended husband, Gui de Fraizmarch. In acknowledgement of that responsibility, Sier Gace has brought word of the many grievous errors this Chatelaine has made in the supposed attempt to fulfill the terms of her penance, terms which she herself vowed to accept and to honor before she left with her escort for the Holy Land.

In recognition of the many services Sier Gace has done Gui de Fraizmarch, said Gui has petitioned Reis Phillippe on Sier Gace's behalf, so that a grant of lands will reward his fidelity, and an augmentation of arms will bear testimony to his worthiness. Said augmentation is a cross raguly vert in the dexter chief, in token of his time in the Holy Land. This augmented device is entered in the annals and rolls of Reis Phillippe's pursuivant herald. The land granted to Sier Gace by his Grace Reis Phillippe is apportioned from the lands of Bueveld, in recognition of the dishonor of the Chatelaine Fealatie Bueveld and the justice of the advancement of Sier Gace.

From the private purse of Gui de Fraizmarch, Sier Gace is offered ten golden Angels for the time he spent in the company of Fealatie Bueveld for the expenses he bore on her demand, as well as a ring of gold and chalcedony as proof of the obligation of Gui de Fraizmarch to Sier Gace, since the said Fealatie has not accomplished her penance and is not willing to do so, thereby disgracing her escort.

From this time until the Trumpet of Judgment sounds, Fraizmarch is ever a haven to Sier Gace and his descendants, the members of this House forever in the debt of de Heaulmiere.

Gui de Fraizmarch

At his behest by the hand of the herald Gaucelm de Excideul and under the seal of Fraizmarch and Reis Phillippe, on the 26th day of June, the Feast of the Martyrs John and Paul, in Our Lord's year 1192.

· 18 ·

Wrapped in the black-and-white mantel of the Hospitalers, Olivia made her way through the streets of Attalia, starting at every sudden noise, but heedless of what way she went, for as much as she did not wish to admit it, she was lost. Once, as she crossed a small square, the doors of a little church burst open and a dozen Cassian monks filed out, singing the Hour. Olivia had shrunk back into the shadows, her throat suddenly tight-constricted, her head buzzing with ache. She leaned back against the stone wall of the building behind her and tried to calm her thoughts, to quiet her mind.

She took more care, going more slowly, behaving as if there was nothing suspicious about being on the street after dark, as if she was entitled to be where she was. In a still and distant part of her mind, she recalled growing up, when such fears, such doubts would have been unthinkable. At the same time, she began to think of a reasonable excuse to offer anyone who challenged her, though she knew there was none.

Eventually she found her way toward the docks, in the hope that there would be a ship she might stow away on. Any lingering trust she had that Fealatie or one of her two escorting knights would find her had faded. Whatever the intentions had actually been, there was not enough time or opportunity to bring their plans to anything more than suppositions, vaguely explored.

As she stopped near one of the warehouses, Olivia found her thoughts turning again and again to Rainaut. Was he still alive, or had the insidious malady finally taken him beyond all help? She did not want to imagine him dead, no matter how much she hoped he suffered no longer. Quite suddenly she saw his device in her memory, the severed arm. She tried to put it out of her mind, but it remained, fixed with her last sight of Orval, Sier de Monfroy with his arm cut half off. Olivia had lived long enough to have lost any faith in fate or destiny, but she could not rid herself of the impression that the device had been an omen. She huddled in the side-street, a warehouse on one side, a chandlery on the other, and ordered herself to find some way to get aboard a ship bound westward. But her mind was sluggish, and the demands she had made on her lowered reserves were taking their toll now. No matter how sternly she admonished herself to act before her crime was discovered and the city sealed, all that was real to her was her exhaustion and pain. It was oddly amusing, she thought, that a vampire should not be able to deal with a little loss of blood. Her eyes were half-closed and she had slipped down the wall.

Though she was unaware of it happening, she assumed she must have dozed, for the sound of nearby footsteps wakened her abruptly. She sat up, biting her lip to keep from moaning at the pain in her back and shoulders.

"There's another footprint," whispered someone.

"I see it. And another, just beyond." Both voices were so soft that Olivia had to strain to hear them.

"Do you suppose they're hers? What if—"

"Quiet, Giralt," hissed his companion. "We've been following these from the stable of the house where de Monfroy was killed. Look how small the feet are. It has to be her." He held a shaded oil lamp so that only a small circle of light was cast near their feet.

"But considering where we've gone—" Giralt objected.

"She's hurt, by Christ's Winding Sheet. You should have come up to the room. It was a slaughterhouse." Sigfroit stopped. "There. Over there."

"Where?" Giralt asked, peering into the dark side-street.

Olivia could not believe what she heard. She lifted one hand to wave, and came close to fainting as hurt rolled through her. Steadying herself, she clenched her teeth and waved again, holding her hand up as the two men drew nearer.

"There she is," Sigfroit exclaimed. "There. Do you see?"

Giralt nodded. "Bondama," he called out in as low a voice as he could.

Olivia was on one knee, her shoulder pressed against the stones of the warehouse. "Here," she murmured. "Over here." The bobbing light swam in her vision and she reached out for the two men, hoping they would reach her before she toppled.

"It is good we found you," said Sigfroit, the first to reach her side. He lifted the shaded lamp to look at her and his eyes widened as his face went white. "Christ in Limbo," he said under his breath.

Now Giralt had joined him, and his expression was as horrified as Sigfroit's. "Saint Alexander! all that blood."

Olivia held out her hands to them, and for the first time saw them in the light. Even she was aghast. Her hands were caked red with dried blood. By the feel of it, there was blood on her face, and under her mantel she knew everything she wore was stained with it. Without thinking she started to rub her hands on the mantel.

Sigfroit stopped her. "No. Nothing that can be seen," he whispered. "If they see blood on the mantel, there will be questions to answer."

"Who sees?" Olivia asked, looking from Sigfroit to Giralt.

"They found de Monfroy. Shortly before compline," Giralt said. "We were at the chapter house when word was brought. Fealatie told us to look for you."

Olivia was pleased that she did not tremble or cry out. "Oh. And who else is looking?"

"No one yet, that we know of," said Sigfroit. "When we looked outside the house, the Hospitalers were searching it, top to bottom, and questioning all the servants. That will take time. Especially since it was known that de Monfroy had a eunuch with him." He held out his hand. "Come. I'll help you up."

Gratefully she took his hand. "You are very good," she said when she was on her feet. He did not release her hand but stood close to her until she was steady.

"Fealatie said to bring you to the Three Sandpipers. It is a merchants' inn between the chapter house and the docks. She has rooms there." Giralt hesitated. "Fealatie wants us to bring you to her. So that we can arrange passage together."

"And you don't approve?" Olivia said, watching Giralt

closely, aware now of his ambivalence and something more, a deeper emotion that was the source of his reaction.

"I . . . I fear for her; I have sworn to protect her and to guard her. I have been with her—as has Sigfroit—from the start, and we know how much she has endured. I . . . we are seeking an alleviation to her travail. You, Bondama, make my task more difficult," Giralt said in a rush, obviously stating his side of an argument he had been having with Sigfroit.

"Would you leave anyone with de Monfroy?" Sigfroit asked sharply. "I've told you some of the things he has done in the past, things which have gone unchallenged because he . . . was Sier de Monfroy. He has not been treated in any way he did not deserve. This woman has avenged many others."

"True, whatever he did, he will not do it again," said Olivia, fighting new dizziness. She mastered herself and addressed Giralt. "I would not expose any of you to danger on my account. I thank you for your warning; I am grateful to the Chatelaine. You need not stay with me if you would rather not."

"We've been deserted by one already," Giralt said, his eyes on his feet. "If Fealatie wants to aid you, then aid you we will, for her sake if not for yours." He directed his next words to Sigfroit. "I will not do anything to endanger us—any of us."

"I didn't think you would," said Sigfroit. He had slipped his arm around Olivia. "Come. We must hurry. If we are caught here, there is nothing we can do to save you."

"Yes," said Olivia, needing all her concentration to walk with Sigfroit. "Who is looking for me?"

"The Hospitalers, of course." Sigfroit glanced at her in surprise at Olivia's single laugh. "What is it, Bondama?"

"The Hospitalers. They would not be pleased to find me for more reasons than de Monfroy," she said, lifting her feet woodenly as she strove to keep up with Sigfroit. "I'm sorry. I did not think—"

"Quiet," ordered Giralt in an abrupt hush. "I hear someone approaching."

The three halted, Olivia leaning heavily against Sigfroit,

her bloody face turned toward his shoulder. She wanted to think of reasonable explanations to account for their presence, but nothing occurred to her. To her amazement, Sigfroit began to hector her.

"It isn't enough that you decide to get into a fight with a sailor with a knife, oh, no. You have to do it when you have more wine in you than water, and with most of the men in the tavern sailors like the fool you fought." He kept his voice low but his vehemence was more stinging for it. "You're fortunate all you'll get for your idiocy is half a dozen scars, when the cuts heal. If we hadn't been with you, you'd be fishbait by now." He kept on in this manner as a group of Hospitalers came along the street.

"You there!" the sarjeant called out. "Stop and account for yourselves."

"Now what!" Sigfroit burst out. "Be damned to you, cousin, for the whole of this night." He shook Olivia, holding her so that she faced him and not the Hospitalers. "It was bad enough that you went to the tavern, but now this!"

Giralt hung back, confused and worried but appearing to be embarrassed. "We're sorry, good Hospitalers."

The sarjeant came a few steps closer. "Who are you?"

"I am Sigfroit de Plessien, and this disgraceful creature is my cousin." He let Olivia sag against him, saying, "I have not seen him for five years. The last time we spoke, he was a beardless youth still learning to handle a horse and a sword at the same time. I was told he would be here, and I look forward to our reunion. But see what I have found!" He made a gesture of disgust. "What can have happened? The first thing he did was drag us off to a seamen's tavern, where he had wine and more wine, and then challenged one of the sailors . . . well, I am amazed that we got out with most of our skin."

The sarjeant tried to look disapproving but there was a twinkle in his eye. "You know how young men are, Bonsier. They have to prove their mettle."

"On a tavern full of angry sailors?" Sigfroit asked. "He is fortunate we did not leave him to fend for himself. If I were not of the cadet branch of the family, I might have." He snorted. "The lad's hopeless."

"Wait until morning," said the sarjeant wisely. "Then talk to him while his head is numbering his sins for him." He gave Sigfroit a measuring look. "He ought to be reported, but since you haven't mentioned a name, there's no way I can do it, is there." He nudged one of the men-at-arms beside him.

Sigfroit looked up, seemingly surprised. "Why . . . Good sarjeant, I do not ask for any indulgence of this rash fellow."

The sarjeant waved this honest protest away. "Another time I might have made note of it, but tonight we're looking for more deadly game than a wild boy. There is a eunuch in Attalia who has murdered—" He broke off. "Have you seen a man, a eunuch, in the streets tonight?"

"I have seen sailors tonight, and the inside of a tavern. There may have been eunuchs there. I didn't try to find out." He suddenly lifted Olivia and slung her over his shoulder. "I had better take him back to his quarters before he gets any worse."

Giralt continued to watch in stony silence. He glared at the sarjeant, but said nothing.

"Well, God keep and bless you, Bonsier," said the sarjeant. "We won't get to our beds until lauds, by the look of it."

"Sarjeant," said Sigfroit, turning back after he had started away, "what has this eunuch done?"

"Murdered a Master of our Order. By the look of the room, de Monfroy put up quite a battle before the villain got him." He shook his head. "De Monfroy saved the wretch, too, and brought him to Attalia out of charity."

Sigfroit paused thoughtfully. "I suppose I have something to be grateful for—this one only brawls and drinks." He motioned to Giralt to come with him. "Good hunting, sarjeant."

"Good of you to say it, Bonsier." The sarjeant and his men continued down the street, away from Sigfroit, Giralt, and Olivia.

"Why did you—" Giralt began, only to be cut short by Sigfroit.

"Wait until they are gone." He craned his neck, addressing his burden. "I'm going to carry you this way, in case we encounter more patrols."

"And if we do?" she asked. She found Sigfroit intriguing; she had not suspected so quick a mind in the Franconian knight.

"I will tell them the same thing." He shifted his arm so that he held her a little more securely.

"You mean you will lie," said Giralt. "And expose every one of us to greater risk."

"There's less risk in this . . . diversion, than in trying to explain what we are doing on the street with a woman in men's clothes who is being sought as a murderous eunuch." He waited while Giralt considered what he had said. "You're worried for Fealatie. Aren't you?"

"She is our Chatelaine and we're . . ." He faltered and stopped.

"She is my Chatelaine. For you she is much more," said Sigfroit, giving Giralt no chance to deny it. "I won't endanger her, but I won't abandon this woman to the Hospitalers, not on de Monfroy's account." He patted Olivia's leg. "Have patience, Bondama. We'll win free. We have so far, and so have you. Together nothing will stand before us."

Olivia hesitated, then said, "I am in no position to argue."

"How true." He chuckled. "Come, Giralt. Fealatie is waiting for us. And we must be away on the morning tide."

When they reached the Three Sandpipers, only a sleepy porter was awake to unbar the door to them. He nodded toward one of the private reception rooms. "She's in there," he said through a yawn before he tottered off toward the back of the inn.

Fealatie sat with her unsheathed sword across her knees, her mail harness on, but her head uncovered, revealing tousled braids of dark reddish-brown, like polished rosewood. She rose as Giralt held the door for Sigfroit. "Is she—"

"Merely part of a small deception," said Sigfroit, bending to let Olivia off his shoulder. "We found her where you suspected she had gone."

"The docks," said Fealatie.

"Near them," Giralt confirmed.

"And was she pursued?" Fealatie asked, looking at Giralt for the answer.

"A sarjeant and men-at-arms stopped us. They were looking for her, though they called her a eunuch." He grudgingly went on. "It was Sigfroit who thought of a way to deal with them. And it worked."

"Behold us," said Sigfroit, who was still enjoying himself, "having to bring home a debauched younger cousin, a disgraceful fellow, given to fighting in taverns."

"Very clever," said Fealatie with approval.

Olivia had been trying to straighten her mantel and put some order about her appearance. She broke off these thankless tasks to speak seriously to Fealatie. "I am very much in your debt, Chatelaine. When we spoke earlier, I doubted that—"

Fealatie waved this aside. "If you are grateful, then your aid in Roma would be more than sufficient to fulfill any sort of obligation you might have for the service we have been fortunate to offer you."

"I don't know how fortunate you are," Olivia said, finding herself truly smiling for the first time in days. "I have no doubt that I have been very fortunate indeed." She took care to frame her next question precisely. "There was no reason for you to aid me: why did you do it?"

"For honor?" Fealatie said. "I have learned what it is to be without help and without friends. Sigfroit told me about de Monfroy, after you left. He is not one I would want to take orders from."

"No," said Olivia drily. She glanced inquisitively at Sigfroit. "What do you know of him, and why did you try to stop him now?"

Sigfroit folded his arms, the amusement gone from his face. "De Monfroy always keeps women. There's no fault in that; half the chivalry of France keeps women. The rest keep boys. But de Monfroy made prisoners of them, and hurt them for his pleasure. I knew one woman, just out of girlhood, and of a gentle and pious nature. She longed for the cloister, but her family had long-standing agreements to uphold, and she was supposed to marry. The man who was betrothed to her is my step-brother." He took a long breath. "It was at Mass that de Monfroy saw her, and wanted her. He had her abducted, and used her for his pleasure. I saw her, when he had finished with her." He fixed his eyes on the opposite wall where wooden trenchers hung from hooks. "Her father challenged de Monfroy, but de Monfroy would not accept a challenge from a man of such great age. My step-brother could do nothing because they had never been married, nor marriage contracts signed. Eventually she had her first wish, and was sent to the convent, where the Sisters care for those who are mad. I saw her when they took her there; my step-brother asked for my company. She was scarred like a soldier who has been thrown onto caltrops." His face was set. "De Monfroy said she had taken the pox, but no pox leaves scars like that, in long, straight grooves."

Olivia sat down, trembling. "It . . . it is nothing. It will pass."

"I should not have spoken," Sigfroit apologized.

"No; no, you're not to blame." She held her arms crossed, fingers fixed above elbows, cold spreading through her. "I knew what he was." It took more courage than she realized to say, "My husband was very like him."

Giralt swore, going to Fealatie's side.

Sigfroit stared at her, his face darkening.

It was Fealatie who was able to speak. "Many husbands are demanding and harsh. But what recourse have we?"

Olivia held back her first response. "You have a demanding and harsh husband as well, don't you?"

"I have a husband who has made demands; I believe they are harsh, but he does not." Her hand brushed Giralt's once, and she went on. "And because my husband has such demands, we must leave for Roma. If there is any way to mitigate my penance, it will be decided there. My husband will oppose any change, but he has not been to the Holy Land." This last was as critical as she would ever permit herself to be.

Giralt placed his hand on the hilt of his sword. "What do you want us to do?"

"There is an usciere leaving for Ragusa and then to Ancona. It is almost empty; our horses will have three stalls apiece." Now that she was discussing plans, Fealatie was starting to be enthusiastic once again. "They leave tonight, when the tide turns. They will carry us, but it will take most of our money to pay for the voyage."

"Once we are in Roma, there will be no trouble with

money," said Olivia. "What accommodations are we to have?"

"Grooms' cabins," said Fealatie. "We will be able to have one apiece." She saw something in Olivia's face. "What troubles you now, Bondama?"

"I am a very poor sailor," she said, thinking that once again she was destined to be seasick.

*   *   *

Text of a coded message to Reis Phillippe of France.

To my most puissant lord, Your Grace Reis Phillippe, I have just returned from a gathering of knights called in Acre, and it is my estimation that all opportunity to reach Jerusalem has been lost. There is at this time no means by which the Christian forces currently on Crusade can breach the Islamite barriers and reclaim the city.

As you may have heard, Saladin recently found another means to insult Reis Richard when Coer-de-Leon was unhorsed in the fighting. Saladin, learning of this, had one of his horses sent to Reis Richard as a replacement. Richard's anger was only greater than the amusement of the Islamites, for none of the Islamite horses is large enough or strong enough to carry a man in armor, let alone wear the bard. This insult has caused more acrimony than a host of defeats, since it is now assumed that the Islamites are playing with us and hold us in contempt.

The flux continues to claim lives, as do the sweating fever and putrescent wounds. Recently an apothecary with the English was accused of witchcraft because of the treatment he had developed, which he said he was taught by an herb woman. He had been told that packing open wounds with mouldy bread would lessen the mortification, since the mould would take the pus to itself. However it was, he did save more soldiers than any other of his number, and this caused many to be jealous and suspicious. When he could not prove that he was not a sorcerer, he was burned for his demonic healings. The priests and monks have blessed this death, but there are those among the knights and men-at-arms who would prefer that they had left the apothecary alive. God offers salvation to the last breath of life; the apothecary gave some hope of life continuing.

It is being said that an end is in sight, and that those few of us remaining will be permitted to leave before another year goes by. Some have suggested that the current makeshift truce will become formal and that will permit us to return either to France or to the Frankish cities. I have heard that Saladin is willing to permit Christians to retain the coastal cities that are currently in Christian hands. The merchants are all for that, and the Courts of Bourgesses have urged that the terms be formalized as soon as possible, before the Islamites change their minds and demand control of the ports.

It is disheartening to be here now, to see the destruction of the cities and all the huts and hovels where the people live who used to have houses within the walls. Many of the simple folk, farmers and smiths and artisans, are angry and displeased about the whole venture, and they blame Reis Richard more than they blame you.

Also, most of the people are afraid of the Templars, who are worse than pagan warlords in their conduct. While the Order is regarded as being in French hands, I warn you that they are beyond any control but the Will of God. They live in great luxury, for all their vows of poverty, and their Order has so much treasure amassed in their chapter houses that it is said that they could buy Jerusalem from the Islamites. No matter what the official reports tell you, or what the heralds say, I am warning you that the Templars are more treacherous than any Islamite warrior.

The Hospitalers are another matter, for they continue to uphold their rule of protection and defense, and have not yet been lured into battle. The day they are permitted to attack is the day they will become one with the Templars, in act if not in habit.

I pray that I have said nothing to offend the King's Grace, nor to bring about any mistake in judgment. I swear by God *and the honor of my House that what I have said is the truth and I will stand by my Word at the Last Trumpet. God save and protect you, Reis Phillippe.*

Your martlet

By my confessor's hand and under confessional seal and arms seal, on the 2nd day of August in the 1192nd year of Our Lord.

· 19 ·

AMONGST

They came on the Via Flaminia, with one horse between the four of them; of the three they had taken aboard the usciere at Attalia, one had taken colic aboard ship and died; the other had been sold for traveling money when they arrived in Ancona. The remaining gelding was showing ribs and sweating readily in the high summer heat. Olivia's suggestion that they travel only in the early morning and late evening, Fealatie did not bother to discuss; she told Sigfroit and Giralt to find them all satisfactory places to rest at the hottest hours.

"That's for farmers," said Sigfroit. "What are we, hod carriers? that we must drop into the shade once the sun is overhead? We have been in the Holy Land, and this is pleasant by comparison." He had hooked his thumbs into his belt and rocked back on his heels to show his disgust.

"I was more concerned for the horse than for you," said Fealatie. "He's straining, and if we want to be able to ride him to Roma, he had best not be hard-driven now."

Giralt took Fealatie's position. "We have come this far, and there is no reason we should bring ourselves to the brink of failure now. If resting for a time spares the animal's and our own strength, then why not?" He patted the neck of the gelding. "He has served us well and has earned our consideration."

Olivia, who felt as if she had succumbed to fever, though she knew it was the sun leaching her vitality, interjected her observation. "The horse is worn out. He cannot be pushed, but then, neither can we. Think of how hungry and thirsty we have been. If we are sensible now we will not have worse to suffer before we reach Sanza Pare."

"Are you certain we will be welcome there?" Giralt asked, his doubt plain on his good, square countenance.

"I have said so," Olivia reminded him, as tired of defending herself as she was of walking in sunlight. The one thing sustaining her now was the sense of nearness of Roma. It was stronger than the tug of a magnet, and she welcomed it.

"But there might have been some change," Giralt said, then added, "We have no money left, and if there can be no aid from you, we are no more than mendicants."

"The estate is mine," said Olivia, and heard the exclamation of shock and denial. "It is mine," she repeated when they let her speak again.

"You have said that your husband was a patrician," said Giralt, more critically.

"Yes, so I did. But he has been dead some time, and I have decided how the money is to be spent. I have had to use sponsors and intermediaries to accomplish my purpose, but I am the owner of Sanza Pare and the major domo there is my bondsman." She stumbled and righted herself by grabbing hold of the gelding's stirrup. "I tell you that you will be welcome there, that you will be given horses and money for all you have done, and whatever aid I can extend to bring you to a Cardinal or the Pope. If you do not believe me now, reserve your opinion until we reach the estate."

Giralt was about to question this, but Fealatie silenced him. "You gave Olivia your help because I asked it of you. Now I ask that you defer your arguments. There is time enough to cavil when we reach this Sanza Pare." She straightened in the saddle and pointed to the mountains ahead of them. "We have a long way to go before we reach Roma. Nothing can be settled before we get there."

Sigfroit, who had remained silent, now added his own comments. "Whether or not we have succor at this estate she speaks of, we will be near Roma, and that is what we wish to be. Giralt, no matter what else may happen, we have escorted Fealatie this far."

"It isn't enough to guard her, we have obligations to her, duties that extend beyond—" Giralt exclaimed only to be cut short by Fealatie herself.

"You have served me well, and in ways no oath can define. You have done far more than my husband required of you, and for longer." She looked straight ahead between her horse's ears. "I can no longer ask anything of you but what you wish to give. Any other obligation is owed not to me but to my husband." This reminder of Gui de Fraizmarch's existence caused an awkward moment; Fealatie did her best to lessen the discomfort they all felt. "I am thankful with all my soul that you are willing to remain with me on this journey, that you did not follow Gace and return to France when we were forbidden to enter Jerusalem."

Both Giralt and Sigfroit were sufficiently abashed that neither spoke for some time, and when they did, it was of minor and diverse matters; the subject of their service did not arise again, though now when Fealatie prayed at shrine, she added her thanks for the constancy of her two companions.

At last they reached Spoleto, where troops of the Holy Roman Emperor Henry VI were massing for yet another attack on the Kingdom of Sicilia in the south. Soldiers, knights, men-at-arms, armored bishops, and nobles were everywhere. The city was in an uproar, and what few accommodations were to be had were disastrously expensive. Everywhere they were asked if they were part of the Emperor's forces and when they admitted they were not, they were refused what few lodgings were left.

"We could seek refuge at a monastery," suggested Sigfroit when they had exhausted all but the brothels of the city in their search for rooms for the night.

"There won't be room; the families and dependents of the soldiers will be there, and half the merchants, no matter where you look," predicted Fealatie, recalling similar times in the Holy Land. "We are French vassals, these are German," she went on. "It would be wiser to find another place."

When it was evident that they would not find room, Olivia

ventured a suggestion. "There are a few small villas through the mountains. Most of them won't be safe, but I know of one or two that are—or were—protected."

The place where she led them was an ancient guard station, sunk into the side of the hill and overlooking Termi and the Nera. There was no place to stable the horse, but the six-sided squat building was relatively untouched and large enough to hold many more than their number.

"How did you know of this?" asked Giralt with increased respect.

Olivia was trying to decide on an answer when Sigfroit said, "Old Roman families always know about the bolt-holes, don't they?" His wink took any insult out of this observation.

"Yes, and with good cause." She looked away. "Everywhere you look, there is war—Crusades and campaigns and aggressions—and nowhere can you escape it. It is all around us. Why not have a hiding place?" She had been driven here five times in the last three centuries, and each time the cause had been war.

Fealatie inspected the largest of the three rooms of the guard station, nodding her approval as she stood by the shuttered windows. "In this location, with walls this thick and those heavy wooden shutters, it might be possible to hold off an army."

"A squad," Olivia corrected, "at most a century of legionnaires."

"It's stone, so it's hard to burn . . ." Fealatie continued her appraisal, favorably impressed. She opened the door to one of the other two rooms. "A hearth. Spits. A kitchen?"

"And a place to keep warm in the winter," said Olivia. "It probably isn't safe to start a fire—the flues haven't been cleaned in a long time."

"The third room is a dormitory?" asked Giralt.

"Yes," said Olivia, holding the door open for them. She was the last to step through, and as her feet once again touched Roman earth, the first returning of her inner power began, like a freshet from snow at the start of spring thaw. How foolish she had thought she was when she had brought Roman earth to line the foundation for the dormitory, and now how relieved she was that she had done it. While it would not restore her to full strength, she would not be so drained as she had been.

"This was built by your House?" asked Fealatie, obviously evaluating the potential of the little guard station.

Olivia shrugged. "Indirectly, yes." It would be good to sleep here, she said to herself. The presence of her native earth under the stone floor was not unlike a distant humming, as if a nest of bees were hidden there.

"How indirectly?" Giralt wanted to know.

"This guard station is more than seven hundred years old. It's been changed a little between then and now, but is basically the same building. Seven hundred years is a long time." Olivia crossed the room to where a few planks revealed where the beds had been. "Think of how much has been lost in seven hundred years. The roads are not the same, the cities are not the same. Except for the hills themselves, this place has changed the least of anything. Or so I have been told."

The next morning the sky was cloudy, threatening a summer storm, and during the first quarter of the morning, they grew denser, as if dark canvas sails had been inexpertly stretched from horizon to horizon. After a brief conference, the four agreed to remain at the guard station one more day; trudging along muddy roads in a downpour did not appeal to any of them. So while the thunder trundled around them and lightning lanced through the clouds, Fealatie, Giralt, and Sigfroit feasted on the half-dozen rabbits Olivia caught for them.

"What can Roma offer better than this?" asked Giralt as he held up the last bits of his meal. "Where did you find the berries to crush onto the meat?"

Olivia waved in the direction of the drenched hillside. "I grew up not far from here," she said, not inaccurately if she stretched a point. "You could probably do the same for me in France."

Giralt chuckled. "But the berries would not be so sweet."

"A shame you did not eat them," said Sigfroit, a keen, speculative light at the back of his eyes.

"Oh," said Olivia with feigned insouciance, "it doesn't bother me. I used to like berries when I was young, but then I . . . lost my taste for them."

"Too bad; they're excellent," said Fealatie. "We'll have enough left over to be able to take food with us tomorrow." She indicated the last two rabbits on the spit over the fire in front of the guard station. "It's been some time since we had such luxury."

Olivia nodded, wishing Sigfroit was not studying her as closely as he was doing, and that his attention were not as acute as she feared it might be.

"How long will it take us now, do you know?" asked Fealatie, trying to disguise her eagerness.

"Three to four days, depending on the weather and how much traffic there is on the Via Flaminia," said Olivia. "If we encounter more of the army, we could take twice that time."

"Three or four days," said Giralt. "A full day's walk, I suppose?"

"Yes," said Olivia, filled with sudden and engrossing nostalgia. At that realization, she had to resist the urge to leave at once and walk day and night until she was truly home.

Three days later, with the walls of Roma visible in the distance, Olivia began to stop those met on the road to ask them if they knew the location of Sanza Pare. The first man was not from the area and knew nothing about the place, the second was from the south side of Roma and had no knowledge of the north side of the city. The third, a lanky fellow with a large brindled dog and a wicker basket over his shoulder, pointed out a side road.

"Go along there; it's that way. Look for a place where the road turns west and another road from a church joins it at a square-fronted shrine. There are two crosses flanking the shrine instead of one atop. The next gate is for Sanza Pare. But they take no soldiers there." He looked at Fealatie. "It is a noblewoman's estate. They have no place for improper women." The condemning expression he wore revealed that he disapproved of Fealatie wearing mail.

"They will admit us," said Olivia. She motioned for the other three to follow, and led the way along the road they had been told to take. Now that she was nearing her home—a home she had never seen—Olivia was unable to believe that her long journey was coming to an end. It did not seem possible that she should be walking on familiar roads, with Roma, beloved Roma a day's walk from her land. Her satisfaction was dream-like, and she was not wholly convinced that she would not awaken shortly to discover that she was alone in the mountains, Atlas lamed by broken feet, and no sanctuary of any kind for her.

"That's the shrine," said Fealatie, pointing to the two crosses flanking the small structure of stone and wood. "I wonder who it honors?"

"Probably the Virgin," said Olivia, recalling how over the centuries the harvest statues of Ceres had been changed to shrines to the Virgin. "Or one of the local saints."

"I must stop," said Fealatie, pulling up the horse. "I ought to offer prayers here." She had been trying to keep to the requirements of her penance and to pray at every shrine she passed. Giralt held the gelding's reins while Fealatie went to kneel before the weathered statue that was so ancient it was impossible to tell the identity of the saint it represented.

This was so like the delays in dreams that Olivia found it difficult to believe once again that she was not about to waken. She did not pace or fret, but the hope that had been burgeoning within her faded as she watched Fealatie kneeling before the shrine.

"Bondama?" Sigfroit asked, cutting into her ruminations. "Are you ready?" There was a slight edge of doubt in his question, as if he was not certain she would take them to her estate, or that the estate truly existed.

"Oh, yes," said Olivia softly. She fidgeted as Fealatie remounted and then signaled to her. "We're almost there." Her stride lengthened, and at the next gate, she stopped, as she had been told to do. After a short hesitation, she reached for the chain that rang the bell for entry.

"How much room is there in the house?" asked Giralt while they waited.

"I . . . I don't know," Olivia admitted. "Enough, I am certain."

"How can you not know?" Giralt demanded, his voice growing sharp.

"It has been . . . a long time since I have lived in this

country," said Olivia, not quite sure how best to answer him. She was spared further explanation by the appearance of a house slave. "God give you good day," Olivia said when the slave unbarred the door.

"What business have you here?" the slave inquired in an unencouraging manner.

Giralt exchanged quick looks with Fealatie, but said nothing when she gestured him to silence.

Olivia made herself speak calmly. "I . . . we wish to speak to the major domo here, the bondsman Niklos Aulirios," she said with careful precision. "It is important."

"Aulirios is busy in the fields," said the slave at his most daunting.

"Then please fetch him. I bring him word from the Holy Land." She knew it was useless to reveal who she was—the disheartening experience of the past had taught her that such statements were rarely believed and often escalated to angry confrontations—but hoped that her knowledge of Niklos would be enough to cause the slave to bring him. How amusing, she thought with wry irritation, that she should come this far and be balked by a slave at her own gate.

"If it is not, Aulirios will see that you suffer for this intrusion," the slave promised before going away from the gate.

"Your household is courteous to strangers," Sigfroit said sarcastically. "But that must be the habit of caution."

"I assume so," said Olivia, doing her best to seem unperturbed by the slave's actions.

"How long will he take?" asked Giralt.

"I don't know," Olivia admitted, and schooled herself to wait without fretting.

It took longer than the first half of the Mass for the slave to return, decidedly flustered. He unbarred the gate and drew it open. "Aulirios said you are to be admitted. I am to take you to the vestibule of the villa."

"You are kind," said Olivia, thinking that if they looked as scruffy to the slave as they did to her own eyes, his reluctance to admit them was understandable, and his disapproval in taking them into the villa itself.

"This is beautiful," murmured Fealatie as the gates were

closed behind them and the gardens and court came into view.

"Yes," said Olivia with a faint smile. "Yes, it is."

At the slave's instructions, the horse was relinquished to the care of grooms with the assurance that he would receive proper care. This last was said pointedly, showing the slave's lack of satisfaction with the way the gelding looked now.

"There is a vestibule by the inner garden," the slave went on as the front door of the villa was opened by a footman. "Aulirios will meet you there. He has instructed that you be given refreshments." With that, he made a short bow and went away into another part of the building.

Fealatie stared around the entrance to the villa. "This is . . . more than I anticipated."

It was all Olivia could do to keep from concurring. She indicated the door the slave had pointed out. "We're to wait here," she said, looking at the handsome paintings on the walls and the ornate patterns inlaid on the floor. What a splendid home Niklos had made for her! Her smile was almost painful.

Two kitchen slaves had just withdrawn from the vestibule, leaving Fealatie, Sigfroit, and Giralt more food to sample than they had tasted in days, when the door to the inner garden opened and a moderately tall man in old-fashioned dalmatica came in, his handsome face frowning with concern.

The three strangers looked up, their expressions uncertain, and for a moment no one spoke.

"You are from the Holy Land?" Niklos said without any formal salute or greeting. "Why have you come here?"

A voice on the other side of the room answered. "They brought me home, Niklos."

With a glad shout, Niklos spun around, opening his arms as he did. "Olivia!"

She had decided she would not be overcome by seeing him once more, that she would walk to him, quickly but not too quickly, and take his hands in hers. "Niklos!" she cried, and hurtled across the room into his arms.

That night, when her chagrined but delighted guests had been fed, bathed, clothed, and sent to their various rooms, Niklos walked through the gardens with Olivia beside him.

"I was afraid for you," he said. "I've had Ithuriel Dar—do you remember him?—searching every port in the Holy Land."

"I remember him very well," said Olivia, her hazel eyes distant. "How will you send him word that he can stop hunting?"

Niklos considered his answer, knowing that her question was serious. "I will probably alert all our ships and the ships of our new partnerships to ask for him at every port. He'll turn up soon enough." He hesitated. "I am truly grateful to him for all he did. It's my pleasure at having you back that makes me flippant."

"I know that," Olivia assured him.

"It was an ordeal," he said, speaking of her last few years, not his own.

"Yes," she said quietly. "I'll tell you all of it, but not just now." She raised her head as an owl swept overhead on silent wings. "You have done a magnificent job here. I am overwhelmed."

"Thank you," he said. "But something does not satisfy you."

"I didn't say that," she told him.

"It's true, whether you say it or not." He stopped walking and looked down at her. "Tell me."

She did not speak at once. "Villa Ragoczy. Have you seen it? Is there anything left of it?"

"Not much," he said, making the news as gentle a blow as he could. "It was badly damaged before you went to Tyre, and it has not improved since then."

"Ah." Olivia walked a few steps away, then came back. "Niklos, buy it. I want to have it, to restore it."

"Sanct' Germain is far away, Olivia," Niklos pointed out with great kindness.

"Yes, but he may be back one day. Buy it, and make it as beautiful as you have made Sanza Pare. It truly is without equal." She leaned her head on his shoulder. "I have missed you so much."

"And I you," he said.

Shortly before they went back into the villa, Niklos said, "What about those three you brought with you? From what they said, they're not going to return to France, not for a long while."

Olivia smiled briefly. "And they may or may not be granted a change in her penance, even if you can aid them in petitioning a Cardinal."

"What, then? I know you, Olivia, and you have something in mind for them." Niklos grinned widely. "It is so good to hear your schemes once more. Tell me what you've decided for them."

"I've decided nothing for them," Olivia said in a prim manner that was so unlike her that Niklos had to stifle a laugh. "But should they want to make use of the house I have at Bergamo, or the old farm in Carinthia, I will let them know that they are available."

Niklos hesitated. "That's well enough for Fealatie and her besotted Giralt. But what of Sigfroit? He is fascinated with you."

"Or suspicious," Olivia corrected him.

"Fascinated," Niklos insisted. "Suppose he would rather remain here for a while? He would be good for you, Olivia. I know you. You are brittle as a leaf now, all for loneliness." His face changed, growing more loving and concerned. "If he asked it, would you let him stay?"

Olivia did not quite smile as she answered. "Perhaps."

*   *   *

Text of a letter from Kalere Navrentos to Olivia Clemens at Sanza Pare, outside of Roma, written in French and in archaic Greek.

Most gracious Bondama, your generous gifts have arrived, and my brother and I have offered up prayers in your name for the great charity you have shown to us and to those who pass through our doors.

You inquire about the state of health and mind of Valence Rainaut who accompanied you here, and we are sad to inform you that his suffering in this world has not yet ended. It will not be much longer, for his body is frail as twigs, and his flesh is as shrunken as fruit left too long on the vine. His thoughts are now quite lost to us, and no words or actions have been able to recall him from his melancholy since before the start of summer.

You informed us that the messenger who came here seeking you late in the spring has recently returned to Roma. Certainly this man will tell you more than anything I might say in a letter about the great burden God has put on Valence Rainaut. Your funds to provide Masses for the repose of his soul upon his death are not necessary, but we accept them gratefully, in the name of all those who come here for succor.

With your ordeal behind you, and your fortunes again favorable, the path is smooth and pleasant; in all life this is proof of the joy of the soul [in archaic Greek] *for surely the soul is harlot and virgin, mother and daughter of the flesh, the androgyne, father and mother; the soul is exalted and spurned, is debauched and holy, is knowledge and ignorance, is foolishness and wisdom, and nothing comes in life that is not part of the soul.*

[in French] *For your long fidelity and your devotion without reward, God will show you wisdom and blessing. Those who love without rationing their love will receive love in abundance, for as the stone is hollowed it is filled.*

Be assured that whatever may be done for Valence Rainaut will be done, and that it will be done for as long as it must be done, without stinting, and that when it is over, he will lie quietly and untroubled for the care of your good heart.

In the Name of God, Who is all things, from Muse to the End of the World,

Kalere Navrentos
By my own hand on the Feast of Epiphany, in the Lord's Year 1193.

· 20 ·

At San Stefano in Insula, Fealatie waited restlessly, taking no solace from Giralt or Sigfroit. She fretted in her harness and glared at the Benedictine monks who lived in the tiny monastery.

"They will refuse me again," she said when the monks had retired for their solitary meditations before prayer. "They're keeping the Little Hours, but it won't matter if we wait from prime to compline, it will simply be another delay." Her hands were locked in combat with each other. "It's useless."

"You must not despair," said Giralt, as if talking to a faltering squire. "You have come this far, much farther than any of us thought to go."

Sigfroit, who had been looking out across the narrow bridge toward the western bank of the Tibros, now glanced back. "Olivia said that she would be back by mid-afternoon; I believe she will."

"But what answer will she bring?" Fealatie asked, her voice rising in spite of herself. "This is the fourth time we have tried, and always it has come to nothing." She lowered her head. "Perhaps I should petition my husband to be allowed to enter a convent."

"No," Giralt said at once. "No."

Slowly she looked toward him. "No," she agreed.

Sigfroit paced the narthex once. "His Holiness is a very old man, an ancient man, and they say his strength is not great."

"They also say," interjected Giralt in an undervoice, "that his mind has become childish."

"They say that of everyone with white hair," Sigfroit

reminded him with a significant nod to Giralt's hair that had gone badger-gray in the last six months. "It isn't always so."

Giralt got to his feet, his newly polished mail jingling as he moved. "He has many souls under his wing, Fealatie, and age has made him feeble."

"But still," she sighed, letting herself have the luxury of leaning against his shoulder. "Still."

A discreet cough gained their attention as the porter, a tertiary Brother, came from the chapel. "There will be food for you shortly. The Abbot has ordered that I bring you wine." He indicated the tray he had set down. "Deo gratias."

All three armored guests made the Sign of the Cross, murmuring "Deo gratias" in response.

When the porter had left them alone, Sigfroit poured out the wine for them. "It has a good scent," he commented. "Not that sour fare most monks drink."

"That's fortunate." Giralt took the cup offered him.

"What if we were to go to San Cristofo?" Fealatie said abruptly. "What if we were to ask for the audience ourselves, rather than waiting for Olivia to arrange matters for us? Might we not prevail?"

Sigfroit put a cup of wine in hand. "We might," he said in a skeptical tone. "But if we do not prevail, we would never again have the opportunity to approach His Holiness."

"But it's been four times; we have been at Roma now for seven months. How much longer will we have to remain?" There were tears on her cheeks. "God does not hear me." She drank suddenly and deeply as if to drown any more blasphemous words.

"It is not God, but the Pope you are trying to see," Sigfroit pointed out, sounding very much like Olivia for an instant. "God will hear your prayers, but it will take the Pope's approval to—"

Giralt motioned him to silence. "Horses coming." He took the winecup from Fealatie's hand and set it with his own on the tray.

Sigfroit had stopped still. "Olivia," he said quietly.

The rattle of trotting hooves on the bridge grew louder, then slowed to a halt at the gate to San Stefano in Insula. The clang of the visitors' bell echoed off the walls.

"Bondama Atta Olivia Clemens returns," Niklos called out. "The Abbot has already given permission for her entry."

"Saints aid me," whispered Fealatie, unaware that she had taken Giralt's hand in her own.

"Never mind the Saints, hope that the physicians who serve the Pope will aid you," said Sigfroit, setting his cup aside and striding toward the chapel door. "Where are they?"

"With the porter, probably," said Giralt. "The porter has to admit her."

"Both of them," corrected Fealatie. She took a long, deep breath and let it out slowly, unsteadily. "I despise having to wait. I believe I have spent all my life waiting and waiting and waiting."

Giralt tightened his hold on her hand. "God give us all courage."

"Amen," said Fealatie automatically, listening to the sound of approaching steps.

The warder monk, a hunchbacked fellow with a ferret's face and the manner of a general, opened the side-door to the narthex of the chapel. "Your friends await you once you have finished your prayers," he said in a pointed way.

"Pax vobiscum," said Niklos as he came through the door, holding it open for Olivia. "At last," he said to the others. "If you are half so tired of waiting as we are, you must be halfway to madness by now."

"Yes, halfway," said Fealatie.

Olivia lifted the long veil that covered her head and shoulders. "Magna Mater, what a terrible fuss it is." She ran her hand over her fawn-colored hair, securing a few wisps under the crespine net that held her coiled braids.

"What fuss?" asked Giralt in a sharp tone.

"The entire Papal court," said Olivia with asperity. "The Curia has always been difficult, but now—" Her gesture was aggravated.

Fealatie released Giralt's hand. "Tell me. It's another delay, isn't it?"

"Not precisely," said Olivia, her hazel eyes lingering briefly on Sigfroit's face. She turned to Fealatie again. "I have arranged a meeting at vespers with Cardinal Ermano

Trivento. He is one of the secretaries to His Holiness and he has said he will decide if your case merits the attention of the Pope."

"But without the Pope—" Fealatie began.

Giralt interrupted her. "Doesn't the Cardinal understand that without the Pope, Fealatie will have no means to fulfill the conditions of her—"

Olivia held up her hand to silence them both. "I have explained your situation to everyone I could force or cajole into hearing me. You have my word that he knows the particulars of your situation, Fealatie." She paused, weighing her next words. "But sadly there are many petitioners, and the Pope is in frail health."

"I know, yes." Fealatie nodded slowly. "Of course. I did not want to appear ungrateful."

"Oh, for the mercy of Miner—" Olivia exclaimed. "What has gratitude to do with it? If it comes to gratitude, I owe my life to you." She met Fealatie's eyes directly. "If it were up to me, I would challenge the Pope on his way to Mass. But that is not what you wish, is it?"

"No," said Fealatie, then, very suddenly, she laughed. "You, stopping His Holiness. I can almost see you doing it."

"Don't encourage her," said Niklos from his place by the door. As the others turned toward him, he said, "If we are going to reach San Cristofo in time, we should leave as soon as the monks will permit it. It's time to be at prayers."

"Niklos is right," said Olivia with determination. "I ought to have suggested this."

Fealatie nodded, starting toward the chapel. Then she stopped. "Do you think this will do any good?"

"It may," said Olivia candidly. "It is closer than we have come before. Each step is progress, no matter how small it is." She did her best to smile just before she genuflected and crossed herself. "In Roma, long ago, they were content to let you burn a pinch of incense without the chants and the kneeling."

"Olivia," Niklos warned her.

"Yes, yes," she said quietly as she bowed her head and began the long and tedious recitations in the corrupted Latin the Church used.

The road to San Cristofo was fairly crowded, for although it was just after the heat of the day, the late spring had brought traders onto the road. Merchants with mule trains and peasants with ox-carts all jostled to or from the Papal court attending on His Holiness who had come to San Cristofo for the sake of the hot springs which were said to ease diseases of the joints. By the time they dismounted in the old courtyard of San Cristofo, the sun had slid well down the western sky.

As grooms took their horses in charge, Olivia said to the others, "Speak as little as possible until I have presented your case. They consider silence to be a sign of virtuous patience here; it will strengthen your case if you say nothing until it is required of you."

"And you?" Fealatie asked.

"It's best if I can keep quiet, as well. A sore trial, isn't it?" She gave Fealatie a swift, encouraging smile, then started toward the massive wooden inner door.

The monks who greeted them with elaborate courtesy were Ambrosians, sleek and elegant in their simple habits, their tonsured hair glossy and their bodies rounded with good living. "God give you welcome in this place and vindicate your cause. Pax vobiscum," said the senior of the two, addressing Olivia. "Bondama Clemens, your party is awaited in the reception hall of Cardinal Trivento. He and Cardinal dei Conti are already there."

Olivia, who had donned her veil once more, made a gesture of compliance. She motioned to Fealatie and the others to join her as they went down the frescoed corridor.

"An unusual place," murmured Sigfroit, staring at the faded and very secular illustrations on the high walls.

"Long ago, when the Caesars reigned, it was a famous bath for the infirm," said Olivia, keeping her voice low. "Some of the buildings are of that time."

"Strange pictures for a monastery," Sigfroit observed, then said nothing more as he caught a cautioning sign from Niklos.

The reception hall of Cardinal Trivento was on the second floor of the building, smelling of iron and sulphur from the baths below. The walls were whitewashed and the only ornamentation was a large crucifix between two tall, narrow windows. Cardinal Trivento was seated at his writing table, and he looked up as Olivia paused in the door.

"Bondama Clemens," said the Cardinal, rising ponderously to his feet. He was a massive man, big-framed and heavy-bodied; he inspected her companions through the tangle of his eyebrows.

"It is my honor to present the Chatelaine I spoke of earlier. You know her tribulation; without the attention of the Pope, she must continue in disgrace."

"Yes, yes," said Cardinal Trivento. "Come in." He held out his hand so that all could genuflect and kiss his ring. When that was done, he nodded toward the far end of the room. "That is Cardinal dei Conti. He will also receive your obligations." Once again the ritual of kneeling and ring-kissing was repeated, but this time with greater curiosity, for Cardinal dei Conti was little more than thirty, a handsome, auburn-haired man with large gray eyes and a grave manner. When this was done, Cardinal Trivento said, "I have asked Cardinal dei Conti to be with us for two reasons: first, he is the nephew of His Holiness Clement III, who reigned before our Celestine III. Second, he has studied law at Paris and Bologna, and is better able to advise you than I am."

"You underestimate your skills," said dei Conti with dignity. "However, it is my duty to impart whatever information may benefit you." He walked to the window and looked out toward the roof of the opposite building. "His Holiness has requested that where matters of law are concerned that he be given the opinions of two or more Cardinals."

"Very wise," said Sigfroit.

Dei Conti regarded him narrowly. "If you are insolent, this inquiry is over."

"I am not insolent," said Sigfroit at once, bowing his head as much to hide the angry light in his eyes as to show respect. "We have experienced delays and disappointment. I am concerned for the welfare of my Chatelaine, as my oath requires me to be."

"Commendable," said the young Cardinal dryly.

Cardinal Trivento shuffled through the vellum sheets on

his writing table and finally drew out one. "Ah, here it is. This is your complaint and petition, at least as far as Bondama Clemens had communicated it to us. Chatelaine, you are to give close attention to the reading and correct any error or misconception that may appear here."

Fealatie bowed her head, giving Olivia a startled look as she did. "As God guides me, and with Him to witness the truth," she said.

Cardinal Trivento read steadily and on a single note so that Fealatie's case sounded much the same as a household inventory. The Cardinal did not look up from the page as he read, even on those rare occasions when Fealatie made meticulous corrections or qualifications, all of which were painstakingly noted in the margins of the petition. This took some time; bells were sounding for private devotions by the time Cardinal Trivento put down the pages and addressed Fealatie directly. "You vow to God that what has been read here is true, without lie or misrepresentation, as you expect to be judged on the Last Day?"

"Yes, I swear on my salvation it is accurate," said Fealatie, feeling a little breathless.

Cardinal dei Conti, who had remained silent with the rest of the company, now came forward. "What is the wish of your husband in this matter, do you know?"

"I believe he is adamant; he demands that I enter Jerusalem under the terms originally set forth." She looked over at Giralt. "My escort has been loyal beyond any duty of rank. Let their testimony be heard, as well, in order to know how much I have tried to obey the mandate of my husband."

"Do we have any record of the Fraizmarch orders or requests?" wondered Cardinal Trivento.

"I will require it," said Cardinal dei Conti.

Fealatie's hands clenched. "That would be another delay," she said, doing her best to keep her voice level no matter how much she wanted to rage.

"This is a serious matter," said Cardinal dei Conti. "It cannot be decided on a whim. Therefore we must learn how your husband is disposed in regard to your penance. If we judge in haste, we court damnation."

Giralt shook his head. "We have been threatened with damnation since this journey began; that is why my Chatelaine is here, so that honor and salvation may both be served. If we must wait, then there is nothing to do but bow to the will of God and the wish of the Pope." As he said this, he watched Fealatie until he was confident that she had control of herself again.

"A most pious sentiment," said dei Conti in his imposing way. "And you?" This was addressed to Sigfroit.

"And I?" Sigfroit answered. "I am a sworn knight. What Chatelaine Fealatie requires of me I will do."

Cardinal dei Conti folded his hands in his enormous sleeves. "We will review this case and pray for guidance. If it appears that His Holiness is disposed to inquire about this, then you will be notified."

"Notified?" Fealatie echoed in disbelief.

"What?" Giralt demanded at the same instant.

Cardinal Trivento glared at them. "Are you questioning the conduct of the Papal court?"

Before Fealatie or Giralt could answer, Olivia spoke. "You must understand, Eminence, that they fear to give offense to Gui de Fraizmarch, who has laid this burden upon them. If they do not act with dispatch, it might be regarded by him as lack of zeal on their part, and would lessen the chance that he would agree to an alteration of the terms of the penance." She paused, and when she went on, she was more emphatic than before. "Without the assistance and succor of these good Christians, I would have perished. For that alone I am disposed to plead their case. But I esteem them as well, and count them my friends. I am beholden to them for many things, and none greater than the bonds of proved affection."

Cardinal dei Conti cleared his throat. "I will do what I can, Bondama Clemens."

"Deo gratias," said Olivia, with the accent she had learned so long ago. As Cardinal dei Conti swept out of the room, she genuflected with the others.

"I will do my utmost, Bondama Clemens, Chatelaine de Fraizmarch. There are many difficulties, but I will do my best." He seemed a smaller, more ordinary man now that dei Conti was gone; he lost some of his ferocity and gained a gentler mein.

"May God reward you for your charity," said Olivia, making a covert signal to the others. "We will be at the Regina dei Fiori," she added, naming the most luxurious inn near San Cristofo. "We will wait for your answer there." Cardinal Trivento tapped his writing table with his stubby fingers. "It will take some time. You might wish to return to your estate."

Olivia concealed her irritation. "If that is what Your Eminence advises, then we most certainly shall do it."

The Cardinal chose his words very carefully. "Were it not that you, Chatelaine de Fraizmarch, are living under the roof and protection of Bondama Clemens, then there might be more reason for dispatch, for although your knights have accompanied you in the Holy Land, it is not fitting that you remain in their company without proper assurances of your conduct. As long as Bondama Clemens is prepared to extend her hospitality to you, there can be no question of your virtue or the virtue of those with you. If this were not so, it would be required of you that you enter a nunnery until your case is decided." He looked from Fealatie to Olivia. "Is it your intention to permit Chatelaine de Fraizmarch to remain with you?"

Olivia smiled; she was looking at Sigfroit as she answered, "Yes; for as long as desired."

"A most Christian sentiment," said the Cardinal with approval. "It is unfortunate that others are not as eager as you to obey the dictates of Our Lord."

"I thank God for your kindness," Fealatie said formally to Olivia. "I am forever in your debt."

"Nonsense," said Olivia affectionately. "No one is in my debt."

The Cardinal placed the flat of his big hands on his writing table. "So. It is settled then."

"If you must speak with us, word will reach us at the Regina dei Fiori," Olivia said, adjusting her veil and folding her hands piously.

"But you will return to your estate?" suggested Sigfroit.

"It seems wisest," Olivia said, her eyes once again meeting his through the tissue gauze that covered her face.

"Yes," he agreed.

Fealatie was the first to kneel to the Cardinal and to kiss his ring in obedience. "I was near despair. I thank God that you have listened to my petitions."

The Cardinal blessed her automatically. "God answers all prayers in due season, Chatelaine."

She took Giralt's proffered hand as she rose. "Yes," said Fealatie quietly, and for the first time her face bore no trace of apprehension or dissatisfaction.

"Give thanks then, for your guidance and deliverance." The Cardinal was no longer much interested in his visitors. He held out his hand as a gesture of dismissal.

"I give thanks every night," said Sigfroit, the last of them to kiss Cardinal Trivento's ring.

The Cardinal sketched a benediction toward his departing company; he was more intrigued by the legalities of Fealatie's predicament than by the woman herself: which was just as well.

*   *   *

Text of a note from Sigfroit de Plessien to Olivia.

To Olivia whom I cherish more than honor or justice or blood, my plea to you: you have warned me that the time would come when the Pope would make a pronouncement and when that happened, I would be obliged to follow the dictates of His Holiness. To be honest with you and with myself, I did not think it would happen. I was beginning to believe—wanting to believe—that the old man cared nothing for Fealatie's trouble and would pass to glory in Heaven without making a decision about it. It was a pleasant fable, and it has sustained me these last three years.

But now word has come, and I am bound by my oath and my allegiance to accompany Giralt and Fealatie to the Holy Land once more, for the purpose of visiting Bethlehem and Jerusalem on foot.

I would rather remain here. I would rather abandon everything from my past and stay with you. But if I did that, you would not pardon me, would you? To keep you I would lose you. Olivia, do not despise me for loving you to distraction. I beg you to understand that if I did not dread your disfavor more than I fear the odium of the whole world and the might of the Church, nothing could take me from you.

Dar's ship will carry us away in two days, and I have only tonight to spend with you. We are long past the point where another night together would endanger me, for that danger was met and passed more than two years ago. Let me come to you, let me hold you beside me, beneath me, above me from sunset until dawn, and let me try to sate myself with you; I never will, but let me try before I leave you.

Olivia, Olivia, you are a fever in my soul, and my loving you trembles in me like the wings of angels. Nothing in my life has greater meaning than you, and without you, nothing else has any meaning at all. You are my touchstone.

Know that I will come back to you. I must go to the Holy Land, and then return to Fraizmarch, but then, when I am released from my obligation, I will come to you as swiftly and as truly as an arrow flies.

What will be the most awkward for me, being gone from you as I must be, will be to remain in the company of Giralt and Fealatie, for they are so consumed with their own love that it will make being apart from you that much more intolerable. How odd that I should think that I will never have enough of your love, and yet chafe at being around the love of others.

In the name of that treasured friend of yours who brought you to your life, may all the benign forces in the worlds visible and invisible guard you, and in token of that, I send you this ring. Wear it until I return. And if I do not return, send it to your treasured friend with my endless gratitude.

Sigfroit

By my own hand on the 21st day of September in the Lord's Year 1196.

Epilogue

Text of a letter from Olivia in Roma to Saint-Germain in Lo-Yang. The mendicant friar carrying the letter to the merchant outpost in Turkestan was captured by deserting European soldiers from the Fourth Crusade; the friar and the letters entrusted to him were destroyed.

To Ragoczy Sanct' Germain Franciscus in the city of Lo-Yang, which may or may not exist, Olivia sends her most earnest greetings from Roma:

Your letter, which has been on the road more than two years, surprised me, and made me aware of how very much I miss you. Your memory has lain in the back of my mind, dozing, and needed only the sight of your eclipse seal to come fully awake.

Perhaps I should tell you that the last letter I had from you before this one arrived more than twenty years ago, at which time you informed me that you were going east along the Old Silk Road. It was shortly after the Jews were banished from France and that mob in Lyon put three of our blood to the torch. You told me that the knights were spoiling for another Crusade, and that they would probably practice on anyone they could label a heretic. Well yes, you were right about that.

Tell me, have you found the haven you wished for? When

you were there before, you said that the people respect learning and put a high value on tolerance. But that was centuries ago, my friend. Is it as you remember? I confess that I hope it may be, so that you will not have to bear so much. The suffering endured by those of our blood is terrible to think of, but is isolation the only alternative? I have lived in Roma a very long time and have learned, as you said I would, to live in a way that attracts little notice. Surely you could live here with me. After all, this is your house, and has been for more than a thousand years. Come here to me and return to a familiar place. I promise you that you will be protected—I will let it be known that an eccentric relative will be sharing the villa and your way will be smooth.

By the way, I think you will like the way the north wing has been rebuilt. You gave me permission to make alterations, and I think that what has been done will please you. The builders were most upset, but followed the orders they were given. The atrium has been widened and is a proper court now. There is a gallery around the second floor so that all the rooms have access to the court. It is not unlike the house we shared in Tyre. You see, I have never forgot. Though I have not seen you, heard your voice or your footfall for more than four hundred years, yet they are familiar to me, and I catch myself waiting for them.

You have probably not heard that the English King John has at last submitted to the Pope. Everyone in Roma is busy taking credit for this, and His Holiness is unbearably smug about it. I don't mention it, of course, but I feel sympathy for John. That brother of his was impossible. He put all of his kingdom in debt and went off to war with never so much as a moment's doubt that his debts would be paid. And to make it worse, he never made a wife of his Queen. If Richard Lion-Heart had been able to overcome his inclinations long enough to produce an heir, matters would be different in England. Certainly Richard was a splendid leader in war, very brave, a superb warrior, and so forth. But these Crusades are insanity, and Richard's devotion to war, I think, was at least partly spawned by his reluctance to touch Barengaria. It is an unfortunate prejudice in a king. Other men may have their pages and apprentices and students and urchins, but for a king to spurn his wife, that is another matter. If he could not endure her at all, he could have found her a discreet lover and said the child was his. That has happened often enough before. So England went to John and now Pope Innocent is preening like a cock on a dunghill.

Tomorrow I will give this letter into the hands of a Cypriot bound for Thessaly. He has promised to hand it to a merchant or a friar going east. He has warned me that there are not so many travelers now, as there are rumors of great wars in the East and devils coming out of the desert to plunder the land. For your sake, I trust that this is not the case, and that a small band of brigands has been improved upon in the telliing until a handful of men have become an army. It will take time for this to reach you, but when it does, know it for what it is, dearest Sanct' Germain—the cry of my soul to you.

Perhaps it is true that we are doomed to live as outcasts much of the time, and perhaps it is true that if our natures were generally known we would be loathed, hunted, and killed by those who believe the worst of what is strange. But, Sanct' Germain, no one has loved as devotedly as you have. The bond that began that night when I watched you come into my chamber and was filled with terror has never been broken. Do you remember how kindly you used me that night? Without the strength of your love, I would have died before I was thirty. And do not remind me with that wry smile I like so well that I did die before I was thirty. It is not the same thing, and you know it. No one, my friend, no one has loved me as you have. That has sustained me for more than a thousand years, and will doubtless continue to do so until the true death claims me.

How morbid I sound, and here I am trying to persuade you to return. Pay no attention to anything I say, but that I love you, have always loved you.

I must end this before I become maudlin. It would not do for me to attend the reception for the King of Aragon in a distraught humor. It is times like these when I wish I had not lost the ability to weep, for tears might cleanse me. But red and swollen eyes will not become me, so I will tell myself that I was fortunate when the change deprived me of weeping, and my soul will mourn. Doubtless someone will provide me a distraction, and, who knows—I may find someone who will want to share my pleasures.

And you, my dearest, have you found someone to share your pleasures, or are you still alone? If there were anything I might do to give you that which you seek, though it ended my life, I would do it. Empty words, with you so far away from me.

I have sent for my servant and have given orders for my palinquin, so I must bid you farewell for a time.

From my own hand on the Feast of Saint Matthew, in the 1214th year of Our Lord, in Roma.

Olivia